WINDS OF
CHANGE

WINDS OF CHANGE

Book Two of The Mage Winds

MERCEDES LACKEY

DAW BOOKS, INC.

DONALD A. WOLLHEIM, FOUNDER

375 Hudson Street, New York, NY 10014

ELIZABETH R. WOLLHEIM
SHEILA E. GILBERT
PUBLISHERS

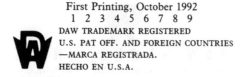

Dedicated to the Tayledras and Heralds of *our* world: police, firefighters, and rescue workers everywhere, whose accomplishments in everyday life outdo anything in fiction.

OFFICIAL TIMELINE FOR THE

by *Mercedes Lackey*

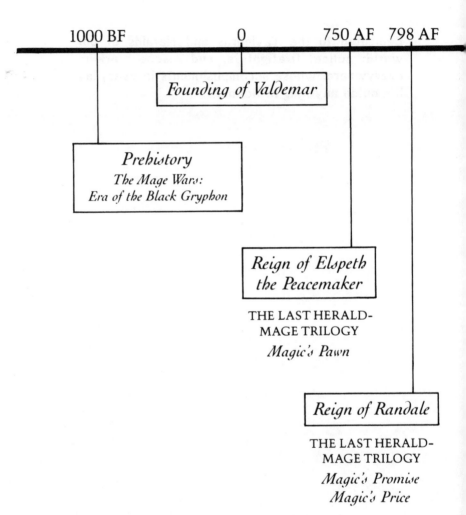

1000 BF   0   750 AF   798 AF

Founding of Valdemar

Prehistory
The Mage Wars:
Era of the Black Gryphon

Reign of Elspeth
the Peacemaker

THE LAST HERALD-
MAGE TRILOGY
Magic's Pawn

Reign of Randale

THE LAST HERALD-
MAGE TRILOGY
Magic's Promise
Magic's Price

BF   Before the Founding
AF   After the Founding
 *   Upcoming from DAW Books in hardcover

HERALDS OF VALDEMAR SERIES

Sequence of events by Valdemar reckoning

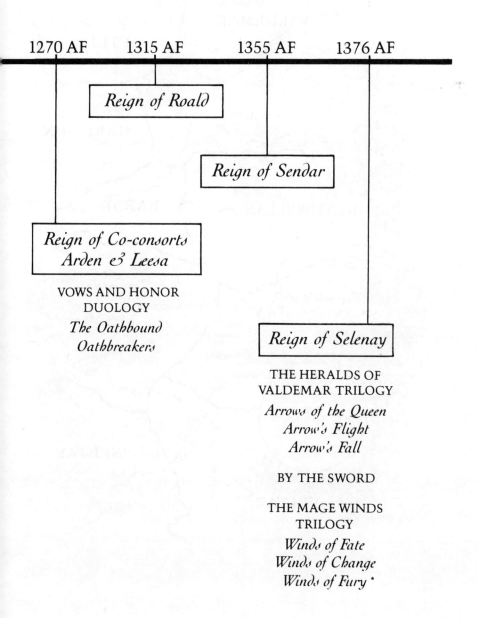

1270 AF   1315 AF   1355 AF   1376 AF

Reign of Roald

Reign of Sendar

Reign of Co-consorts
Arden & Leesa

VOWS AND HONOR
DUOLOGY
The Oathbound
Oathbreakers

Reign of Selenay

THE HERALDS OF
VALDEMAR TRILOGY
Arrows of the Queen
Arrow's Flight
Arrow's Fall

BY THE SWORD

THE MAGE WINDS
TRILOGY
Winds of Fate
Winds of Change
Winds of Fury ˙

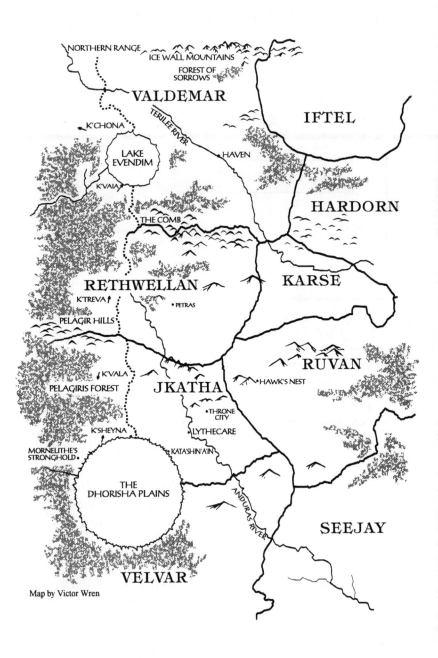

NORTHERN RANGE

ICE WALL MOUNTAINS

FOREST OF
SORROWS

VALDEMAR

IFTEL

K'CHONA

TERILEE RIVER

LAKE
EVENDIM

HAVEN

K'VAIA

HARDORN

THE COMB

RETHWELLAN

KARSE

K'TREVA

• PETRAS

PELAGIR HILLS

RUVAN

K'VALA

• HAWK'S NEST

PELAGIRIS FOREST

JKATHA

• THRONE
CITY

K'SHEYNA

• LYTHECARE

MORNELITHE'S
STRONGHOLD •

KATA'SHIN'A'IN

THE
DHORISHA PLAINS

ANDURAS RIVER

SEEJAY

VELVAR

Map by Victor Wren

Map by Victor Wren

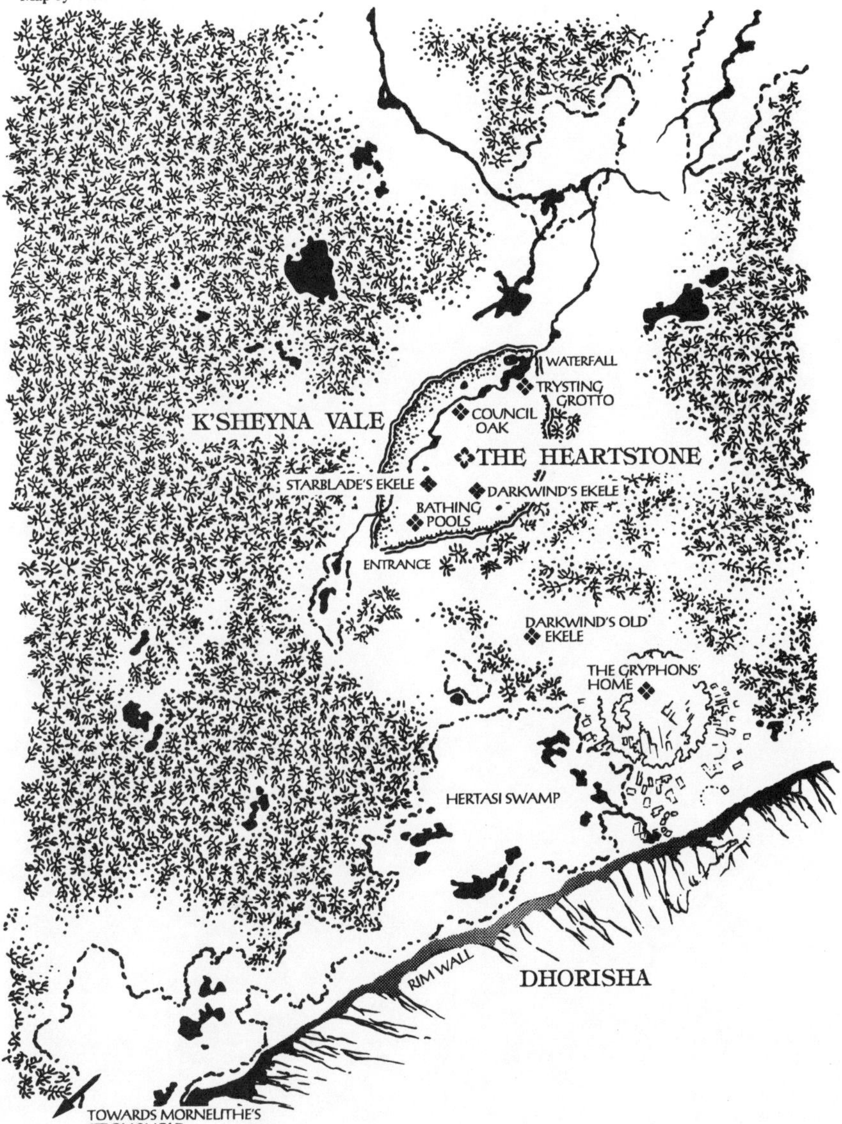

WATERFALL

TRYSTING GROTTO

COUNCIL OAK

K'SHEYNA VALE

THE HEARTSTONE

STARBLADE'S EKELE

DARKWIND'S EKELE

BATHING POOLS

ENTRANCE

DARKWIND'S OLD EKELE

THE GRYPHONS' HOME

HERTASI SWAMP

RIM WALL

DHORISHA

TOWARDS MORNELITHE'S STRONGHOLD

Prologue

For long years, the rich northern kingdom of Valdemar, ruled by Queen Selenay and her consort Daren, had been under siege by the forces of Hardorn (*Arrows of the Queen, Arrow's Flight, Arrow's Fall, By The Sword*). Ancar, its ruthless and cunning leader, had first tried treachery against the rival country's court; that had been foiled by the Heralds of Valdemar, the judges, lawgivers, and law-enforcers of their people. He could not corrupt them, for it was not in the nature of the Heralds, Chosen for their duties by the horselike creatures called "Companions," to be corrupted. He then tried direct attack—that was foiled by the forces of neighboring Rethwellan to the south, brought by an old promise of aid, long forgotten in Valdemar. Those forces included the mercenary company of the Skybolts, commanded by Captain Kerowyn, grand-daughter of the mage Kethry (whose own story is related in *The Oathbound* and *Oathbreakers*). Kerowyn brought more with her than just arms and fighters; she brought with her an ancient and powerful enchanted weapon, the sword her grandmother had borne; Need, who for reasons then unknown could be commanded only by a woman. With her she brought the King of Rethwellan's own brother, Prince Daren, the

Lord Martial of his country, also the younger brother of Selenay's former treacherous husband.

The result was the successful defeat of Ancar's forces—and the Choosing of both Daren (for he was nothing like his brother) and Kerowyn by Companions, much to the consternation of some of Selenay's nobles.

And Daren and Selenay had loved each other at first sight.

Five years later, they had produced both progeny and an uneasy peace, although Ancar continued to make attempts across the border, and insinuated spies inside Valdemar. But the one thing of which all felt sure, was that they were safe from magic.

In fact, few people in Valdemar even believed in "real" magic, although the mind-magic of the Heralds was commonplace. An ancient barrier, attributed to the work of the legendary Herald-Mage Vanyel, seemed to hold the *working* of real magic at bay inside Valdemar's borders, if not its effects. Further, it seemed as if there was some prohibition about even *thinking* of real magic; those who discussed it, soon forgot the discussions; those who witnessed it soon attributed their memories to dreams. Even old chronicles that spoke of it were forgotten, and those who tried to read them found their interest lagging and put them away without a memory of why they had sought them out in the first place.

But one day, it became plain that this barrier was no longer as effective as everyone believed and hoped. The Queen's Heir, her daughter by her first marriage, made the decision that the time had come for Valdemar to have the same manner of magic its enemies wielded (*Winds of Fate*), and perhaps new magics as well.

She fought for the right to seek out the mages of other lands herself—more successfully, after a magically-enhanced assassin sent by Ancar nearly killed her—and set off with the sword Need and one other Herald, Skif, to find mages for Valdemar.

She had not gone far beyond Rethwellan when she deduced that she had not done this alone—that the Companions had acted on her behalf, and were, in fact, forcing her toward a goal only they knew. Angered by this, and swearing that she would follow her own path in this venture, Elspeth turned off the road she had been intended to take, and headed instead for Kata'shin'a'in and the nomads of the Dhorisha Plains—who, she hoped, would lead her to the mysterious Hawkbrothers of the Pelagirs. The last of the Herald-Mages, Herald Vanyel, had been reputedly taught by them (*Magic's Pawn, Magic's Promise, Magic's Price*) and she hoped that she could find either allies or teachers there.

The Shin'a'in had their own set of plans for her, once they learned of her destination. They intended to test her, watch her, and allow her to face some of their enemies as she crossed their land.

Meanwhile, the sword she carried, that she had thought was "only" a magic weapon, proved to be more than that. In her hands it awakened—and proved to be a once-human mage of times so long past that there was no record of her previous life, or anything Need referenced, in the Chronicles of Valdemar.

Together the Heralds, their Companions, and the newly-awakened blade crossed the Dhorisha Plains, only to find themselves going from old dangers into new—for the Tayledras territory they headed for, following a map that the Shin'a'in shaman Kra'heera and Tre'valen gave to Elspeth, was as much under siege as the kingdom of Valdemar.

Among the Hawkbrothers, a former mage, Darkwind k'Sheyna, had been fighting his own battle against enemies within and without. Without, were the forces led by the evil Adept and Changemaster, Mornelithe Falconsbane—not the least of which was his half-human daughter, the Changechild Nyara. Within, the Clan was split—physically, for more than half their number, including all of the children and lesser mages, were stranded in the intended site of a new Vale when their Heartstone cracked. And split in leadership, for Darkwind was the leader of a faction that wanted to bring in help from outside to heal their Heartstone and bring back the rest of the Clan—while his father, who led the mages, swore this could not be done.

But Darkwind's father had been subverted by Falconsbane, and even in the heart of the Vales was still under his control. It was Darkwind's father, the Adept Starblade k'Sheyna, who had actually *caused* the fracturing of the stone.

Darkwind was aided by a pair of gryphons and their young, who had served as surrogate parents to him when his own mother died and his father turned strange and alien. Treyvan and Hydona did their best to support him, but despite being powerful mages in their own right, there were few in the Vale who would listen to their advice.

Falconsbane elected to close his hand tighter around k'Sheyna Vale, and sent his daughter—under the ruse that she was escaping his power— to seduce young Darkwind. Nyara herself, sick of her father's mistreatment, was not aware of Falconsbane's larger plan. Loyalty to his lover

Dawnfire kept Darkwind from succumbing to his attraction to Nyara, but by Falconsbane's reckoning, it was only a matter of time before he had both father and son in his grasp.

Elspeth, bearing an enormously valuable artifact, and a powerful, if untrained mage herself, aroused Falconsbane's avarice as soon as she came within his reckoning. He turned some of his creatures that had been searching the Plain for the artifacts guarded by the Shin'a'in to pursue Elspeth. And meanwhile, in pursuit himself of an old hatred for gryphons, he launched an attack on Treyvan and Hydona and their young. And in the wake of the attack, he managed to trap Dawnfire's spirit in the body of her bondbird, and slay her human body along with the spirit of the bird.

On discovering that the young gryphlets had been contaminated by Falconsbane's power, Nyara confessed her hand in the matter, and was confined in a corner of the gryphon's lair.

Elspeth, Skif, and the rest arrived at the borders of the k'Sheyna territory, pursued by Falconsbane's creatures. Darkwind and the gryphons came to their rescue, and recognized both the sword and the Companions for what they were. Unsure of what to do with them, Darkwind led them back to the lair. There, Skif met Nyara and fell in love with her—and the fascination was mutual.

Things that Nyara knew and confessed proved to Darkwind that his father was in thrall to the evil Adept. He succeeded in breaking Falconsbane's hold on his father and in destroying the creature through which the control had come, but that alerted Falconsbane to the fact that they now knew who and what he was and, presumably, what he had planned. He permitted Dawnfire to overhear that he was planning to meet with Ancar of Hardorn to discuss an alliance—then allowed her "accidental" escape.

The name meant nothing to Dawnfire, but a great deal to the Heralds. This was their worst fear realized; that Ancar should unite with a truly powerful Adept—

But Need, who had centuries of experience recognizing trickery, pointed out that Dawnfire's "escape" was a little too easy—and that they would be leaving both the gryphlets and possibly even herself unguarded to disrupt a spurious "meeting."

So the allies planned a reverse ambush; lying in wait for Falconsbane when he came to take the young ones.

Falconsbane was cannier than they thought; he detected the ambush at the last moment, and mounted an effective counterattack. He attempted to take control of the gryphlets, but Need deflected the magic, and turned it against him, using it to purge the unsuspecting young ones of his taint. He attacked Skif, but before he could kill the Herald, he was attacked by his daughter Nyara, in the first open act of defiance in her life. Nevertheless, Falconsbane's powerful magics and allies succeeded in taking down both Companions and trapping Hydona.

All would have been lost but for the tenacity of Darkwind and the gryphons—and the intervention of the Shin'a'in Swordsworn, the black-clad servants of the Shin'a'in and Tayledras Goddess, who had been secret players in events all along. They surrounded the combatants and forced Falconsbane to a stalemate.

Snarling in rage, the Adept escaped—barely—leaving behind a trail of blood and the survivors' hope that a Shin'a'in arrow had been fatal.

But the intervention of the Shin'a'in was not complete. The Swordsworn and the two shaman took up Dawnfire—who, trapped in a bird's body, was fated to fade and "die," leaving nothing of her human self behind. Before the eyes of the Heralds and the rest, the Goddess herself intervened on Dawnfire's behalf, transforming her into a shining Avatar in the shape of a vorcel hawk, the symbol of the shamans' clan, Tale'sedrin.

And in the awed confusion afterward, Nyara vanished, taking Need with her—at the blade's parting insistence that Nyara required her more than Elspeth did.

But the Clan was united once more, and Darkwind agreed to take up his long-denied powers again, to teach Elspeth the ways of magic, that she might return home an Adept.

So dawns the new day. . . .

Elspeth & Gwena

Chapter One

Elspeth rubbed her feather-adorned temples, hoping that her fears and tensions would mercifully go, and leave her mind in peace for just once today.

This isn't what I expected. I wish this were over.

Herald Elspeth, Heir to the Crown of Valdemar, survivor of a thousand and one ceremonies in her twenty-six years, brushed nervously at a nonexistent spot on her tunic and wished she were anywhere but here. "Here" was the southern edge of the lands held by the Tayledras, whom Valdemarans spoke of as the fabled Hawkbrothers. "Here" was a rough-walled cave, presumably hewn by magic, just outside the entrance to k'Sheyna Vale. "Here" was where Elspeth the Heir was stewing in her own juices from anxiety.

Elspeth was still getting used to these people and their magic. As far as she could tell the cave hadn't been there before yesterday.

Then again—the walls didn't have that raw, new look of freshly cut stone, and the sandy, uneven floor seemed ordinary. Even the entrance, a jagged break in the hillside, appeared to be perfectly natural, and healthy plants lined the edges. Greenery grew anywhere roots could find a pocket of soil to hold onto. And the smell was as damp and musty as any cave she'd ever seen during her Herald's training.

Maybe she was wrong. The cave might always have been there, but its entrance may just have been well-hidden.

Now that she thought about it, that would be a lot more like the style of the only Hawkbrother she knew, Darkwind k'Sheyna. He wasn't inclined to waste time or energy on anything—much less waste magical power. He took a dim view of profligate use of magery, something he'd made very clear to Elspeth in the first days of their acquaintance. If something could be done without using magic, that was the way he'd do it—hoarding his powers and doling them out in miserly driblets.

That was something she didn't understand at all. When you had magic, shouldn't you use it?

Darkwind didn't seem to think so.

Neither did the Chronicles she had read, of Herald-Mage Vanyel's time and before. Incredible things were possible to an Adept—and that, of course, was *why* she was here. If she'd dared, she'd have used her powers now, to shape a more comfortable seat than the rock she perched on, just inside the cave's entrance.

That at least would have given her something to *do*, instead of working herself up into a fine froth of nerves over the coming ceremony.

She glanced resentfully at Skif; *he* looked perfectly calm, if preoccupied. His dark eyes were focused somewhere inward, and if he was at all nervous, none of it showed on his square-jawed face. In fact, the only sign that he wasn't a statue was that he would run a hand through his curly brown hair once in a while.

Elspeth sighed. It figured. He was probably so busy thinking about Nyara that none of this mattered to him. The only thing that being made a Tayledras Wingbrother meant to him was that he'd be able to stay in Hawkbrother territory for as long as it took to find her.

Assuming the sword Need *let* him find Nyara. The blade not only used magic well, it—she—was a person, a woman who'd long ago traded her aging fleshly body for the steel form of an ensorceled sword. It wasn't a trade Elspeth would have made. Need could only hear, see, and feel through the senses of her bearer—and in times when her bearer wasn't particularly MindGifted or when she had no bearer at all, she had drifted off into "sleep."

She'd been asleep for a long time before Elspeth's teacher, Herald Captain Kerowyn, had passed her on to her pupil. But something—very probably something Elspeth herself had done—had finally roused her from that centuries-long sleep. Once she was awake, Need was a hundred times more formidable than she had been asleep.

She had quite a mind of her own, too. She had decided, once Elspeth was safely in the hands of the Hawkbrothers and the immediate troubles were over, that the Changechild Nyara required her far more than Elspeth did. So when Nyara chose to vanish into the wild lands surrounding the Tayledras Vale, Need evidently persuaded the catlike woman to take the sword with her.

That left Elspeth on her own, to follow her original plan; find a teacher for Valdemarans with mage-talent, and get training herself. Among the few hundred-odd things she hadn't planned on was being made a member of a Tayledras Clan. *How did I get myself into this?* she asked herself.

:Willingly and with open eyes,: her Companion Gwena replied, the sarcastic acidity of her Mindspeech not at all diluted by the fact that it was a mere whisper. *:You could have gone looking for Kero's great-uncle, the way you were supposed to. He's an Adept and a teacher. You could have followed Quenten's very clear directions, and he would have taken you as a pupil. If necessary, I would have made certain he took you as a student. But no, you had to follow your own path, you—:*

Elspeth considered slamming mental barriers closed against her Companion and decided against it. If she did, Gwena would win the argument by default.

:I told you I wasn't going to be herded to some predestined fate like a complacent ewe,: she snapped back, just as acidly, taking Gwena entirely by surprise. The Companion tossed her mane as her head jerked up with the force of the mental reply, her bright blue eyes going blank with surprise.

:I also told you,: Elspeth continued with a little less force and just a touch of satisfaction, *:that I wasn't going to play Questing Hero just to suit you and the rest of your horsey friends. I will do my best by Valdemar, but I'm doing it my own way. Besides, how do you know Kero's uncle would have been the right teacher for me? How do you know that I haven't done something better than what you planned by coming here and making contact with the Shin'a'in and the Hawkbrothers? Vanyel was certainly a well-trained Adept, and the Chronicles say that the Hawkbrothers trained him.:*

Gwena snorted scornfully, and pawed the ground with a silver hoof. *:I don't know whether you've done better or worse,:* she replied, *:but you* *were asking how you got yourself into this—this—brotherhood ceremony. And I told you.:*

Elspeth stiffened. Gwena had been eavesdropping again. *:That was a purely rhetorical question,:* she said coldly. *:Meant for myself. I wasn't broadcasting it to all and sundry. And I'd appreciate it if you'd let me keep a few thoughts private once in a while.:*

Gwena narrowed her eyes and shook her head. *:My,:* was all she said in reply. *:We're certainly touchy today, aren't we?:*

Elspeth did not dignify the comment with an answer. If anything, Gwena was twice as touchy as *she* was, and both of them knew why. The only way for Elspeth—or Skif—to be able to remain in the lands guarded by the Tayledras was to be made Wingbrothers to the Clan of k'Sheyna. But that required swearing to certain oaths—which none of their informants had yet divulged, saying only that they'd learn what those pledges were when they actually stepped into the circle to *make* them.

Elspeth had been trained in diplomacy and statecraft from childhood, and undisclosed oaths made her very nervous indeed. It wasn't so bad for Skif—*he* wasn't the Heir. But for her, well, the things she pledged herself to here could have serious consequences for Valdemar if she wasn't very careful. She carried with her the Crown's authority. The fact that a *forgotten* oath had made a crucial difference to Valdemar in the recent past only pointed up the necessity of being careful what she swore to here and now.

"Nervous?" Skif asked in a low voice, startling her out of her brooding thoughts.

She grimaced. "Of course I'm nervous. How could I not be? I'm hundred of leagues away from home, sitting in a cave with you, you thief—"

"*Former* thief," he grinned.

"Excuse me. *Former* thief and a bloodthirsty barbarian shaman from the Dhorisha Plains—"

Tre'valen cleared his throat delicately. "Pardon," he interrupted, in the Tayledras tongue, "But while I am both shaman and bloodthirsty, I am not, I think, a barbarian. We Shin'a'in have *recorded* history that predates the Mage Wars. Can you say as much, newcomer?"

For a moment, Elspeth was afraid she had offended him, then she saw the twinkle in his eye, and the barely perceptible quirk of one corner of his mouth. Tre'valen had proved to have a healthy sense of humor over the past few days, as they waited out the response of the k'Sheyna Council of Elders to their petition to remain. She had heard him refer to himself as bloodthirsty *and* a barbarian more than once. In point of fact, the shaman seemed to enjoy teasing and challenging her. . . .

"I stand rebuked, oh Elder of Elders," she replied formally, bowing as deeply as she could. She was rewarded with his broad grin, which grew broader as she continued, "Of course, the fact that you don't *do* anything with all that recorded history has no bearing at *all* on whether or not you're barbarians."

"Of course not," he replied blandly, evidently well-satisfied with her return volley. "Dwelling overmuch upon the past is the mark of the *decadent*. We aren't that, either."

"Point taken." She conceded defeat, and turned back to Skif. "So I'm here in a cave waiting for some authority to come along and demand that I swear something unspecified, which may or may not bind me to something I'd really rather not have anything to do with—why should I be nervous?"

Skif chuckled, and she restrained herself from snarling. "Now think a bit," he told her, fondly, but as if she were thirteen again. "You've read the Chronicles. Both Vanyel and his aunt swore the Wingbrother Oaths. They *had* to, or they couldn't have gone in and out of the Vales the way they did. If there was nothing in the oaths to bother them, why should you be worried?"

"Do you want that alphabetically or categorically?" She kept herself from reminding him that she *was* the Heir. After all, she had tried long and hard to make him forget that very thing. Instead she continued, "Because that was a long time ago, and a different Clan. We don't know if things have changed since then, or whether the oaths differ from Clan to Clan."

"They do not differ," Tre'valen said serenely, "and they have not changed in all of our *recorded* history. Many shaman of the Shin'a'in swear to Wingsib; and believe me, the oaths our Goddess requires of us bind us to far more than your own oaths to your Crown and country. And *She* can move her hand to chastise us at her will. I think you need not be concerned."

Well, that was some comfort, anyway. Elspeth had seen for herself how the Shin'a'in Goddess—who was, so Darkwind said, also the Goddess of *his* people—could and did manifest herself in very tangible fashion. And she had a sure and certain taste of how seriously the Shin'a'in took their oaths to protect their land from interlopers. Well, if Tre'valen knew all about the oaths and felt comfortable with them, she probably didn't have to worry.

Much.

This would be the first time she and Skif had been permitted inside the Vale of k'Sheyna itself. The Hawkbrother Mage—or was it Scout?—Darkwind had dismissed it with a shrug as "not what it once was" with no indication of what it could be like; and Tre'valen, if he knew what the Vale was like in its prime, was not telling. Descriptions in the Chronicles of Vanyel's time had been sketchy, hinting at wonders without ever revealing what the wonders were.

:Probably because they didn't know,: Gwena said, most of the sarcasm gone from her mind-voice. :Vanyel and Sayv—Savil had too much on their minds to give descriptions of where they'd been. Besides, why describe somewhere no one else would be allowed to visit? It might tempt them to try, and that would be fatal. The Tayledras tend to perforate first and apologize after.:

:Are you snooping in my head again?: Elspeth replied, with a bit less venom than before.

:No, you're echoing at me,: Gwena told her candidly. :I can't help it if your surface thoughts echo down our link unless you block them. And I can't help it if you forget to block because you're nervy.:

:All right, all right. I stand rebuked. I apologize.: Elspeth carefully put up her lightest shields, and went back to her brooding.

There was a fourth party sharing the title of Wingbrother with them, but shaman Kethra had sworn her vows a long time ago. She was considerably older than Tre'valen, though not as old as his superior, Kra'heera, and she had been a wingsib for at least a dozen years. *She* was a Healer as well as a shaman, and she was tending to Darkwind's father, Adept Starblade. Darkwind seemed reluctant to discuss what Mornelithe Falconsbane had done to his father, and Elspeth wasn't about to press him for answers. She did want to know, however, and badly; not because of morbid curiosity, but because one day she might need to know just how one Adept could so completely subvert another. One of Weaponmaster Alberich's precepts was that "anyone can be broken." If it was possible she might find herself on the receiving end of an attempt to break her, she'd like to know what she could expect. . . .

Elspeth had been a bit surprised that Tre'valen was staying on, though. He had said only that his own master had asked him to remain with k'Sheyna "because it is important." Whatever it was, it couldn't have anything to do with what Falconsbane had done to the Clan—Darkwind and Kethra were tending to that.

Could it be because of what had happened to Dawnfire?

The memory was so vividly etched in her mind, she had only to think of the hawk Dawnfire to relive what she'd seen.

The Shin'a'in stood in a rough circle below Dawnfire's perch. The red-shouldered hawk had taken a position just above the door of the gryphons' lair, her head up and into the wind, her wings slightly mantled. Then one of the Shin'a'in, a woman, put her hand up to the hawk.

Dawnfire stared measuringly at her for a moment, then stepped down from her perch onto the proffered wrist. The woman turned to face the rest.

Like all the other Shin'a'in who had come to their rescue, this one was clad entirely in black, from her long black hair to her black armor, to her tall black boots. But there was something wrong with her eyes. Something odd.

Elspeth had sensed a kind of contained power about her; the stirrings of a kind of deeply-running energy she had never felt before.

The woman raised Dawnfire high above her head and held her there, a position that should have been a torment after only a few moments, no matter how strong she was. Tayledras hawks were the size and weight of small eagles, and Dawnfire was by no means the smallest of the kind. But as the woman continued to hold Dawnfire aloft, the entire group began to hum— softly at first, then as the volume increased, and as the ruins rang with harmonics, Dawnfire started glowing.

At first Elspeth had thought it was just a trick of the setting sun, but the light about the bird grew brighter instead of fading. Then Dawnfire spread her wings and grew larger as well as brighter.

Before long, Elspeth couldn't even look at her directly; she had averted her eyes, for the light from the hawk was bright enough to cast shadows.

Kra'heera had looked at her and said, "Dawnfire has been chosen by the Warrior." She hadn't known what that meant then. She did now.

When the light and sound had faded, and she was able to look at the bird again, she saw that it was no longer a red-shouldered hawk. It was a vorcel-hawk, the emblem of Kra'heera's Clan, and the largest such bird she had ever seen. Although the light had dimmed, it had not died, and there was an otherwordly look in the hawk's eyes that had made her start with surprise.

It was the same look as in the eyes of the female warrior who held her— their eyes held neither whites, iris, or pupils—only a darkness, sprinkled with sparks of light that were visible even where Elspeth stood. As if instead of eyes, they had fields of stars.

That was when she had remembered the description of the Shin'a'in Goddess—and had realized exactly what she was looking at. Small wonder the memory was as vivid as it was; it wasn't every day an ordinary mortal saw a living Goddess and her Avatar.

She eyed Tre'valen with speculation. No matter how casually the elder shaman had treated the event afterward, she wondered if he hadn't been just as surprised as everyone else by the appearance of his Goddess. From what little she understood, change came to the Plains seldom and slowly. When Kerowyn had regaled them with tales of her Shin'a'in cousins, had she ever said *anything* about their Goddess creating Avatars? Elspeth didn't remember anything like that. . . .

So maybe this was something new for them. Maybe that was why Tre'valen was here; to watch for Dawnfire, and to try and figure out the reasons behind his Goddess' actions.

Well, if that was the case, he must have told the Hawkbrothers, or at least their leaders. On the surface none of this seemed to have anything to do with her—but Elspeth didn't take anything for granted anymore. After all, why should the Shin'a'in have shown up at all then? Who could have predicted she'd get involved with the Tayledras, and wind up adding their enemies to her own rather formidable list? *I ought to ask him later if I'm right about all that. Maybe we can help each other out.*

Gwena walked to the entrance of the cave and looked out—impatiently, Elspeth thought. Her Mindspoken words to her Chosen confirmed that. *:I wish I knew what it was they were spending so much time doing in there,:* she said. *:They've certainly been keeping us cooling our heels long enough. At this rate, that ceremony of theirs won't be over until dark.:*

Elspeth wondered why *she* was so impatient—the Companions weren't the ones being sworn in, even though they wouldn't be permitted in the Vale until the Heralds were. Evidently, by common consensus, the Tayledras regarded the Companions as creatures that simply didn't require oaths to hold them.

Hmm. That requires thought. Do they think Gwena is some kind of Avatar herself? The idea was kind of funny. *If they ever listened to her moaning and griping they'd soon lose that particular illusion! I rather doubt Gwena's hiding that kind of secret.*

Not that she hadn't been hiding other kinds of secrets. This "plan" for Elspeth's future that the Companions had been plotting, for one. And there were others. . . .

Shortly after Nyara had vanished, taking Need with her, Elspeth noticed that Gwena was missing. Worried about her—since Gwena had been injured in the fight with Falconsbane's mage-beasts—she had tried to find her Companion, and when she failed, tried to Mindtouch her. When *that* failed, she had been alarmed and had gone looking for her.

Gwena had been perfectly all right—but she'd been locked in a self-induced trance, shielded even against the prying of Elspeth's thoughts. And when she'd come out of it, she'd been very unhappy to find her Chosen standing there, tapping her foot impatiently, waiting for an answer.

Under pressure from both Elspeth and Skif, she reluctantly admitted that she had been in contact with another Companion in Valdemar all during this journey. Elspeth had expected that Companion to be her mother's—and had been both surprised and relieved to find that it was actually Rolan, the Companion of the Queen's Own Herald, Talia.

Then she had been annoyed, though she hadn't made much of an issue about it. She hadn't known that Companions could relay messages that far—and so far as she was aware, *no one* knew that little fact. Was it just Gwena and Rolan, or could others do it, too? One way or the other, it was one more thing that the Companions had been hiding. So how much more could they do that they hadn't revealed?

Gwena had said crossly that Elspeth should have expected that "arrangements would be made." And Elspeth had been forced to agree. After all, she was the Heir, and she'd been allowed to go haring off into the unknown with only one Herald to guard her back. For all that she'd managed to get complete agreement from the Council and Heraldic Circle, it was still rather irresponsible. If Queen Selenay had *not* had a way to get news about her errrant offspring, she'd likely have had strong hysterics before a month was out. Especially after Elspeth departed from the agreed-upon itinerary, and "vanished" into the Dhorisha Plains.

Still, she hadn't much liked the idea that little reports on her progress were being sent back home, as if she was some kind of child on her first outing without Mama.

On the other hand, Gwena had told them, when Elspeth pressed her for *exactly* what she'd been telling Rolan, that the "reports" she'd been sending Rolan were edited. "Heavily edited," in fact, was what the Companion had said, rather glumly. Which was just as well. If Selenay had the smallest inkling just how much danger Elspeth and Skif had gotten themselves into—

She'd have found a way to haul me back, that's what she'd have done, and plunked me down in nice safe embroidery classes for the rest of my natural life.

How could she possibly explain to her mother that ever since she'd started on this trip—even before she'd started—she'd had the feeling that the Crown wasn't something she was ever going to wear? Even if she had tried to tell her, Selenay would have taken it the wrong way; she'd have been sure that Elspeth had some premonition of doom, and there she'd be in embroidery class again, away from all possibility of danger.

What an awful idea.

And it wasn't a premonition of "doom," or anything like one. It was just the feeling that she was never going to rule. That one of the twins was going to have the throne, and the other—

The other would be King's Own. Not a bad arrangement, since they aren't at all alike. Wouldn't be the first time that sibs were Monarch and Monarch's Own.

Her fate was something else entirely—though what, she hadn't the faintest notion. Even though her conscience bothered her now that she was so far away from home, she'd been doing some useful work, assigned to Kerowyn and the Skybolts. And, though she would never have believed it when she left Haven, she was homesick.

She kept telling herself that there wasn't much she had been doing that couldn't be done by Talia and Daren . . . and that though she wasn't a ForeSeer, she'd never been wrong when she got really strong feelings about something. There was something she had to do, and it was tied up with learning magic.

She'd said as much to Gwena, who'd agreed with her. "Even though you *aren't* following the course we'd planned for you," she'd added.

Too bad. So I'm a stubborn bitch. I do things my way, or not at all, and if Mother, Gwena, and Rolan don't like it, I'm not at all sorry. So there. Nyah, nyah. She grinned to herself at her own childish thought. Really, it was a very good thing that the messages were going through Rolan to Talia and only *then* to Selenay. Rolan had more of a sense of humor than Gwena—and a little more tolerance. And Talia knew her former charge very well indeed. Further, Talia had told Elspeth privately that she thought the Queen was reacting like most mothers to the evidences of her daughter growing up and developing a mind of her own.

Badly.

Oh, not as badly as she could have, but all things considered, it was much better for Elspeth to be off beyond Mama's reach for a while. By the time she returned, it might be possible for Queen Selenay to admit that her daughter wasn't a foolish, headstrong, *stupid* child anymore.

I've managed to acquire a little sense, anyway. . . .

:Gather yourself, my dear,: Gwena Mindspoke, interrupting her thoughts. *:They're coming for you. Finally.:*

Elspeth glanced out of the corner of her eye at Skif and Tre'valen. Skif looked as if he were concentrating on every word that the Hawk-brother called Iceshadow spoke. Actually, he probably was; his command of the Tayledras tongue wasn't anywhere near as good as hers. Odd; she'd slipped right into the language as if she had known it most of her life.

Oh, that's probably because it's like Shin'a'in, and Kero taught me some of that.

Tre'valen wore that inscrutable face that Kero always put on when she was determined not to let anyone know what she was thinking. "Gambling-face," she called it.

The more she thought about it, the better she liked the idea of approaching Tre'valen later to see if they could do anything for each other. She felt a lot more comfortable around him—around any of the Shin'a'in, really—than she did around the Tayledras. That was probably because she *could* read him, a little. He and Kethra reminded her of Kero; well, that shouldn't surprise her. Kero had trained *her*, and Kero had, in turn, been trained by a Shin'a'in Swordsworn, so there was a lot of Shin'a'in attitude and thinking patterns in the way Kero looked at things. A good bit of that had rubbed off on her pupil, without a doubt. The Tayledras, however, were very exotic, and Darkwind had been so hard to read that Elspeth had given up even trying.

I wonder if they seem that way to Tre'valen?

They hadn't had much of a chance to see the Vale; as Gwena had predicted, it was sunset when the Hawkbrothers came for them, and most of the Vale was shrouded in shadows as they passed through it. Elspeth had gotten some impressions that had taken her breath away, however—of luxuriant growth that made any forest she'd ever seen look sparse by comparison, and trees so enormous her mind refused to accept their size. The Companions had trailed along behind as they followed a well-worn path past curtaining vines covered with cascading flowers the size of her hand, and bushes with leaves bigger than a saddle. Elspeth couldn't wait to see the place in the daytime.

Darkwind himself had come to fetch them, as their sponsor into the Clan; Kethra was Tre'valen's. With him had come at least a dozen more Tayledras—and Elspeth had done her best not to stare, but it had been very difficult. She had thought that Darkwind was a typical Hawk-brother, and she had been just a little disappointed, given the hints in the Chronicles of how strange the Hawkbrothers were, at his shoulder-length, mottled-brown hair and his drab clothing. The Chronicles had talked about Moondance and Starwind being as "brightly plumaged as firebirds" and she'd cherished images of brilliant colors and weird cloth-ing, maybe things that didn't look like clothing at all.

She wasn't disappointed any longer. The dozen Tayledras with Dark-wind had been garbed as wildly and beautifully as she could have wished. Every one of them had hair that was waist-length or longer, white as ice, and twined with feathers, crystals, bells, slender chains, or strands of silk matching their—costumes. That was the only word she could arrive at. "Clothing" certainly wasn't adequate—not for robes with layered sleeves that trailed on the ground, hugged the arm like silken skin, were scal-loped, bejeweled, embroidered, and tapestried. "Garb" didn't describe tunics and gowns that mimicked feathers, leaves, flower petals, frozen waterfalls. Every one of the dozen was unique; every one was incredible and complex. And yet, the costumes weren't any less functional than, say, Valdemaran Court gear; although she wouldn't have known how to move in those outfits without tripping over something.

She felt for the first time as if she had truly left the world she knew and had stepped into the pages of a tale.

Even Darkwind—drab, disappointing Darkwind—had been trans-formed. Although his hair was still shoulder-length, he had somehow managed to get *patterns* dyed into it. She assumed it was dye; it might not have been. How would she know? It might have been magic. Birds flickered whitely against a dark gold background every time he moved his head, as if his hair was a forest in autumn with doves flying through it. And his costume was as fanciful as the rest—although a little more practical. He had eschewed trailing sleeves and hemlines for embroidery and something that stayed fairly close to his body. But he was just as eye-dazzling in his way as the others were in theirs.

He smiled shyly when he saw the surprise and approval in her ex-pression, but said nothing, simply gesturing for her and Skif to follow him into the depths of the Vale. Kethra led Tre'valen in a similar fash-ion; the rest of the Tayledras came behind, with mage-lights bobbing above their heads, and the Companions bringing up the rear. Above the walls of the valley and the tops of the towering trees, the sky still glowed blue, with the west a warm gold—in the shelter of the massive branches, dense blue shadows obscured all but the trail they walked.

They had emerged in a clearing, ringed and paved with stone. In the very center of the circular area stood a cracked and half-broken stone with a brazier at its foot, all of it lit by more mage-lights. This strange monolith, she assumed, was the Heartstone—damaged, its wild energies barely restrained by multiple layers of shielding. Darkwind had warned her to keep tight personal shields about her when she was near it; she saw no reason to argue with him. Even through her protections she felt something vaguely *wrong* with the stone, a kind of sickness about it. It wasn't something she could put a finger on, or point to, but the uneasy feeling was definitely there.

Iceshadow—wearing an elaborate costume that made him look as if he was half a man and half a delicate, frozen fountain—took his place before the stone. In the transparent, unwavering illumination of the mage-lights, he could have been a dream, an illusion—an ice sculpture brought to life. Then he moved, gracefully, holding up his hands—and with no more preparation than that, Elspeth found herself surrounded by a blue glow that was quite familiar.

Truth Spell? Bright Havens, did we get it from them, or did they get it from Vanyel?

The other question that occurred to her, with a touch of envy, was how Iceshadow had managed to call the spell up with no preparation and in no more than a heartbeat. It took her a good bit of time to call up a Truth Spell, and she was one of the best in her class at that particular exercise. Iceshadow hadn't even needed to *think* about it, so far as she had been able to tell. He just gestured, and there it was. That was as impressive as all the lightnings and thunders she'd seen—and cast—fighting Falconsbane and his creatures. Iceshadow had not only cast the spell as easily as breathing, he had made it *look* effortless.

Iceshadow lowered his arms, and a white horn-tufted owl drifted down out of the trees to land on his shoulder. He watched the three of them serenely for a moment, and then folded his hands in his sleeves. "Do you bring any ill-intent into this Vale?" he asked, conversationally.

Was this the beginning of the oathtaking? It must be. She shook her head, and Skif mouthed the word "No."

Iceshadow smiled slightly, and continued; still calm, still casual. "Is it your wish to be made a brother of this Clan?"

They both answered with nods.

Now Iceshadow sobered; the owl settled itself and turned unblinking eyes upon them, as if it, too, was weighing the truth of their intent. Elspeth was suddenly hyperaware of everything about her; the faint, cool breeze on her back, the way it stirred Iceshadow's clothing, Skif's hair, the fringe on Tre'valen's sash. The way the blue light from the spell reflected in the onlookers' eyes. The call of a bird, somewhere out in the Vale. Iceshadow took a deep breath, and spoke, in a soft voice that still carried incredible intensity. "Hear, then, the privileges of brotherhood: to come and go freely within all lands held by Tayledras k'Sheyna; to call upon your brothers in times of need; to ask of us teaching; to make your home among us. Hear also the responsibilities of brotherhood: to keep the secrets of the Clan; to neither bring nor lead strangers among us; to keep our lands and guard them as we do; to answer to our need if no other oath prevents; to teach when it is asked of you, aid when it is asked of you, give shelter and succor to your brothers of the Clan, of Tayledras, and of Shin'a'in. Can you be bound to these conditions?"

"Yes," Elspeth breathed. It would not have been unreasonable to swear them to absolute secrecy, or to require that they pledge a formal and complicated alliance to the Clan. Skif seemed just as surprised as he answered in the affirmative.

The breeze gusted past again, and the owl roused its feathers, shaking himself vigorously before settling down to resume his stare at them. Iceshadow watched them as unblinkingly as his owl. "Then there is another vow you must make," Iceshadow continued. "But it is one that you must not make in ignorance. So listen—watch—and heed—"

He gestured again, and as Elspeth caught her breath in startlement, a globe of glowing white mist rose up from the pavement between them, obscuring everything on the other side of the circle. As Elspeth turned her attention from the Hawkbrother to the globe of starlight, she saw that there was a picture forming in it—

She bit her lip when the picture cleared, this time with a feeling of incredulity and horror; she had seen her own land ravaged by warfare, but this was beyond anything she had ever dreamed in her worst nightmares. Encased in the glowing globe was the image of a devastated land; the viewpoint was from the edge of a blasted crater so wide she literally could not see the other side. She blinked and swallowed, finding it hard to comprehend destruction on so vast a scale, and nauseated by the very idea that such a thing could have happened. To see a place that must once have been green, been full of people, animals, trees and plants—to see it not only ravaged, but utterly *annihilated*—the shock of it drove any real thoughts from her head for a moment. Beside her, Tre'valen started in surprise, as if this was something *he* knew about but had not expected to see here.

"This was the homeland, long and long ago." Iceshadow's voice drifted across the silence, a voice filled with such sadness and loss that it seemed as if what Elspeth saw might have happened a day ago, rather than centuries ago. "This was the homeplace of the people called Kaled'a'in. This was all that remained, at the end of the First and Last conflict, the Mage Wars."

The scene shifted, to a group of armed, subdued people, all with the long black hair and golden skin of the Shin'a'in, gathered on the edge of the crater. There was some confusion as they and their animals— horses, huge dogs, hunting cats, and birds of prey—milled about, and then it was apparent that about half of them were packing up and moving off, away from the crater, while the rest stayed.

"We fled from the destruction, and returned when we could. This was what we found, and there was mourning and confusion. Then came anger, at what had happened, at what had caused it. There was dissent over what the people should do. Some wished to renounce all magic; some, to make *further* use of magic to keep the Clans alive in this new and alien world. There was no compromise possible between those positions—dissent became argument, and argument became hate. That was when, rather than turn dissent to feud, the two sides agreed to divide, and with this decision came the Sundering of the Clans. Those who renounced magic became the Shin'a'in, while those who sought magery removed themselves from the rest, calling themselves *Tayledras*, after the birds that they had helped to bring into being. These, our Fathers and Mothers, went north."

Again the scene shifted, to something that had probably been a forest. Once.

Now it was another kind of nightmare; instead of lifelessness, twisted and contorted wildlife ran riot. The vegetation grew so thick it formed a solid green wall on either side of the road, except that it was hard to tell some of the flora from some of the fauna. There were plants that groped after the passing Clansfolk, and animals that were rooted to the spot like plants, some watching them with indifferent eyes, others that screamed unendingly. There were creatures she half-glimpsed through the veils of vines hanging from every branch that made Elspeth shudder. As she tried to make sense of confusion of color and motion, the group shown was attacked by things that were horribly worse than the creatures Falconsbane had sent against them—things that seemed to be nothing but teeth and claws, with armored plates covering everything but their joints.

Iceshadow's voice made her jump. "The five Clans that were now Tayledras found that the lands beyond the homeland were ravaged by the forces of twisted and tainted magic. No human or bird could survive there for long. Either they must starve, for they could not spare a moment from defense to grow or hunt their food, or they must give up defense and perish at the hands of the monsters that inhabited these lands. They despaired, for there was nowhere else for them to go."

The scene fogged for a moment, and re-formed. The band of Tayledras had made a camp on the top of a hill, the earth scorched bare by fire, with a temporary palisade of thorny branches about the camp—but it was obvious it could not last for long against any kind of attack.

"They knew they could go no farther," Iceshadow concluded. "So, as their kindred that would become the Shin'a'in would do, they prayed to their Goddess. And She answered. Here is her answer to their plea."

Nothing Elspeth had watched prepared her for what happened as the mist clouded again.

Suddenly there was no ball of glowing mist with pictures in it before her; suddenly there was no clearing, no Hawkbrothers, no Skif—

—no light, no sound, no *world*.

Only herself, a sky full of stars stretching in every direction—

—including *down*—

And out of this starry nothingness arose a white-hot flame that was somehow also a woman. Too bright to see clearly, She changed from moment to moment, and the raw Power emanating from Her made Elspeth tremble. She'd have fallen to her knees—if she could have figured out how to do so in the midst of all this starry space.

I have heard your prayers, She said, in a voice that filled Elspeth's mind, leaving no room for anything, not even fear. *There is a price to be paid for what you ask, and that price is in your lives, and your freedom.*

She gestured, and in the palm of Her hand was cupped the weirdly twisted landscape of the forest the Clansfolk had entered. *Terrible magics have warped this land, and only magic can heal it again. Therefore I offer this, that you have asked of me. I shall grant you safety here, long enough to establish each of you a Clan holding. I shall teach you the means of creating a place in the midst of the holding wherein you shall dwell in protection. I shall grant you the knowledge of Adepts, to use and concentrate the magic— and a knowledge even Adepts have not—to create a center of such power that the greatest of the mages who caused these changes would look upon you with envy.*

To this you shall swear, in return. You will cleanse these lands—restore them to what they were before the Wars. You shall destroy the creatures of evil intent, cherish and succor the innocent victims of this catastrophe, and find shelter for those that are merely animals, meaning neither good nor ill. You shall destroy those old weapons you may find, that they may not be misused again. You shall cleanse the land you hold—and then you shall move on, to another place, to begin again. All of your children that are Mage-Gifted shall follow this path. All who are not shall guard and aid the ones who are. You shall be the Healers and Protectors—and you shall never permit the magics you manipulate here to be used for ill, nor shall you permit strangers within your ranks, unless they be sworn to the Clans. This you must do, at whatever cost to yourselves.

Abruptly, the vision was gone. Elspeth shook her head, blinking and still trembling with reaction; more than a little disoriented. There was nothing now in the clearing but what had been there when they entered; even the glowing mist was gone.

She tried to shake off the effect of the vision—if that was what it had been. She had *been there* for a moment; she didn't at all doubt that she had experienced exactly the same thing as those long-ago Hawkbrothers had. What she couldn't understand was why Skif didn't seem particularly affected, but Tre'valen looked just as dazed and bedazzled as she felt. Long ago, when she was younger, she had first heard the story of King Valdemar and the first appearance of the Companions, and had thought it a very pretty tale. *Now* she had the glimmering of what King Valdemar just *might* have experienced when his prayers were answered. It shook her to the soul. It made her understand why some people became ardent, abject devotees of deities.

Iceshadow was silent for a long moment, while she and Tre'valen gathered their scattered wits. Elspeth thought that he watched her particularly closely, although she couldn't be sure of that. Finally, he spoke again.

"This is the last oath you must swear—that you will aid your brothers of the Clan in their duty, as your own oaths permit—and that *never will you use what is taught you here for the sake of your own power, pride, and status.*"

He held his hand up, to forestall their immediate answers. "I shall not ask you to swear never to use it to harm—for one day you may find yourself facing an enemy who would destroy far more than you if he is given the opportunity to do so. But you must *never* use your learning for selfish purposes, to increase your own importance, to make your life one of pointless leisure, to merely indulge your fancies. Can you swear to that?"

Elspeth heaved a sigh of relief; that was enough like the Oaths a Herald took before the Circle that the wording made very little difference. She gave her assent with a much lighter heart, grateful that all of the vows she'd been asked to make seemed to take into account the fact that those outside the Clan had other duties and oaths of their own that might take precedence.

Now as long as both sets of promises never come into conflict, I should be all right.

Throughout the entire oathtaking, the blue glow of the Truth Spell remained steady around all three of them. Now Iceshadow banished the spell with another gesture, just as the deepening blue of the sky above them took on the golden-red streaks of the last moments of sunset. Elspeth looked up for a moment, as some movement against the luminous blue above caught her eye, and discovered that what had attracted her attention was the steady circling of a bird over their clearing. A bird of prey, by the shape.

Nothing unusual, not here in the heart of a Tayledras Clan territory, but something about the bird made her take a second, closer look.

It was big; much bigger than she had thought, at first. In fact, it was easily the size of the largest eagle she had ever seen. But it had the distinctive tail-striping of a vorcel-hawk; that was *one* bird she would never again mistake for anything else.

A vorcel-hawk the size of an eagle, or larger—and unless it was a trick of the light, it was glowing.

Dawnfire? The thought was inevitable. She glanced back down at Tre'valen, only to see that he was watching the hawk as well, though no one else seemed to notice that it was there. The expression on his face was a most peculiar one; he looked both excited and obscurely disturbed, at one and the same time.

The hawk made a final circle above, then spiraled upward, to be lost in the scarlet-and-golden glory of the sunset. Tre'valen licked his lips and looked down again; reluctantly, it seemed to her. He caught her watching him before she could look away, and something in his eyes made her nod, once, slowly; admitting, without actually saying anything, that she had seen the bird as well.

His lips formed the merest ghost of a smile, and he turned his attention back toward Iceshadow.

Less time had passed than she had thought. The Tayledras Adept was only now finishing *his* words of acceptance, admitting them into the Clan as Wingsiblings, and welcoming them as allies and friends.

She shook her head again, feeling another shiver of disorientation. Time was doing strange things around her, today. And Skif didn't seem to be affected by any of it. Was it because she was a mage, or was it something else entirely?

Or was it just nerves?

Not that it really mattered at the moment. The ceremony wasn't *quite* over yet, although the formal pledging of vows was. Darkwind had explained this afternoon as he brought them to the cave to wait, that Iceshadow wanted to talk to her, Skif, and their Companions before he unleashed the rest of the Clan on them.

"He wants to give you a clearer idea of what you've getting involved with," he had said; she had wondered at the time if he was joking a little or being completely serious.

But Iceshadow was, indeed, walking across the paving toward them with another strange Hawkbrother at his side, and Darkwind and the Companions following behind. The other Tayledras drifted off, seeming to melt into the luxuriant foliage.

"So, I meet the Heralds at last," the Adept said, as he got within easy conversational distance of them. "The last of your kind to be within a Clan was—what?" He looked to the other Tayledras for an answer.

"Near seven hundred years ago," the stranger supplied. Elspeth noticed, now that he was near enough for her to note details, that he was very pale, very tired-looking; there were lines of pain around his eyes and mouth. He made a little grimace. "That was k'Treva, though. They always were—hmm—unconventional."

"I would say, innovative, Starblade," Iceshadow chided gently. "The experience certainly did them no harm and much good, from all I have heard out of the tales."

At his naming the stranger, Elspeth took a moment for a second, closer, but covert examination of him. So this was Darkwind's father? They didn't look all that much alike, but that could be illness and the differences in their hair as much as anything. Starblade was wearing a more—conservative costume than the rest of his fellows; in fact, there was something about it that seemed very similar to the one Darkwind was wearing; something that invoked birds and their wings, without actually imitating feathers. As if they had been designed by the same mind. Interesting.

"The k'Treva Tayledras that welcomed the Heralds back then—that would have been Moondance and Starwind k'Treva, wouldn't it?" she replied, obviously startling all three of the Hawkbrothers, and earning a covert grin of approval from Tre'valen. "That was in the Chronicles of Herald Vanyel's time; I read them, and that was why I came here, to try and find more Tayledras, if I could. The Heralds were Vanyel Ashkevron and his aunt, Savil—Vanyel was the last of the Herald-Mages. The Chronicles said that he spent quite a lot of time there, in k'Treva Vale, especially when he was young, and that Starwind taught him most of what he knew about magic."

"That is quite true, young one," Starblade replied, his voice warming a little with what sounded to her like approval. "Or at least, that is what *our* records told me. Iceshadow, my friend, would it be possible for us to move to somewhere a little less formal for the rest of this?" He gestured apologetically to her, and to Skif and Tre'valen, "I am sorry, but I fear I must beg your indulgence and find a place to sit."

"What about the fishpond over there?" Darkwind asked, pointing with his chin somewhere behind Iceshadow's shoulder. "It's quiet enough, and there shouldn't be anyone there after the sun sets."

"Good enough," his father replied—gratefully, Elspeth thought. "There should be room for your large friends, and seating enough for all of us."

Iceshadow gestured to the younger Hawkbrother to lead the way; Elspeth followed him, and the rest trailed behind her. By now it was becoming quite dark, and she was grateful for the mage-lights Iceshadow and Starblade produced. She found that distances were deceptive in the Vale; the ornamental fishpond Darkwind spoke of was actually hardly more than a stone's throw away from the Heartstone circle, and yet it might easily have been halfway across the Vale. Once they had arranged themselves around it, there was no way of telling that the Heartstone was anywhere nearby.

"Well," Starblade said, once he had settled himself in a comfortable "chair" formed of the roots of a tree with moss cupped where a cushion would be. Elspeth took a second, similar seat, and found it incredibly comfortable. "Iceshadow has asked me to explain to you just what sort of a—ah—situation you have unwittingly involved yourselves in. And since I am the partial cause of that situation, I think it only fair that I make the attempt."

Elspeth met his eyes and recognized what she saw there. Pain, mental and physical. This conversation was going to cost him something—but she had seen some of that same pain in Darkwind's eyes whenever he had spoken of his father, and she knew that Starblade had put that pain there. The man was right. It *was* only fair.

She settled herself and nodded to him, decisively. "Go ahead," she said. "I don't think anything you say is going to make us change our minds, but I was trained as a tactician; I like to know what I can expect." She smiled, slightly. "Good or bad."

Starblade nodded gravely, and leaned forward. He cradled his right hand around his bandaged left hand—surely there must be a story behind that as well. This was either going to be very short, or very long. Whichever it was, it was going to be interesting.

She had told the truth about not changing her mind; she only hoped what she learned wasn't going to make her regret her own decisions. It was a little too late for regret now.

It was not, however, too early for strategy. It was *never* too early, or too late, for that.

The Celebration

Chapter Two

"I know you are an Outlander . . . but I know not how much my son has told you of our troubles here," Starblade began, with a sober glance at Darkwind, "so I shall tell my tale from the outset, and beg your patience if I repeat what you know." He glanced down at the pond, with its patient, colorful carp skimming just below the surface of the water. "I shall be as brief as I can."

He paused for a moment, clearly organizing his thoughts. "Mornelithe Falconsbane," he said at last. "It all comes down to him."

Darkwind nodded grimly, but said nothing.

"The Heartstone—" Starblade closed his eyes, but not before Elspeth had seen another shadow of pain pass across them. "Its shattering is his doing, but by my hand. I was foolish and vain; I thought myself clever, and I found out differently. He caught me through my foolishness, and my pride. He broke me, and he used me."

Terse speech, but obviously each word cost him dearly. "Through me, he set his darkness upon the Heartstone, disrupted our magics, broke it from the inside, and in so doing, caused the deaths of many of our mages. Because of me, three-fourths of the Clan are lost somewhere in the wilderness."

"How?" Elspeth asked, puzzled. "I mean, how could you lose that many people?"

Starblade toyed with a glass-beaded feather braided into his hair. "When a Clan moves, it is our way to establish the children, the lesser mages, the weak and the old, with the bulk of our scouts and warriors to protect them, at a new site. We send them by means of a Gate, we drain the Stone of its power and send it to the new Stone, then we follow. But when we filled the Stone with all the Clan's power in preparation for diverting the power to the new site, the Heartstone shattered, and the Adept holding the Gate open died with the shattering. We had no one among us who could use the Heartstone, damaged as it was, to go to them by Gate. We barely know the true location of the rest of the Clan, for the scouts who had found the new place were with them."

"And they couldn't reach you without sending badly-needed fighters," Elspeth supplied. "I take it none of the lesser mages were able to build these Gate things?"

"Only an Adept can master the Gate Spell," Iceshadow replied. "And we fear that even if they had one who could cast it, the Stone is too unstable and there may be no way of bringing a Gate near to it."

"All the scouts that knew the overland way to the new Vale are at that Vale," Darkwind repeated. "Our number would be decimated trying to get to them by foot—leagues traveled are hard-won going North—and they cannot come to us, burdened with the old, the young, the sick."

His father nodded. "Indeed. So—to make the bad much the worse, Falconsbane continued to work through me, keeping the Clan from reaching for help, keeping the Adepts still remaining from stabilizing the Stone, and keeping those who knew me well at a distance." Starblade averted his eyes from Darkwind, but the reference was plain enough. "He hoped, I think, to wear us down until he could penetrate our defenses at his leisure and usurp the Stone and the power it still held. But he had not reckoned on our clever allies, the gryphons—and he had not reckoned on the courage and good sense of my son."

"He couldn't have guessed Nyara would turn against him, either," Skif put in, with a hint of pride.

"No—nor the appearance of you and all that you represented," Tre'valen told him, his eyes showing a hint of sardonic humor. "To tell you true, there was an unexpected marshaling of powers from all sides.

Falconsbane certainly did not plan on that, nor the involvement of the Shin'a'in. That was his downfall."

"If he lives still, he cannot be prospering," Iceshadow put in. "Shin'a'in arrows found a mark in him; that much we know. And he has lost much in the way of power and creatures."

"I wonder at that; Shin'a'in do not often miss in such attacks, their Goddess oft assists the arrow to the mark. But, despite that, I doubt that he lives," Starblade sighed. "I think that the arrows of the Shin'a'in found their mark; that he fled only to die. There has been no sign of him or his creatures, and his escape was by blood-magic . . . with his own blood. That is an act of finality among mages."

Elspeth shrugged. "I don't know one way or the other about him, but the point, it seems to me, is that he has left the Vale in one snarled mess."

Starblade nodded, and smoothed his braided hair back behind his ears. "My son has said he will teach you in the use of your Mage-Gift; that is a good thing, I think—but he will need to relearn much as he teaches you. It would be hazardous for you to do much practice of that learning within the Vale itself; though you would be protected from threats that are outside the Vale, the Stone is yet dangerous."

Gwena stamped a hoof and snorted agreement, bobbing her head vigorously. Elspeth nodded; she felt the same. Starblade bore many years' experience, and knew the magics involved as only a Tayledras Adept could. Better to err on the side of safety.

"I think," Darkwind said slowly, "that we may practice outside the Vale for some time in relative safety. It will only be as we approach the greater Adept-magics that we will need the shieldings of the Vale."

"By then, the Council and I should have come to some decision on the Stone," Iceshadow told them. "Either we shall have begun to heal it ourselves, or we shall have found a way to deal with it."

He glanced at Elspeth, with a certain amount of expectation in the look. She sighed, knowing what that look meant. "If you're wondering if you can count on my help with this Heartstone of yours, I *do* remember those oaths I just took," she said, with a little shake of her head. "I can't say I *like* the idea of mucking about with that much power gone wrong, but what I can do, I will."

Both Iceshadow and Starblade gave her nods of approval, but she wasn't quite done. "What I need to know, here, is this—how much more trouble from outside can we expect while we're doing all this? Starblade,

I hope you'll forgive my asking this, but you were a point of weakness before. Just how vulnerable are you to more meddling?''

Starblade wet his lips with the tip of his tongue before replying. ''To meddling—I would say not at all. Even if Falconsbane still lives, and as I said, I do not think that he does, Iceshadow and Kethra have changed all the paths that made me open to him. To have me so his slave again, he would have to have me in his hand. He would break me faster—for I am that much more fragile than I was—but he would have to have me to break me.''

''And?'' Elspeth raised an eyebrow.

''And I shall not leave this Vale until I walk through the Gate to a new one,'' he told her. ''I have been broken and am mending, but I am still weak to be broken again, and I will not chance it, for the sake of all of us.''

Elspeth nodded, satisfied, but Skif frowned. ''What about attack?'' he asked. ''Are you weaker to attack than—say—Iceshadow?''

Starblade looked mildly surprised by the question. ''I—think not,'' he said immediately. ''The weaknesses I have still require someone who *knows* me to exploit, and to have me, if not within physical touching, certainly within sight.''

Skif glanced over at Tre'valen, who shrugged. ''The only magics I know intimately are those of the Goddess,'' he said. ''I am of no help nor hindrance in these things. These are good things to know, Starblade. I thank you for telling them.''

''I can't think of any more questions,'' Skif admitted. ''I'm no mage, and I'm no help to you. Frankly, I'll be a lot more help in finding Nyara and that damned sword she carries.''

''Now *that* I need to know something of,'' Starblade said immediately. And Elspeth found herself the focus of every eye in the little clearing.

She fidgeted a little, uncomfortably. ''I don't know as much about Need as I'd like,'' she replied, reluctantly. ''She predates the Mage Wars, I think. At least, I didn't recognize anything she showed us when she let us into her memories. So she's either very old, or from awfully far away.''

''I would say, very old,'' Darkwing opined, toying with a feather in a gesture uncannily—and probably unconsciously—like his father. ''I would say, she is as old as the oldest artifact I have ever seen. She gave me the impression of great age, as great as any of the things I have stumbled upon in the ruins.''

Elspeth tilted her head back and took a deep breath of the cool, flower-scented air, using the moment to think. "What I do know is she was a member of some kind of quasi-religious order, with gods I never heard of—male and female twins."

She gave the Hawkbrothers a glance of inquiry; all three of them shrugged as if the reference meant nothing to them either. "Well, even though at one time she'd been a warrior, she called herself a Mage-Smith." Elspeth closed her eyes for a moment, to call up the memories that Need had shared with her and Skif. "As to how she became a sword in the first place—someone attacked the Order while she was gone—wiped out the older members, enslaved the young girls, stole everything they could carry. The only ones left were Need, who was too old to fight, and a young apprentice. So Need took a special sword that she'd forged spells into, spells of healing and luck—and forged *herself* into it as well."

"How?" Iceshadow asked, genuinely interested.

Elspeth shook her head. "It wasn't something I'd have done. She did some kind of preparation, then she killed her human body with the blade so that she could move her spirit into the sword. Then as long as the girl carried her, Need could give her both the skills of a fighter and of a Mage-Smith."

All three of the Adepts looked startled at that. "How could that be?" Starblade asked.

"Well, she could operate on her own as a mage, or through her bearer," Elspeth told him. "Or she could direct her bearer, if the bearer was Mage-Gifted—that was how she worked with me, after I refused to let her take me over. But for fighting skills, you had to let her completely take control of your body." She grimaced. "I'm afraid I wouldn't let her, artifact, mage, or no. She didn't much care for my attitude."

A hint of smile appeared around Starblade's mouth; Darkwind grinned openly. "Why am I not surprised by that?" the younger mage said, to no one in particular.

Elspeth was glad that the darkness hid her flush; Darkwind seemed to have an uncanny ability to poke pins into her pride. Maybe it was just ill-luck, or bad timing.

She licked her lips and kept her temper. "I think that she wasn't used to being thwarted," she said carefully. "Captain Kerowyn, who had her before I did, told me that I would have to be prepared to counter her, that she'd have me haring off to rescue whatever female nearby was in trouble, whether or not it was a good idea to poke my nose into her problems. That, though, was while she was still—'' Elspeth thought a moment. ''As I remember, she called it 'being asleep.' I gathered that the personality was dormant, unconscious for a long time. Need never told me why.''

''The blade may not have wanted you to know why,'' Tre'valen said smoothly. ''Certainly, if you contradicted her will, she would not be so free with revealing secrets.''

''That's true,'' she acknowledged. ''Anyway, she didn't start to wake up again until I was at Kata'shin'a'in. So I don't know as much as I'd like to about her. I think she *is* likely to take over Nyara; I think that after years of her father molding her to his whim and will, Nyara is inclined to be manipulated like that.''

Skif bristled, and started to say something. Darkwind's thoughtful statement forestalled him.

''That would not be entirely ill for her,'' the Hawkbrother said quietly. ''Especially since—it seems, at least to me—Need has no intention of doing anything detrimental. I think she seeks to make her bearer a stronger woman. It is just that she does not like to have *her* will thwarted.''

Elspeth smiled ruefully. ''I can testify to that,'' she said.

''It seems to me this might be a good thing for the Changechild,'' Starblade added thoughtfully. ''Despite what has happened, I—I can feel pity for Nyara. She and I—'' he faltered ''—we have much, much in common. What Falconsbane did to her—it is very like what he did to me. It may be that this sword, if it has healing magics like those of Kethra and Iceshadow, can reverse some of the things that were done to the girl, even as Kethra is aiding me. I hope that is so. For her sake, and for ours.''

There didn't seem to be anything else to say; Elspeth sat there awkwardly for a moment, until Iceshadow cleared his throat conspicuously. ''If there is naught else that we can tell you—'' he said.

Elspeth shook her head; so did Skif. ''Not that I can think of,'' she replied. ''Although I probably will come up with a dozen questions I should have asked just before I drop off to sleep tonight.''

Iceshadow chuckled; Starblade nodded knowingly. ''If you can recall them when you wake, feel free to ask them,'' Iceshadow said, rising. ''In the meantime—we hold celebration, to welcome you to the Clan and

Vale. Your fellow K'Sheyna are anxious to see you; they are as curious about you as you are about them."

In a way, that statement was something of a relief. It meant that the secretive Hawkbrothers were human enough to be curious. For all the time she had spent in Darkwind's presence, there was more that was a mystery about him and his people than there was that was familiar.

"In that case," she replied, rising from her own seat, "let's not keep them waiting any longer."

Elspeth followed Darkwind's direction, as Iceshadow escorted Starblade in another direction—presumably, to rest. "We have had little enough to celebrate, of late," Darkwind told the two Heralds and their Companions in a quiet voice, as he shepherded them down yet another path bordered by wild growth. "The stalemate with the Stone, the constant harassment on our borders, the separation—it has been difficult for everyone here. Add to that my father's attempt to foster dissension between the scouts and the mages, and there was more tension than many could bear."

"That particular dust-up was all because of Falconsbane, wasn't it?" Skif asked. "I hope that's been settled. I'd just as soon not find myself in the middle of a private quarrel."

"You won't," Darkwind actually chuckled, as Elspeth hid a sigh of relief. "It's been settled. I can pledge you, everyone is ready for a good celebration. The fact that you are the cause of it—*and* are strange Outlanders into the bargain—will make you very popular."

That gave Elspeth a bit of a qualm; not because she was ill-at-ease at the idea of being the focus of so many strangers, but because of what Darkwind had called her.

Outlander.

She was a stranger here. There was nothing in this place that would remind her of home. If Darkwind seemed alien to her, his words were a reminder that she must be just as alien to him, and by extension, to his people. *She* wasn't used to being the stranger; it made her feel disconnected and unbalanced.

And now, for the first time since she had arrived, she felt completely alone, completely without roots. And felt a wave of terrible homesickness wash over her.

At that moment, she was within a breath of weeping. Her throat closed, and she couldn't speak. Her eyes clouded, and she stumbled—

But when she looked up, she found herself on the edge of another clearing, but this one was full of light—people.

Her training took over; there were people waiting to meet her out there. She was the Heir to the Throne, she was a Herald. Her homesickness could wait. She must put on a good face for them, impress them, so that they would see that Valdemar was worth aiding.

She blinked once or twice, clearing her eyes. The Companions, Skif, and Darkwind got a pace or two ahead of her, giving her the chance to compose herself further. She took a deep breath, another, then followed them out into the radiant clearing.

She had expected mage-lights, and mage-lights there were in plenty, but the chief illumination came from the moon. The soft, silvery light blurred and softened details; and as she looked around her, she suddenly realized that not all of the exotic occupants of the clearing were human.

Hertasi, the shy lizardlike creatures that were roughly half the height of a very tall man, she had seen once or twice before, in colored beads and satins—and the gryphons of course.

Their presence was a welcome surprise, and she waved at Treyvan when she knew he had seen her. She hadn't known that the gryphons were coming, and Treyvan's wide-beaked grin from across the clearing chased away the last of her homesickness. She couldn't help herself; the gryphon grin was so contagious it left no room for such trivialities. Hydona saw that Treyvan was staring in their direction and turned to see what he was looking at. When she saw them, she nodded; her smile matched her mate's and welcomed the newcomers with a warmth that surpassed species boundaries.

The gryphons occupied one entire nook of the clearing all by themselves, but beside them were three graceful, horned creatures that Elspeth guessed must be *dyheli.* And scattered among the Hawkbrothers were a handful of two-legged creatures whose feathers were real, and growing from their heads, not braided into their hair.

Tervardi! Elspeth's years of protocol schooling kept her from staring, even though she would dearly have loved to. Along with the gryphons and the *hertasi,* these creatures were the stuff of legend in Valdemar. Legend said the *tervardi* were shapechangers, that they sprouted wings and turned into real birds when they chose. One of them turned, and Elspeth caught sight of a still, serene face with a mouth rimmed by something that was either a small, flexible beak, or hard, stiff lips. The creature gestured before she turned back to her conversation-group, and

Elspeth saw the stunted, colorful feathers, the last vestige of her wings, covering her arm.

As she moved hesitantly into the clearing, she realized that the previous occupants were—not ignoring her, but permitting her politely to fit into their group. That was certainly more comfortable than being mobbed and was exactly what a similar gathering of Heralds would have done.

She looked around; there were birds everywhere, some sleeping on perches, some awake and perched on shoulders or poles. The Companions both had joined a small group of mixed humans and nonhumans, along with Tre'valen; somehow, Darkwind and Skif had vanished, she had no idea how, but it left her on her own. With all those people carefully, politely, *not* looking at her, she felt more conspicuous than she would if they had been staring at her.

She hurried across the rest of the grassy space between her and the gryphons. Odd that of all of that gathering, they were the strangest physically, and the most familiar in every other way. . . .

"Sssso!" Treyvan greeted her, extending a taloned foreclaw in a token of welcome. "You are now Tayledrasss, Clansssssib! Do you feel any different?"

"Well, yes and no," she replied. "No—I mean, I'm still a Herald, and I'm still everything I was before."

"But yesss?" Hydona spoke gently. "I think perhapsss it isss home-sssicknesss?"

She blinked, surprised, and in an odd way, grateful. "How did you guess?"

The female gryphon nodded at the rest of the gathering. "We arrre the only two of *our* kind herrre asss well, except for the little onesss. We know how ssstrange you musst feel."

She flushed, embarrassed that she could have missed something so very obvious. "Of course. It's just that you and Darkwind are such friends, it never occurred to me—"

Treyvan laughed. "If it neverrr occurred to you, then I would sssay that iss a compliment on how well we have come to fit in herrre!" he exclaimed. "And trrruly, the humansss of the Valesss arrre not that unlike the humansss of our own landsss."

"Ah," she replied vaguely, not knowing what else to say. "Oh, where *are* the little ones?"

"Therrre." Hydona indicated another corner of the clearing with an outstretched talon; there, in the shadows, the two young gryphlets were sprawled on the grass, listening sleepily to what appeared to be—

A *very* large wolf?

—except that it wasn't speaking, so how could they be listening?

"That isss a *kyree;* they arrre not often in thisss Vale," Hydona said, as if she had heard Elspeth's unspoken questions. "It isss a neuter. It hasss taken a liking to the little onesss and hass been kind enough to tell them taless sssince we arrived. I believe it iss called—" She turned to her mate for help.

"Torrl," Treyvan supplied promptly. "It wass a great friend of Dawnfire, and iss sstill a great friend of Darrrkwind. *Kyree* neuterss are often verry fond of little oness of any speciessss; it iss a good thing the childrren arrre both sstrong Mindspeakersss."

And that, of course, was how the *kyree* was "telling tales" to the young gryphlets; directly mind-to-mind, as the *kyree* who helped Vanyel at the last had spoken to Stefen. Elspeth's mouth had gone very dry; this was like being inside of a tale herself, the experience being made even more dreamlike under the delicate illumination of mage-lights and moonlight.

She managed not to jump, as something tugged at the hem of her tunic. She looked down quickly; it was one of the *hertasi,* carrying a tray laden with fruits and vegetables that had been carved into artful representations of flowers. It offered the tray to her, and she took one; she hadn't the faintest notion of what she'd taken, but she didn't want to offend the little creature by refusing.

It slipped into the crowd, and she bit cautiously into her "prize." Crisp and cool, it had a faint peppery taste, and a crunchy texture; encouraged by her success, when the next *hertasi* came by, this one with a tray of drinks, she took a glass with more enthusiasm.

This proved to be a light wine; she sipped it and continued to chat with the gryphons, deliberately keeping the subject light, asking innocuous questions about the *kyree* and the other nonhumans, until other Tayledras drifted up to join the conversation. Gradually she began to relax, and to enjoy herself.

When a touch on her elbow made her turn, she found that Darkwind had found his way back to her. He handed her a slice of something breadlike, with something like a tiny, decorative flower arrangement atop it, and slid into the group beside her.

"Your friend Skif and my brother seem to have discovered that they have much in common," he said by way of joining the conversation, "And they have gone off to discuss weaponry. Knives, I think."

She shook her head. "That figures. Offer to talk about knives, and you'll have Skif's undivided attention for as long as you like. Do I eat this, or wear it?"

He chuckled. "You eat it. I think you will like it; it is smoked fish."

She nibbled the edge of it, tentatively. The smoked fish *she* was used to generally had the consistency and texture of a slab of wood, and tasted like a block of salt dipped in fish oil. She was pleasantly amazed at the indescribable blend of delicate flavors. As Darkwind chuckled again at her expression, she devoured it to the last shred.

"I have been asked," he continued, both to her and to the gryphons, "to request the presence of my good friends Treyvan and Hydona at the waterfall, and my wingsib Elspeth at a gathering of the scouts."

"Ssso?" Treyvan replied. "What isss at the waterrfall? And whom?"

"Kethra, Iceshadow, and my father, among others," Darkwind told him. "And, I am told, a very large selection of fresh fish and uncooked meat and fowl. Some of our more sensitive guests, like the *dyheli* and *tervardi*, might be distressed by refreshments of that nature, so we took them out of the way."

"Wissse," Hydona acknowledged. "But the little onessss—"

"Torrl assures me that they are not too far from falling asleep," Darkwind answered, "And when they do drift off, the *hertasi* have promised to keep an eye on them."

"I am *famisshed,*" Treyvan said, with a look of entreaty at his mate.

Across the clearing, Elspeth noticed the *kyree* raising its head from its paws, and looking directly at them.

:*Every parent deserves some time without the young,*: she heard, just as clearly as if the *kyree* was her own Companion. :*They are too tired to get into mischief that I cannot distract, and anything that wishes to harm them will have to come at them through not only me, but all the defenses of the Vale. And, I suspect, the large white hooved ones.*:

Hydona gave in; Elspeth readily understood her reluctance to have the gryphlets out of her sight, considering all that had happened to them, but the *kyree* was right. If the little ones weren't safe *here*, none of them were. They rose to their feet, folded their wings tightly against their sides to avoid knocking anything or anyone over, and took their leave.

Darkwind led the way up and down yet another path; this one ended beneath one of the enormous trees she had only glimpsed through curtains of bushes and vines. There were quite a few Tayledras gathered beneath it, but for the first few moments, all her attention was taken up by the tree itself.

Simply put, it was so large that an entire house could have been built within the circumference of its trunk. A curving staircase had been built around it, leading up to a kind of balcony three stories above the clearing. Soft lights hung from the bottom of the balcony, preventing her from seeing anything above that level, but she had the feeling that the staircase continued upward. When she shaded her eyes and peered upward, she caught sight of other, fainter lights near the trunk, half-obscured by the enormous branches. The Chronicles had once referred to the Hawkbrothers as the "tree-dwelling Tayledras," and she knew that Darkwind lived in a kind of elaborate platformed treehouse. So it looked as if that was the norm for the Hawkbrothers, rather than a concession to danger.

At least now she knew *why* they made a point of cultivating those enormous trees. Such marvels could support not one, but several dwellings.

When she turned her attention back to the gathering, she discovered that most of the Tayledras here were dressed very like Darkwind; in relatively "plain" clothing, and with hair either cut or bound up to be no longer than just below the shoulders, dyed in patterns of mottled brown and gold. They looked more like the Shin'a'in than the mages did, and it wasn't just that their hair wasn't white. . . .

It's because they're scouts, fighters, she realized, after a moment. Like Darkwind, they couldn't wear clothing that interfered in any way with fighting movements, nor could they afford to indulge themselves with elaborate hairstyles. Like Darkwind, they had a certain economy of movement; nothing dramatic, nothing theatrical—nothing done just for the effect. There were strong, well-trained muscles under those silken tunics, hard bodies that saw furlongs of patrolling every day.

She felt herself relaxing further in their presence, even before Darkwind began introducing them to her. These were people who, although they were familiar with magic, had very little to do with it; they were somehow more down-to-earth than the mages in their sculptural robes. And they were more like Heralds than anyone she had met yet.

She took careful note of the names as they were introduced to her, the habit of someone born into politics. Winterlight and Stormcloud, Brightmoon and Daystar, Earthsong, Thundersnow and Firedance—she matched names with faces, with smiles shy or bold, with personality quirks. Darkwind had explained the Tayledras habit of taking use-names, names that described something of what the person was like. She had to admit that it wasn't a bad system; it was much easier to match a name with a face when Winterlight (one of the few scouts to grow long hair) had a thick mane that when he was persuaded to unbraid and unbind it, looked like moonlight pouring down on snow—when Daystar was as sunny of disposition as the twins—and when Firedance was always in motion, never quite still, mercurial in temper and bright with wit. She wondered if she ought to take a use-name as well, though it shouldn't be hard for *them* to remember Elspeth, Skif, Gwena, and Cymry. Four names were easier to remember than an entire Clan-full.

"These are the k'Sheyna scouts," Darkwind said, when he'd finished the introductions, confirming her guess that there wasn't a mage among them. "Not all of them, of course; we still have a full patrol out tonight. But enough for now, I think; any more of us, and you would be overwhelmed with names and faces."

She smiled, but said nothing. This wasn't the time to point out that she'd coped with four times their number at ordinary state dinners. True, she had Talia's and Kyril's help, and the nobles and dignitaries didn't look quite so alike. . . .

"You are lucky, Els-peth," the young fellow called "Stormcloud" told her. "Truly. We are in festival gear now. If you were to see us tomorrow, you might find it hard to tell one from the other."

Earthsong nodded vigorously. "There is a tale among Outlanders that we are all mage-born copies of a single Tayledras."

"I can see how they would think that," she replied after a moment of consideration, imagining them all garbed in Darkwind's drab scouting clothing, with their hair bound up against snags. If the women—already slender and athletic—bound their breasts, it would even be difficult to tell male from female. "Of course, I'm sure you don't do a *thing* to encourage that now, do you?"

She was pleased when they laughed at her sally; sometimes the most difficult thing about dealing with a new people was finding out what they considered funny. And as she had discovered on her own, knowing what made someone laugh was the surest shortcut to making him your friend.

"Oh, no, of course not!" Firedance exclaimed, eyes wide and round with mock innocence. "Why would we ever do anything like that?"

The others laughed again at his disclaimer, then settled themselves back where they'd been before Darkwind brought her into the clearing. "We were just having some music and a little dancing," Earthsong said, as he picked up a flat drum. "We thought you might like to see and hear some of it, so we asked Darkwind if he'd go pry you away from the gryphons."

"Not that we're great artists," Winterlight spoke up quietly, "But we do enjoy ourselves, and I think music is better than any amount of words at telling people about each other. A language that needs fewer words."

"That's what our Bards say," she replied, looking for an inconspicuous spot to put herself, and finally giving up and taking a seat on one of the tree's enormous roots.

Winterlight gestured in agreement, and picked up something that she didn't recognize; a trapezoidal box strung like a harp. He set it on his lap and pulled a couple of hammers from under the strings, then glanced at Earthsong. The young scout evidently took that for a signal; he began to produce an elaborate rhythm on his flat drum with a single, double-ended stick; Winterlight listened for a moment, then joined him, not by plucking the strings as Elspeth had expected, but by striking them deftly with the hammers. Within a few moments, others had joined in, either on instruments of their own or simply by clapping. Some of their instruments were things that Elspeth recognized; most weren't, with sounds that were not—quite—like anything she knew.

The music was far from unpleasant. There were unexpected bell-sounds in the rhythm, a wailing wind instrument that added an unearthly element like a singing hawk's scream, and the occasional whistling improvisation by one of the scouts. It was quite infectious, and she found herself clapping along with it.

It wasn't much longer before the Tayledras got up to dance. Here was another difference between the Hawkbrothers and her own people. At home, folks danced in groups—ring dances or set-pieces, with a definite sequence to the steps. The Tayledras danced singly, or in couples, or trios at most, and there was no set-pattern to the dance steps. The nearest she had ever seen to this kind of exuberant chaos had been at a Herald celebration when a number of the younger Heralds just in from the field had gotten involved in a kind of dancing contest, demonstrating the wilder steps from their various home villages.

Two or three songs later, she noticed that some of the original contingent had vanished somewhere, and there were a few additions, wearing costumes more like those of mages than of scouts.

She started watching the onlookers as well as the dancers, and figured out from overheard bits of conversation that there were dozens of these little gatherings, scattered all around the Vale, although this was probably the most lively. Several scouts turned up in the next few moments with wet hair, attracted by the sounds of the music from the pools in which they had been swimming. That, it seemed, was the essence of a Tayledras celebration; to roam. People came and went; sampling little bits of this and that, food, music, conversation. . . .

She decided to do as the natives were doing, taking the opportunity to explore the Vale a little, and slipped off by herself, wandering down a randomly chosen path until she heard the sounds of a softer melody than the dancing music.

She discovered a single singer, a woman in silvery-gray, slender as a birch tree, playing a huge diamond-shaped wire-strung harp. There were a half dozen of the mages listening to her, sitting on benches arranged in a half-circle around her, and Elspeth stayed through three songs before moving on.

She found her way back to the original clearing. By now the gryphlets were sound asleep, oblivious to all the light and movement and the sounds of conversation around them. Both Companions were still there, with that relaxed attitude and cheerful, ears-up, tail-switching pose that told her they were enjoying themselves. Their conversational partners were Torrl, the *kyree*, two of the mages, one of the scouts, and an old *hertasi*. Seeing them, she relaxed as well, since they were enjoying themselves. As she wandered off again, it occurred to her that this was the one thing that was often missing from parties that the Heralds held— Dirk and Talia's wedding had included the Companions, but all too often, they were left out of things. As she watched Gwena and Cymry, she made a mental note; when she got home again, that was one thing that would change. She'd find a way to make certain they weren't left out again. They were as responsible for the success of the Heralds as the Heralds themselves. Surely they deserved that much consideration.

Gwena turned around at that moment and gave her an unmistakable wink before returning to her conversation.

Even if they do snoop in our heads.

But she was smiling as she chose another path, not looking for anything in particular, but thinking that a swim might be nice.

She heard water trickling, off to one side, and someone giggling; she didn't really stop to think, she just started to make her way down the little path.

Suddenly Darkwind slipped in front of her, stopping her before she could part the branches that shielded the end of the path. "Pardon," he said apologetically. "The marker beside the path—it was turned to face red. It means that—"

The giggling changed to an unmistakable gasp of pleasure. Elspeth found herself blushing. "Never mind," she whispered, backing up hastily. "I think I have a good idea what it means."

She turned, and started back toward the clearing; Darkwind intercepted her again. "Oh, no," he said earnestly. "No, if they had not wanted to be disturbed, the marker would have been blue. No, the red marker means that they would welcome—ah—all other—" he coughed "—participants—"

She blushed even deeper; her ears and cheeks aflame. She'd always been told that the Heralds were uninhibited. It seemed that the Hawk-brothers had even fewer inhibitions.

"I thought perhaps no one had warned you," he continued. "If, perhaps, you might want to enjoy one of the hot springs, I can take you to one where there is nothing more active than hot water."

What else could she do but accept gracefully, and hope that by the time they reached this spring, her blushes would have cooled?

A curtain of steam announced the location of the spring, but when Darkwind pulled aside the branches at the entrance and waved her into the area around the pool, she found herself flushing all over again. There were about ten of the Hawkbrothers she remembered seeing at the dancing, all soaking muscles that must certainly be complaining, but they weren't wearing much except hair.

"Darkwind!" one of them hailed. "Fifteen split-jumps! Beat that, if you can!"

"Oh, yes," the young woman next to him said mockingly. "Fifteen split-jumps indeed—and now you see him soaking here, because he could scarce walk when he completed the fifteenth!"

"Sunfeather!" the young man exclaimed indignantly, "You weren't supposed to tell him that!"

Darkwind peeled off his tunic, as Elspeth averted her eyes and slowly took off her boots. "Perhaps you should think less about split-jumps, and more about what Sunfeather's expectations for the evening were *before* you tried to displace your hipjoints," he suggested mildly. "Then you might have the answer as to why she revealed your secret."

As the rest of the Tayledras teased the discomfited dancer, Darkwind removed the rest of his clothing and slid into the water beside Sunfeather. The spring-fed pool was quite a large one; the dozen Tayledras were scattered about the edge of it, each one of them lounging at full length, and they were hardly taking up more room than a dozen peas in one of the Collegium kitchen's biggest pots.

The analogy to a pot was a lot more apt than she had thought; when she finally got up enough courage to shed the rest of her clothing, she slid into an unoccupied niche. The hot spring was a good deal hotter than she had thought; not *quite* painful, but not far from it.

Steam rose about her face and turned her hair limp, but after a moment she stopped thinking she was about to have her hide boiled off, and began to enjoy the heat.

She slipped out again, after a relatively short time; she was *not* used to turning herself into a scalded turnip. Much to her surprise, someone— perhaps one of the ubiquitous and near-invisible *hertasi*—had left a towel and robe beside her clothing.

For the rest of the evening, she alternated between the larger clearing, and the one the scouts had taken for their dancing. One of the mages treated the group to a guided flight of befriended firebirds—like the fireworks displays at home, except that these fireworks didn't fade or die. Gwena loved every moment of it, although Elspeth would have liked to have seen the firebirds come closer. The demonstration was very impressive, especially when they flew among the branches of the huge, shadow-shrouded tree. *That* wouldn't have been possible with real fireworks.

She lost track of time, wandering around the Vale, as fatigue caught up with her and her nerves relaxed. Finally she found herself back beneath the tree; most of the lights hanging from the balcony had been extinguished, but there were more people, human and not.

They were all "people" to her now, after an evening of trading jokes with *hertasi*, commiserating with *tervardi* on the likelihood of a bad winter, and telling the *dyheli* exactly what had happened to Nyara. So far as the *dyheli* were concerned, Nyara was still their heroine. *She* hadn't known that their entrapment had been a set-up by her father, to ensure that the k'Sheyna would look on her favorably. She had acted in the belief that she was saving them. They knew that, and honored her for it.

So the facts of her disappearance were of great interest to them; they promised Elspeth that they would watch for signs of the Changechild, and report anything they learned back to the Tayledras scouts.

All but the most die-hard of dancers had given up by now; Elspeth found herself a seat in the shadows. Tre'valen was the center of a cluster of the scouts, who were trying to persuade him to dance. Finally he shook his head, shrugged, and gestured to the musicians. "Hawk Dance?" Iceshadow called back.

Tre'valen laughed. "Indeed!" he said, taking a stand in the middle of the illuminated area. "What else would I do for you? But only on condition that Darkwind follow with a Wind Dance."

Elspeth hadn't seen Darkwind before Tre'valen called out his name, but when he waved agreement from across the clearing, she saw that he had stripped off the fancier overtunic, and now looked more like the Darkwind she knew, in a deep-cut sleeveless jerkin and tight breeches, his only ornaments the feathers in his hair.

Tre'valen had changed after the ceremony into his Shin'a'in finery of scarlet, black, and gold; embroidered vest with fringe to his knees, fringed and belled armbands. Loose breeches with fringed kneeboots, all of it topped with a horsehair and feather headdress like some strange bird's crest—he was a striking sight.

The drummer began first; Tre'valen marked the time with one foot, the fringe shivering with each beat. When the instruments came in, Tre'valen leapt into action.

Elspeth soon saw why it was called the "Hawk Dance." Tre'valen was aloft more often than he was on the ground; whirling, flying, leaping. He never paused, never rested; no sooner did his foot touch the ground than he was in the air again. His arms curved like wings cupping the air. Elspeth's heart kept time with the beat, her eyes unable to leave him. He didn't seem much like a human at the moment—more like a creature akin to the *tervardi* or the firebirds. But then, perhaps that was the essence of being a shaman.

The dance came to an end on a triple beat and one of the highest leaps of the dance that left Tre'valen standing still as stone, exactly in the same place where he had begun the dance. Elspeth had no idea how he had known the music was about to end; she had heard nothing to signal the end of the piece. It left her staring, dumb with astonishment and delight.

Tre'valen sat down on a root amid the shouts and applause of the others. Darkwind took the shaman's place in the center of the circle; composed himself, and nodded to the musicians.

This time the music began slowly, with a glissando on the odd hammered instrument, followed by another on the harp, a softer echo of the first. Then Darkwind began to dance.

The Tayledras and Shin'a'in music were related; that much was obvious from a root similarity of melody, but dancing and music had changed from the time the two races were one. Either the Shin'a'in had gotten wilder, or the Tayledras had become more lyrical, or both.

Darkwind didn't leap, he floated; he didn't whirl, he flowed. He moved as if he had no bones, flew like his own bird, glided and spun and hovered. There was nothing feminine in the dance, for all of that; it was completely, supremely masculine. Besides his supple grace, what Elspeth noticed most of all were his hands—they had to be the most graceful pair of hands she had ever seen.

Darkwind finished the dance like a bird alighting for the night; coming to rest with a final run from the harp. There was a faint sheen of sweat over his body and face, shining in the moonlight. As he held his final pose, he was so completely still that he could have been a silver statue of a forest spirit, looking up in wonder at the stars.

That was the image that Elspeth took with her, as she slipped out of the clearing and found one of the *hertasi*. She asked the little creature to show her the quarters Darkwind had promised were waiting for her here.

The little lizard grinned at her, and led her down so many twisting, dark paths that she was soon lost. Not that it mattered at the moment. Darkwind had also pledged that he would send someone to lead her about until she knew her own way.

She recognized the area, once they got near it; they were very close to the entrance to the Vale, the farthest they could be from the Heartstone and still be inside the Vale shields. The *hertasi* showed her a staircase winding up the side of a tree. For a moment she was afraid that she would have to climb up several stories, and she wasn't sure she had the head for it.

But the *hertasi* scrambled up ahead of her, and her waiting quarters proved to be a mere single story above the floor of the Vale, a set of two rooms built just off the stairs, lighted and waiting for her.

She fell into the bed as soon as the *hertasi* left her—but for a surprisingly long time she lay looking at the moon, as sleep deserted her.

She felt a little less like a stranger, but no less lonely. Skif had Nyara—or at least, he had the dream of Nyara, wherever he was now. She still had no one.

Only her duty, her omnipresent duty. To learn everything she could about magic; learn it quickly, and bring it home to Valdemar.

That was cold comfort—and no company—on a silvered, moonfilled night. . . .

Darkwind & Vree

Chapter
Three

Darkwind accepted the applause of his fellow scouts along with a damp cloth and a healthy gulp of cold water. It had been a long time since he had performed the Wind Dance in full, although dance was a part of his daily workout. He enjoyed it, and enjoyed the applause almost as much. It was good to know his skill could still conjure approval from his brethren.

The Outlander, Elspeth, had been watching the dancers when Tre'valen began his display. He knew she had enjoyed the Hawk Dance; from the look on her face, she had probably never seen anything quite like it before. He thought she'd enjoyed *his* dancing as well—and he meant to talk to her afterward. He was disappointed, after he'd caught his breath, to find she had gone.

He settled for a moment to let his muscles recover; he felt them quivering with fatigue as he sat down. He had pushed himself in this Wind Dance, to far closer to his limits than he usually tried to reach. The steps which appeared deceptively easy, required perfect balance and control and required fully as much effort to sustain as Tre'valen's more energetic Hawk Dance.

He listened to some of the others discussing dances and dancers past, nodding when someone said something he particularly agreed with. No one else wanted to follow his performance, and some of the players took that as a signal to put their instruments away and rest their weary fingers. As Darkwind settled his back against the tree and slowly sipped his water, he considered the Outlanders—Elspeth in particular. They were less of an enigma than he had feared they would be, although he still wished he knew a great deal more about their culture.

Elspeth was more of a problem than her friend Skif, simply because of her position as his student. She was sometimes fascinating, sometimes infuriating, often both.

She compounded his own problems as he resumed his position as an Adept. As his father had pointed out, he had a great deal to re-learn; how much, Darkwind was only now figuring out. What Starblade didn't know was that his son was already giving Elspeth lessons, even while he was retraining his own powers.

Elspeth posed a peculiar hazard, that of half-knowledge. She had full training in the Gifts of mind-magic, though no true training in her mage-powers—but some of the Mind-Magic disciplines were similar enough to give her a grasp on magery, but without controls. Her sword had at one time provided some guidance and tutelage, but Elspeth had a great deal to learn about even rudimentary magics. Without the blade Need about to keep her in hand, he had not felt safe about having Elspeth walking around loose without beginning those early lessons in basic control.

What he had not reckoned on—although, given her quick temper, he should have anticipated the difficulty—was her impatience with him.

She wanted answers, and she wanted them immediately. And when he was already impatient with himself, he didn't feel like explaining himself to an Outlander who had barely even seen magic in action before she came south.

Her insistence on forcing years' worth of learning into a few weeks was enough to drive the most patient of savants to distraction, much less her current teacher. *She can be so irritating. . . .*

He leaned his head back and stared up into the pattern of faint light and deep darkness created by moonlight, mage-lights, and tree branches. There was randomness, no discernible pattern, just as there was no discernible pattern to his life. A season ago, he would never have been able to imagine the events of the past several weeks. A year ago, he never would have believed his life would change in any meaningful way, except for the worse.

He sighed, and ran his hand through his hair, fluffing it to cool and dry it. Elspeth was a disruption to an already confusing situation. The problem was, she had the infuriating habit of being *right* now and again in matters of magic—matters in which she had no experience and little knowledge.

He'd dismissed all of her suggestions initially. Then, when she'd been proven right a time or two, he'd thought at first that it was pure luck. No one could *always* be right or wrong after all, but a day or so ago, he'd finally seen the logic to her ideas' successes. In general, when she saw something that she thought could be done magically, but that *he* had never learned, her theories turned out to be, in principle, correct.

One case in point that still annoyed Darkwind was treating the lesser lines of power as if they were a web, and the mage was a spider in the midst of that web. She'd reasoned that anyone working magic within the area a mage defined as his "web" would create a disturbance in the lines of power, which the mage at the center would feel, in the same way a spider felt an insect in its web. The advantage of this was that it was a passive detection system; there was nothing to alert the intruding mage that he'd been detected.

It was nothing he'd been taught. He'd been certain it wouldn't work— until she sketched a diagram, extended a few tendrils of energy, and proved to him that it would. It had been something of a shock to his already-bruised pride, and he followed along numbly as she refined the idea.

As if it weren't enough that she was attractive, in her unadorned way. She had to be innovative, too.

The mage-lights dimmed, sending the boughs above vanishing into shadows; and he looked back down from his perusal of the branches to find that everyone had left the clearing but him. The celebration was winding down, as couples and groups sought *ekeles* or hot springs, and the rest, not ready to seek beds, gathered in the meeting-circle or beside the waterfall.

He stretched his legs, carefully, to make certain they hadn't stiffened up on him. They weren't cramping as he'd feared; he was in better shape than he'd thought, apparently. But he didn't feel much like rejoining the rest who were still celebrating; he rose slowly, and began pacing, making a point of walking as silently as he could. It was a lot easier to do that here, on the clear paths, than out in the forest. There was no point in losing his hard-won scouting skills just because he was resuming his position as an Adept. There was a Tayledras saying: "No arrow shot at a target is ever wasted, no matter how many break." It meant that no practice or lesson, however trivial it might seem, was a loss.

Now, reclaiming his magery, he was discovering the downside of that saying.

I didn't realize how much I'd forgotten until I started trying to teach her, he admitted to himself. *If she'd just be a little more patient with me. . . .*

When something went wrong, Elspeth wasn't particularly inclined to sit and wait quietly until he got it right again. Magic wasn't simple; spells had to be laid out methodically, and when something got muddled, a responsible mage couldn't just erase things and start over. Spells gone awry had to be unmade. Generally Darkwind had to retrace his steps carefully, in order to find out exactly where he'd made those mistakes. Only then could he undo what he'd done, go back to the beginning, and start again, constructing correct paths.

Whenever he was forced to do that, Elspeth would invariably ask questions at the worst possible time, when interruptions would be the most irritating. She never seemed to know when to keep quiet and let him work. Why was she in such a hurry to master every aspect of magic? Mastery took time and practice; surely she was bright enough to realize that.

Even now, he realized she was irritating him. *How can she do that?* he asked himself, pausing in his pacing for a moment to examine his reaction. *How can she annoy me when she isn't even here? It has to be me, not her—*

As he folded his arms and pondered the question, he recalled something that seemed to have nothing to do with Elspeth. It was the reason why he had given in so quickly to the demand that he perform the Wind Dance. And it had nothing to do with Tre'valen's request, either; he'd have found some excuse to perform that dance before the evening was over, no matter what.

The reason? Stormcloud's boast of fifteen consecutive split-jumps.

Challenge. He couldn't resist it. And Elspeth annoyed him because she challenged him in a way no one else ever had—or at least, no female ever had. He wasn't facing the challenge of a teacher toward a student's potential, nor, precisely, was he facing the risks of an explorer. There was, though, that annoying realization that he didn't have the safety of being able to lord skill over her; he was as uneducated in *his* way as she.

It didn't sit well with him, but that was the truth of the matter. Therein lay the challenge: she was a virtual equal.

Now that he had identified the source of his irritation, he realized that he wasn't going to be able to do anything about it. Perversely, he enjoyed the frustration, just as he enjoyed Elspeth's company though she grated on his nerves.

She was too impatient, but that was not damning. There was no reason why she shouldn't intrigue him, just as what he was teaching should be a challenge to her. She was, after all, a bright student. Alert and eager.

Hmm. That's not the only challenge she represents. He enjoyed her company quite a bit more than he was fully willing to admit. Of all the possible partnerings he could have made tonight, he had only considered one. She attracted him quite as much as she irritated him, although he was certain that he was not ready emotionally for anything as deep as he had shared with Dawnfire. And there had only been one consideration that held him back from offering Elspeth a feather tonight.

Sadly, that consideration was a major one; one that was going to require any association with her—other than pure friendship—to be choreographed as carefully as any major spell. She was an Outlander; he had no idea of the ways of her people. It might be that the folk of Valdemar took sexual liaisons very seriously; they might even reserve sexual activity for formal bondmates only. Until he knew more about her and her people, he was not going to take the risk of offending her or her country by propositioning her. Even if she would accept an apology, the offense would continue to taint everything he did or said to her.

Lust is easy to come by, after all. I couldn't enjoy it with too much worry, anyway. There is simply too much at stake to permit a night of pleasure to complicate matters.

Not to mention the possible repercussions of bedding the designated heir to a foreign monarchy. Who knew where that would lead? He doubted anyone would declare war over it, but what if a liaison with Elspeth would make her subject to problems when she returned home? She was too important a personage.

Ah, now there's another thing that irritates me!

He began walking again, turning his steps out of the clearing and down the path that led to the waterfall at the end of the Vale. Now that he'd figured out what it was that was bothering him, it might help to have a talk with someone about it. He could do his best to try to watch his own reactions, but there wasn't a great deal that he could do about Elspeth's attitude.

It's this Heir To The Throne business. She never actually says anything about it, but she radiates it. As if—she doesn't wear a crown, but she carries herself as if she did. As if she is always *thinking that she's being watched and admired, that she is an important person, and expects everyone else to be aware of that.*

Never mind that the only Tayledras around who knew of her land were Starblade and Iceshadow, who had studied the old histories. Never mind that even those two had no interest whatsoever in her country and the Heralds who populated it, except as a curiosity and as it had impact in the past on Tayledras concerns.

Treyvan and Hydona might have some ideas about his concerns; they were ambassadors, of sorts—Hydona was female. That could help. In either case they might have some idea how to deal with another Outlander. Particularly an impatient, high-ranking, annoyingly impressive female Outlander.

At the waterfall, all the mage-lights had been extinguished. The moon was still high overhead, though, providing plenty of illumination, pouring down over this end of the Vale and touching the mist rising from the falls with silver. The two he sought were still there, lazing beside the pool like a pair of creatures from legend; both gryphons looked up at his footfall, but to his disappointment he saw that they were not alone. The shaman Tre'valen was with them, and he felt a certain reluctance to discuss one Outlander in front of another. For that matter, he wasn't certain he wanted to discuss Elspeth with anyone except the gryphons. He trusted them unfailingly.

Nevertheless, since they had seen him and nodded greetings, it would have been impolite to ignore them and walk on. It would be even worse to return the way he came. *It isn't going to do any harm to make some idle chat. And Her Highness Elspeth isn't a problem I can't cope with on my own, if I just think carefully before I say or do anything.*

So he approached the little group—which, he saw as he grew nearer, included the gryphlets. The little ones were tucked under their mother's wing, quietly sleeping, curled together into softly huffing balls of wings and limbs.

"Tre'valen brought the younglingsss when they began to fret and did not want to sssleep without usss near. And have you had enough of cccelebration?'' Treyvan said softly as he neared. The shaman lounged beside Hydona, along the edge of the pool, his hair wet and rebraided.

Looks as if Tre'valen has been swimming. I didn't know that the Shin'a'in knew how to swim. I didn't think there were any bodies of water on the Plains deep enough for them to learn.

"Quite enough, I think," he replied, and nodded to the shaman. "Your Hawk Dance is very good, Wingbrother. In fact, I don't know that I've ever seen better. I should like to see you dance one day in full home regalia, with a proper set of Shin'a'in musicians and singers."

"If you enjoyed my dance, you should see my brother; I learned it from him." Tre'valen stretched, and turned to look him straight in the eyes. "I have been greatly curious, Wingbrother, and I think you will be willing to answer an impertinent question. Was it my imagination, or was there an air of desperation about all of this? As if folk were doggedly determined to enjoy themselves?"

Darkwind had been wondering if he was the only one to notice that. "It was not your imagination," he replied quietly.

"I thought not." Tre'valen nodded. "Your people escaped the hand of Falconsbane by a very narrow margin. Whether it was the hand of the Goddess or of chance, or both together, there was little they could have done of themselves to free this Clan from his influence. I wondered if they knew how narrow their escape was. Your father, for instance—"

"They know," Darkwind replied, carefully steering the conversation away from his father. That was another whole situation he was not quite ready to deal with yet. "They simply don't dwell on it. And they know that our troubles are not yet over, which accounts for that desperate enjoyment you noted."

"But the urgency iss lesss," Hydona said. "All that hass occurrred, hass bought k'Sheyna time. Thisss celebrration—it wass a good thing. It iss a relief from the tenssion. Bessidesss . . . other changess arre coming."

Darkwind decided to leave that typically gryphonish—meaning cryptic—remark alone.

"You could be reading Iceshadow's mind," he smiled. "After all the troubles, the fear—"

—and the other things no one wants to talk about, like discovering what had been done to my father—

"It was just a good idea to give everyone something pleasurable to think about for a little while. A relief." He scratched Hydona's neck-ruff absently, and she half-closed her eyes with pleasure. One of the gryphlets rolled over, chirring contentment in its sleep. "A day or two of rest isn't going to alter the Heartstone question, but it might make all the difference in letting us gain a fresh outlook."

Tre'valen raised an eyebrow, but said only, "Some look as if they need a rest more than a fresh outlook. Starblade, for instance."

Don't ask too many impertinent questions, shaman. I might answer them, and you might not care for the answers. I am not altogether certain that the Shin'a'in are ready to embrace the problems of their cousins, no matter how many Wingsib Oaths are sworn. What you do not officially know, you need not act upon.

Treyvan raised his head from his foreclaws. *"You* look rrready for a frresh outlook, Darrkwind," he said, as Darkwind tried unsuccessfully to suppress a yawn. "The outlook you may have frrom yourrrr bed."

"I think you're right," he admitted, glad of the excuse to escape from a conversation that was becoming increasingly uncomfortable. *He* didn't particularly want to discuss the problems of k'Sheyna, at least not now, when his tired mind and tongue might let things slip he would rather were not revealed.

The way he felt about Starblade, for instance. His heart was still sore and shaking from the revelation that the cold, critical "father" of the past several years had *not* been the father who had taught him his first lessons in magic—and who had worn the costumes his son had designed for him with such open pride.

The fact that Starblade had worn one of those costumes tonight, which was not only the Wingsib Oathing, but the first time he had taken part in the social life of K'Sheyna since Darkwind had freed him, had left him on very uncertain emotional ground. In a very real sense, he had a new father—but Darkwind was years older, and there was deepset pain between them. It was going to take some time before his feelings were reconciled.

He imagined it was much the same for Starblade. The only difference between what he and his father had to cope with was that Starblade had known the truth but had not been able to act upon it, while Darkwind had been able to act but had not known the truth. Equally painful situations.

He yawned again, and this time did not take the trouble to hide it. "I think I must be getting old," he said. "My ability to celebrate until sunrise is not what it once was. And I did promise young Elspeth that her lessons would continue when we both arose from sleep—'' He ignored Tre'valen's suggestive smirk. ''—so rather than finding her waiting at the foot of my *ekele,* I think I will seek my own bed and see if I might wake before she does.''

''A good plan,'' chuckled Tre'valen. *''Zhai'helleva.''*

''And to you, all,'' he replied, and rose from the soft turf beside the pool, brushing off his seat. He retraced his steps, this time heading for the path that ultimately led out of the Vale. Even though he was reconciled with Starblade, the fluctuating power of the Heartstone made him uncomfortable, and he disliked having to sleep near it. Starblade and the rest understood, and his ''eccentricity'' of maintaining a dwelling outside the safe haven of the Vale was no longer a subject of contention.

His path tonight, however, was not a direct one. Three times he had to interrupt his path with detours to avoid trysts-in-progress. He should have expected it, really; the end result of a celebration was generally trysting all over the Vale, of whatever tastes and partners.

So why am I going back to my ekele *alone?*

He'd never lacked for bedmates before. Actually, if he hadn't been so choosy—or was it preoccupied—he wouldn't have lacked for bedmates tonight.

He could say that he mourned for Dawnfire, and that would have been partially true. He missed her every time he thought of her, with an ache that he wondered if he would ever lose. She had been the one that he'd thought would actually work out as more than a bedmate; their interests and pleasures had matched so well. The fact that she hadn't *died* made the situation worse, in some ways. She had become something he could see, but could not touch. Now at least, after much thought, the first, sharp sorrow had passed, the sorrow that had been like an arrow piercing his flesh. Now what he felt was the pain of an emotional bolt lodged in place, poisoning his blood with regret.

He also knew that Dawnfire would have been the first to tell him to get on with his life. If she had been with him, if he had lost another lover, she would whisper to him to take a bedmate, and some pleasure, to ease the pain. That was just her way, another thing he had loved her for.

So why hadn't he taken one or more of those offers for companionship tonight?

Because he didn't *want* any of them. They simply didn't fit his real, if vaguely defined, desires.

And to tell the truth, he wasn't sure what he wanted. Elspeth was the only person tonight who had attracted him. But along with every other way she made him react, he was afraid—afraid that she might draw him into a deeper relationship than he intended.

She would leave the Vales and return to her Valdemar; and his people were here. There could be nothing lasting between them emotionally, save wistfulness over what might have been. But they would be spending most of their time together, now that she was a Wingsister; it was his duty to teach her, and hers to help defend the Vale for as long as she dwelled here. The Council had made it clear that *he* was responsible for her. If it turned out that Elspeth was equally attracted to him—that her ways were similar to his people in the matter of loveplay and they became more than casually involved—perhaps they could pursue some of the techniques in which sexual magic could be tuned and sublimated, and in so doing—

No. I couldn't do it. I just lost Dawnfire, I can't lose another lover. I'm not made of such stern stuff.

He finally reached the path to his *ekele* without incident—without encountering anything more hazardous than a flight of moths. That in itself was a pleasant change. The sharp bite to the air and the faint aroma of leaves in their turning reminded him that there were other changes on the wind that were not so pleasant. Autumn was at hand; winter would follow, and although the Vale would remain green and lush, outside it, the leaves would fall, and snow and ice-storms would come. Winter would bring a new set of dangers from outside; predators would grow hungry, and the fear that kept them away from the Vale in the summer might not be enough to overcome their hunger's insistence. Winter would make it difficult for infatuated young Skif to track the Changechild. And it would be much harder for the remains of k'Sheyna to trek across the country in search of the rest of the Clan, if that was ultimately what they had to do to reunite.

Despite the fact that k'Sheyna territory was now much safer than it had been before the confrontation with Mornelithe Falconsbane, Darkwind had reverted to his old habits the moment he passed the barrier at the mouth of the Vale. It only took one slip at the wrong time to make someone a casualty. Tayledras had been killed even in tamed territories, simply by thinking they were secure. He kept to the deepest shadows, walked silently, and kept all senses alert for anything out of the norm. The moon was down beneath the level of the trees by the time he reached his *ekele;* he kindled a tiny mage-light in the palm of his hand and—with some misgiving—loosed the ladder from its support above and lowered it by means of another exercise of magic. With a tiny spell, he tripped the catch that held the rope-ladder in place.

If this had been in daylight, he'd never have used magic, he'd have had Vree drop the trigger-line to him. He still felt uneasy about using anything except mage-shields outside of the Vale. True, Falconsbane was no longer out there, watching for the telltale stirrings of magic-use and waiting to set his creatures attacking anything outside the protection of the Vale. But caution was a hard habit to break, especially when he wasn't certain he truly wanted to break it.

Still, the presence of the mage-light made climbing the ladder a lot easier, and the use of the spell eliminated the need to scale the trunk in the dark to release the ladder. It was worth the risk, at least tonight.

Perhaps, now, there were many things that were worth the risk of attempting them. . . .

Skif could hardly believe what he'd just heard. He rubbed his tired eyes, and stared across the tiny firepit at his new friend. The conversation had begun with knives in general, proceeded to other things, such as forging, tempering, balance and point structure, throwing styles—but it had just taken a most unexpected turn. "Forgive me, but I'm not— ah—as good in speaking Tayledras as Elspeth. Did you say what I think you said?"

Wintermoon chuckled, and passed him a cup of a spicy—but, he'd been assured, nonalcoholic—drink, poured from a bottle he'd asked one of the *hertasi* to bring. "I will speak in more plain words," the scout told him, slowly, reaching for one of the sausages warming on the grill above the coals of their fire. "I wish to help you to find the Changechild Nyara. If you tell me 'aye,' I shall come with you. You say you have no true learning in woods-tracking; I am not a poor scout. I think I would be of real help."

:*He's one of the best scouts and trackers in k'Sheyna, Chosen,:* Cymry told him. Her ears were perked up, showing her excitement and interest. :*He's being very modest. The* dyheli *told me he's one of the few that can even hunt and track by night, maybe even the best.:*

He wanted Wintermoon's help—wanted it badly. He *needed* it. Without it, all he'd do would be to crisscross k'Sheyna territory, virtually randomly, hoping to come across some sign of Nyara. With Wintermoon's skillful help, he would be able to mount a systematic search. But was this a test of his oaths and his loyalties?

"I—uh—I don't know what to say," he stammered, watching the tall Tayledras with his strange hair and pale eyes. "Wintermoon, I want your help more than I can say, but you're a scout, a hunter, a good one. What about the Clan? Don't they need you? I mean, I'm a Wingbrother, but doesn't that mean I need to think of the good of the Clan first?"

Wintermoon blinked slowly, and turned away toward the trees. He held up a gauntleted wrist. That was the only warning Skif had that something was happening; a heartbeat later, a huge white shape hurtled by his ear, soundlessly. As he winced away, the shape hit Wintermoon's wrist and folded its wings. It resolved itself into a great white owl, which swiveled its head and stared unblinkingly at him before turning back to Wintermoon, reaching down with its fierce hook of a beak and nibbling the fingers of his free hand gently.

"This is K'Tathi," Wintermoon said, stroking the owl's head gently. "Corwith is in the tree above. There are not many Tayledras who bond to the greater owls."

"You didn't answer my question," Skif said pointedly.

"Ah, but I did." Wintermoon transferred the owl from his wrist to his shoulder, where it proceeded to preen his hair. He sighed, and gave Skif a look full of long-suffering patience.

"There are not many Tayledras who bond to the greater owls. While my bondbirds can hunt by day, they prefer not to. They are also a different species from the hawks and falcons, and there is instinctive dislike between them and the birds of other scouts. It can be overcome, but it requires great patience." He shrugged, as the fire flared up for a moment from the cooking. The flare flushed the owl with ruddy light. "More patience than I care to give. Thus, I hunt by night, and mostly alone. That makes me something that can be done without when times are not so chancy."

"In other words, your absence won't cause any problems?" Skif persisted, clutching the cup.

The owl found Wintermoon's ear, and began nibbling it. Wintermoon sighed, and gave it his finger instead. "The new plan is for mages to help the scouts," he explained. "There will be more watchers. Your friend, Els-peth—she is clever, and will make up for my absence. So, I am free to aid you.''

:*There is a hole in this, somewhere,*: Cymry said.

Skif agreed; he could sense it. "What is it that you aren't telling me?'' he demanded. "Is it something about Nyara?''

The owl let go of Wintermoon's finger, roused its feathers, and settled, staring at Cymry as if it found her fascinating. Wintermoon nodded. "I thought perhaps you might think that, and yes, it concerns the Changechild. But you must pledge not to take offense.''

:*Offense?:* he asked Cymry. :*Why would I—oh. Of course. They still don't trust Nyara, they want her under control, and they probably feel the same way about that damn sword.*:

:*Can you blame them?:* she asked reasonably.

:*About the sword, no,:* he replied. Then, to Wintermoon, "You Tayledras don't trust Nyara or the blade, do you? The rest of the Clan wants you to go along and make sure she isn't out there trying to set up some more trouble for you.''

Wintermoon nodded. "Quite. I beg pardon, but that is only the truth of the matter. But, Skif—I do wish to help you, for yourself. You are not schooled in tracking, you have said as much yourself. Think of it this way,'' he grinned. "I have no wish for your friend Els-peth to be sending me out in an ice-storm to *find* you!''

"Oh, I'm not that bad,'' he replied with a rueful smile. "I've had *some* field training. But it was all in Valdemar—there were Herald waystations all over.''

"And you cannot track or trail,'' Wintermoon repeated. He turned to Cymry. "Lady, you cannot track or trail, either. Nor can you see as well at night as my Corwith and K'Tathi can. Nor do you know our territory.''

Cymry bowed her head in agreement.

"And Skif, I would like to help you, for I know that you feel very much for the Changechild.'' His face sobered. "I do not know if the Changechild is near as dangerous as the Council think she might be. I think she deserves to have someone looking for her that will give her that benefit. I think it is a good thing for her to have someone besides yourself that will do that. You are a Wingbrother—but an Outlander as well. I am k'Sheyna.''

Skif was well aware of what the Tayledras meant; just as his own word would hold more weight in Valdemar than Wintermoon's, no matter how many oaths the latter swore, so Wintermoon's held more weight here. If there were any doubt as to Nyara's allegiances, Wintermoon's opinion might well be the deciding factor.

And it would be a very good thing to have company out there in the wilderness. . . .

:*Take his offer,*: Cymry urged. :*He's a good man; he could become a good friend.*:

"All right, Wintermoon," Skif said decisively. "I would be very, very glad to have you help me. Cymry wants you along, and I never argue with her."

:*Never?*: she snorted.

:*Well—I never argue with you when you're right.*:

"Good," Wintermoon rose to his feet, then held up his wrist again. For the second time, a white shape dove past Skif's ear; this time the owl came in from the side, then swooped up and alighted on Wintermoon's gauntlet with grace and silence. "This is Corwith," he said, transferring the owl to his other shoulder. "We three will be most happy to give you our help. Then I shall see you in the morning?"

"Make that when we wake up," Skif amended. "It's already morning."

Wintermoon squinted at the west, where the moon was going down. "So it is. Well, the night is my chosen time of departure, when I am given a choice. That will be good. There will be fewer eyes that will see us leave. *Zhai'helleva*, Wingbrother. May your dreams bring you peace and good omens."

"And yours—friend." On impulse, Skif offered his hand; Wintermoon took it after a moment, clasping first his hand, then his wrist.

As Wintermoon vanished into the darkness under the trees, and Skif turned to climb up into the *ekele* that had been given him, Cymry reached over and nuzzled his shoulder. :*That was well done,*: she said warmly. :*I like him. I think we might have accomplished more than we realized.*:

:*I think you're right,*: he answered, yawning. :*I've got a good feeling about this.*:

So good a feeling, that for the first time since Nyara disappeared, he fell asleep immediately, instead of lying awake and staring at the darkness. And for the first time, it was a calm sleep, untroubled by dreams of silken skin and crying, cat-pupiled eyes.

Skif & Cymry

Chapter Four

Skif tied the final knots on his packs, expecting at any moment to have a *hertasi* pop its head over the edge of the treehouse with a summons from Wintermoon. It was difficult to tell time here, where the position of the sun was obscured by the towering trees and where the temperature seldom varied by much, but he thought he'd awakened about noon. There had been cheese, fruit, and fresh bread waiting in the outer room of his little treehouse along with all of his belongings and Cymry's tack, brought from the gryphon's lair. By *hertasi* or one of the scouts, he presumed; they were the only ones who knew where his possessions were, besides, of course, the gryphons. He and Elspeth had stayed with the gryphons since they had first arrived here in k'Sheyna territory; they were kindhearted creatures, but certainly not pack animals; he'd assumed he would have to go fetch all of the gear himself. This was yet another instance of Tayledras thoughtfulness; or at least, of *hertasi* thoughtfulness. He was even more surprised and delighted to discover that every bit of his clothing had been cleaned and neatly folded before being put in the pack, and all but one of his hidden knives and garrottes from said clothing laid out neatly by the pack.

Old habits die hard.

He descended long enough to clean himself up at a hot spring set up as a kind of bathhouse—and to thank the first *hertasi* he saw for having his things brought. He found the lizard first. He was a little ashamed that he couldn't tell the difference between individual lizard-creatures; surely there was a way, and it seemed doltish not to know it. He covered it as best he could by asking the diminutive creature to pass on his thanks to the others. The *hertasi* didn't seem to mind. In fact, it thanked *him,* and showed him where to go to bathe and find provisions for his journey.

Back in the treehouse, he launched into packing feverishly. The strange provisions he'd gotten from a hidden kitchen area—learning only then where all the food for the celebration had come from—weighed much less than the dried fruit and beef and travelers' bread that the Valdemaran forces, Heralds and Guards alike, carried into the field.

Just so that they were marginally edible. Marginal was all he asked for. *They can't taste any worse than the clay tablets they expect Karsite troops to eat. Starch for shirts or old glue would taste better.* That much he was certain of; some folks would rather eat their saddles than the Karsite field rations.

"I trust you are ready?" Wintermoon called up from below, startling him. He went to the balcony, and looked over the edge.

Beneath him were the scout—now with his hair bound up in a tail and wearing clothing identical to the kind Darkwind had worn—and a pair of handsome *dyheli* stags. One carried a light pack, the other did not even have a cloth on its back. Beside them was Cymry, looking up at him with merry blue eyes, as if she was amused by his startlement.

"I'm ready," he replied to all of them. "I'm pretty much packed. Look out, I'm going to toss the stuff down."

Wintermoon and the rest backed up a little, giving him room for the drop. He dropped the saddle and the pack containing his clothing and nonbreakables over the edge of the balcony; he brought the rest down the staircase, slung over his back.

By the time he reached the ground, Wintermoon had already saddled Cymry for him, and was waiting for the rest of the gear. "You should try the Shin'a'in saddles," the Tayledras scout observed, as Skif pushed aside an enormous leaf that overhung the trail to join them. "I think you both would find them more comfortable."

"Maybe," Skif replied, dropping his pack on the ground, and holding up the hackamore for Cymry so that she could slip her nose into it. "But the Shin'a'in don't have to contend with anything other than the plains. We've got a lot of different terrain to cross, a lot of jobs to do, and sometimes we have to be able to sleep in the saddle or strap ourselves on because of wounds." He faltered for a moment, as an ugly memory intruded; he resolutely ignored it, and continued. "I'll try their saddles some time, but we've put a lot of time and work into that design, and I'm not sure there's any way to improve it."

Cymry nodded, which apparently surprised Wintermoon. Skif was going to ask where his birds were, when one of them dropped down out of the tree to land on the laden *dyheli*'s pack, and the other followed to land on the unladen one's horns. The stags were both evidently used to this; the second *dyheli* held his head steady until the owl hopped from the horns to Wintermoon's shoulder. "Mobile tree branches," the Tayledras grinned.

"So I see. I told Elspeth that I was going out to hunt for Need," Skif told the scout, "I told her that I didn't think we could afford to have a major power like that out loose and not know where it was or what it was doing. She agreed, but I don't think she believed that was the only reason."

"I doubt you could fool your friend on matters of the heart," Wintermoon replied. "At least, not for long. Except, perhaps, for her own; I have noted that few people are good judges of their own hearts."

Skif flushed, and decided not to answer that statement. "Have you got any ideas about where we should start looking?" he asked instead. "I mean, I know you haven't had much chance to think about this since last night, but—"

"Actually, I have," Wintermoon interrupted, surprisingly. "I spent some time last night reviewing what I would do if I were in her place. So I know where she might be, I think—or rather, I know where we need not look. Here—"

He pulled out a map from a pouch at his belt and spread it on the ground. Skif pulled the last buckle on Cymry's packs tight and crouched down on his heels beside the scout. Cymry craned her neck around to look over his shoulder.

"—here, is the Vale." Wintermoon pointed at an oval valley on the rim of the crater-wall that marked the rim of the Dhorisha Plains. "Nyara will not have run to the west, neither south nor north; to the west and south were her father's lands. To the west and north, *that* is untamed, unhealed, tainted land, full of creatures that are as bad or worse than anything that her father commanded.''

''And she knows this?'' Skif asked.

Wintermoon snorted. ''She cannot have avoided knowing. No matter how closely he kept her mewed, if she had any contact with the world outside his walls, she would have known. We had intended to bracket the area between this Vale and the new one—well, that is of no matter now. She will not have gone west unless she is an utter fool. Nor will she have gone south.''

''Because that's the Dhorisha Plains,'' Skif said, absently, studying the map.

''Yes. So, that leaves east and north. She may have gone east—she *can* go east—but here—'' he indicated a shaded area on the map. ''This pattern means that the lands here *are* healed. If she goes there, she will encounter farms and settlements. If she goes further, she must meet towns, villages, and people who are unused to seeing creatures that are not wholly human. She will surely encounter trade-roads, traders, caravans. No, I do not think she would go very far to the east.''

''And if she went due north?'' Skif asked.

''Ah—again, she will encounter a border, this time the territory guarded by another Clan. They may not be as kindly disposed toward her as we. Certainly, since they will not know her, they will regard her with suspicion and even hostility.'' Wintermoon sat back on his heels. ''So you see, she must be within *this* area.'' His forefinger described a rough oblong on the map. ''Those are the lands we once claimed, but we have let run wild, as we pulled back our borders. *That* is where I think we shall find her.''

Skif nodded, and considered the map. ''None of it is very far from where the scouts patrol,'' he observed. ''In fact, we *could* go out there and start our search, and come back to the Vale every few days to see how matters are progressing here—and whether or not we're going to be needed after all.''

''My thought exactly,'' the scout said, picking up the map and folding it. He stood up, stowing the folded parchment in his pouch again. ''In this way we fulfill our own wishes and our duty to the Clan as well.'' He gave Skif an odd sideways grin that Skif returned.

''Why do I have the feeling that you're as good at that as I am?'' he asked slyly. ''Getting your own way by threading through rules and obligations, I mean.''

"What, I?" Wintermoon replied, widening his eyes innocently. Then he laughed. "Come, we are birds of the same flock, you and I. We know each other. Yes?" He turned and mounted the second stag bareback, saving Skiff from having to answer that question.

Skif took his time mounting, settling himself into the saddle with a sigh. Not that he didn't enjoy partnering with Cymry, but it had been a long journey and he'd been glad it looked as if they were staying in one place for a while. Well, it *had* looked that way, until he'd realized that Nyara was gone and wasn't coming back. Now they were on the trail again. . . .

:*Oh, you won't be in the saddle as much as you think,*: Cymry told him affectionately. :*Don't forget, Wintermoon is going to have to look over the ground out there very closely for clues. Actually, if I were you, I'd let him teach me about tracking in the wild; I think you could learn a lot from him. I know I'll be paying attention.*:

Skif was a little surprised at her matter-of-fact acceptance of this excursion. He had more than half expected her to object to leaving Elspeth on her own—after all, he was supposed to be looking after her, wasn't he? He was supposed to be her bodyguard, *and* he was supposed to keep her from getting into too much trouble.

:*Elspeth's quite capable of taking care of herself, Chosen, as she has reminded you more than once.*: This time the tone was teasing, lighthearted. But she quickly sobered. :*There is no way that Ancar can get to her here— even if he could learn where she was. She's got to go her own way now, you know that. You know she's going to have to deal with things you can't even guess at. Whatever trouble she's likely to get into, I don't think it's going to be anything a couple of arrows or knives would fix.*:

Skif ducked out of the way of a branch stretching over the path, and sighed. That, no matter how his pride felt about it, was only the truth. She was a mage now, under the protection and tutelage of mages. He would be as out of his element as if he tried to teach a candlemaking class.

:*And I don't have any of this Mage-Gift, whatever it is,*: he added. :*Probably I'd only be in the way. Probably I'd get myself in trouble without ever helping Elspeth.*:

:*Probably,*: Cymry agreed. :*Nyara, now—that's something you can do something about. I think you should. If nothing else, when you find her, you'll discover for yourself if there can be—or ever was—anything between you two. And you'll finally stop worrying about her.*:

While her words were practical, the tone of her mind-voice was un-expectedly sympathetic.

She was his best friend, barring no one else. She knew all of his secrets, even the ugly ones. He stared at the trail ahead and at Winter-moon's back for a while, thinking about that, thinking about how close they were. *:Cymry, were you ever in love?:* he asked abruptly.

:Bright Havens, what a question!: she exclaimed. *:Me? In love? Why do you want to know?:*

After all these years, he'd managed to surprise her. *:Because—I don't know if I'm in love or not—or if I was ever in love with anyone.:* Silence fell between them for a heartbeat. *:I thought if you were ever in love, you'd be able to tell if I was. Am. Whatever.:*

They reached the barrier-shield at the end of the Vale at that moment; the tingling of energies as they crossed it distracted Skif from his question.

When they emerged into slightly cooler air on the other side, Cymry shook her head, and shivered her skin as if she was shaking off flies. *:Skif, yes, I do know something of emotional involvement. That doesn't simplify matters any. You weren't in love with Elspeth, I can tell you that much,:* she said, slowly. *:That was a combination of a lot of things, includ-ing, my dear Chosen, the fact that you finally saw her as a very attractive woman for the first time and had a predictable reaction.:*

He choked; turned it into a cough when Wintermoon looked back at him in inquiry. Cymry wasn't usually so frank with him.

Or blunt. *:You made matters worse, I'm afraid, by acting far too strongly upon those feelings.:*

:I'd kind of figured that part out,: he replied wryly. *:But now, this time?:*

She shook her head. *:I honestly don't know. You have some very strong feelings, but I can't sort them out any better than you can.:*

Well, at least the Companions didn't know everything. Sometimes he wondered about that. They certainly didn't go out of their way to dispel the idea that they did.

Skif turned his attention to the woods surrounding the trail; trying to get used to these new forests, so that he could learn to identify what was a sign of danger and what wasn't. He did the only thing he could do; he assumed that this area was safe, and studied it. Anything that differed from this might be dangerous.

Most of his experience outside of towns consisted of the single circuit he'd made with Dirk when he first got his Whites, and his occasional duty as courier and messenger. At neither time had he really had to deal with *wilderness*; with places where people simply did not live. He had traveled roads, not game-trails; spent nights in way-stations, not in a tent, or a blanket roll under the open sky. Even on the journey here, the first time he had encountered true wilderness was when they descended into the Dhorisha Plains.

There, on that trackless expanse of grassland, there had been no real sign of the hand of man. Perhaps that was why the Plains intimidated him so much. Never had he felt so completely out of his element.

Maybe that had been why he had persisted in clinging to Elspeth. . . .

Well, here was wilderness again; once outside the Vale, there were no tracks of any kind, for the Tayledras went to great lengths to avoid making them. The only creatures making trails of any sort were wild ones: deer, bear, boar. Even the *dyheli* did their best to avoid making trails, for trails meant places they could be ambushed. Skif couldn't help wondering if the only reason Wintermoon rode the *dyheli* stag now was to keep from leaving human footprints.

The signs of fall were everywhere; in the dying, drying grasses, in the leaves of the bushes which were just starting to turn, in the peculiar scent to the air that only frost-touched leaves made. This wasn't a comfortable time of the year to be traipsing about in wild country.

On the other hand, it would be harder for anything hostile to hide, once the leaves started falling in earnest. If there was anything noisier for a skulker than a carpet of crisp, freshly-fallen dry leaves, Skif had yet to run into it; even in his days as a thief and a street brat, he'd known that, and stayed clear of rich folks' gardens in the fall. And he was not looking forward to camping out in the cold, riding through chill autumn rains. . . .

On the other hand, it probably wouldn't get horribly cold this far south, at least, not for a while yet. Game would be plentiful at this time of year, a lot of it birds and animals in their first year—inexperienced, or just plain stupid, which to a hunter translated as "easy to catch." Darkwind had quoted a Shin'a'in saying about that, one day when Vree brought back a rabbit that couldn't have been more than two months old: "If it gets caught, it deserves to be eaten." On the whole, Skif agreed. With fresh meals volunteering their lives to their owls, arrows, and snares, they might not even need to resort to their traveling rations much. Maybe this wasn't going to be so bad after all.

Cymry's ears flicked, the way they did when she was Mindspeaking, and he caught the barest edges of something in the back of his mind. But he couldn't make anything out; just a mental "sound." It was as if he was several rooms away from two people having a conversation; no matter how hard he strained, all he could hear was a kind of murmur in the distance.

:Who are you talking to?: he asked her, puzzled. He hadn't thought Cymry could Mindspeak with anyone except himself and another Companion.

:Elivan,: she replied, shortly.

Elivan? Who—

Then the *dyheli* that Wintermoon was riding turned its head on its long, graceful neck and gave him a look and a nod.

The *dyheli?* She was Mindspeaking the *dyheli?* Frustrated, he tried to make sense out of the far-off murmuring, unable to make out a single "word." Even more frustrating, he caught Wintermoon in a kind of "listening" attitude, and heard a third "voice" join the other two in what sounded like a brief remark.

Whatever they were saying, Wintermoon seemed vastly amused; Skif got a look at his expression as he ducked to avoid a low-hanging vine, and he looked like someone who has just been let in on a private joke.

Skif felt a surge of resentment at being left out. Just how much mind-magic did the Hawkbrother have? Why couldn't he hear the *dyheli*, if Wintermoon and Cymry could? And was it only Wintermoon who had that particular Gift, or did all the Tayledras share it?

They'd been free enough with information about real magic; why keep this a secret?

Except that they weren't exactly keeping it a secret—not from Skif, anyway.

Unless they couldn't block what they were doing. But in that case, why did Cymry tell him matter-of-factly that she was talking to the stag?

The murmur of far-off voices stopped; finally Wintermoon signaled a halt at the edge of a tiny, crystalline stream. The Tayledras dismounted, and the two *dyheli* moved up side-by-side to dip their slender muzzles into the water. Another sign of the stags' intelligence—the pack-laden stag was not being led, and Wintermoon made no move to limit their drinking.

:I could use a drink too, dear,: Cymry prompted him. Skif slid out of his saddle to let Cymry join them. Wintermoon strolled over, stretching to relieve the inevitable stiffness of riding any distance at all.

"We are at the edge of the territory k'Sheyna still patrols," he said. "After this point, the hazards begin. It may be dangerous to break silence; if I note anything, I shall warn your lady mind-to-mind."

"Why not warn me?" Skif asked, doing his best not to sound sullen, but afraid that some of his resentment showed through anyway.

Wintermoon only looked mildly surprised. "Because I cannot," he replied. "The mind-to-mind speech of the scouts is only between scouts and those who are not human." His brow furrowed as he thought for a moment. "Perhaps you caught the edge of my conversation with Elivan. I apologize if this seemed rude to you, but your Cymry told me that you did not share the Gift of Mindspeech with one other than her—or perhaps another Herald. I thought, then, that you did not hear us." He shrugged, apologetically. "I am sorry if you thought we had left you out a-purpose. Many Tayledras have this Gift, but I am one of the strongest speakers, as was Dawnfire. Sometimes it only extends to bondbirds. I am fortunate that I share my brother's ability to speak with other creatures as well, although I do not share his gift of speaking with other humans."

Skif flushed. That was one possibility that simply hadn't occurred to him—that Wintermoon might not know that he was aware of the conversation without knowing what was being said. *Well, now I feel like a real idiot. . . .*

"Is that what makes the nonmages scouts, and not something else?" he asked, trying to cover his misstep.

Wintermoon shook his head, and smiled. "All Tayledras have mind-to-mind speech, usually only with their bondbirds," he replied. "It is a part of us; one of the many things that the Goddess granted to us to help us survive here. but although those who can speak with other creatures make the best scouts, if they are also mage-born, then mage-craft is oft the course of their life."

Skif looked beyond him for a moment, across the stream. It didn't seem any wilder or more threatening there than it did on this side. Frost had laced the trees on both sides of the stream, perhaps because they were more sensitive to it; the leaves were a yellow-brown, and some had already fallen, carpeting the ground and occasionally drifting off on the current of the brook. Jays called somewhere out there—or at least, something with the same raucous scream as a scarlet jay. A hint of movement on the other side of the water caught his eye, and he turned his head slightly just in time to catch the tail of a squirrel whisking over to the opposite side of the trunk—presumably, with a squirrel attached to it, although if what he'd been told was true, that didn't necessarily follow.

"Just what's so bad out there?" he asked, curiosity overcoming pride. "It doesn't look any different to me, but I wouldn't know what to look for."

"There—not much," Wintermoon replied, scanning the trees and the ground beneath them with eyes that missed nothing. "Farther out—I've heard there are *wyrsa*, though at this season they do not run in packs. Bears, of course, and Changebears. Treelions and Changelions, wild boars and Changeboars. Perhaps *bukto*, and—"

"Wait a moment," Skif interrupted. Those names—that was something he'd been wanting to ask about, and hadn't had an opening. "Changebears, Changelions, Changeboars—what are you talking about? Darkwind called Nyara a 'Changechild,' does this have anything to do with her?"

"Yes and no," Wintermoon replied maddeningly. Skif stifled his impatience as Wintermoon paused, as if searching for the proper words. "Do you not recall what you were shown by Iceshadow? How magic, uncontrolled and twisted, warped all that it touched here?"

"Yes, but wasn't that a long time ago?" he said, thinking back to those images, strange and only half understood. The part where that bright light had appeared to the Hawkbrothers—he'd understood what the Goddess had asked of them, but he hadn't seen more than that light. Elspeth and the Shin'a'in had plainly experienced more than that.

"Not long enough," the scout replied, looking soberly out at the innocent-looking land beyond the stream. "There was a time when magic in all its 'colors' and 'sounds' worked together. The time we call the Mage Wars shattered that order. The structure of magic—and its energies—were stressed to their limits. In the great disaster that ended the Final War, those bonds were broken. Their crystalline patterns, like branches of light to a mage, became as distorted as pine needles dropped to the ground. And every place they touched, on a scale vaster than we can see, they made the land dangerous, and caused creatures that should never have lived to appear."

Skif shook his head, unable or unwilling to comprehend it. Wintermoon continued.

"When we first came here and established this Vale, the land hereabouts was as fearful as anything you saw before the Lady appeared. We have tamed it somewhat, and it is a fortunate thing that few of the magic-twisted creatures breed true. That also is due in part to Tayledras magery.''

"But some do?" Skif asked.

Wintermoon nodded. "Those, we call 'Changebeasts.' They plainly have parentage of normal creatures, but they have new attributes, generally dangerous. Changelions, for instance—oft they have huge canine teeth, extending far beyond their jaws, and have a way of being able to work a kind of primitive magic that can keep them invisible even when one looks directly at them, so long as the Changelion does not move. That is . . . a common Change. Some are unpredictable or unrecognizable." He hesitated, gathering his thoughts. "When the parentage was human, we call the result a 'Changechild.' And—in general—true humans do not—mate with them."

He glanced sideways at Skif, gauging the effect of his words. Skif didn't take offense, but he wasn't going to accept that particular judgment without a fight, either. "Why not?" he asked, bringing his chin up, aggressively. "I mean, what's the difference? Who would care?"

Wintermoon sighed. "Because it is said that to mate with a Changechild is the same as mating with a beast, because the Changechildren are one with the beasts." He held up a hand to stop the angry words Skif started to speak. "I only say what is commonly thought, not what I think. But you must know that it *is* the common thought, and there is no escaping it."

Skif frowned. "So most Tayledras would think—if Nyara and I made a pair of it—that I was some kind of deviant?"

The Hawkbrother sighed. "Perhaps fewer in this Clan than in others, but some would. And outside the Clans altogether, among Outlanders who live in Tayledras lands and hold loyalty to us, or among those who trade with us—there would be no escaping it. They would all feel that way to some degree."

So I'll deal with it when—if—it happens. He nodded his understanding, but not his agreement.

Wintermoon continued. "There is another problem as well; there are either no offspring of such a mating, or as often as not, they truly *are* monsters that are less able to reason than beasts. This, I know, for I have seen it. The few children of such a union that *are* relatively whole are like unto the Changechild parent. And that is only one in four."

Not good odds. . . .

Wintermoon flexed his hands. "The likeliest to happen is that there are no children of the union. I would say that is just as well."

"So Nyara is a Changechild," Skif said, thinking out loud. "Just what makes her that, and not some—oh—victim of an experiment by her father on a real human child?"

"That there are things the human form cannot be made to mimic," Wintermoon replied too promptly. "Her eyes, slitted like a cat. Fur-tufts on her ears."

"Oh?" This time Skif expressed real skepticism. "That's not what Darkwind told me. He said that it *was* possible that she'd been modified from a full human. He said that it would take a lot of magic to do it, but that if Falconsbane was using her as a kind of model for what he wanted to do to himself, he might be willing to burn the magic."

"He did?" Skif's assertion caught Wintermoon by surprise. "That— would make things easier." The Hawkbrother chewed his lip for a moment. "That would make her entirely a victim, among other things. That would bring her sympathy."

"I've got another question." Cymry returned from the stream and came to stand beside him; he patted her neck absently. "What if she wasn't a Changechild—but she wasn't a human either?"

Wintermoon shook his head in perplexity. "How could she not be either?"

"If she was someone from a real race of her own—" He chewed his lip, and tried to come up with an example. "Look, you don't call the *tervardi* Changechildren, or the *hertasi*. What makes them different from Nyara?"

"There are many of them," Wintermoon replied promptly. "They breed true; they have colonies of their own kind, settlements."

"So how do you know that there *aren't* settlements of Nyara's kind somewhere?" he interrupted. "You didn't know there were gryphons before Treyvan and Hydona arrived!" He smiled triumphantly.

"Gryphons were upon a list handed down from the time of the Mage Wars," Wintermoon said immediately, dashing his hopes. "As were the others. Every Tayledras memorizes it, lest he not recognize a friend—or foe. There is nothing on that list that matches Nyara."

Well, so much for that idea. At least she isn't on the "foe" list; I suppose I'd better consider us fortunate.

Nevertheless, he couldn't help wondering if there *could* be creatures that were like the *hertasi* that simply hadn't made the all-important list.

Or if there were creatures that had developed since the Mage Wars that couldn't have made the list because they hadn't been in existence then. . . .

Oh, this is ridiculous. It doesn't matter what she is. What matters is what she does. Every Herald he'd met had told him that as he grew up in the Collegium. They had been right then; that should hold true now.

"It will be dark, soon," Wintermoon said, glancing at the sky. While they had been talking, the quality of the light had changed, to the thick gold of the moments before actual sunset. Filtered through the golden-brown leaves, the effect was even more pronounced, as if the very air had turned golden and sweet as honey.

"Are we going to camp here, or go on?" Skif asked. The question was pertinent; if this had been an expedition with two Heralds, they would camp now, while there was still light. But it wasn't; Wintermoon had abilities and a resource in his bondbirds that no Herald had.

"We go on," Wintermoon replied promptly. "Although we will feign to make camp. If there is anyone watching us, they will be deceived. Then once true night falls, we shall move on."

It didn't take them long to unload the packs and Cymry's saddle and make a sketchy sort of camp; Wintermoon unstrung and tied out a hammock, and padded it with a bedroll, then produced a second one and guided Skif in setting it up. That done, they cleared a patch of forest floor and built a tiny fire.

As they sat beside the fire, one of the owls lumbered into their clearing, laden with a young rabbit. It dropped its burden at Wintermoon's feet, and before it had taken its perch on his shoulder, the second followed with a squirrel in its talons.

"Well," Wintermoon chuckled, as the second owl dropped its burden beside the first and flew to a perch in the tree above Wintermoon's head, "It seems that my friends have determined that we shall have a meal, at least."

"That's fine by me," Skif said, and grinned. "I was about to dig out those trail rations."

"I thought I heard something growling—I thought it might be a beast in the bushes. 'Twas only your stomach," Wintermoon teased as he began gutting and skinning the rabbit. Both owls hopped down from their perches to stand on the ground beside him, waiting for tidbits.

They took the proffered entrails quite daintily; seeing that, Skif had no hesitation about picking up the squirrel and following the scout's example. When the darker of the two owls saw what he was doing, it joined him, abandoning Wintermoon.

Skif got two surprises; the first, that this little "squirrel" was built more like a rabbit than the scrawny creatures he was used to—and the second, that the owl took so much care in taking its treats from him that its beak never touched his fingers. "Which one have I got?" he asked Wintermoon. "How hungry is he likely to be?"

"K'Tathi," the scout replied without looking up. "The scraps will suffice for now; they will hunt again after we make our second camp, this time for themselves. Give him what you wish to spare from your meal."

Head, entrails, and the limbs from the first joint out seemed appropriate. K'Tathi took everything that was offered with grace, never getting so much as a spot of blood on his gray-white feathers. Skif offered the skin as well, but the owl ignored it, so Skif quickly tossed it into the bushes as he saw Wintermoon do. That would have been foolhardy if they had been planning to stay, for the bloody skins might well attract something quite large and dangerous. But since they weren't—well, there was sure to be something that would find the skin worth eating, and if there *was* someone watching them, possibly following them—

Well, if they try to go for the camp and there's something big, with teeth, still here, they're going to get a rude surprise.

When he finished his task, he once again followed Wintermoon's example and spitted it on a sturdy branch to hold over the fire. Meanwhile, the sun continued to set, the sky above the trees turning first orange, then scarlet, then deepening to vermilion-streaked blue. By the time the meat was done, the sky was thick with stars.

He was halfway through his dinner when Wintermoon said abruptly, "I envy you, did you know that?"

He looked up, a little startled, into the ice-blue eyes of the man across the fire. There was no sign of Wintermoon's dinner, other than the pile of small, neatly-stacked bones at his feet, each of them gnawed clean.

What did he do, inhale the thing?

On the other hand—it was in the interest of the scout's survival to learn to eat quickly. No telling when a meal might be interrupted by an uninvited, unwelcome dinner-guest.

"Why?" he asked, puzzled by the question. "What is there about me to envy? I'm nothing special, especially around Heralds."

"My—liaisons—tend to be brief, and informal," the scout replied.

"One reason I wished to guide you was because Starsong returned my feathers, and I am at loose ends."

Skif wondered if he should tender sympathy, surmising from the content that "returned his feathers" meant his lover had dissolved the relationship. But Wintermoon evidently saw something of his uncertainty in his expression and shook his head, smiling.

"No, this was not painful. I have no wish to *avoid* the Vale, or her. But I simply have no partner now, and there is no one else I care to partner with at the moment. So I am at loose ends, and would just as soon have other things to think on." He wiped his fingers clean on a swatch of dry grass, and tossed it into the fire. "That is what I envy you, do you see," he said, watching the grass writhe and catch. "Strong feelings. I have never experienced them."

Skif coughed, a little embarrassed. "I don't know that this is anything other than infatuation or attraction to the exotic."

"Still, it is strong," Wintermoon persisted. "I have never felt anything strongly. Sometimes I doubt I have the ability for it."

The statement was offered like a gift; Skif was wise enough to know that when he saw it. He searched his mind for an appropriate response.

:The birds,: Cymry prompted.

"You feel strongly about Corwith and K'Tathi, don't you?" he countered.

Wintermoon nodded slowly as if that simply hadn't occurred to him in such a context.

"Well then," Skif said and gestured, palm upward. "Then I wouldn't worry. You're capable. The way I see it, we all feel strongly about things, we just might not know we do. Valdemar is like that for Heralds; we lay our lives down willingly for our country and Monarch when we must, but most of the time, we just don't think about it. If you encounter someone you *can* feel strongly about, you will. You haven't exactly been given much of a choice of potential mates what with three-fourths of the Clan gone, and your tendency to, well, stay to yourself."

"True." The scout sat back a little, and only then did Skif realize, as he relaxed, that he had been tensed. "My father thinks that being born without the Gift for magery shows a serious lack in me. Sometimes I wonder if I have other, less visible lacks."

Before Skif could change the subject, Wintermoon changed it for him—to one just as uncomfortable. "What do you intend when we find Nyara?" the scout asked, bluntly. "We shall, I promise you. I am not indulging in vanity to say that I am one of the finest trackers of k'Sheyna.''

"I—uh—I don't know," Skif replied. "Right now, to tell you the truth, all I'm thinking about is finding her. Once we do that—" He shook his head. "It just gets too complicated. I'm going to worry about it when it happens. What she says and does when we find her will give me my direction.''

"Ah," the scout replied, and fell silent.

After all, I spent less than a week in her company, he thought. *I could have been misreading everything about her.*

Except that she had saved his life at the risk of her own. She'd attacked her *own father,* a creature that had held absolute control over her all of her life, and for Skif's sake.

She'd gone after Falconsbane with nothing; nothing but her bare hands—

—or rather, claws—

And thoughts like that made him realize all over again just how alien she was, yet that realization didn't change how he felt in the least. Whatever it was, it was very strong and very real.

What's going to make a difference is what's happened to her—and what happens to us. If she's handling the things her father did to her. And if we can find someplace where people will accept her—and maybe even us.

That place might not be Valdemar; that was something he was going to have to admit. They might not be able to deal with someone who had tufted, pointed ears, catlike eyes, and a satiny-smooth pelt of very, very short fur. It wasn't obvious, but a close examination would show it. The Heralds were open-minded, but were they open-minded enough for *that?* To accept someone who looked half animal?

And he was going to have to go home eventually. . . .

That question kept him thinking until Wintermoon shook his shoulder. After that, he was too busy breaking camp and following the scout through the darkness to worry about anything else. And when they finally made camp again, he was too *tired* to think at all.

Wintermoon, Corwith, & K'tathi

Chapter
Five

The two hunters began using a different pattern than a follower might expect; they were on the move from about midafternoon to after midnight. With the owls helping him, Wintermoon was completely happy doing most of his scouting after darkness fell, and even Skif's night-vision gradually improved with practice. He would never be Wintermoon's equal, but he grew comfortable with searching the forest in the darkness. There were advantages to this ploy that outweighed the disadvantages; the strongest advantage being that with K'Tathi and Corwith scouting for them, there was nothing that was going to surprise them—and nothing that would be able to follow them easily. Few creatures hunted the night by preference, and those few, though formidable, could be watched for. So for several days, they hunted and camped, and remained unmolested even by insects. But Skif knew that the situation could not last. Sooner or later, they were going to run into one of the kinds of creatures that had driven the Tayledras borders back in the first place. Sooner or later, something was going to come hunting them.

That, in fact, was what he was thinking when they paused along a deer trail, and Wintermoon sent the owls up to quarter the immediate vicinity, looking for disturbed areas or other signs of someone who was not especially woodswise. Cymry began acting a little nervous, casting occasional glances back over her shoulder. But Wintermoon, who was sitting quietly on Elivan, didn't seem to sense anything out of order.

His first real warning that something really was wrong and that Cymry just wasn't being fidgety was when Wintermoon suddenly tensed and flung up his hand, and Corwith came winging in as fast as slung shot, landing on his outstretched arm, and hissing with fear and anger. Skif held out his hand as Wintermoon had asked him to do if one of the owls ever came in fast and showing distress. K'Tathi arrived a moment later, and K'Tathi hit his gauntleted wrist as if striking prey. It was the first time that the owl had landed on Skif, and nothing in his limited experience in hawking with merlins and kestrels prepared him for the power and the weight of the bird as it caught his wrist and landed. Those thumb-length talons closing—even with restraint—on his wrist could easily have pierced the heavy leather of the gauntlet. They did not although the claws exerted such powerful pressure that Skif could not possibly have rid himself of the bird short of killing it. K'Tathi hissed angrily, and swiveled his head away from Skif, pointing back the way he had come.

Before Skif could ask what was wrong, Wintermoon cursed under his breath and the *dyheli* stag he rode tossed its antlers and reared, its eyes shining in the moonlight, wide with fear. Wintermoon kept his seat easily, but Corwith flapped his wings wildly to keep his balance.

Tilredan, the second stag, the one laden with their provisions and extra gear, bolted; it was Skif's turn to swear, and not under his breath. But he had reacted too soon; in the next breath, Wintermoon's mount followed the other stag, and Skif only had Cymry's warning Mindcall of *:Hold on!:* before she was hot on his heels.

Hold on? With an owl on one arm?

He dropped the reins—useless in a situation like this one—and grabbed for the pommel of the saddle with his free hand, deeply grateful that he had *not* given in to Wintermoon and exchanged Cymry's old saddle for a Shin'a'in model. Shin'a'in saddles had no pommel to speak of. . . .

K'Tathi continued to cling to his wrist, mercifully refraining from using his wings to keep his balance. One strong buffet to the head from those powerful wings would lay Skif out over Cymry's rump before he knew what had hit him. Instead, the owl hunched down on the wrist, making himself as small as possible, leaning into the wind of their passing. Skif tried to bring him in close to his body, but he wasn't sure how much K'Tathi would tolerate.

:What in—: Skif began.

:A pack of something, that scented us and is hunting up our backtrail,: Cymry answered shortly. *:Not something we've seen before, but something Wintermoon and the others know. Worse than wolves, worse than Change-wolves. And smart—we're running for a place where we can defend ourselves. K'Tathi found it just before Corwith sighted the pack.:*

He could only hope that an owl's idea of what was defensible and theirs was the same; sheer cliffs were fine if you could scale them, and a hole in a tree would be all right if the tree was the size of a house, but otherwise they'd be better off making a back-to-back stand.

And he hoped his idea of "nearby" and the owl's was the same, too.

For behind him, he heard an uncanny keening sound; not baying, not howling, not wailing—something like all three together. The noise gave him chills and made the hair on the back of his neck stand up, and it sounded as if it was coming from at least eight or nine throats. He glanced back over his shoulder and saw nothing, but his imagination populated the darkness. If he heard eight, how many were really in the pack? Twelve? Twenty? *Fifty?*

K'Tathi clutched his wrist a little harder, and the deadly talons pricked him through the leather. This was not a good way to carry the bird, but there was no way to turn K'Tathi loose to fly. The *dyheli* were nearly a match for a Companion in speed, and they were going flat-out; neither owl could have hoped to keep up with them by flying through the canopy, which was why both birds were clinging desperately to their perches on his wrist and Wintermoon's. But K'Tathi, at least, was having a lot of trouble holding on. If the owl exerted a little more pressure—

:Cymry! Can you talk to K'Tathi?: he asked Cymry, frantically.

Her mind-voice was colored with surprise and annoyance at what probably seemed like a supremely inappropriate question. *:Yes, but this is no time—:*

He interrupted her. *:Tell him not to move, I'm going to try something with him, before he goes through my wrist.:*

He pulled his arm to his chest, and brought the bird in close to his body, sheltered against his body. This left the owl unbalanced, with its face shoved against his tunic, but K'Tathi displayed his agility and intelligence; somehow he managed to get himself reversed, so that his head faced forward and his tail and wings were tucked down between Skif's wrist and his chest. Now the bird wasn't having to fight the wind by himself, he was braced against Skif. The painful pressure on Skif's wrist relaxed.

That takes care of one problem.

Cymry's muscles bunched and flexed under his legs, the sound of hooves drowning out anything else except the chilling cries behind them. The wailing behind them seemed closer. Skif didn't ask Cymry if it was; it wouldn't make any difference. They'd either reach safety in time, or not.

He just wished he knew how far it was to that promise of "safety." If he knew, he might be able to guess whether they had any chance of making it, or whether it might be better to turn and make a stand.

And he wished that he had Wintermoon's night-sight, far superior to his own. To him, the moon-filled night was full of shadows his eyes couldn't penetrate. There could be nothing in those patches of darkness, or an enemy, or a hiding place. Though the moon was bright, there were still enough leaves on the trees to keep most of the light from reaching the ground.

The pack behind them cried again; this time there was no doubt in his mind about the peril of their situation. They were closer; if he looked back, he might be able to see them. The brush obscuring the path behind them didn't seem to be slowing the pack at all. In fact, they were probably breaking a trail for the pursuers to follow along. He'd learned long ago that being the pursued in a chase was more difficult than being the pursuer.

He crouched a little lower over Cymry's neck; as low as he could without flattening the owl. K'Tathi seemed to realize what he was doing, and didn't object or struggle, only giving him a warning stab with his talons when he crouched too low for the owl's comfort. Soft feathers pressed against his chin, and K'Tathi hunched down on his wrist so that the bird's chest-feathers warmed his hand.

He glanced up; saw the gray bulk of a rock formation looming ahead of them through the trees. In this light, it looked very like the one in which he and Elspeth had sheltered when they first arrived in Tayledras territory. A moment later, he saw that this one was bisected by a good-sized crack. Just like the one he and Elspeth had used.

He seemed to spend a lot of time hiding in rock crevices lately. Whatever had happened to hiding in rooms, behind drapes, or under furniture?

He had a moment to think—*Oh, no, not again*—and then Cymry braced all four legs for a sudden stop, skidding to a halt beside the *dyheli*. At least the owls did seem to have some idea of what constituted a good shelter for the rest of the party. The crevice would be a little crowded for three plus the two humans, but it was better than facing what howled on their backtrail with nothing to protect their backs!

All three of them crowded into the narrow crevice between two halves of a huge boulder; the rock was easily two stories tall, and the crevice ended in the stone face of a second stone that was even taller. There was barely enough room for Cymry to turn around, but that was fine; less room for them meant less room for those things out there to try to get past them.

A strangled hoot and the booting of K'Tathi's head against his chest reminded him to turn the poor owl loose. He raised his arm and launched it clumsily into the air, thrown off by the confined quarters and the fact that the owl was considerably heavier than a merlin. It wasn't much of a launch, or much help to the owl in gaining the air; K'Tathi hit him in the side of the head with a wing, recovered, and got free of the crevice, just as the pack reached them.

Skif looked up when a note of triumph entered the wailing. A strange, yellowish flood burst through the bushes and into the area around the rocks. *Dear gods—*

He needn't wish for night-sight after all. The damned things glowed. Now that he saw them, he wished, perversely, he didn't have quite such a good view.

They looked—superficially—like dogs; they had the lean, long-legged bodies of greyhounds, the close-cropped ears, the long, snaky tails and pointed muzzles. But their faintly-glowing, pale yellow hides were covered with scales, each scale outlined by a darker yellow. Their heads, shaped like an unholy cross between dog and viper, held eyes that burned a sulfurous yellow much brighter than the bodies, and rows of sharply pointed fangs.

They flowed, they didn't run; they drifted to a halt outside the entrance to the crevice and wound around each other in a vicious, impatient, ever-moving tangle. A snarl of ropes, with teeth at one end. A ball of vipers. They confused the eye and baffled the senses with their hypnotic restlessness. Wintermoon slid off the back of his mount; Skif followed his example a moment later.

They couldn't get in; the sharp hooves of Cymry and the *dyheli* bucks awaited them if they tried, not to mention the bows that Skif and Win-termoon unlimbered from the sheaths at each saddle. But those who had taken refuge here couldn't get out, either.

Stalemate.

Skif strung his bow and nocked an arrow to the string, Wintermoon shadowing every movement. *All right, here we are. Now what?*

"What are those things?" Skif asked quietly, as the creatures contin-ued to mill about in front of the crevice. He blinked his vision clear as they blurred for a moment. Was that just his tired eyes acting up, or were they doing it?

"Wyrsa," Wintermoon replied, frowning as he sighted along his ar-row. He loosed it in the next moment, but the *wyrsa* that was his target writhed aside literally as the point touched its hide, evading the deadly metal hunting point in a way that Skif would have said was impossible if he hadn't seen it himself. He'd never seen anything move so fast in his entire life.

Wintermoon muttered under his breath; Tayledras words Skif didn't know, but recognized for intention if not content.

The Tayledras nocked another arrow, and sighted, but did not fire. "They have no magic weapons, but they do not tire easily, and their fangs are envenomed," Wintermoon continued, watching as the beasts flowed about each other. "Once set on a quarry, they do not give up. They know how to weave patterns that confuse the eye, and as you see, they are swift, agile. Alone, we do not consider them a great prob-lem, but together in a pack, they are formidable."

"Great," Skif replied, after a moment. "So what do we do about them?"

"We kill them," the Hawkbrother said calmly, and loosed his arrow. This time, although the beast he aimed at evaded the shaft, the one that was behind it could not get out of the way, and took the arrow straight in the chest.

In any other beast, the wound might not have been fatal. There was no blood, and Skif honestly thought the creature was going to shake the strike off, even though it had looked like a heart-shot. But it stood stock still for a moment, jaws opening soundlessly, then toppled over onto its side. The light died from its eyes, and a moment later, the light faded from its hide, until it was a dull gray shape lying on the darker ground, revealed only by the moonlight.

The entire pack surged to one side, leaving the dead one alone. For a moment they froze in place, unmoving and silent.

He thought for a moment that they might prove Wintermoon wrong, that after the death of one of the pack, they might give up and leave their quarry to go its own way.

But then they all turned burning, hate-filled eyes on Wintermoon, then pointed their noses to the sky and howled again.

The sound was much worse at close range; it not only raised the hair on Skif's head, it rang in his ears in a way that made him dizzy and nauseous. The pack of *wyrsa* wavered before his blurring eyes, and he loosed the arrow he had nocked without even aiming it.

Luck, however, was with him. Two of the *wyrsa* dodged aside, accidentally shoving a third into the arrow's path. A second *wyrsa* dropped to the ground, fading as the first had done the moment it dropped. The pack stopped their howling, and tumbled, hastily, out of the way.

They stood near the bushes at the head of the path, this time staring at the cornered quarry. Skif got the feeling that there were cunning minds behind those glowing eyes; minds that were even now assessing all five of them. *Two down—how many to go? I can't make out how many there are of them, they keep blurring together.*

They advanced again, as a body, but with a little more separation between each of the beasts, so that they could dodge out of the way without sending another into the line of fire. He and Wintermoon loosed another five or six arrows each without hitting any more of the beasts. At least they had stopped their howling; Skif didn't think he could have handled much more of that. After the last fruitless volley, Wintermoon nocked his arrow but did not bother to draw it. Instead, he looked out of the corner of his eye at Skif and said, "And have you any notions?"

Skif had been trying to think of something, anything that could be done about the beasts, shook his head, wordlessly. Wintermoon grimaced.

One of the *wyrsa* separated from the pack, when they held their fire, and slunk, belly-down to the ground, to stand just in front of the crevice, as if testing them. When they didn't fire on it, another joined it, and another, until all of them had gathered directly before the entrance to their shelter. While they were moving one at a time, Skif got a chance to count them. There were eight in all, not counting the two dead.

He'd gone against worse numeric odds, but never against anything with reactions like these creatures had. *We're rather outnumbered.*

"If this were a tale," he offered, "our rescue would come out of the woods at this point. A herd of *dyheli*, perhaps, something that would come charging up and flatten everything in sight. Or a mage that could kill them with lightning."

"Would that it were a tale," Wintermoon muttered, his eyes following every move the beasts made. "The things move too swiftly to shoot."

If we had a way to distract them, it might be possible to get at some of them before they figured out what we were doing. "Are K'Tathi and Corwith fast enough to avoid those things?" he asked. "Could they—oh, fly down and make strikes at their heads and eyes, keep them busy while we tried shooting?"

Wintermoon shook his head, emphatically.

"No," he replied. "Owls are agile flyers, and silent, not swift. If they were to dive at the *wyrsa*, the beasts would have them. I will not ask them to do that."

Well, so much for that idea. Unless—well, they don't have to dive at them to distract them.

"All right, what about this," he said, thinking aloud. "Can they fly just out of reach, and hiss at them, get them worked up into forgetting about keeping an eye on us, maybe tease them into trying to make strikes even though they're out of reach?"

"Not for long." Wintermoon frowned. "Not long enough for us to pick off all the *wyrsa* with arrows."

"But what if we used the last of the arrows, waited, got the owls to tease them again, then charged them, all of us? Cymry and the *dyheli*, too?" Skif had a good idea that the hooved ones might account for as many as one *wyrsa* apiece—that would leave less for him and Wintermoon. "We can always retreat back here if we have to."

"It is worth a try." Wintermoon left his arrow nocked, but did not sight it. Even as Skif did the same, two ghostly white shapes swooped down out of the dark treetops, hissing and hooting. The *wyrsa* looked up, startled, as the owls made another swoop. At the third pass, even though they were plainly out of reach, the nearness of the owls, and the taunting sounds they made, broke through their control. They turned their attention from their trapped quarry and began lunging upward at the birds.

Wintermoon gave the *wyrsa* a few moments more to fix their attention on the "new" targets—then pulled up his bow and fired his last three arrows, just as fast as he could get them off. Skif did the same.

The *wyrsa* quickly turned their attention away from the owls, but it was already too late. Each arrow had found a mark; two more *wyrsa* lay dead, and four were wounded. It seemed that only a heart-shot was effective in killing them; the wounded *wyrsa* limped, but did not bleed, and in fact took a moment to gnaw off the shafts of the arrows piercing front and hind-quarters.

Now they were even more angry; Skif felt the heat of their gaze as a palpable sensation on his skin, and the hatred in their eyes was easy to read. As he put up his now-useless bow and drew his sword, he thought he read satisfaction in those eyes as well.

Wintermoon drew his sword as well, and K'Tathi and Corwith swooped down again, harrying the *wyrsa* from above, carefully gauging their flights to keep them just barely out of range. Skif would have thought that the ploy wouldn't work the second time, but either the *wyrsa* had not made the connection between the owls and the attack, or now that the last of the arrows was spent, they had reasoned as a human would that the quarry would not be able to use the owls as the cover for an attack.

They grew frustrated by their inability to do anything about the flying pests, and, sooner than Skif would have thought, turned their full attention back to the owls. That was when Wintermoon gave the signal to charge.

Cymry, larger and heavier than the *dyheli*, charged straight up the middle of the pack, striking with forehooves and kicking with hind, before whirling and retreating to the safety of the crevice. The *dyheli* came in on either side, just behind her, and trampled the *wyrsa* that dodged out of the way. They too retreated, as Skif and Wintermoon followed as a second wave, swords out and swinging.

Skif's world narrowed to his enemies and himself; nothing more. As always, fear temporarily evaporated, replaced by a cool detachment that would last only as long as the battle. Talia had told him that he was really temporarily insane when this came over him—as emotionally dead and uncaring as an assassin. He hadn't always been this way, but like so many in Valdemar, the war with Ancar had changed him.

He ducked away from snapping jaws, and decapitated one *wyrsa*. Two more came for him, poisoned fangs gleaming in the moonlight, but one of the *dyheli* got in a kick that distracted the first, and he fatally disemboweled the second when it couldn't limp out of the way fast enough.

Cymry screamed a warning, and he ducked the one that the *dyheli* had kicked; hit it with the flat of the blade, and knocked it into Cymry's path. She trampled it; bones crunched and popped, and a hoof crushed its skull as it snapped at her.

He saw movement out of the corner of his eye, and struck at a third as it jumped for Wintermoon's back. His strike wasn't clean; he only sliced at its foreleg, but that disabled it. Wintermoon finished that one off, and Skif looked around for more of the beasts.

There weren't any more.

"We did it." Skif could hardly believe it. It had happened so quickly—he leaned on his sword, panting, his heart still in his mouth over the near-misses he'd had with the creatures' poisoned fangs. Very near-misses; the cloth of his breeches was torn in one place, and his tunic damaged by claws.

"We were lucky," Wintermoon said flatly. "Very, very lucky. Either these were very stupid *wyrsa*, or your tactic took them by surprise. One touch of a fang begins to dissolve flesh far worse than any poisonous serpent. And *wyrsa* often travel in packs twice the size of this one. We would not have defeated a larger pack this easily."

Skif nodded, and the battle fever that had sustained him drained out of him in a rush, leaving him weak-kneed and panting. He cleaned his sword on a handful of dry grass, and sagged against the stones that had sheltered them. "Havens. No, if there had only been one more of those things, I don't think we could have done this. I've never seen anything move as fast as they did." He closed his eyes as a rush of exhaustion hit him.

"I think," Wintermoon said, in a voice as drained-sounding as Skif felt, "that we should camp now."

Wintermoon decreed a fire, after they cleared the carcasses of the *wyrsa* out of the way, pitching them into the forest, upwind of the camp, for scavengers to squabble over. Not the easiest task in the dark; they were heavier than they looked, and their fangs were still deadly and had to be avoided. Then they collected arrows and arrowheads, all that could be found. There were more arrows in their packs, but every arrow was precious, and every broken-off head might be needed. By the time they had the fire going in front of their crevice, there was *something* out there, fighting over the remains with other *somethings*, all of them squalling and barking. Skif wondered how they would dare to sleep; he kept glancing at the forest where the noises were coming from, even though he knew the chances that he'd actually see anything were remote. Hopefully, they hadn't attracted anything *too* large. . . .

"We stay awake until they carry away the remains," Wintermoon said, as if answering his thought. Skif was only startled by it for a moment; he was probably pretty transparent, and Wintermoon had read his expression. "Once the carcasses are gone, the scavengers will go. The fire will keep them away until then. The night-scavengers are cowards, and fear fire. We had best not move away from it."

The Hawkbrother settled down on his blanket roll, got one of his packs and took out a small, fire-blackened pair of pots, and filled both with water from one of their bottles. He looked up to see Skif watching him with puzzlement.

"So long as we are confined to the fire we might as well make use of it," he said. "The owls will only be able to hunt enough to fill *their* bellies; they are too weary to hunt for us tonight. I prefer not to resort to unembellished trail rations if I have any choice at all."

With that, he reached into his pack for a slab of dried venison and a few other things. He broke off bits of meat and dropped them into the first pot, which was already simmering, following that with the multi-colored contents of a gray paper packet, and a sprinkling of what looked to be herbs. Into the second pot went more herbs, dried fruit, and several small, round objects that Skif didn't recognize.

"Can I help?" Skif asked. "I should warn you, I tend to ruin anything I cook on my own, but if you keep an eye on me, I should do all right."

The scout chuckled, and handed him a wooden spoon. Skif pulled the edges of his cloak a little closer around his body, and stirred the meat pot as he'd been directed. He was very glad of the fire; now that they weren't moving or fighting, the air, though windless, was very chilly. He expected to see thick frost on the ground in the morning.

"I have needed this myself," Wintermoon said, breaking the silence. "I am often out alone, and the *hertasi* do not care to be outside the Vale or their settlements. My lovers have always been casual, so there has never been anyone to share such—domestic chores with."

"Forgive me if I am stepping beyond the bounds," Skif said, "But I can't imagine why. You seemed popular."

Wintermoon coughed politely. "Well, none of the scouts have felt easy about having long-term affairs with one who hunts the dangerous hours of night by choice, and no woman of the Clans would ever consider a long liaison with a man who has no magic.''

"But you have magic,'' Skif felt moved to protest. "Better than mine, in fact.''

Wintermoon shrugged. "It is not magic by Starblade's definition,'' he said, too casually. "I do not know how these things are reckoned in other Clans, but it is that way in k'Sheyna.''

Skif stirred the pot vigorously, and tried to think of a tactful way to approach the subject of Starblade. Darkwind had been so relieved at the release of his father, that he was likely to look no further, but Skif did not trust Starblade's ability to assess his own strengths and weaknesses. Tact had never been his strong suit; he finally gave up searching, and tried bluntness instead.

"What do you think of Starblade?'' he asked. "Now, I mean—now that he isn't being manipulated. Do you trust him?''

"Much the same as I have always thought of him,'' came the surprising answer. "Not often, and not a great deal. This revelation has changed very little between Starblade and myself, whatever it has done for Darkwind.''

"But—'' Skif began. Wintermoon looked up from his task, briefly, and the firelight flickering over his face obscured whatever faint expression it might have held.

"Starblade disassociated himself from me when testing proved me to have no real magic,'' he said carefully. "Do you really wish to hear this? It is not particularly interesting.''

"Why don't you let me judge that?'' Skif replied, just as carefully. "It will help me to know k'Sheyna through you.''

Wintermoon raised an eyebrow at that, but made no other comment. "So, then,'' he began. "My mother was a k'Treva mage, who came to k'Sheyna to look for a father for outClan children. She bargained with Starblade for twins, male and female, the male to leave, the female to take back with her. I do not know if my sister had mage-powers, but *I* did not, and I am told I was a great disappointment to my father. *I* did not know that, and I only knew he was my father because I was told, for I scarcely saw him.''

"At least you know who yours is,'' Skif replied, with a bitterness that took him by surprise. "I don't. If I have any sibs, I don't know that, either. Mother never got around to telling me anything; she was too busy

teaching me to pick pockets. Then someone decided to get rid of her—
a rival thief—and I was on my own.''

He snapped his mouth shut, appalled at the way he had simply blurted
that out to a near-stranger; things he hadn't told anyone except his dear
friend Talia.

"You were a thief? In a city?" Wintermoon seemed more intrigued
than anything else. "I should like to hear of this one day. I have never
seen a city.''

"You haven't missed much," he replied. "Cities aren't all that impressive. And I'd give a lot to have a brother.''

Once again, the Tayledras dropped his eyes. All of Wintermoon's apparent attention was again on his half of dinner. "At least I do have
Darkwind, that is true. I am actually glad that I am so much older than
he; if I had been younger, I would have hated him for stealing Starblade's love and care. But I was old enough to know that what occurred
was no one's fault, that without magic, I would never represent anything
but failure to Starblade, and that Darkwind was no more to be blamed
for that than the magic itself, which declined to manifest in me. Still, I
stay away a great deal. It is very easy to find myself envying him, and
envy oft turns darker.''

He sighed, as Skif nodded. He stared into the fire for a moment and
continued. "I think I will never have other than mixed feelings for Darkwind. I do love him. When he was very young, it was easy to love him,
for his disposition was sunny, and his mother treated us both as if we
were sons of her body. Even as he came into his power, he was not
prideful—he rather delighted in the learning, in finding what could be
done—in showing it to me, like any young man with a new accomplishment. Magic was like a huge and complex puzzle to him. But at the
same time, there was always the envy. . . .''

"I don't see how you could have gotten away from it," Skif put in
quietly, hoping he wasn't going to break Wintermoon's mood by speaking. This was instructive; it gave him an idea of how some of the more
complex situations in the Clan had evolved.

"Ah, but I am also jealous," Wintermoon said with a lightness that
did not in the least deceive Skif. "Darkwind has so many things come
easily to his hand, from his bondbird to his magic. Things that I must
struggle to achieve, and often have not even a hope of having. Women,
for instance. If you have gotten the impression that he could have any

partner in the Vale that he chose, you are substantially correct. That is not the least because he was—or is—a powerful mage.''

They sat in silence for a while as their dinner cooked, and ate in silence. Finally Wintermoon broke it. "I think, perhaps," he told Skif, slowly, "that I have said too much. You must think badly of me. I do not ordinarily speak of such things even to friends; I cannot think why I did so now.''

"Maybe because we're more alike than either of us guessed," Skif replied. "And, if you don't mind, I think I'd like to talk. There's been something bothering me for a long time, and I can't really talk about it to anyone—at home. They wouldn't understand." He looked straight into Wintermoon's eyes. "I think you might.''

Maybe it was that Wintermoon was *so* strange—and yet so very like him. Maybe it had something to do with everything the entire Clan had just endured. Maybe it was just time. Skif didn't know, but when Wintermoon nodded, he drew a deep breath and began choosing the simple, painful words to tell the story of his failure.

"You know we are at war with a country to the east of us, right?"

Wintermoon nodded.

"And I told you that I was a thief, once. Well, for a little while, I was working across the Border, because I'm used to doing things that are—outside a Herald's usual skills." He paused for a moment, then continued, keeping his voice as expressionless as he could. "I was supposed to be helping people escape across the Border, and I was working with a series of families that were providing places for escapees to hide as they fled across the country. I lived with one of those families. Hunters, the husband and wife both—he hunted game, she hunted herbs that won't grow in gardens. They had two children, an older boy and a little girl. They were—kind of the family I never had.''

Wintermoon nodded knowingly. "As Darkwind's mother played mother to me.''

"Exactly." His stomach churned, and a cold lump formed in his throat. "I never thought I'd like living out in the middle of nowhere—and I used to tease them about being backwards—but I kind of got to enjoy it. Then we got a message saying there was someone waiting at the next house in, waiting for me to guide him to the place on the Border. I went and fetched him—and damn if he wasn't *just* like me. Same background, used to be a thief before he joined Ancar's army, all that.''

I trusted him. I should have known better, I should have, but I liked him, I trusted him. . . .

"He had to stay a couple of days before it was safe to make the crossing. We talked a lot."

He acted and reacted just like me, teased the kids, helped with the chores—but I should have known, I should have—

"Anyway, it was finally clear, and he went off. I *thought* he made the crossing. I left him, though, because I had to check back with the people he'd stayed with before, bring them some news and money. That was when I found out—"

"That they were no longer there," Wintermoon interrupted. "That the plausible fellow you had trusted was a traitor."

"How did you know?" Skif's jaw dropped, and Wintermoon grimaced.

"Because I am older than you, by more than you know," the Hawkbrother said, gently. "I have seen a great deal. Remember who was the unwitting traitor in *our* midst. To be effective, one who would betray others must be likable and plausible—while all the time actually being something else entirely. He must be a supreme actor, projecting warmth and humanity, while having a cold, uncaring heart. Someone who was a criminal is likely to be all of these." He looked up at Skif, thoughtfully. "I do not think he was likely to have been a thief, though he may well have associated enough with them to have collected the tales he traded with you. He is likelier to have been something darker. I would say, one who kills in cold blood for pay."

Skif blinked, and tried to collect his thoughts. All he could think of to say, was, "How old are you?"

Wintermoon did not seem surprised at the non-sequitur. "You are Darkwind's age, I would guess. I am sixteen summers his senior." He half-smiled, wryly. "It is difficult to determine the age of a Tayledras, even if you are of the Clans yourself."

"Oh." Skif gathered his scattered and perambulatory wits, and continued his story, but this was the most difficult part to face.

"I—I went back, as fast as I could—but—" He swallowed the knot of grief in his throat. He didn't close his eyes; if he had, he'd see them, hanging from the crossbeam of their own barn. See what had been done to them by Ancar's toadies before they were hanged. He still saw them, at night. "The only one left was the little girl; the family had managed to get her out before the troops caught them, and she was hiding in the woods." *Thank the gods, she never saw any of it, never knew what had been done to them.* "I got her across the Border; left her with friends. Then—then I went back. Against orders. The bastard shouldn't have told so many stories; he gave me more clues than he knew, and I *know* cities. I tracked him down."

And I did to him what had been done to them before I killed him.

Wintermoon nodded, and waited.

Skif hesitated, then continued. "Nobody ever said or did anything, even though they must have known what I did. And I'd do it again, I swear I would—"

"But part of you is sickened," Wintermoon said softly. "Because what you did may have been just, in the way of rough justice, it may have been—excessive." He stared up at the sky for a moment. "It is better to kill cleanly," he said, finally. "If you did not, you are at fault. A creature like the one you described is not sane, any more than Mornelithe Falconsbane is—was—sane. But you do not torment something that is so crazed it cannot be saved; you kill it, so that its madness does not infect you."

Skif was astonished. "After all he did to your people—if you had Falconsbane in front of you now—"

"I would kill him cleanly, with a single stroke," Wintermoon said firmly. "I learned this lesson when I was a little older than you, now—when I visited similar retribution on a very stupid bandit that had been tormenting *hertasi* and killing them for their hides. It does no good to visit torments upon a creature of that nature. It teaches him nothing, and makes your nature closer to his. And that is why you are troubled, Wingbrother. You knew this all along, did you not?"

Skif hung his head, and closed his eyes. "Yes," he admitted, finally. "I did."

Wintermoon sat in silence a moment longer. "For what it is worth," he said finally, "What was done, was done in the heat of anger, and in the heat of anger, one loses perspective—and sanity. *Now* you are sane—and sickened. Do not forget the lesson, Wingbrother—but do not let it eat at you like a disease. Let it go, and learn from it."

Skif felt muscles relaxing that he hadn't known were tensed, and a feeling of profound relief. There. It was out in the open; Wintermoon had guessed most of it without Skif having to go into detail. And the result: he had just discovered he wasn't alone in depravity after all.

"I visited similar retribution upon a stupid bandit, who had been torment-
ing hertasi *and killing them for their hides."*

He would never have guessed from Wintermoon's serene exterior.

"Others will forgive you this, Wingbrother," the Tayledras said softly,
"but only you can forgive yourself. You must never, never forget."

"I won't," Skif promised, as much to himself as to Wintermoon. "I
won't . . ." He shook his head, in part, to clear it. "I—after that,
though—I got myself assigned back at the capital. I just lost my taste
for adventure."

Wintermoon chuckled. "In that case, Wingbrother, why are you
here?"

"I also couldn't resist Elspeth. It's strange how, even if you know
inside that there isn't a chance, you'll pursue something anyway because
the thought of it is so attractive. I've known it for a long time, but I
wouldn't admit it to myself. Elspeth has her own plan for her life, and
my role in it is not as her lover. Still, there it is. The only way they were
going to let her make this journey was if I came along." He smiled, and
shrugged. "But, when this is all over, if I'm given a choice, I'd like to
have a place like that family had. For me . . . or maybe for their memory." Skif pursed his lips, then looked back up at Wintermoon. "Oh,
I'd probably be awful at country living—I'd probably have everyone in
the county laughing at me, but it would be good trying. I know I'd like
to have a home. A family." He smiled, a little wistfully. "Nobody at
Haven would believe that of me."

"You have seen enough blood, enough death," Wintermoon surmised. "You fought in battles, as a soldier?"

"Yes." Once again he was amazed at Wintermoon's insight. Or was
it something more? "Are you talking with Cymry?"

The other man nodded, and poked at the fire.

:I told him only a few things.: Cymry didn't sound at all apologetic.
*:When you started talking to him and it looked like you were going to talk
about That—I prompted him a little.:*

:Why?: He wasn't angry, not really; Cymry was in and out of his
thoughts so much she was part and parcel of him. She was his best and
dearest friend; he loved her so deeply that he would sooner cut off his
arm than lose her. And if he knew nothing else, he knew that she would
never, ever do anything to harm him in any way. She had been a part
of the revenge scheme, although she had not known his plan until he'd
ambushed the bastard and begun. And even then, she kept silent after

her initial protests. He didn't think she'd even betrayed his secret shame to other Companions. So why reveal it now?

:Because I thought it sounded and felt like you were ready to speak, and he was ready to hear,: she replied, matter-of-factly. *:And as much as being ready to speak, you were ready to listen. Was I wrong?:*

He shook his head. *:No. No, you were right. Thank you, love.:*

Wintermoon sat quietly through the silent exchange, and watched Skif and Cymry alternately. When the Companion nodded, he sighed, and smiled thinly. "I hope you are not angered with us," he said, in half apology. "You see, I had a similar discussion after *my* ill-conceived vengeance, with Iceshadow. He is not a Mind-Healer, but he is closer to being one than he thinks. He has the insights, at least."

The Hawkbrother fixed him with a penetrating stare. "I will tell you this, out of my own experience. Although you feel relief now, this is likely to be the source of many sleepless nights for you. You will lie awake, look upon your heart, and find it unlovely. You will be certain that, regardless of what I have said, you are the greatest of monsters. This is a good thing; although you may forgive yourself, you must never come to think that your actions were in any way justifiable. But—" He chuckled, ironically. "As Iceshadow told *me*, being a sane, honorable human is not always *comfortable.*"

:He should go set up shop on a mountaintop somewhere,: Cymry said. *:He'd make a prime Wise Old Teacher. He's already got the part about tormenting the students down perfectly.:*

Wintermoon drew himself up and stared at her in mock affrontery. "I heard that," he protested.

:I meant you to.:

Skif grinned, and the grin turned into a yawn. Wintermoon caught it, and pointed an admonishing finger at him.

"We still have work ahead of us, and that work requires rest. As you *both* know." He spread out his bedroll by way of making an example, and climbed into it. "Stars light your path, Wingsibs," he said pointedly, and made a show of turning on his side and closing his eyes. "*Wyrsa* have no respect for crisis of conscience."

Well, that about sums the evening up, he thought as he rolled out his own bedroll and crawled into its warmth. And then he thought nothing more, for sleep crept up and ambushed him.

Nyara & Need

Chapter Six

Nyara slicked back her sweat-soaked hair, hardly feeling the cold as the chill breeze dried her scalp. She licked salt from her lips and crouched in the shelter of the bushes for a moment, surveying the open expanse of cracked and crazed pavement that kept the forest from encroaching on the foot of her tower. Though the stones were fragmented, even melted in places, they must have been incredibly thick, for nothing but grass grew in the cracks. It looked similar in construction to the ruins around the gryphons' home, though the tower's age and makers were unknown to her.

There was no sign of anything waiting for her, but she had learned to leave subtle telltales, things easily disturbed by interlopers. The "random" lines of gravel, for instance; not so random, and placed so that one or more of them would be scuffed by anyone crossing the paving. The faint threads of shields that would vanish if breached—or, just as importantly, if even touched by a mage's probing. With her feeble command of magic, she could scarcely hope to build a shield that would hide her presence from a greater mage, so she didn't even try. Instead, she concentrated on things that would let her know if she had been discovered, so that she had the time to run and hide somewhere else.

But once again, her refuge seemed secure; the threads were still in place, the pavement clear. Nevertheless, she stayed in the shelter of the evergreen bushes, and sent a careful probe up into the heart of her shelter.

:*Well?*: That was all she Mindsent. Anything more could reveal her location to lurkers. There were creatures—some of them her father's—that were nothing more than compasses for the thoughts of those who could Mindspeak. Normally only the one Spoken to could Hear, but these creatures could Hear everything, and could follow the thoughts of a Mindspeaker from leagues away.

:*All's clear,*: came the gravelly reply. :*Come on up, kitten. I trust you had good hunting.*:

Now she relaxed; nothing got past her teacher. :*Quite good,*: she replied shortly. :*No visitors?*:

:*None,*: came the answer. :*Unless you count our daily cleanup committee.*:

She would have worried if *they* hadn't shown up. Anything bad enough to frighten off a vulture was a serious threat indeed. :*I'm coming up,*: she Sent, and only then arose from her shelter, pushing through the bushes and trotting out into the open—as always, with a thrill of fear at leaving her back exposed to the forest, where someone *else* could be lurking.

She padded quickly across the paving, taking care to avoid her own traps. The less she had to redo in the morning, the sooner she would be able to get out to hunt. The sooner she got out to hunt, the more practice she would have. She was under no illusions about her hunting successes; the colder the weather grew, the scarcer the game would become, and the harder it would be for her to catch it. She had never truly hunted for her meals before this, and was no expert. She was lucky; lucky that game was so abundant here, and lucky that she was getting practice now, while it *was* abundant, and a miss was not nearly so serious as it would be later in the winter.

The wall of her tower loomed up before her, the mellowed gray of weathered granite. The tower had that look about it of something intended to defend against all comers. She took the neck of the pheasant she had caught in her teeth, and set her finger- and toe-claws into the stone, and began climbing. The scent of the fresh-killed bird just under her nose made her mouth water. Just as well there had been no blood, or she would have been in a frenzy of hunger.

As she climbed, it occurred to her that it was not going to be pleasant, if indeed *possible*, to make the climb in winter. Ice, snow, or sleet would make the rock slippery; cold would numb her hands and feet. The prospect daunted her.

Well, no point in worrying about it now; truly dismal weather was still a few weeks off, and anyway, there was nothing she could do about it at the moment. Not while she was clinging to sheer stone, three stories above the pavement, with another to go.

Perhaps a ladder, like the Tayledras outside the Vale use for their tree-houses. True, she did not have a bird to let the ladder down for her, or to hide the line that pulled it up, but she had magic. Not much, but she was learning to use every bit of what she had, and use it cleverly. A bit of magic could take the end of such a ladder up, and drop it down again when she returned.

So many trips up and down that stone had taught her where all the holds were, and now she didn't even need to think about where she was putting her hands and feet. This was the most vulnerable moment in her day—this, and the opposite trip in the morning. There was a staircase up the inside of the tower, but although it looked sound, appearance was very deceptive. It was, in fact, one more of her traps and defenses, and anyone chancing it would find himself taking a two- or three-story drop to the ground, depending on how far he got before the weakened stone gave way beneath him.

But then, she privately thought that anyone trusting his weight to an unproven stair—in a ruined tower, no less—probably deserved what he found.

Her mind wandered off on its own, planning lightweight ladders and imagining what she might use to make them, discarding idea after idea. She came to the conclusion that she might be trying to make things a little *too* elaborate; after all, by virtue of her breeding she was a much better climber than the best of the Tayledras. A simple, knotted rope might serve her better.

At that point, her hand encountered the open space of her window, and she grasped the sill with both hands, and hauled herself up and over the stone slab. She swung her legs inside and dropped down to the floor, crouching there for a moment. She took the pheasant out of her mouth and grinned, as her teacher and weapon growled in her mind :*I hate it when you do that. You look like a cat that's just caught someone's pet bird.*:

"But it is not a pet bird, Need," she replied pertly. "It is my dinner."

:So is the pet bird for the cat,: the sword said, *:But nobody ever asks the bird how it feels about the situation.:*

She sat down cross-legged on the bare stone of the floor, and began industriously plucking her catch. "If it gets caught, it deserves to get eaten," she told the sword.

:You stole that from the Hawkbrothers.: Need accused.

She shrugged. "So? That does not make it less true. And like all Hawkbrother sayings, it is double-edged. If it gets caught, it *deserves* to be eaten—to be appreciated, used entirely and with respect, and not robbed of something stupid, like a tail-feather, and discarded as useless. I honor my kill, and I am grateful that I caught it. If it has a soul, I hope that soul finds a welcome reward."

Need had nothing to say in reply to that. Nyara smiled, knowing that "no comment" was usually a compliment of sorts.

She put the best of the feathers aside; the large, well-formed ones she would use to fletch arrows, the rest would go to stuff her carefully-tanned rabbit hides. Need had been teaching her a great deal; she had come to this tower with nothing but a knife she had filched from Skif and the sword. Now she had clothing made from the hides of animals she had caught; a bed of furs from the same source, with pillows of fur stuffed with feathers on a thick pallet of cured grasses. And that was not all; over in the corner were the bow and arrows Need had taught her to make and was teaching her to use. Need had already taught her the skills of the sling she had used to take this pheasant.

The sword had also unbent enough to conjure—or steal by magic—a few other things for her, things she couldn't make herself. Not many, but they were important possessions; a firestarter, four pots, three waterskins and a bucket, one spoon, a second knife, and a coil of rope. The latter was precious and irreplaceable; she had used it only to haul heavy game and her water up the side of her tower.

:Are you going to eat that raw?: Need demanded. She licked her lips thoughtfully; she was very hungry and had been considering doing just that. But the way the question had been phrased—and the fact that her teacher had asked the question at all—made her pause.

"Why?" she asked. "Is there something wrong with that?"

If the sword could have moved, it would have shrugged. *:Not intrinsically,:* Need replied. *:But it gives the impression that you are more beast than human. That is not the impression we are trying to give.:*

Nyara did not trouble to ask just who would be there to observe her.

True, there was no one except herself and her mentor at the moment, but she sensed that Need did not intend either of them to be hidden away in the wilderness forever.

She doesn't want me to seem more beast than human. Need had been trying to reverse the physical changes Nyara's father had made to her; now she had an inkling of why. Need wanted to make her look. . . .

Less like an animal. Perhaps she should have been offended when that thought occurred to her, and she was, in a way, but rather than making her angry with Need, it made her angry at her father. *He* was the one who had made so many changes to her body and mind that Need had been incoherent with rage for days upon discovering them. *He* was the "father" that had made her into a warped slave, completely in thrall to him, often unable even to act in her own defense.

Need had done her best to reverse those changes; some she had, but they were all internal. There was no mistaking her origin; the slitted eyes alone shouted "Changechild."

If the world saw a beast—the world would kill the beast. It was not fair, but very little in Nyara's life had ever been fair. At least this was understandable. Predictable.

Mornelithe Falconsbane had never been that, ever.

No one was here to see her now except Need, but when she finished plucking the pheasant, instead of tearing off a limb and devouring it raw as her stomach demanded, she gutted and cleaned it as neatly as any Tayledras hunter or *hertasi* cook, and set it aside.

She tried not to think about how loud her stomach was complaining as she uncovered the coals in her firepit and fed them twigs until she had a real flame. Once she had a fire, she spitted her catch, and made a token effort to sear it.

Once the outer skin had been crisped, she lost all patience; she seized the spit and the bird, and began gnawing.

Need made an odd little mental sound, and Nyara had the impression that she had winced, but the sword said nothing, and Nyara ignored her in favor of satisfying her hunger.

But when she had finished, sucking each bone clean and neatly licking her fingers dry, the blade sighed. *:Tell me how the hunt went,:* she said. *:And show me.:*

"I saw the cock-pheasant break cover beside the stream," she said, picturing it clearly, as she had been taught. "I knew that the flock would be somewhere behind him. . . ."

The stalk had taken some time, but the end of the hunt came as swiftly as even Need could have wanted. She had lost only one of her carefully rounded shot, which splintered on a rock, and took one of the juvenile males with the second. She felt rather proud of herself, actually, for Need was no longer guiding her movements in hunting, or even offering advice. Although the blade could still follow her mentally if she chose, it was no longer necessary for her to be in physical contact with her bearer to remain in mental contact.

When Nyara had fled from the Tayledras as well as her father, she had no clear notion of where she was going or what she would do. She had only known that too many things were happening at once, and too many people wanted her. Their reasons ran from well-intentioned to darkly sinister, and *she* had no real way of telling which from which. So she ran, and only after she had slipped out of Darkwind's ken had she discovered herself in possession of Elspeth's sword. She honestly had no memory of taking it; the blade later confessed to having influenced her to bear it off, making her forget she had done so.

At first she had been angry and afraid, expecting pursuit; the blade was valuable enough that her father had wanted it very badly. But pursuit never came, and she realized that Elspeth was actually going to relinquish the blade to her. Such unexpected generosity left her puzzled. It would not be the last time that she was to be confused over matters in which Need was involved.

Nyara had found the tower after a great deal of searching for a defensible lair. Need had rebuilt the upper story with her magic, strengthening it and making it habitable. It still looked deserted, and both of them had been very careful to leave no signs of occupancy. Any refuse was taken up to the flat roof and left there; vultures carried off bones and anything else edible, and the rest was bleached by the sun and weathered by wind and rain. Eventually the wind would carry it away, and it would be scattered below with the dead leaves.

:You're doing well,: the sword said, finally. *:Even if you do eat like a barbarian. I don't suppose table deportment is going to matter anytime soon, though.:*

Nyara was silent for a moment; now that her stomach was full and the little chamber warmed by the fire, she had leisure to consider the blade's remarks, and feel a bit of resentment. Nyara appreciated all that Need had done for her, attempting to counter the effects of twenty years of twisting and abuse, teaching her what she needed to survive. Still, sometimes the sword's thoughtless comments hurt.

"I'm not a barbarian," she said aloud, a little resentfully. "I've seen Darkwind bolt his meals just like I did."

:*Darkwind is fully human. You are not. You are clever, intelligent, resourceful, but you are not human. Therefore you must appear to be better than humans.*:

Once again, Nyara was struck by the injustice of the situation, but this time she voiced her protest. "That's not *fair*," she complained. "There's no reason why I should have to act like some kind of—of trained beast to prove that I'm just as human as anyone else!"

:*You* were *a trained animal, Nyara,*: Need replied evenly. :*You aren't any longer. And we both know why.*:

Nyara shuddered, but did not reply. Instead, she cleaned up the remains of her meal, saving a few scraps to use as fishing bait on the morrow, and took everything up to the roof. As Need had mentioned, the vultures had been there already; there was little sign of yesterday's meal.

Although the wind was cold, Nyara lingered to watch the sunset, huddled inside her crude fur tunic with her feet tucked under her. Need was right. She *had* been little more than a trained animal. Her father had controlled her completely, by such clever use of mingled mind-magic, pain and pleasure that a hint of punishment would throw her into uncontrollable, mindless lust, a state in which she was incapable of thinking.

Need had freed her from that; Need had worked on her for hours, days, spending her magic recklessly in that single area, to heal her and release her from that pain-pleasure bondage. Need had watched the nomad Healer working on the Tayledras Starblade from afar, studying all that the woman did and applying the knowledge to Nyara.

In this much, she was free; she would no longer be subject to animal rut. Although Need had not been able to "cure" her tufted ears, pointed canines, or slit-pupiled eyes, the blade had put *her* in control of her emotional and physical responses.

Must I really be more than they are to be accepted as an equal? Nothing less would do, according to Need, and as she watched the stars emerge, she came to the reluctant conclusion that the blade was right. She *had* to be accepted as at least an equal to claim alliance with the Hawkbrothers. She needed them, and knew it, although they did not yet know how much they needed her. She had information that would be very useful to them, even if some of it was information they might have to get at using Need's mind-probing tactics. She would gladly submit to that, to have their protection.

But to earn that, did she have to give up what she was, to take on some kind of mask of what *they* considered civilized? That simply wasn't fair, not after everything she had already been through! What Falconsbane had done—she didn't want to think about. And under Needs' tutelage, she had not only undergone the pain that preceded Healing, but nightly—and sometimes daily—vision-quests. She had to admit there was one positive result of that; her real dreams were no longer haunted, and her nightmares had vanished completely. The sword was as hard a teacher as she could have imagined; driving her without allowance for weakness. Not only did she take Nyara through trials in her dreams, and teach her the skills that helped her survive on her own, but she launched Nyara like an arrow against whatever target she deemed suitable, giving her lessons in real combat as well as practice. Nyara had already defeated a wandering bandit and a half-mad hedge-wizard. Both had been left for the vultures when they had seen only a female alone, and attempted to take her. In both cases, Need had ultimately taken command of her body, as soon as she reckoned that Nyara had gone to the very edge of her abilities, and moved her with a skill she did not, herself, possess. There would, doubtless, be more such in the future.

So why must she prove that she was something other than she was to be accepted?

No, she decided as she watched the moon rise above the horizon. It was *not* fair. Need wanted too much of her.

She descended to her tower-top chamber only to find the fire burning down to coals and the sword silent. She watched it for a moment, then shrugged philosophically and heated just enough water for a sketchy sort of bath. One advantage of her breeding, besides her owl-keen nightsight, was that the pelt of very short, very fine fur that covered her body made bathing less of a chore than it was for full humans. And one had to be very, very close to her to learn that it was fur, and not just smooth skin. She wasn't entirely certain that either Skif or Darkwind had figured it out. Well—perhaps Skif had. He hadn't seemed to mind.

Morning would arrive far too early. Although she intended to fish and not hunt, it would still be better to do so in the early morning when the fish were hungry. So as soon as she had cleaned herself, she banked the fire, and crawled into her bed of furs.

Only then did Need speak, just as she was falling asleep.

:*Let's explore that business of "fair,"*: the sword said, with deceptive mildness. :*Shall we?*:

Nyara was no longer Nyara; no longer a Changechild. In fact, she was no longer in the world or the body she knew.

Except that she *was* Nyara; she was herself and someone else, too. She relaxed; this was something she had experienced in Need's dream-quests many times, although this was someone she'd never been before. Then she realized that this was different; strange, in a way she could not quite describe. This life—was ancient, heavy with years, and faded. She felt the experience as if through a series of muffling veils, each of which was a century.

Her name was Vena; she was once a novice of the Sisterhood of Spell and Sword. Now she was alone, except for the sword that had once been her teacher, the Mage-Smith Sister Lashan—and ahead of her was an impossible task.

A mage that Lashan identified as Wizard Heshain had come to the enclave of the Sisterhood with an army of men and lesser mages, capturing the Sisterhood's mage-novices and slaughtering everyone else. Vena had escaped mostly by luck, and by hiding in the forest surrounding the enclave until they all left. She had thought she was completely alone until Sister Lashan had come riding up, returning from her yearly trip to the trade-markets where she sold her bespelled blades to weapons' brokers to profit the Sisterhood.

When she saw her teacher, she'd had no thought but to escape with her to somewhere safe. But Lashan had other ideas.

She had questioned Vena very carefully, probing past the girl's hysteria to extract every possible detail from her. Then she had sat in silence for a long, long time.

Her decision had not been the one that Vena had expected; to make their way to some other temple of the Twins, and seek shelter there, since it was plainly impossible for anyone to rescue the captured novices from such a powerful mage-lord. Sister Lashan had told her stunned apprentice that they—the two of them—were going to rescue their captive Sisters. She admitted that she did not know what he planned to do with the novices exactly—mostly because there were so many things he *could* do with a collection of variously mage-talented, untrained, mostly virginal young women. But all of the fates she outlined to her apprentice were horrible. Eventually, even Vena had to agree. They could not leave their Sisters in Heshain's hands.

Rescue *was* possible. Especially if rescue could come before the caravan reached Heshain's stronghold. But there was no time to gather another small army to rescue them, assuming that anyone could be found willing to commit themselves and their troops against a mage like Heshain.

That had left only Vena and Sister Lashan, who had decided, unbeknownst to her bewildered apprentice, that her old, worn-out human body was just not going to be up to the task. So instead, she had chosen a new one; a body of tempered steel. A sword, to be precise; a bespelled blade, the kind she had been teaching Vena to make.

Vena was still not certain how Sister Lashan, who had ordered her to forget that name and call her "Need" now, had ensorceled herself into the blade. She wasn't certain that she *wanted* to know. It had certainly involved the death of the mage herself, for she had found the Sister spitted on her own sword. She had thought that despair had overcome her mentor, and had been overwhelmed with grief—when the sword spoke into her mind.

Now she was on the trail of Heshain and his minions, armed with a blade she scarcely knew how to use, ill-provisioned, and without the faintest idea of what she was doing. And winter was coming on. In fact, since the trail led northward, she would be walking straight into the very teeth of winter.

But if she did not try to do something, no one would. She had no choice.

No choice at all.

All this, she knew in an instant, as if she had always known it. And then, she was no longer aware of Nyara—only of Vena. Only of a moment that was dim and distant, and yet, Now.

Vena crouched above the road, belly-down in the snow, and tried to think of nothing. There was no sign that Heshain had any Thought-seekers among his men—but no sign that he didn't, either. Despite her wool and fur-lined clothing, she was aching with cold. It had been a very long time since she'd last dared to light a fire, and she couldn't remember when she'd last been warm.

She was hungry, too. The handful of nuts and dried berries she'd eaten had only sharpened her appetite. And down below her was everything she craved. Shelter, a roaring fire, hot food—

Trouble was, it was all in the hands of the enemy.

And the enemy wasn't likely to share.

She Felt Sister Lashan—or rather, Need—studying the situation through her eyes. She wasn't certain how Need felt about it, but it looked pretty hopeless from here. The group that had captured the novices seemed to have divided up. This was the hindmost bunch, and the girls they guarded seemed to be the ones in the worst shape. Most were in deep shock; some were co-matose, and carried on wagons. The rest hardly seemed aware of their sur-roundings. None of them were going to be of any help at all—at least, not until Vena could physically get Need into their hands, for contact-Healing was one of Need's abilities. But that could only happen after they were rescued, and not before,

So just how was one half-trained Mage-Smith apprentice going to success-fully take on twenty or more well-trained fighters?

:Cleverly, of course,: *Need's voice grated in her mind.* :There are twenty or more tired, bored, careless males down there. What do you think would distract them the most?:

"Women?" *she whispered tentatively, thinking of conjuring an illusion of scantily-clad girls, and getting into the camp under the cover of the excite-ment. But then what? The illusion wouldn't hold past the first attempt to touch one of the girls, unless Need could somehow make it more than a mere illusion—*

Her teacher made a mental sound of contempt. :And a troupe of dancing girls rides up out of nowhere. I don't think so, dear. These are also seasoned fighters; they're suspicious of anything and everything. Try to think like one of them. Look at their camp; what are they doing?:

As if she hadn't been doing just that, ever since they cleared a space for the first tent, and freezing her rear off, too. "They're eating," *she offered tentatively.*

:Closer. What are they eating?:

Vena's mouth watered as she stared down at the common fire. "Looks like winter-rations. Beans and bread, I think." *Oh, she would gladly have killed for some of those hot spiced beans and a piece of bread. . . .* "I don't see—"

:Meat, Vena. They don't have any. They're on winter-rations, and they haven't been allowed time to hunt, so they don't have any meat. And these are fighters; they're used to having it. They don't seem to have any wine, either, but I can't think of a way to get that to them without making them suspicious of their good fortune. Back down the ridge, slowly. I'm going to try calling in an elk. I used to be good at this.:

In the end, it was a deer Need managed to attract, and not an elk, but in all other ways it was precisely what she wanted. Old, with broken antlers, already looking thin this early in the winter, the aged animal would not have outlasted the snows. Vena followed her directions carefully, as they poisoned the poor beast by means of counter-Healing, hamstrung one leg, as if it had just escaped from a wolf, and drove it over the ridge and down into the enemy camp.

The men there fell on the weakened beast, seeing only their good luck, and never thinking that there might be something wrong with it other than exhaustion and injury. The toxin Need had infused into the deer's blood and flesh was only slightly weakened by cooking. A clever poison, there was little or no warning to the victims of their fate; most ate, fell asleep, and never woke. By daybreak, all twenty men were dead or dying—and Vena came down into the camp to dispatch the dying, and found herself in charge of eleven of her fellow novices.

Not one of whom could be trusted even to look after the others, much less find her own way back to safety.

Confidently, she turned to Need for advice.

:Damned if I know what to do with them,: *the blade replied.* :I can Heal their injuries, but the rest is up to you. Demonsbane, girl, I only made blades before I made myself *into* one! You're the one with the hands and feet, and they know *you*, they probably never even met me! I'm fresh out of clever ideas. Time for you to come up with one or two.:

So it was up to Vena to deal with the girls; to try to rouse some of them from their apathy, and to figure out what to do with the rest. And to drag the bodies of the poisoned fighters out of the camp, to get her eleven charges fed and sheltered, to make sure the horses were tended to.

It was nothing less than hard labor, although she gave herself a selfish moment to build the fire back up, and warm herself by that fire until her bones no longer ached. Then she took a little more time to stuff herself on the bread and oat porridge (not beans, after all) that was cooking over the fire—avoiding the charred venison and the pot of venison stew.

She freed the novices from their cages in the four prison wagons, but most of them didn't recognize her, and the ones that did reacted to her as if they'd seen a ghost—terrified and huddling speechless in the corners. She tried not to look too closely at them after the first encounter; the girl wasn't one she had known, but her eyes were so wild, and yet so terrified, that she hardly seemed human anymore.

She led the girl, coaxingly, away from there, across the snow, and into the only wagon without bars and chains; the one that held the provisions. When she offered the girl a blanket, taken as an afterthought from one of the bedrolls beside the fire, the poor child snatched it from her, and went to hide in the darkest corner of the wagon.

She repeated the process until she got them all herded into the wagon, where they huddled together like terrified rabbits, their eyes glinting round and panic-stricken from the darkness of the back.

During the long process of getting her former fellow students into the pro-vision wagon, she'd tossed out everything else that had been in there. Now, in the last of the daylight, she sat on a sack of beans and went through everything she had thrown on the ground, and all the personal belongings that were still in the camp. She felt very strange, rifling through other peoples' possessions, at least at first. But soon sheer exhaustion caught up with her and she no longer saw them as anything other than objects to be kept or discarded in the snow. Blankets went straight into the wagon behind her; hopefully, the girls still had enough wit left to take them. The best blankets she kept for herself, as well enough food for the girls for a few days more, and in a separate pack, provisions for herself.

Finally, the unpleasant job she had been avoiding could be put off no longer. She tethered all the horses next to the wagon, then harnessed up one, the gentlest, the one she had marked for her own. Trying not to look at the bodies of her former enemies, she threw a hitch of rope around their stiffening feet, and towed them one by one to a point far beyond the camp, leaving them scattered around a tiny cup of a valley like dolls left by a careless child.

Then she returned to the shelter of the wagon, and the non-company of her charges. All of that work had taken another precious day. She got the girls fed and bundled up in blankets as best she could, spending a sleepless night listening to the screams of scavengers when they found the bodies, and making *sure none of the eleven wandered off somewhere on her own. It was, possibly, worse even than the nights she had spent waiting for the raiders to return.*

In the end, it was the horses that gave her the idea of how to move them, and what to do afterward. Vena was a country girl; where she came from, a horse was a decent dowry for any girl. A pair of horses apiece ought to be enough to pay for their care until someone could come get them, later.

She roused six of the girls to enough self-awareness and energy that they could cling to the saddle-bow of a horse—even if half the time they stared in apathy, and the other half, wept without ceasing. The other five she put in one wagon, with the rest of the horses following behind, tethered in a long string. Then she coaxed Need into using her magic to find the nearest farm. It proved to be a sheep-farmer's holding rather than a true farm; hidden away in a tiny pocket-valley, she would never have found it if not for Need.

To the landowner she told the truth—but cautioned him to tell any other inquirers a tale she and Need concocted, about a plague that caused death and feeble-mindedness, killing all the men of a village where she had relatives, and leaving only the healthiest of the girls alive. She offered him the entire herd of horses (save only the one she had chosen for herself) to tend to the novices. Her only other condition was that as soon as possible he was to send a message to the nearest temple of the Twins, telling what had happened and asking for their aid for the girls.

As she had expected, the offer was more than he could possibly refuse, and when Need read his thoughts to be certain he would keep the bargain, she found no dishonesty. Winter was an idle time for farmers and herders; he had a houseful of daughters and servants to help tend the girls. And sons to find wives for . . . it would be no bad thing to have a mage-talented girl for a bride for one of his boys. Such things tended to breed true even if shock made the girl lose her own talent, and a man could do much worse than have a wife who could work bits of magic to help protect herself and her home, and to enrich the family, if she was able to keep practicing. Hedge-wizardry and kitchen-witchery was easy to learn; it was having the power to make it work that was granted to only a few.

She agreed on their behalf that if any of them chose to stay with him and his boys, there would be no demands for reparations from the Sisterhood. Then she saddled and mounted her horse, and turned back to the hunt.

They were now weeks, not days, behind the enemy, but he was burdened with wagons and hysterical girls, and Vena was alone, and now a-horse. As she turned her mare's head back along the trail, Need finally spoke.

:Demonsbane, girl! Why didn't you put that fatuous sheep-brain in his place? Brides for his sons—what did he think you were, some kind of marriage-broker? And where did he ever get the idea any of them would want to live out their lives making herb-charms and tending brats and lambs?: *The sword grumbled on, for a while, and Vena let her. The novice had plenty of other things to think about; most notably, finding the now-cold trail of the rest of the captives. It wasn't easy, not with two weeks' worth of wind and weather eating at the signs.*

But she had the right gear for the job, at last. Sheepskin boots and coat, woolen leggings, sweater and cotton undertunic. And all the provisions and equipment she needed.

Or at least, all that she needed until the next encounter.

But she told herself she wasn't going to think about that until it happened.

Finally she found the track, half-melted prints of hooves and wagon-wheels in the snow, and Need finally finished venting her spleen.

Vena waited for a moment, both to be sure she had the trail and to be certain Need was talked out. "Look," *she pointed out,* "After everything those girls have been through, one or more of them are bound to change their minds about a life dedicated to High Magery and the Sisterhood. That farmer was trustworthy and kindhearted; not a bad thing in a father-in-law. And the boys were a little rough around the edges, but no worse than the lads in my home village. You and I can never give back what those girls—our Sisters—have lost, but we can at least give them options."

Need stayed silent for a moment. :You could be right,: *she finally said, grudgingly.* :I don't like it, but you could be right.:

Vena decided not to tell her that she was having second thoughts, herself . . . she doubted she'd survive long enough to consider being a farmer's wife. Right now, despite this early success, she wasn't going to give herself odds on that.

Nyara woke with the sun in her eyes, and for a moment, her arms and legs still ached with that long-ago cold; her hands expected to encounter those heavy blankets instead of furs, and she was exhausted with a phantom weariness that vanished as soon as she realized who she was, and where.

Phantom weariness was replaced by real weariness. She lay where she was for a moment, despite her resolution of the night before to get up early to fish. Dream-quests did not, as a rule, leave her tired. Nor did they leave her feeling a weight of years. . . .

:*That's because I never took you back so far before,*: Need said, and it seemed as if the sword was just as tired as her student. *:I've granted you what I seldom grant my bearers; now you know the name I had forgotten, my name as a human.:*

But that wasn't what mattered to Nyara; suddenly she sat bolt upright and stared at the sword leaning against the wall with a feeling of anger and betrayal. "You didn't help her!" she accused. "You didn't help her at all!"

:I did what I could,: the blade replied, calmly. *:I was new to my form and my limitations. I had as much to learn as she did, but I didn't dare let her know that, or her confidence would have been badly undermined. I've had a long, long time to learn more of magic, Nyara. I didn't know a fraction then of what I know now.:*

Nyara stared at the sword propped in the corner, aghast. "You mean— you did not know what you were doing?"

:Oh, I knew what I was doing. I was herding us both into trouble. But what else was I going to do? There were all those youngsters in danger, and if Vena and I didn't do something about it, nobody would.:

Nyara blinked, and started to say, "But that's not f—"

:Fair? No, it wasn't. Not to Vena, not to me, and certainly not to the novices.: The blade's matter-of-fact attitude took Nyara aback.

She climbed out of her bed of furs as her thoughts circled around something she could not yet grasp. Need was not cruel—not on purpose, at any rate. She *was* driven by expediency, and by a dedication to the longer view. But she wasn't cruel. . . .

So what was she trying to say?

She had sacrificed herself for the bare chance of saving the novices through Vena. The girl herself had done the same. And it was all so unf—

It was unfair. But so was what Father did to me, what he did to the Hawkbrothers, what happened to the gryphons. . . .

Life was unfair. She *knew* that, and so did Need. But she'd been complaining about that unfairness a great deal lately.

:Very good, kitten,: Need said in her mind. *:You've figured that part out. I find it a wonder that you can even grasp "unfairness", knowing so little else in your life besides it. I am still working on that; it seems inconsistent with what your thrice-damned father taught you. Know this, though: often- times the concept of fairness can be a wall to accomplishing what must be done. Worrying over fairness can sometimes impede justice, and that in itself is not fair.:*

Nyara nodded, as more awareness of Need's teaching came to her. *:Now let me show you what* real *unfairness is.* . . . *:*

Vena clung with her fingers and toes to the side of the cliff, and prayed that Heshain's Thought-seekers would not find her. . . .

Treyvan, Hydona, Jerven & Lytha

Chapter
Seven

Darkwind had been struggling for several days now to maintain his dignity, his composure, and above all, the signature Tayledras detachment, and failing dismally. The cause, ever and always, was Elspeth. He wondered if all teachers felt like this, or if he was particularly blessed— or cursed—with a student so intelligent and quick that she threatened to run right over her hapless instructor.

"I can't keep ahead of her, and sometimes it's all I can do to fly apace with her," he confessed to Treyvan, as he helped the gryphon affix a set of shelves onto a wall of an interior room, a bit of work that only small, nimble, human hands could manage. Treyvan and his mate had expanded the original lair quite a bit since things calmed down, reconstructing the original walls of the building that had stood here, then creating several rooms where there had once been only two. Why the gryphon would want shelves, he had no idea—but then, there were a great many things he still didn't know about the gryphons. For all he knew, they collected *hertasi* carvings and wanted to display them.

Darkwind hammered on a stake and tied support cords from it. Finished, flat boards such as the gryphons had discovered were hard to come by, and he wasn't going to waste them on wall mounts; he was using a variation on the Tayledras' *ekele* construction, that of anchored, co-supporting lines.

"Ssso what iss the trouble?" the gryphon asked genially. "You have had much more tutelage than she, and access to more knowledge." He lounged in the corner and watched Darkwind with half-lidded golden eyes, not out of laziness, but because he had just eaten, and the gryphons, like the raptors Darkwind knew so well, rested after filling their crops.

"I can't do everything," Darkwind admitted, with a touch of annoyance. He shook his hair out of his way, and aligned the support he was working on with the others. "I haven't actively worked magic in years, and my memory of what to do is a little foggy. My magical skills are—well—as stiff as muscles get if not exercised regularly. And, the Mage-Gift fades if not used."

"Asss any other attribute," the gryphon agreed. "Asss in hunting, sswordsskill, or musssic."

"Well, mine's creaky with disuse," Darkwind sighed, "And I can't re-learn everything I'd forgotten *and* teach Elspeth, too. It was all right when she didn't know anything about mage-craft, because I could set her to work on something basic, while I practiced something else. But now—that won't work anymore."

The gryphon stopped in the middle of a lazy stretch, and blinked at him, claws still extended, back arched. "Ssshe isss that quick?"

"She's that quick," Darkwind told him, setting the last support firmly into the wall. "The problem is that her people have made quite a science of mind-magic, and she's very good at it. Although she says she isn't particularly outstanding." He snorted. "Either it's the one and only time I've caught her being modest, or her people are frightening mind-mages. Good enough to stand equal with an Adept."

"And in mind-magic there isss enough sssameness to give her a basssisss in true magic," Treyvan supplied. "Isss there alsso enough sssameness to causse her trouble?"

Darkwind wedged the heavy shelf into the support-loops and eyed it critically, ignoring the question for the moment. "How level do these have to be?" he asked. "What are they for?"

"Booksss," Treyvan replied, completing his stretch. "Jussst booksss, many of them. Ssso long asss they do not fall, it iss level enough."

Books? Where is he getting books? He sighted along the shelf again. It slanted just a bit, but not enough for most people to notice. Or it just might be the uneven stone floor that gave the illusion that it slanted; it was hard to tell. It would certainly do for books—wherever the gryphons had gotten them. And whatever they planned to do with them. He couldn't imagine them reading, either—

"Yes," he admitted, finally. "There is just enough that mind-magic has in common with true magic to make her ask me some really difficult questions and to occasionally get her in trouble. And that's the problem—if she's asking me questions, I'm distracted from polishing my own skills. And when she gets into trouble, it's sometimes difficult to get her out again, because I am, well, rusty. I've forgotten most of the specifics. It's more annoying than anything else at the moment, but it's going to be dangerous when facing an enemy."

And how would I explain that to her countrymen? "*I'm sorry, but I seem to have let your princess get killed. I hope you have a spare?*"

"Can you not asssk anotherrr Adept to train herrr?" the gryphon asked, his crest-feathers erect with interest.

He sighed, put his back to the wall, and slid down it to sit braced against the cool stone. "That's just the difficulty, you see. I sponsored her as Wingsib; unless I *really* get into trouble, she's my problem and my responsibility. We don't have that many Adepts in the first place, and, frankly, none to spare to teach Elspeth."

Besides, I can just imagine what would happen if she were to pull one of her impertinent little questions on, say, Iceshadow. And how would I explain that? "*I'm sorry, but your princess seems to have gotten a bit singed. Don't worry, truly, I'm sure everything will grow back as good as new.*"

Treyvan scratched meditatively for a moment, then said, "Well, what of me?"

Darkwind frowned, not understanding the gryphon's question. "What about you?" he asked.

The gryphon coughed, and cocked his head to one side. "It ssseemsss to me that I could train herr. I am Masssterrr, and my ssskillsss, while not Adept-classs, arrre quite finely honed and in usssse. I am sssurely good enough to answer herr quessstionsss, get her out of tanglesss, and drill you both. Anything I cannot deal with, you can sssurely anssswer, sso long as the child isss not breathing firrre down yourr neck." His beak gaped in that familiar gryphon grin. "Bessidess, I doubt ssshe will give me asss much backtalk asss ssshe givess you!"

This was the answer to all his problems. He'd known the gryphon was *some* kind of mage. He'd seen it proven, and levels were largely a matter of power rather than skill, once one reached anywhere near to Master.

"Would you?" he said eagerly. "Would you really do that?"

The gryphon made a chirring sound, something between a snort and a chuckle. "I ssssaid that I would, did I not? Of courssse I will. It will be amusssing to teach a human again." He eyed Darkwind speculatively. "What isss more, featherrrless sson, I sshall drrrill you asss well. I sshall assk Hydona to help me."

Darkwind suddenly had the feeling a sparrow must have when caught out in a storm. He could bluff Elspeth when he didn't know an answer or concoct a spur-of-the-moment fake that would hold until he recalled the real answer. He wouldn't be able to do that with Treyvan.

And what was more, by the glint in Treyvan's eye, the gryphon knew he'd been doing exactly that.

On the other hand, he needed the drill badly, and Treyvan was the only one likely to offer. He didn't like to go to the other mages and beg for their help; many of them were working themselves into the ground, first shielding, then trying to Heal the Heartstone. The rest, now that the rift between mages and non-mages had been dealt with, were often working the borders with the scouts. Thanks to them there were proper patrols and reasonable work shifts, and the scouts were no longer spread so thin that if one of them were ill or injured, it meant a gaping hole in their border coverage. Those holes were how Falconsbane had gotten in and out of their territory at his leisure.

But that meant there was no one Darkwind really wanted to ask to help him re-train. Except Starblade—but there were too many things between Starblade and he that had yet to be resolved. Besides, Starblade had task enough in simply being healed.

"There isss ssomething more about Elsssspeth, iss there not?" Treyvan asked. The gryphons' perceptiveness was a constant source of annoyance for Darkwind. It was impossible to be self-indulgent around them. "You have feelingsss beyond the ssstrictly necesssarrry. Sssomething—hmm—perrrsssonal?"

He flushed. "Not really," he replied, more stiffly than he would have liked. "I'm attracted to her, of course. But that would happen with any beautiful young woman that became my pupil. It's a natural occurrence in the student-teacher relationship, when both student and teacher are young, and their ages are close." He winced at saying that; he'd sounded pompous, and he'd come perilously close to babbling. But better that than have Treyvan think there was more between them.

"Of coursse," Treyvan said blandly. Too blandly. He could hardly take exception to that. He could suspect that Treyvan was teasing him, but he could prove nothing—which was, of course, exactly what Treyvan wanted. So long as Darkwind couldn't prove a real insult, the gryphon could tease all he wanted.

Crazy gryphon. Treyvan and his sense of humor, he thought sourly. *He'd laugh at his own funeral.*

"Anyway," he continued, as if Treyvan had said nothing at all, "With you drilling her, that won't come up. I will be too busy with my learning, as will she, and I sincerely doubt she will have any interest in you as a . . . uhm. . . . I wouldn't worry about it, if I were you."

"Oh," Treyvan replied, a definite twinkle in his eyes, "I won't."

Darkwind gritted his teeth; Treyvan was trying to annoy him, and there was no point in letting the gryphon know he was succeeding. That would only encourage him.

And after all, Treyvan had put up with plenty of harassment from Darkwind's bondbird, Vree. The forestgyre had a fascination for Treyvan's crest-feathers, and attempted to snatch them any time he had the chance, no matter how often or forcefully Darkwind warned him off. Sometimes, much to Treyvan's discomfort, he succeeded in getting a claw on them, too. Once when Treyvan was in molt, he'd even managed to steal one.

I suppose I can put up with a little teasing. Unlike Vree, Treyvan is at least not snatching at body parts in his joking.

But he would rather that Treyvan had chosen another subject for the teasing besides his feelings toward Elspeth. . . .

Hydona hissed and clacked her beak to get Elspeth's attention; Darkwind ignored her, for he had learned that Treyvan would use any moment of distraction to send lances of carefully tempered power at the Hawkbrother's shields. And Treyvan was watching him very carefully without seeming to; the advantage of the placement of the eyes on gryphon heads. They had excellent peripheral vision; a full three-quarters of a circle, and sharper than Darkwind could believe.

Despite Treyvan's comment about asking his mate, Darkwind had not expected that both gryphons would show up to tutor them. But when he and Elspeth traveled across the pass-through to the Practice Ground, four wings, not two, lifted to greet them.

"Hydona hass more patience than I," Treyvan had said jovially. "And ssshe hasss taught morrre than I. Ssshe thought ssshe might be a better teacherr for Elsssspeth." His eyes glinted. "That leavesss me morre time to tutorr *you*."

Hydona trilled. "Tutorr orr torturrre?"

"What about the young ones?" Darkwind had asked, worriedly, trying to ignore Hydona's remark. "The Heartstone still isn't safe for little ones to be near, even with all the shielding we've put on it."

"They are at the lair," Treyvan had replied. "The evening of the celebrrration had an unexpected outcome. The *kyree*, Torrl, hasss decided to ssstay with usss to aid yourr folk in ssscouting, and hisss young cousin, Rris, arrrrived yesssterday to join him. Rris watches the younglingsss. He ssays he isss glad to do ssso." Treyvan grinned hugely. "It ssseemss that we are sssuch thingss of legend that it isss worrth it to him to be the brrrunt of the younglingsss' gamesss to be nearrr usss."

Darkwind could only shake his head. The *kyree* were large, yes, but by no means the size of a half-grown gryphlet. Lytha and Jerven could bowl *him* over without even thinking about it; they would certainly give that poor *kyree* plenty of reasons to regret his offer.

I can just imagine the games they'll get up to. Pounce and Chase, Scream and Leap, Who-Can-Send-Rris-Rump-Over-Tail. . . .

Unless, of course, Rris was very agile—or very clever. If the former, he could probably dodge the worst of their rough-and-tumble games, and if the latter, he could think of ways to keep them out of mischief without getting flattened.

"I hope this Rris has a great deal of patience, my friend," was all he had said. "Your offspring are likely to think he's some kind of living tumble-toy."

Treyvan had only laughed. "Think on Torrl," he had replied. "Young Rrisss isss asss clever asss hisss cousin, and verrry good, I am told, with younglingsss. All will be well."

Then Darkwind had no more time to worry about the well-being of the brave young *kyree* who had taken on the task of tending Jerven and Lytha, for their father launched him straight into a course of practice aimed at bringing him up to full and functional Adept status in the shortest possible period of time. It was aggressive, and Treyvan proved to be a merciless teacher.

Interestingly enough, he proceeded very differently from the way that Darkwind had initially been taught. In his years of learning before, he had mastered the basics of manipulating energies and shielding, then learned the offensive magics, *then* the defensive. But the first thing that Treyvan drilled him in were the Master-level *defensive* skills.

As now; he was constructing a structure of shields, onionlike in their layering, while Treyvan watched for any sign of weakness in them and attacked at that point. The object was to produce as many different kinds of shields as possible, so that an enemy who might not know every kind of shield a Tayledras could produce would be defeated by one, perhaps the third, fourth, or fifth.

The outermost was not so much shield as misdirection; it bent the mental eye away from the wearer and refracted the distinct magical image of the mage into resembling his surroundings, as if there was no one there. Beneath that was a shield that deflected energy, and beneath that, one that countered it. Yet deeper was one that absorbed energy and transmuted it, passing it to the shield beneath *it*, which simply resisted, like a wall of stone, and reflected the incoming energy back out through the previous layer. It was the transmutational shield that was giving Darkwind trouble. It would absorb Treyvan's attacks, right enough, but it wasn't transmuting the energy-lances into anything he could use.

"Hold," Treyvan said, finally, as Hydona lectured Elspeth on the need to establish a shield and a grounding point *first*, before reaching for node-energy. He had been trying to get that through her head for the past two days; finally, with someone else telling her exactly the same thing, it looked as if she was going to believe that he was right.

No, she's going to believe the information was right, he chided himself. *That's what's important, not the source of the information. If hearing it from Hydona is what it takes, then fine, so long as she learns it now and not the hard way—*

No one in k'Sheyna had ever learned that lesson "the hard way," not within living memory, but there were tales of a mage of k'Vala who had seized a node without first establishing a grounding point, and discovered that the node was rogue. Nodes could go feral, flaring and dying unpredictably, without the stabilizing focus of a Heartstone. The node he seized had done just that; it flared, and with no ground point to hold him and shunt the excess away and no shield to shelter him, he had burned up on the spot, becoming a human torch that burned for days— or so the tales said.

In fact, it had probably happened so fast that the mage had no notion of what had gone wrong. But whether the tales were true or not, it was still a horrible way to die.

Maybe all she needed was for it to be a female that taught her, he thought, watching as her grave eyes darkened and lightened according to her mood. *Her weapons' teacher, the Tale'sedrin-kin that she worships so, is a female; and so is her oldest friend. And her Companion is female. Maybe she just responds better to female teachers.*

A reasonable thought—

Thwap!

A mental "slap across the side of his head" woke him to the fact that he was supposed to be working, not woolgathering. Once again, Treyvan had taken advantage of the fact that his attention had wandered to deliver a stinging reminder of what he was supposed to be doing.

Damn you, gryphon. That hurt.

With his "ears" still ringing, he turned his attention back to his teacher, whose twitching tail betrayed his impatience.

"If you do not pay heed, I ssshall do more than ssswat you, Darrrk-wind," Treyvan warned him. "That isss the third time today your thoughtsss have gone drrrifting."

He grunted an assent, without mentioning that each time Elspeth had been the cause of his wit-wandering. He needn't have bothered. Treyvan brought it up on his own.

"Can you not worrrk about a young female without having yourrr mind drrrift?" he asked acidly. "Humanss! Alwaysss in sseasson!"

Darkwind felt his neck and ears heat up as he flushed. "That's not it," he protested. Treyvan cut his protests short.

"It mattersss not," the gryphon growled. "Now *watch* thiss time. *Thiss* is how the transsssmutation ssshould look to you. Crreate the texturrre *sso,* pussh it frrrom you asss if rrreleasssing a brreath. Halt it *herrre* frrrom yourr body."

Darkwind blotted everything out of his mind except the sense of the power-flows, and the magic that the gryphon manipulated. As Treyvan built the proper shield, step by slow, tiny step, Darkwind finally saw what he had forgotten.

Treyvan had woven a complex texture into the shield, in one area directing power only *in,* and in another place filtering it *out,* giving him *two* power flows—one from himself, the other ready to take in energy directed at him by an enemy, and transmute it. That was the problem;

he'd only allowed for the single power-flow from himself. The energy coming in from outside took over the field that was supposed to channel power from himself into the first shield. Back-pressure, as in a well-spring, with only the inevitable leaks to relieve that pressure. Once there, since it wasn't shield-energy, it eddied or stood idle—or worse, waited to react with another "color" of magic—in all cases, more than frustrating. Potentially deadly, in fact. It never reached the transmutational part of the Working; so it never channeled to the last shield.

Mentally cursing himself, he rebuilt his shields; this time the transmutational shield worked correctly, giving him two shields for the personal-energy cost of one. At least for as long as the enemy chose to sling spellweapons at him.

"Now, you know how thisss ssshield can be countered, yess?" Treyvan asked, when the shields had been tested and met with his approval.

"Two ways—well, three, if you count just blasting away with more energy than the shunt can handle," Darkwind replied. "The first is to find the shunt—where he's grounded—and use it to drain energy out of the shield—hooking into it yourself, and taking the energy back. If that happens, the shield starts draining the mage that's holding it. If you do that fast enough, all his shields will collapse before he can react."

Treyvan's crest-feathers rose with approval. "And?"

"Attack where the mage isn't expecting it," he said. "That can be one of two things—attacking through the shunt, which is structurally the weakest part of the shield, or attacking with something else entirely." He thought for a moment. "At this point, if I were the attacker, I'd go for something completely unexpected. Like . . . a physical attack. Send Vree in to harass him. Toss an illusion at him. Demonsbane—throw a *rock* at him to make him lose his concentration!"

Treyvan laughed. "Good. Now—could you have done what the sssword Need did? Could you now transssmute the energy of an attack and sssplit it?"

He thought about that for a moment; thought about exactly what the sword had done. "Yes," he said finally. "But only by doing what she did—holding no shields at all between the attack and the transmutation-layer. That might work for a thing made of metal and magic, but it would be pretty foolhardy for a flesh-and-blood creature."

Treyvan nodded. "Neverrrthelesss," he said, pointing a talon at Darkwind, "It did worrk. And ssso long asss Falconsssbane kept launching magical attackss against herr, it continued to worrrk. Only if he had ssseen what ssshe wass doing and launched a physical attack, or ssome otherr type of magic, would he have failed. He ssufferrred frrrom sshort sssight.''

Darkwind countered that statement with one of his own. "We were lucky,'' he said flatly. "Falconsbane was overconfident, and we were *damned* lucky. I have the feeling that if he'd had the time to plan and come in force, he could have taken us, all the Shin'a'in, and maybe even their Goddess on, and won.''

Treyvan hissed softly. "Your thoughtsss marrch with mine, featherlesss ssson,'' he said, after a pause. "And it isss in my mind that we ssshall not alwayss be ssso lucky.''

"In mine, too.'' Darkwind nodded toward Elspeth, and tried to lighten the mood. "For one thing, that woman seems to *attract* trouble.''

The gryphon's beak snapped shut, and he nodded. "Yesss, sshe doess. Sshe hass attracted you, forr one. Ssso, let usss sssee if you can conssstruct thossse ssshields corrrectly a ssecond time—and thisss time, hold them againssst me.''

Elspeth paid careful attention to every hissed word Hydona spoke, finding it unexpectedly easy to ignore the fact that her teacher was a creature larger than the biggest horse she had ever seen, with a beak powerful enough to snap her arm off at a single bite. Even with a motivation to pay attention such as that, the gryphon already made more sense than Darkwind did. Neither she nor the gryphons were native speakers of the Tayledras tongue; Hydona was being very careful about phrasing things in unambiguous terms that Darkwind likely thought were intuitively obvious.

Another case for being careful about what you assume in translation. Interesting. That is a consideration I would expect of a Court-trained person, not a creature like Hydona.

Hydona related everything she taught Elspeth to the mind-magic Elspeth already knew. *That* made a lot more sense than Darkwind's convoluted explanations of power-flows and energy-fluxes. They seemed clear to him, apparently, and seemed to make sense, except when he tried to fake; she had seen bluffs in enough Court functions to recognize the signs.

Hydona clearly detailed making an anchor point and shielding, for instance; that was a lot like grounding and centering, and was done for many of the same reasons. When put that way, Elspeth stopped subconsciously resisting the idea of having to effectively double-shield, once against mental intrusions and once against magical attacks. The other thing that made sense was that Hydona had pointed out the sword Need had done all that *for* her; the sword was in itself a permanent anchor point, radiating a seemingly ungraspable power into the earth, forever acting as a ground for the bearer it was bonded to. Need had shields on it that Hydona doubted were under conscious control anymore—if they ever had been. She seemed to think that they hadn't been; that they were some part of the sword itself, before the spirit came to reside in it.

So that was how Elspeth had managed to work magic without all the preparations the Hawkbrothers and their large friends deemed necessary. The precautions *had* been taken, they simply hadn't been taken by her.

And now that Need was no longer in Elspeth's possession, Elspeth was going to have to learn how to do everything Need had done so that she could manage for herself. With an ironic smile, she thought how easily Need could have become less a sword and more a crutch.

Oh, Need would have forced her to learn it all anyway. The only reason Need had aided her for as long as she had was because they had been in something of an emergency situation. In all probability, Need would have insisted on her learning to fend for herself as soon as there had been some breathing room.

Obediently, she "watched" as Hydona led her through the steps of anchoring and shielding, then practiced until they came easily. First, feeling the stable point in the power-flows about her and setting mental "hooks" into it, then erecting a shield against mage-energies that was remarkably similar to mental shields. Hydona drilled her over and over, and after a while the exercises stopped being something foreign and started feeling like second-nature. Best of all, they took about the same effort it took to stay on a galloping horse. She was a little surprised by how quickly it all came to her, but Hydona said nothing of it. She seemed to think it was only natural.

"Now," the gryphon said, after she'd repeated the patterns until she was weary of them, and thought she could do them in her sleep. "Here isss when you rrreach for powerrr; when you arrre ssafe in yourrr protectionsss, and anchored against fluxesss. Now, there isss a ley-line to the eassst of you; a young one, eassily tamed—but you do not know that. Ssso. Asssssume you know nothing. Searrch for it. When you find it, rrreach forr it, asss Need ssshowed you, and ssample it. Sssee if you can usse it, orrr if it isss too ssstrong forr you.''

She closed her eyes, found the line Hydona spoke of, and *reached* for it, dipping the fingers of an invisible hand into it, as if it were a kind of stream, and she wanted to drink of it.

She "tasted" it; tested the textures, the strength of the flow and the complexity. It was very tame, and bland. Not terribly strong. Kind of boring, in fact, compared with the rush of power she had gotten when she'd tapped into the node under the gryphons' ruins for the first time.

I can't do much with this, she thought, and began to trace it out to whatever node it was linked into, without thinking twice about doing so.

She felt her skull resound with a hard, mental *thwap!* Her eyes snapped open, and she rocked back on her heels for a moment, staring at the female gryphon, aghast.

"What did you do that for?" she cried, angrily. "I was just—"

"You were jussst about to find yourrr way to the Hearrtsssstone," Hydona interrupted. "And *that,* little child, would have eaten you whole, and ssspit out the piecessss. A trrrained and warry Adept can stand againssst it, but not you."

She licked her lips and blinked. "I thought the Heartstone was shielded. I thought nobody but Adepts *could* reach it now. Isn't that what all the mages have been working on since we got rid of Falconsbane?"

"And ssso it isss," Hydona nodded, "But you arrre within the prrotectionsss of the Practice Ground. The ssshieldsss do not extend herrre, so that those who arrre trrrying to Heal the Ssstone can rrreach it without dissrrupting thossse sssame ssshieldsss."

"So the Adepts healing the Stone come *here* to work?" she asked. Hydona nodded. Her voice rose with alarm; if the shields didn't extend here— "Isn't it dangerous for us to be here, then? I mean, what if we interfere with what's going on?"

"Therrre isss no one herrre at the moment," Hydona said calmly. "Arrre you afrrraid?"

Reluctantly, she nodded. After all she'd heard about the Heartstone and how dangerous it was in its current, shattered state, she wasn't very happy being somewhere that had no protections against it. The idea made her skin crawl a little with uneasiness.

"Good," Hydona said, with satisfaction. "You ssshould be afrrraid.

Verrry afrrraid. It isss nothing to disssregarrd, thisss Ssstone. It isss lightning harrnesssed, but barrrely, in itsss perfect sstate." She refolded her wings, and settled her tail about her forelegs. "Now, *why* werrre you wanderrring off like that?"

She shuffled her feet, uncomfortable beneath the gryphon's dark, penetrating gaze. "I—there wasn't much power there," she stammered. "I wanted more than that. I mean, there was hardly enough there to do anything with."

"Morrre than you think," Hydona scolded gently. "Tcha. You arrre a child who hasss alwaysss had a forrrtune at herrr beck, and hasss never learrrned how to make do with less." The gryphon shook her massive head, and the scent of cinnamon and musk wafted over Elspeth. "You musst learrrn to budget yourrrssself." She cocked her head sideways and watched Elspeth with a knowing eye. "The mossst effective mage I know neverr rrossse above Journeyman-classss. He wasss effective becaussse he knew *exactly* what hisss limitsss werrre, and he did everrrything possible insside thossse limitsss. *He* neverrr perrrmitted lack of powerrr to thwart him; he sssimply found waysss for lesss powerrr to accomplisssh the tasssk."

That was the harshest speech she'd ever gotten from Hydona, the closest the gryphon had ever come to giving her a scolding.

Although the *thwap* a few moments ago was a great deal like one of Kero's "love-taps."

She rubbed her temple, and considered the similarities between the two teachers. *"Delivered for your own good,"* Kero used to say. *Well, this is another kind of weapons' work I suppose. And what was it Kero always says? "On the practice ground, the weaponsmaster is the one true God." And this is the same as the practice ground, I guess.* She nodded meekly, and Hydona seemed satisfied, at least for the moment.

"Ssso, do asss I told you in the firrrsst place. Find the line, tesst it, and link with it." Hydona sat back on her haunches and gave her a steady, narrowed-eyed look that Elspeth interpreted as meaning she would not permit the slightest deviation from her orders.

So, with a purely mental sigh, she found the tame, boring line of power again, and tapped into it. The amount of energy possible to get from a source so slight was hardly more than a trickle, compared to the sunlike fury that was the Heartstone. This time, she made the connection without even closing her eyes. The relationship between the inner world of power, unseen by physical eyes, and the outer world no longer confused her. Part of that was simply all the work she'd done with FarSight over the years; another instance of how working with mind-magic made work with *real* magic much easier.

Ah, but as Hydona pointed out, less power does not mean less effective power. Mind-magic is still strong. If there are more Heralds with the Mage-Gift, after this I should be able to teach them in a reasonable length of time—not like the six or eight years it takes Quenten's students to become Journeymen. I could just work from their own mind-magic Gifts outward.

When she finished her assigned task, sealing the connections with a bit of a flourish, Hydona nodded with satisfaction. "Good. Now, channel the powerrr to me." Her beak opened in a hint of amusement at Elspeth's dropped jaw. "What, you did not know sssuch a thing wasss posssible? Becaussse it isss not posssible in mind-magic? Ah, but it *isss* possible in Healing, isss it not? Asss there are ssssimilaritiesss, there are diferencesss asss well, and those differencesss might kill you. Trrrussst yourrr intuition, but neverrr asssume anything."

What Hydona did not say—because she didn't need to—was that Elspeth needn't think she knew everything just because she was well-versed in the magic of her own people.

All right, so I'm a bonehead. She reached a tentative "hand" to Hydona, and was relieved to find the gryphon's shields down, and Hydona waiting for her "touch." She had no idea how to proceed with someone who was uncooperative, or worse, unable to cooperate. It took several false starts before she was able to create a channel to Hydona without losing the first one to the ley-line, but once she had it set up, she was able to redirect the power without too much difficulty.

She was tempted to set up a channel from Hydona to the line, directly, but she had a notion that Hydona would be able to tell the difference, and that the gryphon would not be amused.

Hydona broke the contact, and Elspeth maintained the channel without drawing any more energy from it while she waited for the gryphon's next instructions.

"Ssso, you can ssseek, sssample, channel, and sssend. Now we sssshall practice all of thossse," Hydona said genially. "We sssshall prrractice, and prrractice, until you can ssseek, sssample, channel and sssend underrr any circumssstancesss."

Elspeth smothered a groan, and broke her contact with the ley-line neatly, letting its newly-freed power wisp away harmlessly. This was starting to get frustrating. Hydona sounded more and more like Kero with every passing moment. *If she starts being any more like Kero, the next thing she's going to do is quote a Shin'a'in proverb at me.*

"It isss sssaid that 'Whateverr isss prreparred forr neverrr occurrrssss,' " Hydona quoted. "That isss an ancient Kaled'a'in sssaying. Ssso, let usss prrepare you for finding yourrrssself alone, sssick, wounded, exhaussted, ssssurrounded by enemiessss and needing powerrr, and it will neverrr occurrr. Yesss?"

Elspeth could only sigh.

Later, after the gryphons were gone, Darkwind rubbed eyes that ached and burned with the strain of DoubleSight, and was mildly surprised to find Elspeth still there. She sat quietly on a stone bench, leaning against the curved marble wall of their corner of the Practice Ground with her eyes closed. He wondered if she was waiting for him to show her the way out—or just waiting for him.

He walked up to her, and she stared up at him with eyes as tired as his own. "We should leave, Elspeth," he said carefully, uncertain of her temper, as weary as she looked. "The others will be here soon to work on the Heartstone, and we shall be in the way."

"We'll be more than in the way, if what Hydona said is any indication," she replied, getting slowly to her feet. "We'd be in danger—and a danger to them. Well, I would be, anyway. Like having a toddling baby underfoot on a tourney field. Nobody would ever hit it on purpose, but . . . well."

He nodded, relieved. "There you have it, truly. Would you care to come with me, to find something to eat?"

She hesitated a moment, then shrugged. "I'm not hungry, though."

"All the more reason that you should eat," he told her warningly. "Until you are used to it, the manipulating of mage-energies dulls the appetite. You must take care that you do not starve yourself."

She looked at him in surprise, and must have seen by his expression that he wasn't joking. "Well, that's not such a bad thing if you're on the plump side, but—"

"Hmm. There are no fat mages," he pointed out as he walked, "except those who habitually and grossly overindulge themselves; those for whom overeating is either a self-indulged vice or a disease. Manipulating mage-energies also costs one in terms of one's own energies, which means that you have just done *work*, Wingsib. Very hard, physical work, that deceives your own body.''

He led her to the peculiar Gatelike construction called a "pass-through" that led to the Practice Ground. It was yet another way to ensure that the unwary and unready did not intrude on students at practice, or the Adepts at their work. Because of the wall about it, the grounds could not be seen from outside, nor the Vale from within. They were a place and a time unto themselves. And in fact, he sometimes wondered if time moved a bit differently there.

She shook her head as she recovered from the jolt of disorientation that accompanied the transition across the pass-through. "How do you ever get used to that?" she asked. "That kind of dizzy feeling, I mean."

He raised an eyebrow at her. "We never do," he said simply. "There is a great deal that we never get used to. We simply cease to show our discomfort."

She said nothing, but he caught her giving him a speculative look out of the corner of his eye. For his part, he was more concerned with finding one of the *hertasi*-run "kitchens" before his temper deteriorated. Hunger did that to him, and he couldn't always predict what would set him off when his temper wore thin.

He didn't want to alienate her; the opposite was more like it, but he often felt as if he was dancing on eggs around her. He wondered if she felt the same around him. There was no cultural ground that they could both meet on, and yet they had a great deal in common.

The "kitchen" was not a kitchen as such; just a common area, a room in one of the few ground-level structures, that the *hertasi* kept stocked with fresh fruits, bread, smoked meat, and other things that did not spoil readily. Those Hawkbrothers who either did not have the skill or the inclination to prepare their own meals came here to put together what they pleased. The fare was not terribly varied, but it was good. And at the moment, Darkwind had no inclination to make the trek to his own *ekele* for food. Not while his stomach was throttling his backbone and complaining bitterly.

He indicated to Elspeth that she should help herself, and chose some fruit and bread, a bit of smoked meat, and a handful of *dosent* roots that had a cheesy taste and texture when raw. They found a comfortable spot to sit, in an out-of-the-way clearing, and fell to without exchanging much more than nods.

"So, what was it that Hydona tutored you in?" he asked, when the edge was off his hunger.

"Baby-steps." She made a face. "This is childish of me, I know, but she had me tapping into a very low-power ley-line, over and over, until she was certain that I could handle it in my sleep. But I was working the node under the lair with Need, and she *knows* that!"

"So you wonder why is she insisting that you work with minimal energy?" he replied, trying very hard to see things through her eyes.

Elspeth nodded, and nibbled a *chasern* fruit tentatively.

He licked the juice of another *chasern* from his fingers, and tried to answer as he thought Hydona would. "Firstly, there are some sources of power that are much too dangerous even for a single Adept to handle. Yes, even here, in our own territory. I mean besides the Heartstone." He nodded at her look of surprise. "There are pools of tainted magic, like thin-roofed caves, left by the Mage Wars. Difficult to see from the surface, and deadly to fall into. That is what a Healing Adept must deal with, and at the moment, we have none. There are even perfectly natural sources too strong for one Adept to handle by himself—any node with more than seven ley-lines leading into it, for instance, or rogue lines, which fluctuate in power levels unpredictably. Add in the tendency of lines to move, and you find the only way to use these sources is with a group of Adepts, each one supporting the others, each doing a relatively small amount of work so they have a reserve to deal with emergencies."

"I can see why she doesn't want me to just tap into whatever powerful source I See," Elspeth replied impatiently, "but *why* is she insisting that I only work with a bare trickle of power when energy is everywhere?"

"Ah, but it *isn't*," he replied, happy to at last discover the misconception that was the source of her impatience. "There is a limit on all Gifts, no matter how powerful. There is a limit on how far you, personally, can FarSee, yes?"

She nodded, slowly, and focused on him intently, paying very close attention to his words.

"And when you Mindspeak, you can only do so within a given distance, true?" he continued. "Well, power is *not* everywhere—or rather, great power is not everywhere. There are places where there are not even weak ley-lines for a day's ride in any direction. There are places where even the nodes are weaker than the line you worked with today. We are *Tayledras*, Elspeth, and we are enjoined by the Goddess to cleanse these lands of magic. To that end, we concentrate it here. The energy level is unnaturally high in and around a Vale, even one as damaged as this one, and unnaturally high in and about the lands you call the Pelagir Hills, which we call the Uncleansed Lands.''

She swallowed the bite she had begun with a bit of difficulty. ''So you're saying that when I get home, I might find that there's no magic energy to work with?'' She looked horrified, and he hastened to assure her.

''No. I am saying that when you return, you may find you have lower levels of energy available than you have here. Or the power may be there, but buried deeply.'' He ate the last of his fruit. ''That is why there are schools of mages, who build up reservoirs of power that are available to the Masters and Adepts of those schools. And that is why blood-mages build power for themselves by exploiting the pain and death of others. So, you must know how to work subtly. You must learn that raining down blows with pure power is not always the correct response. It was not with some of Falconsbane's creatures; that you witnessed.''

She shook her head; whether stubbornly or for some other reason, he couldn't tell. ''Listen,'' he said, ''Hydona believes you are doing well. Once you have mastered the fainter sources of power, and in using the energy you yourself have stored within you, she and Treyvan wish us all to take our places on the border.''

She perked up at that, and he smiled to see her interest. ''Really?'' she exclaimed. ''I've felt so useless. I know you have to learn theory before you practice anything, but—''

''But you came here to become a weapon against the enemy of your land, I know,'' he replied. ''Now please—I know that you are impatient, but believe me. It is better to use little power rather than too much. Using a poleaxe to kill small game destroys the game thoroughly, rendering it useless. So it is with magic. Too much can attract things you do not wish to have to deal with, as a dead creature can attract things more dangerous than it was to scavenge upon it. Master the subtlety Hydona tries to teach you. There will be time and more than time for the greater magics.''

He watched her face; she seemed thoughtful, and he hoped she believed him, because whether she knew it or not, her life depended on believing him—and sooner than she might think.

For Hydona had not meant that suggestion in jest, that both of them take up a scout's position on the border of k'Sheyna. When they did that, there were no longer any shields, any protections, or any rules. It would be only themselves and the gryphons, and it might well be that there were things out there that were more powerful and deadly than Mornelithe Falconsbane.

Chapter Eight

So now I'm a scout on the border of the Tayledras territories. In the Pelagirs. Me, who never even rode circuit. Mother would have a cat. Elspeth's heart raced every time a bird called an alarm or a stray twig broke, even though she knew very well that potential danger was likely to be upon them long before there were any such warnings. Gwena was jumpy too, and that didn't help her nerves any. She had all her shields down toward Gwena, and whatever her Companion felt, she felt, and vice versa.

Or was it that Gwena was jumpy after all? The Companion was ill at ease, but it didn't quite have the feeling of nerves.

:*All right,*: she said, suddenly suspicious. :*What are you hiding this time?*:

:*I wasn't hiding it—at least, not from you,*: the Companion temporized. :*I've been keeping something from the others. Well, maybe I have and maybe I haven't—I mean, I don't know how much they've guessed about Cymry and me. So I wasn't really hiding it from you, but—*:

Elspeth choked and coughed to cover it. :*Gwena, dear, you can stop babbling, all right? I'd say the Tayledras know plenty about you two, from the way Darkwind dances around you, and they aren't telling* me *about what they know, either. So you might as well let this great secret out, whatever it is, because even if I don't know about it, they probably do.:*

She couldn't hide her resentment at that, and didn't try. It was obvious—would have been plain even to a child—that the Hawkbrothers considered the Companions something quite special, according them more reverence than they even got at home in Valdemar. But the Tayledras wouldn't discuss the Companions at *all* without one of them being present, as if they were determined not to offend the Companions or reveal something they shouldn't.

And even if there was nothing to this dancing about the bushes, it drove Elspeth to distraction.

:Well,: Gwena said slowly, *:I would have to tell you soon, anyway. It's not really all that complicated. Now that you know how to channel mage-energies, and you know how to feed someone else and be fed in turn—well— I can feed you.:*

Elspeth was past being surprised. She simply nodded. *:And of course it would have been no use telling me this before I had the skill, I know.:* She closed her eyes and counted to ten, very, very carefully. *:You aren't keeping anything else back, are you?:*

:No,: Gwena replied in a subdued voice. *:No, not really. I can feed you if you need it, but I'm subject to the same limitations you are. Except—:*

Elspeth counted to ten a second time. *:Except?:*

Gwena waited a long time, and Elspeth sensed that she was choosing her words very carefully. *:Except that you and I are a special pairing; so special that distance doesn't matter between us. That's all. I'm—different that way. It's like a lifebonded pair working together. Ask Darkwind about that some time, if you like; there are things a pair can do that even two Adepts working together can't do.:*

A vague memory fluttered at the back of her mind; something about a dark, windy night, the night when Gwena had Chosen her.

But the memory escaped before she could grasp it and she gave up trying to get it back after a fruitless moment of concentrating. *:I won't say I'm unhappy to hear that,:* she told Gwena sincerely. *:If things ever go badly for us, you and I might need that edge. I—don't suppose this means you're a mage, too—does it?:*

:Oh, no!: Gwena replied, her mind-voice bright with relief. *:No, not at all! I can just tap into nodes, energy-lines, and fields. All Companions can, just most of them can't use it for more than—oh, the usual. Healing themselves quickly, extended endurance, and running faster than a horse can.*

And they certainly can't feed their Chosen. That's why we're white, you know—ask Darkwind about node-energy and bleaching.:

She sat up straighter, and looked up in the tree above her at Darkwind, who was "taking the tree-road." Except that right now he was just sitting; letting Vree do his scouting for him before they all moved on to another spot on their patrol. "Darkwind?" she whispered.

He looked down at her, but did not give her the hand signal that · indicated she should be quiet.

"Gwena says I should ask you about node-energy and bleaching. She says that's why Companions are so white, because they use node-power to increase speed and endurance." She shook her head, still trying to figure it out.

But Darkwind seemed to get the point immediately; his eyes lit up, and he grabbed the branch beneath him. He swung down off his branch perch like a rope dancer, to land lightly beside her. "So! That is the piece of the puzzle that I have missed!" he said cheerfully. "I think you need not fear lack of nodes and power in your land, if all your Companions are able to tap them to enhance their physical abilities. That must mean that there is no scarcity of mage-energy."

Well, that was a great weight off her mind. "About bleaching?" she prompted.

He tugged at his own hair, and she noticed that white roots were starting to show and that the color had faded to a dull tan. "Use of node-energy gradually bleaches a mage; the color-making dies in skin, hair, and eyes, and the color that is already there is leeched away. I do not lie when I say that magery changes a person. So—your Companions use node-energy, and thus are blue-eyed, silver-coated, gray-hooved."

:Silver-hooved,: Gwena said with dignity. He chuckled softly, and tapped her nose.

"If you insist, my lady." He turned back to Elspeth. "My hair is not white, because as a scout I dye it. Tayledras all *live* with node-energy, whether we are mages or no, so nonmages bleach as well. Mages are silver-haired usually in their fifth year of practice; any other member of the Clan will have made the change at, oh, thirty summers, or thereabouts. Even with dye, I must renew the color every few days now that I am a mage again."

Elspeth could only cast her eyes upward. "It's like continuous sun on them, then? No wonder dye won't take on them," she said. "The gods know we've tried often enough—you know, it's damned *hard* to disguise a big white horse!''

:*Sorry,*: Gwena put in. :*Can't help it.*:

"In a trade-off between endurance and the rest of it, and being unable to disguise them, I think I'll take the endurance," Elspeth said, as much for Gwena's ears as Darkwind's. And for Gwena's ears only, :*I'll take you just the way you are, oh great sneak,*: and felt Gwena's rush of pleasure, much like a pleasantly embarrassed flush.

He shrugged. "It is the choice I would make. Besides, now that you are a mage, you may make her seem any color you choose, by illusion."

Before she could answer that, he was back up in the tree again, swarming up the trunk like a squirrel, and hooking the branches above him with the peculiar weapon-tool he kept in a sheath on his back. She still didn't see how he could possibly climb that quickly, even with the spike-palmed climbing gloves he wore; humans shouldn't be able to climb like that.

She was about to ask him what was going on, when he gave her the hand signal indicating that she should remain quiet. She and Gwena froze, statue still, trusting to the bushes they sheltered in to keep them from sight.

She didn't dare let down her shields to probe about her. Darkwind had warned her of the danger of that, and after hearing more about Mornelithe Falconsbane and the creatures he had commanded, she was inclined to listen to him and believe. But she was free enough to use every other sense, and she did. At first she couldn't tell that there was anything at all out of the ordinary, but then she realized that the forest was a little too quiet. No birdcalls, no wind stirring the branches, nothing but the little *ticks* the red and golden leaves made as they fell.

:*Els-peth?*: came the tentative mental touch, as soft as the caress of a feather. :*Vree has found someone. I sense only a void, which means that there is someone inside a shield where Vree sees a two-legged creature.*:

Darkwind had told her that he would use Mindspeech only if he had determined that an enemy could not hear it, and had explained that he would test with a quick mental probe of his own, too swift to fix on. She had wanted to object, but it *was* his land and he was used to scouting it; she had to assume he knew what he was doing. And evidently he did. . . .

:*We're going to have to work out what I should do if someone ever* does *catch a probe and lock horns with you,:* she interjected, Sending a mental picture of stags in full battle.

A rush of chagrin accompanied his reply. *:You are right. But—not now.:*

:No,: she agreed. *:Not now. What do you want me to do? Should I try a probe? Are the gryphons going to get in on this?:*

:Not unless there is no other choice,: he replied firmly. *:We need to keep their existence as quiet as possible; there are surely others besides Falconsbane who might covet them or the small ones. And you may try a mind-magic probe, but I think you will encounter the same shields as I have. No, you and I will confront and warn him. If he does not heed the warning, we will deal with him—:*

He broke off his link with her so suddenly that she was afraid that something *had* locked him in mental battle after all. But then, a heart-beat later, his mind-voice returned. *:There is an additional complication,:* he said dryly; she looked up to find him looking down at her with a face full of irony. *:It seems our intruder is a Changechild.:*

Her first thought had been: it must be Nyara. Her second thought had been that it couldn't be Nyara, but that it must be another of her father's creatures, running wild with Falconsbane gone. She tried a mental probe and discovered that just as Darkwind had said, the creature had very strong shields, well beyond her ability to counter. So the only way to learn anything about it was to confront it.

As she and Darkwind watched the intruder from their respective hiding-places, she knew all of her guesses about it had been wrong.

She didn't know whether to be relieved that this interloper was not their Nyara, or not. If it *had* been Falconsbane's daughter, the situation between herself and Darkwind would have been complicated enormously. Her own instincts warred with her on the subject; she trusted Nyara to a limited extent, and she certainly felt that the Changechild had been greatly wronged and abused, but—

But Nyara was incredibly, potently, sexually attractive. She couldn't help herself. Elspeth would have to have been blind not to see that Darkwind had wanted her as much as Skif had and that if anything had kept them from becoming intimate, it wasn't lack of attraction. She suspected that his own innate suspicion, lack of opportunity, and perhaps something on Nyara's part had kept him from playing the role of lover. As it was, that night before Dawnfire had returned to them, trapped in the body of her bondbird, it had been Skif, not Darkwind, who had taken that role. And, perhaps, guilt had kept Darkwind at arm's length. Guilt, that kept him from taking a new lover when his former love was a captive, confined to a bird's body by the temptress' father.

But Falconsbane was dead, or the next thing to it, and Dawnfire was out of reach of any of them. That left him free. And if he encountered Nyara before Skif did, would he be able to stand against temptation a second time? Especially if Nyara were to make overtures?

Knowing men, she didn't think so.

But at the same time, discovering that this stranger was *not* Nyara was a disappointment. However brief their acquaintance had been, Elspeth *liked* Nyara, and felt a great deal of sympathy for her. And she sometimes spared a moment to worry about her, out there in the wild lands that k'Sheyna no longer held, with a mage-sword who might not even *like* her. She had few or no provisions, no shelter against the coming winter unless she had somehow found or made one. . . .

Well, this wasn't the time to worry about their errant Changechild. Not with another standing on k'Sheyna lands, within k'Sheyna borders—and by the blood on its hands and the circle about its feet, one who was up to no good.

Elspeth had done enough hunting in her time not to be sickened by the blood of a butchered deer. What made her ill were the fact that it was a *dyheli* that had been slain, and the signs that the butchery had taken place *before* it was dead, not after.

Blood-magic. Wasn't that what Darkwind and Quenten both mentioned, but wouldn't talk about?

Well, here it was—a "blood-mage"—and now that she knew what to Look for, she Sensed the power that the mage had drawn into himself as a result of his work. It wasn't power *she* could have used under any circumstances; in fact, it made her a little nauseous to brush against it just long enough to figure out what it was. But it *was* power, and she had a notion that the death of a thinking, reasoning creature like a *dyheli* would have given this mage four times the strength that a deer would have. Perhaps more, depending on how long it had suffered.

Easy power, easily obtained, from a source you can find anywhere. And if you're sadistic by nature, a source that gives pleasure when exploited. No wonder Ancar is attracted to it.

If Nyara was feline in nature, this creature was serpentine. As he moved about, disposing of his victim, he glided rather than walked, and many of his motions had a bonelessness to them that made her shiver in an atavistic reaction to the evocation of "snake."

Odd. The hertasi *don't do that to me, and they aren't half as human. I wonder why this thing does?*

What exposed skin she saw—mostly hands and a glimpse of cheek—gleamed in the late afternoon light, with a kind of matte reflectivity that hinted at hard, shiny scales.

He dressed for deep cold, rather than the autumnal chill of the season; heavy leather boots, thick hose, a fur-lined tunic and cloak, and a heavy velvet shirt beneath the tunic. The colors were curious; a strange, dappled golden brown shading into deep orange—colors that blended surprisingly well into the foliage. Whatever else he was, this Changechild was canny. If he lay unmoving in the heart of a thicket, no one would ever see him.

The Changechild looked up at the first rustle of leaves, and froze in a combat-ready crouch. Darkwind dropped out of the branches like a great hawk coming to land, his knees flexed, and his hands in front of him, wary and ready to launch into an attack or defense as the need arose. The creature faced her fully now, and she saw that beneath the hood of his cloak, his face was curiously flat, with a thin, lipless mouth, and unblinking eyes as round as marbles. He straightened, but did not relax his wary pose.

Neither did Darkwind.

"You trespass," the Hawkbrother said clearly and slowly, in the most common of the trade-tongues used hereabouts. "You trespass upon the lands of the Tayledras k'Sheyna, and you pollute those lands with blood needlessly spilled."

That thin mouth stretched in what might have passed for a smile in any other creature. He straightened with arrogant self-assurance. "Not needlessly," he said. "and who or what are you to tell me what I may or may not do?"

"Tayledras k'Sheyna," Darkwind replied flatly. "These are our lands. We do not permit this. You will depart, taking your filth with you."

The mouth stretched a little more, and the creature's hands flexed a little. "What? Run from a single foe? I think not."

He made no gesture, but the circle he had drawn about his feet in blood flamed with sullen power—

—and, horribly, the disemboweled *dyheli* on the ground beside him heaved itself to its feet. It stood swaying a little, a gaping hole where its belly should have been, its eyes red with that same sullen power, and a dull glow about its hooves and horns.

"You are only one," the Changechild said softly. "One single Hawk-brother is hardly a threat. This weak creature was not enough. I think you will do to serve me."

Elspeth did not need Darkwind's signal to step from concealment, with Gwena at her side. She took up her position near enough to the Hawkbrother that they could not easily be separated, but distant enough that they would not interfere with each other.

"*We* are Tayledras k'Sheyna," Darkwind said, firmly, but with no hint of anger. "And you will leave now."

This time Hydona was not around to keep her from using the strongest source of power she could Sense, and there was a three-line node not more than a furlong from where they stood. She tapped into it, quickly; to her Othersight it glowed with healthy green fire, and touching it was a pleasant jolt, as if she took a deep draught of cold spring water on a hot day. She established her link and channeled power to herself and her shields before the stranger had a chance to respond to Darkwind's challenge. She kept the level of her outermost shield the same so as not to warn him; at minimal strength, the kind of mage-shield a beginner would build. But, like a paper screen hiding a stone barrier, beneath the disguising energies of the first shield was a second, and it was linked to the node-power.

It was just as well that she did, because the Changechild's reply was to attack.

He was no Falconsbane, but he was no Apprentice, either. He chose his target cleverly, launching his initial onslaught against Elspeth rather than Darkwind. Perhaps he was deceived by the rudimentary outer shield, or perhaps he was under the impression that a female would be less prepared and less aggressive than a male.

If that was the case, he judged wrongly.

She Saw his attack as he launched it; a flight of white-hot energy-daggers that he flung at her with both hands. She anticipated the direction of his attack by his eyes—and was ready in time to reflect them straight back at him, holding up mirror-shielded hands that doubled the flame-bright weapons back on themselves and sent them back on their original path. *That* must have been something of a shock to him, for he did not even deflect them properly, much less reabsorb them. They impacted on his shields, splintering silently into a thousand shard-sparks, and he flinched away.

Before he had a chance to recover from that shock, Darkwind had launched an attack of his own, but not one he likely would have expected. He attacked the mage's shields with a needle-lance of force, not the mage himself, boring through the protections at their weakest point, where some of the energy daggers had impacted. The blue-white lance split the air between them, and Darkwind held it straight on target, despite the Changechild's best efforts to shake it off. Elspeth readied a second attack, arrows of lightning, but did not launch it, holding it in reserve.

The Changechild sent his unliving creature to attack them; the shambling, bloody thing charged with a speed quite out of keeping with the condition it was in. It was halfway to them before Elspeth realized that it *was* an attack, but Gwena intercepted it, like a trained war-horse, as if she had dealt with such things all her life. She sidestepped the wicked horns neatly, and twisted sideways to launch a cruel double-hooved kick with her hind legs as the thing passed, that sundered its hips with a meaty *thunk* and a wet *crack*.

The dead thing staggered and went down again, and tried to heave itself erect. But it could not struggle upright again, for its hip and one of its hind legs were broken and would no longer bear its weight.

At that same instant, Darkwind penetrated the Changechild's shields, and Elspeth launched the lightning-arrows she had been readying, targeting them at the hole Darkwind had bored and was even now spreading open. The first one missed slightly, impacting just to one side of the hole, splintering as had the mage's own energy-daggers.

The second did not miss, nor did Darkwind's fireball that followed in the arrow's wake.

Within the enemy's shields and contained by them, a storm of utterly silent fireworks erupted. The Changechild stood frozen for a moment, a dark silhouette against a background of coruscating energies—

Then he collapsed to the ground as his shields collapsed around him, and, like the *dyheli* that had been his victim, did not move again.

They patrolled the border until nightfall and the arrival of Summersky, the scout that was to relieve them, but there wasn't so much as a leaf out of place. As they headed homeward toward the Vale, Elspeth found herself very glad that she was riding. Although Hydona had warned her that a mage-duel would take *far* more out of her than she would ever believe, she hadn't really understood what the gryphon meant. Now though—now she knew Hydona was not only right, she had understated the case. Mostly all that she wanted right now was a soak in one of the hot springs, a meal, and her bed.

But besides being weary, she was very confused; a poor combination, all things considered. She was dissatisfied with her first foray on k'Sheyna's border. Certainly there were questions that had not been answered adequately.

And as she followed in Darkwind's wake, watching him stride tirelessly along with one hand on Treyvan's shoulder and folded wing, and Vree perched on a padded perch on his shoulder, she tried to reconcile her mixed emotions. It didn't help matters any that from this angle she had such a good view of his tight, muscular. . . .

Hydona trilled to herself, apparently amused by a private joke. The female gryphon walked beside her as her mate strode beside Darkwind, all of them following a dry streambed back to the Vale. Hydona's head was easily level with Elspeth's, which was a little unsettling, since it underscored how very large the gryphon was. It was easy to forget that, when one often saw them lounging about like overgrown house cats.

"And what arrre you thinking?" Hydona asked, as if she were following Elspeth's thoughts.

"I'm not sure," she said, frowning, trying to put her emotional reactions into words. "This isn't the first time I've been in combat—it isn't even the first time I've been in magical combat. I think we did all right—"

"You did," Hydona confirmed. "Verrry well, essspecially forr a beginerrr. But asss you pointed out, you have had combat experrrience, and I expected nothing lesss than competence." She cocked her head at Elspeth. "How do you feel you will manage againssst that enemy of yourrrsss?"

She thought for a moment, weighing what she could do now with what she knew Ancar could produce. "Well, providing Ancar hasn't acquired an army of mages, I should be able to do something about him, if I can keep progressing at this rate. I mean, it isn't easy, but so far I haven't lost any body parts. Provided I don't reach an upper limit to my powers in the near future, and Ancar hasn't learned to tap nodes. I know he should be a Master-class mage by now at the very least."

"One should neverrr trrusst an enemy to be placssid. What about yourrr perrrforrrmance?'' Hydona asked shrewdly. ''How would you rrrate yoursssself?''

''Darkwind and I worked together as a team *quite* well, I think. At least we did once he got around to *doing* something.'' There it was; that was what she had been trying to pinpoint as the root of her discontent. ''But that was the problem; he gave that damned thing a warning even after we knew it had worked blood-magic!''

She couldn't keep indignation from creeping into her voice, and didn't try. Kero would have cut the interloper down where he stood; filled him full of so many arrows that he would have looked like a hedgehog.

''The oddssss werrre two to one,'' Hydona responded. ''Thrree to one, if we count Gwena. Don't you think that the crrreaturrre dessserrved a fairr warrrning with oddsss like that?''

Elspeth shook her head, stubbornly. ''No,'' she said flatly, and her voice shook a little with intensity. ''I don't. We knew he was a blood-mage; there's no point in giving something like that a chance to get away or hurt you. I *sure* as Havens don't intend to give Ancar a shred of warning. In fact, if I get the chance, I'll ambush him!''

As always, the mere thought of Ancar and what he had done made her blood boil. The tortures he had inflicted on Talia—the rape of his own country—the hundreds, thousands of lives he had thrown away— but most of all, the careless *glee* he had taken in it all—

No, when she thought of Ancar, all she could think of was the chance of getting him in her power and shredding him. She hated him, she hated everything he'd ever done, and she wanted him *dead*, safely *dead*, so that he couldn't hurt anyone any more.

Ever.

In fact, if there was a way to destroy his very soul, she'd do it, so that there wouldn't even be a chance he'd be reborn and start over again, as some mages could.

''You arrre angrrry,'' Hydona observed. ''This enemy of yourrrsss angersss you.''

''I'm always angry when I think about Ancar,'' she replied fiercely. ''I can't help it; the man's another Falconsbane, just as evil and as corrupt, and I want him dead as much as any Tayledras could ever have wanted Falconsbane dead.'' She raised her chin defiantly. ''More than that, I want Ancar's liver on a plate, so I can feed it to something vile. I not only want to kill him, I want to *hurt* him so that he knows some of what his victims felt. I hate him, I'm afraid of him, and if there were any way to put *him* through what he has put others through, I'd take it."

Hydona shook her head with open admonition. "You arrre *too* angrrry," she said. "It isss not underrr contrrol, thisss angerrr. Hate will not serrve you herrrre. And ssssuch hate, sssuch angerrr will weaken you. You musst learrrn to contrrrol them, orr they will contrrol you. Thisss I know."

Elspeth grimaced, but kept her lips clamped tight on what she wanted to say. This wasn't the first time she'd heard this particular lecture; the first time, it had come from Darkwind. And it just made her angrier.

How could she *not* hate the bastard, after everything he'd done to her friends and her land? How could she not hate him after seeing what he had done to his own people? How could she not feel enraged at everything he had done?

And how in Havens could an emotion that strong possibly be a weakness? It was a contradiction in terms.

But there was absolutely no point in getting into an argument over it, so she elected to keep her thoughts to herself, and her tongue on a very short leash, until they reached the sanctuary of the Vale.

Hydona said nothing more.

The gryphons left them once they were well within the "safe" area that was kept under close watch by the mages, and full of alarms that would be tripped by strangers. By the time they arrived at the shielded entrance to the Vale it was already dark, and her temper had cooled considerably. Not that she had changed her mind about anything she'd said, but she wasn't quite so ready to bite off someone's head over it.

One thing had calmed her down a bit; she discovered that Gwena felt the same as she did—at least about Ancar. The Companion was of two minds about Darkwind warning the Changechild, admitting that there were good reasons for either decision, whether to warn or not—but on the subject of Ancar of Hardorn, Gwena was in full accord with her Chosen.

:*The man is a mad dog,*: she told Elspeth flatly. :*You don't give a mad dog a chance to bite you, and you don't try and cure it. You get rid of it, before it destroys something you love.*:

That backing of her own thoughts on the matter made her feel a bit more secure about her own judgment, and that Gwena shared her anger eased her own somewhat. That helped her temper to cool a lot faster.

She was quite ready to see the Vale long before they actually reached it. She discovered, somewhat to her surprise, that it was no real effort to keep her Mage-Sight invoked—and since Mage-Sight gave her an enhanced, owl-like view of her surroundings, she left it in force. It occurred to her, as she noted how every living creature and some things that were not alive each bore a faint outline of energy, that this must be what Companions used for night-sight. After all, in order to tap into and manipulate mage-power, you had to be able to See it, and since this kind of Sight worked equally well by day or night, why not use it to give you a nighttime advantage? Yet another Companion power she could explain away, which gave her a perverse feeling of satisfaction.

Once they approached the shields surrounding the Vale, she had to drop the Sight; the energies there were so powerful they threatened to "blind" her.

Well, that's one reason not to count on it for night-sight. And if powerful energies can "blind" you—well, that's something to be wary of. Hmm. And something to keep in mind as a weapon.

The faint tingle of her skin as they passed the entrance to the Vale, as if lightning were about to strike her, told her that they had crossed the shields and protections standing patient guard over the only way in and out. But even if she had not felt that little tingle, she would have known they were inside k'Sheyna Vale, for in the space of half a heartbeat they went from deep autumn to high summer. Suddenly her clothing was much too warm.

Gwena stopped as Darkwind went on ahead, pushing through the foliage draped over the path and vanishing into the shadowy gloom. Elspeth dismounted, unfastened her cloak, and draped it over the saddle. Even then she was a little too warm; she rolled up the sleeves of her shirt and opened the collar to the balmy night air, heavy with the scent of night-blooming flowers she could not even put a name to.

This place was the closest thing on earth that she had ever seen to the Havens of scripture and sermon. *Too bad I can't bring a little bit of this back with me,* she thought wistfully. *Fresh fruit and flowers in the dead of winter, hot springs and cool pools to bathe in—trysting nooks, and I can think of plenty of people who'd enjoy those! Near-invisible servants. Balmy breezes. No wonder Vanyel visited k'Treva whenever he was exhausted.*

Darkwind had said more than once that this Vale wasn't even a real showplace of what the Hawkbrothers could do. K'Sheyna, he'd wistfully related, was the smallest of the Clans even when they were at full strength, and the Vale was neglected and run down. Half tended at the very best, with no water-sculptures, no wind-harps—more than half the *ekeles* untenanted and falling to ruins—no one making vine-tapestries or flower-falls. No concerts except on the rarest of occasions, no artists except Ravenwing and the *hertasi*. Still, Elspeth found it beautiful beyond her wildest dreams.

She could only wonder what the rest of the Vales must be like. And—could the Heralds create something like this, if only in miniature?

But—should they?

She brushed aside a rainbow-threaded dangling vine and wondered about that.

This Vale was a very seductive, hedonistic place, and many people already thought that the Heralds were a bit too randy as it was. It was also a place that could encourage sloth; she found it very easy to justify sleeping a little later, lingering in the hot spring, or sitting and watching a waterfall and thinking about nothing at all.

Her footsteps made no sound on the soft sand of the pathway, sand that cradled her feet luxuriously. Everything about this Vale hinted at luxury—a luxury that few outside the Vales enjoyed. In fact, not even the Tayledras "cousins," the Shin'a'in, got to enjoy this sort of life. For that matter, could the Heralds really justify making themselves a private paradise when there were so many other things that needed doing?

A pair of long-tailed birds sang sweetly nearby, scarcely an arm's length from Gwena, reminding her by their presence that outside the Vale the songbirds had long since gone south. Even if Heralds could justify building a place like this, there was no way that they could justify lounging about in it the way the Tayledras did. Frolicking in flower-bedecked bowers and lounging in hot pools didn't get circuits ridden. Too much living like this, and she'd find herself wasting time designing feather-masks and festival-garb instead of getting her work done.

A feeling of moral superiority crept into her thoughts, and she let it. She led Gwena up the path to her loaned *ekele* and the tiny, sculpted hot pool beneath it, and felt a bit smug.

The stone path wound across another just ahead of her, and the murmur of voices to her right warned her that several folk were going to cross ahead of her. She paused—

And her sense of moral superiority vanished as soon as the Hawk-brothers came in view.

"Els-peth," called the first of the group as he caught sight of her,

"We should like the use of your pool. The *hertasi* are cleaning several of the others, and yours is the nearest that is prepared. May we?"

The mage-light that danced over his head revealed the little group of five pitilessly. The one in the lead, a mage named Autumnwing, was the best off, physically—and he was worn right down to the bone. Overextended, to say the least; his eyes were sunken, his skin pale, and he trembled with weariness. Behind him were two of Darkwind's scouts, both bruised and bloody, and supporting them were two more mages who looked in no better shape than Autumnwing. Even as she watched, one was redressing a wound that gleamed dark and wet, while her partner held the arm steady.

"What in Havens happened to you?" she exclaimed, before she could stop herself.

Autumnwing shrugged. "I have been with the rest on the Heartstone; it fluxed again today. Be glad you were not within the Vale, or we would have conscripted you with or without training. But I am not so bad—these four met with a pack of Changewolves that had cornered one of k'Sheyna's *dyheli* herds, and if it had not been for them, there might have been a score of Changewolves hounding the Vale itself tonight." As Elspeth's eyes widened, he added, "They are very valiant. Had I been in their place, I fear I would have fled."

The arm-wounded woman grunted and said, "Forty-arrow fight." Then she shrugged.

"P—please," Elspeth stammered, "Feel free to use the spring. I was going to find some food; shall I bring you back some, or send a *hertasi* with it?"

"Either," replied one of the scouts wearily. "I could happily eat one of our fallen enemies at this moment, raw, and without salt."

:*I'll take care of it, if you'll pull off the tack,*: Gwena told her. :*I can probably find a* hertasi *before you can.*:

In answer, Elspeth bent to loose the saddle-girth, and saddle and blanket slid to the ground as she unbuckled the hackamore and hauled it over Gwena's ears. The Companion vanished into the undergrowth. "She's gone to recruit you some food," Elspeth told the others, as she bent to retrieve the fallen saddle.

"Our thanks," Autumnwing told her gravely; she waited for them to make their way past her, then gave them a head start, before following in their wake.

Hot pools and life in an eternal summer don't compensate for that, she thought, balancing the saddle on her shoulder. *And given the Goddess' edicts, I suppose that even in Vales where the Heartstone is whole the mages aren't sitting around discussing water-sculpture.*

So much for moral superiority.

The Vales must seem like paradise itself when they're out in the Pelagir wilds—but one that wouldn't be there to return to if they weren't out in those wilds to defend it. Is Valdemar any different to a Herald?

Willfully faulty memory caught up with reality. This wasn't the first time she'd seen Hawkbrothers in such poor condition. The mages, half-Healed Starblade among them, worked themselves to a thread every day, shielding the Vale from attack, and trying to do something about their Heartstone. She had her own experience today to show her the hazards of being a scout on the border of the k'Sheyna territory, where every league held new and deadly horrors.

For that matter, she'd been an inadvertent witness to the worst—save only death—that could befall a Hawkbrother. She'd seen what had happened to Dawnfire, and she'd been asked to feed power to Kethra one day, when the mage that usually augmented the Healer-shaman was too exhausted to continue. Kethra put Starblade through purest agony that day, explaining only that this was a necessary part of Healing what had been done to him. Elspeth still felt uncomfortable with the memory. Although she repeated to herself again and again that it was for the better, she still felt like a torturer's apprentice for it.

We're pampered, we Heralds, she realized, stopping long enough to shift the weight of the saddle to her other shoulder, and shake some of the aches out of the arm that had balanced it. *We have everything we need taken care of for us. We live in prepared quarters, we have servants picking up after us. The Hawkbrothers have Vales; we have our rooms at the Collegium. They have* hertasi, *we have human servants. They have their food and clothing made for them; so do we. Neither of us have physical pleasures that are adequate compensation for what we do.*

She reached the foot of the tree that held her *ekele;* muted voices and faint splashing told her that the pool was occupied. She hung her saddle and hackamore over the railing at the bottom of the stair, and took herself up the staircase.

Darkwind had pointed out something about the Vales; that anyone with sufficient magic power could create one. They were really just very large hothouses, with a mage-barrier serving in place of glass. Nothing terribly exotic about a hothouse—

She pulled aside the door to her *ekele*, and looked down over the edge of the staircase for a moment. Kerowyn's grueling lessons in strategy and tactics caused her to realize something else as well.

The *ekeles* were not simply exotic love nests. They were based directly on the quite defensible treetop homes of the *tervardi*. How defensible they were could be demonstrated by the *ekeles* built outside the Vale; once the ladder to the ground had been pulled up, there was virtually no way to reach them. They were warded against fire, even, by set-spells and a transparent resin painted around the tree trunks well past two man-heights.

Even the *ekele* here could be made quite defensible simply by destroying the rope-and-truss suspended staircases, making them an excellent place to retreat if the Vale defenses were ever breached.

Gwena must have found her *hertasi* right away, for there was a tray of food waiting for her, and the herb tea in the pot was still hot and steeping. She helped herself to bread and meat, and collapsed onto her pillow-strewn pallet.

My people build walls. The Tayledras put themselves up in the trees. Differences in philosophy, really. More like the Heralds than like the ordinary folk of Valdemar. They think in terms of evasion, the way we do, rather than the stand-and-fight of the Guard.

She finished as much of her meal as she wanted at the moment, and stripped off her filthy, blood-speckled clothing. *Dyheli* blood, of course, and not of herself or Darkwind, but it was still going to be a major task to get it out. She could bleach it with magic of course, and she probably would, but that was a waste of mage-power.

Maybe she'd just shift over to scout clothing. It was more practical for all this woods running, anyway.

She wrapped a huge towel around herself and descended the staircase, heading for the spring. Occupied or no, she was going to use it. After all, she deserved a good soak as much as her visitors did; she'd just spent *her* day doing the same things they had done. She had earned a little luxury.

They all had.

Kethra & Rris

Chapter Nine

Vree stayed calm on Darkwind's shoulder after they passed the protections at the entrance to the Vale, even though until recently the bondbird had not wanted to enter the Vale itself. The rogue energies of the Heartstone had disturbed Vree badly, and the bondbirds of every other scout as well, but the additional shielding on the Stone seemed to be having some beneficial effect.

:Are you all right?: he asked Vree, just to be sure. *:We can turn around and leave if you want; I can hold the scouts' meeting at the* ekele *just as well as here. The mages will just have to climb a rope ladder instead of a staircase, and they'll all have to squeeze into my rooms. I think it would bear their weight.:*

Vree ducked his head a little, and yawned. *:Fine. Happy,:* he replied sleepily. Then, anxiously, *:Food soon?:*

:Soon,: he assured the bird. *:Quite soon. As soon as we get to the meeting.:* The other scouts would have hungry birds as well; the *hertasi* would have provided a selection of whole game birds and small mammals for the raptors, along with some kind of meal for the birds' bondmates.

For the first time in a very long time, this would be a meeting of day-watch scouts and scout-mages. Stormcloud would hold a similar meeting for those on night-watch. Yesterday Darkwind had asked them to gather because there was something important to be addressed. He hadn't specified what that was.

He had been the scouts' representative to the k'Sheyna Council during the most divisive period in their history—the period when Starblade, as directed by Mornelithe Falconsbane, was creating rifts between mages and nonmages, to weaken the Clan and make it easier for Falconsbane to destroy them. Darkwind had been willing to serve then, knowing that no one else had the edge he did, having his own father as chief of the Council. It was a bitter truth that his advantage then was not in currying favor, but knowing the other's weaknesses. He had sometimes been able to manipulate his father. Equally painful to recall was the fact that Starblade had done the same to him.

But now that he was devoting more time to mage-craft, he had less time to spend elsewhere. The scouts were his friends and charges, and with his attentions divided so, they could conceivably suffer for it.

It was time for a change. Now the question was whether or not he could get the others to agree with him. In general the kind of person who became a successful scout was *not* the kind who enjoyed being in a position of authority, or who relished dealing with those who were.

The best place for the gathering was the central clearing that had been used for the celebration, but that was closer to the Heartstone than Darkwind liked, shielding or no shielding. So he had asked them all to gather in the smaller clearing beneath the tallest tree in the Vale; the one that the scouts had used for dancing.

When he arrived, he found a near replication of the celebration, except that there was no music or dancing, the clothing was more subdued, and the conversation level was considerably quieter. Birds stood on portable perches, the exposed roots of trees, or in the branches, most of them with talons firmly in their dinner, the rest eyeing the mound of fur and feathers with a view to selecting something choice. Brighter mage-lights than those conjured for the celebration hung up in the branches, illuminating everything below with a clear yellow light, sunlike but for its intensity. Tayledras sprawled all over the clearing, eating, talking, or both. Darkwind did a quick mental tally and came up a few names short, as Vree yearned toward the heap of "dinner," making little plaintive chirping noises in the back of his throat.

:Hungry!: he urged his bondmate, as Darkwind tried not to laugh at the ridiculous sounds he made. The uninitiated were often very sur-

prised at the calls of raptorial birds; most of them, other than the defiant screams of battle and challenge, were very unimpressive chirps, clucks, and squeals. One species, the Harshawk, even croaked, sounding very like a duck with a throat condition. And owls hissed; not the kinds of things one expected to hear from the fierce hunters of the sky.

But silly sounds notwithstanding, Vree's hunger was very real and quite intense, and the bondbird had more than earned his dinner. Darkwind took him on the gauntlet and tossed him into the air, to give him a little height. Vree gave two great beats of his wings, reaching the lowest of the branches, then dove straight down at the pile, shouldering aside lesser and less-famished birds to get at a fat, choice duck. One of the Harshawks quacked indignantly as the tasty morsel was snatched right from under his talons, and two of the owls hissed angrily at being shouldered aside, but Vree ignored them all. The gyre heaved himself and his prize up into the air, and lumbered off to a nearby branch, where he mantled both wings over it and tore into it with his sharp, fiercely hooked beak.

"Here—" Shadowstar shoved sliced meat and bread at Darkwind, and snatched back her fingers, laughing, when he grabbed for it as if he were a hungry forestgyre himself. "Heyla! Sharpset, are we? In yarak?"

"Something like," he admitted, "It's been a long day, with a mage-duel at the end of it." He took a healthy bite of the food, and bolted it, suddenly realizing just how hungry *he* was. "Where are Summerstar and Lightwing? And—ah—" it took him a moment to remember the names of the mages that had been assigned to help the two scouts.

Shadowstar beat him to it. "Songlight and Winddance. Gone to get injuries tended again; they ran into Changewolves. Nothing serious."

A tentative Mindtouch from an unfamiliar source reassured him. *:Songlight here. We are mostly soaking bruises, Darkwind. I will stay in Mindtouch and relay to the others, if you like.:*

:Please,: he replied, taking a seat where he could see the others. *:This shouldn't take long.:*

He took out his dagger and rapped the hilt of it on the side of the tree; it rang hollowly, and got him instant attention and instant silence.

"I hope that most of you have guessed why I asked for these meetings—" he began.

Shadowstar stood up, interrupting him. "We pretty much figured it out," she said dryly, as the others nodded. "We were talking it all over before you got here. And we're all agreed that while we *don't* want to lose you as our leader, you deserve a rest, and you aren't going to get one at the rate you're going.''

Nods all around confirmed her words, and Darkwind felt an irrational surge of relief—both that the scouts still wanted him as leader, and that they were willing to let him go.

"Have any of you got a candidate in mind?" he asked. Surprisingly, it was one of the mages who answered him.

"Winterlight," the young man said promptly. "He did it before you had the position, and now that we aren't at each others' throats, he says he would be willing to take it again.''

Darkwind turned to his old friend, one of the oldest scouts in the Clan, raising an eyebrow inquisitively. Winterlight coughed and half-smiled. "I know the job," he answered, confirming the mage's words. "And since it's no longer the trial that it was—''

Darkwind grinned openly. "Then as far as I am concerned, the position is yours, my friend—if the rest agree, that is.''

He was going to open the meeting up to discussions, but the others forestalled him with their unanimous assent. Even the bondbirds seemed pleased with the choice. It was a good one; although he was not a mage, Winterlight seldom dyed his hair, and wore it long, as a mage did. So he looked like a mage, and he was a contemporary of Starblade and Iceshadow, which made him doubly acceptable to the Elders of the Council.

"As long as the night-watch agrees, then, it's yours," he told Winterlight happily. "And if they come up with a different candidate, you'll have to deal with that yourself.''

"If they come up with a different candidate, we'll split the duties," Winterlight replied immediately. "I've had my fill of dissension.''

Darkwind shrugged. "That's fine with me," he responded.

Winterlight smiled. "It wasn't just a rest that the youngsters decided you need," he said, in a confidential whisper. "I overheard one of them saying that you've been living like a sworn celibate and you needed to take that pretty Outlander off to a bower and—''

The rest of Winterlight's whispered suggestion made Darkwind flush so hard he was afraid he was glowing.

The rest of the scouts howled with laughter.

Winterlight just smiled enigmatically and asked if Darkwind needed to borrow any feathers. Darkwind deliberately turned his attention first to Vree to make sure the gyre was all right, then to his food, both to cover his confusion. When he looked beside him again, Winterlight was gone—

—but the Shin'a'in shaman Kethra had taken his place.

Oh, my. I wonder what I owe this *pleasure to.*

He brushed invisible crumbs from his tunic, self-consciously. Kethra was another source of confusion entirely for him, and not just because she was his father's lover.

Although that was a part of it—

"Is Father well?" he asked her, quickly.

She nodded, her bright green eyes as cool and unreadable as a falcon's, and smoothed her long black hair in back of her ears. She wore a bird-fetish necklace that sparkled in the magelight, and a braided length of cord adorned with feathers hung from her left temple.

"He is relatively well," she told him, as the assembled scouts collected their birds as if at an unspoken signal, and drifted not-too-casually off, back to their respective *ekeles*. There wasn't any people-food left, and the few carcasses that remained were taken by those who lived outside the Vale.

Kethra, however, was not leaving. "There are some things I need to discuss with you before I proceed to the next steps with him. They concern you, and your relationship to him."

"What about it?" he asked, more brusquely than he intended. Suddenly it seemed as if everyone in k'Sheyna was interested in his private life! *Am I to be allowed no thoughts to myself?* He glanced around the clearing, hoping for a distraction, but all of the scouts who had thronged the area had evaporated like snow in the summer sun, as if there was some kind of conspiracy between them and the Shin'a'in. She only pursed her lips and shook her head at him, allowing him no evasions.

"I need to know what you think of him now—and what you think of me." She fixed him with an unflinching gaze. "You know I am Starblade's lover."

He flushed, painfully embarrassed. "Yes," he said shortly. "And Iceshadow told me why—why it was necessary."

"What did he tell you?" she asked. "Humor me."

He averted his eyes for a moment, but she recaptured them. "Because so many of the things that were done to Father, and the magics that were cast to control him, were linked with sex, it has required sexually oriented Healing to undo them. That meant Father's Healer should be a lover as well."

Kethra nodded, and leaned back, her slender hands clasped around one knee. "That is quite true," she said quietly, "And in case you had wondered, I knew that was the case when I came here at Kra'heera's request. But had you also deciphered that I am your father's love as well as his lover, and he has become mine as well?"

Darkwind tried to look away in confusion, and found that he could not. "I—it had occurred to me," he admitted. "I am not blind, and your attitude toward one another shows."

She set her jaw with the perpetual half-smile that shaman always seemed to have. "And what do you think of that?" she asked bluntly, a question he had not expected. "What do you think of me, when you picture me in that role?"

Gods of my fathers. She would ask that. "I am confused," he said, as honestly as he could. "I do not know what to think. I admire you for yourself, shaman. You are a very strong, talented, and clever woman. You force my father to be strong again, as well. I think that he must need this, or you would not do it. I see you encourage him to go to his limits; you permit him to do for himself what he can. Yet you do not let him fall when you can steady him, and you match your talents with his when he cannot do something alone."

"You are describing a partner," Kethra said calmly. "An equal. Someone who is likely to go on being one for the foreseeable future."

He nodded, reluctantly, aware that his uneasiness was making him sweat.

"And this makes you ill at ease." She stated it as an observation rather than a question. "Uncomfortable in my presence whether or not I am with your father."

He sighed. "Yes, lady. It is not just because you are a shaman, though there is something to that."

Kethra chuckled. "Shaman make you nervous?"

Darkwind took a deep breath and chose his words carefully. "Shaman as a rule can make one uncomfortable by seeing more than one would like. That is not the whole of it, though. I do not know what to say to you, or how to treat you. You are the first of my father's lovers who has been a full partner since my mother's death. And when I am looking objectively at my memories, it seems to me that you have more patience and compassion than my mother had. And yet—"

"And yet, what of your loyalty to your true mother, now that I have come to replace her? Surely I seem an interloper. I suffer by comparison with your memory of her.''

"It is easy to regard someone who is dead as without peer,'' he told her candidly. "I have lost enough friends and loved ones to be aware of that.'' He cocked his head to one side, and nibbled his lower lip. This was, possibly, one of the oddest conversations he had ever taken part in. "Say this. I know that I can call you friend. I think if you will give me time, I can even come to call you more than that. Will this serve?''

Her smile widened, and she reached out a hand to clasp his, warmly. "It will serve,'' she told him. "Friend alone would have served; I am pleased you think of me that well. I was not sure, Darkwind. You are adept at hiding your true feelings—you have had need to, I know. That is not unique to Tayledras, Shin'a'in, or any other people. Trust me, we shaman need to hide our feelings ourselves sometimes, to struggle through pain.''

He shrugged. "We all have needed to hide true feelings here, to one extent or another. Events have made it necessary.''

She nodded. "Well, at least you and I have looked beneath the masks, and not run from what we have found.'' He smiled, impressed by her steadfast sense of humor. "Now the unpleasant news. Your father is still far from recovered. It will not take weeks or even months to cure him; it will be a matter of years.''

He took a deep breath and ran his hand through his hair. He felt his shoulders slumping, and remembered that it made a poor impression of strength, but he knew Kethra would see through any attempts to hide his emotions, either by words or body language. He closed his eyes. "I had thought so, but I had not liked to believe it. Father has always been so—strong. He has always recovered quickly from things. Are you quite certain of this?''

A deep, somewhat strained male voice spoke from behind them.

"You must believe it, my son,'' said Starblade. Darkwind jerked his head up and turned to face him. Starblade wore a thin, loose-cut resting-gown that Songwind . . . Darkwind had designed for him a decade ago. The Adept walked slowly into the clearing, and now that he knew the truth, Darkwind saw the traces of severe damage done to him, physically as well as mentally.

Starblade found a space beside Kethra and joined her. "You must. I am but a shadow of what I was. In fact,'' he chuckled as if he found the idea humorous, "I have considered changing my use-name to Starshadow. Except that we already have a Shadowstar, and that would be confusing for everyone.''

Darkwind clenched his hands. It wasn't easy hearing Starblade confess to weakness; it was harder hearing him admit to such profound weakness that he'd thought of altering his use-name. That implied a lasting condition, as when Songwind had become Darkwind, and sometimes an irreparable condition.

Starblade sat carefully down beside the shaman, and took her hand in his. His left hand—the one that Darkwind had pierced with his dagger as part of his father's freeing from Mornelithe Falconsbane. It showed a glossy, whitened scar a half-thumblength long now that the bandages had been removed. "I hope that you and I have reconciled our differences, my son," he said, as Darkwind tried not to squirm, "because I must tell you that I do not trust my decision-making ability any more than I can rely on my faded powers.''

Darkwind started to blurt out a protest; his father stopped him. "Oh, not for the small decisions, the everyday matters. But for the decisions that affect us all deeply—and the ones I made in the past—I do not feel that I can continue without another view to temper mine. In our Healings, I see my actions laid on bare earth, without order. As I am rebuilt, Kethra helps me to understand the motivations behind those actions, and reject those that Falconsbane engineered. It is a slow process, Darkwind. I do not *know* which of the decisions I have made were done out of pride, out of good judgment, or out of the direction of our enemies. I need you, my son; I need your vision, and I need your newly regained powers. More so: k'Sheyna needs them.''

Now Darkwind was numb. At the moment, all he could do was to nod. But this—this was frightening, inconceivable. Even at his worst, when Starblade had been trying to thwart him at every turn, he had been in control, he had been powerful. He had been someone who at least could be relied upon to know what he was doing, a bastion of strength. Full of certainty.

This was like hearing that the rock beneath the Vale was sand, and that the next storm could wash it away.

Kethra and Starblade both were waiting for some kind of response, so he got himself under some semblance of control, and gave them one. "What is it you want me to do?" he asked.

"I want your opinions, your thoughts," Starblade told him, his lined and weary face showing every day of his age. "I need them. The most pressing concern is the Heartstone; what do *you* think we should do about it? You know enough to make some educated guesses about it. We cannot stabilize it, not without help. I do not think that we can drain it, either. When we try, it fluxes unpredictably. And after you have given me your opinion, I want your help in doing whatever it is that we must to end this trouble—I want you to take *my* place as the key of the Adepts' circle."

He shook his head at that, violently. "Father, I can't. I haven't even begun to relearn all I've forgotten and—"

"The strength of your will and youth will counter that lack of practice," Kethra said, interrupting him. "The key need not be the most experienced Adept, but he must be the strongest, and you are that."

Starblade coughed, then settled himself, fixing Darkwind with a sincere look. "I will explain it to you in this light, then. Your mother and I raised you to be a strong and responsible person, Scout or Mage. Now, the strength that I taught you has been taken from me. You are at least in part the vessel of my old personality. I would appreciate relearning what I was from you, and learning your strength."

Given a choice, he would have told them it was impossible; turned and fled from the Vale, back to his *ekele*. But he had no choice, and all three of them knew that. He bowed to their will. "If that is truly what you want," he said unhappily. "If it is, then I shall."

"Thank you," Starblade said, simply. As Kethra stood up, he rose to his feet to place one hand on his son's shoulder. "This—confession has cost me a great deal, but I think it has gained me more. I have given over wanting you to be a copy of me, and I wish that Wintermoon and I had not drifted so far apart that I cannot say those same words to him and be believed. Perhaps in time, he will not be lost to me. I do not wish you to be anything but yourself, Darkwind. Whatever comes of this, it will have happened because you went to the limit of your abilities, and not the sum of my expectations. In all that happens, I shall try to be your friend as well as your father."

With those words, which surprised him more than anything else that had happened tonight, Starblade turned and walked slowly back into the shadows, with Kethra at his side.

Vree swooped down off his perch, and backwinged to a new one beside his bondmate. He swiveled his head, turning it upside down to stare at Darkwind from a new angle, as only a raptor would do. Hard to manage, with his crop bulging as if the bird had swallowed a child's ball. And possibly the silliest pose any bird could take.

:*Sleepy,*: he announced. :*Sleep now?*:

Darkwind held out his gauntlet automatically, and Vree swiveled his head back and hopped onto his bondmate's wrist. :*I think so,*: he replied, absently, all the while wondering if, after all this, he still *could* get to sleep.

He flailed up out of slumber, arms windmilling wildly, with sparkling afterimages of confused dream-scenes still in his mind and the impression of someone shaking him.

Someone *was* shaking him. "What?" he gasped. "Who?" The hammock-bed beneath him felt strange, the proportions of the room all wrong.

Light flared, and he blinked, dazzled; the shaker was Sathen, the *hertasi* who usually tended Starblade's *ekele* for him. The little lizard was holding a lit lantern in one claw, with the other on Darkwind's shoulder. And the proportions of the room were wrong because he was not in his own *ekele*, he was in Starblade's, in the guest quarters. Vree dozed on, oblivious, on a block-perch set into the wall, one foot pulled up under his breast-feathers and his head hunched down so far there was nothing visible in the soft puff of white and off-white but a bit of beak.

I need to find Father a new bondbird, came the inconsequential thought, as Sathen waited patiently for him to gather his wits and say something sensible.

"What?" he obliged, finally. "What's wrong?"

"Trouble," the little *hertasi* whispered. "Trouble-call it is, from Snowstar. Needing mage. Needing *mages*," he corrected. "More than one."

Marvelous. Well, I'm probably the least weary. "What for?" he asked. It couldn't be for combat; by the time he reached Snowstar's patrol area, any combat would have been long since resolved. He reached for his clothing and pulled on his breeches. *Well, at least this means that someone else will have to take our patrol in the morning. And I don't have to be the one to decide who it is.*

"Basilisk," Sathen said, his nostrils closing to slits as he said it. The lizard-folk did not like basilisks—not that anyone did, but basilisks seemed to prefer *hertasi* territories over any others.

Darkwind groaned, and pulled his tunic over his head, thinking as quickly as his sleep-fogged mind would permit. "Go leave a message for Winterlight that—ah—Wingsister Elspeth and I went out to deal with the basilisk, and he'll have to get someone else on day-watch to cover for us. Then go wake up the Outlander and tell her I'll be coming for her in a moment."

Fortunately Elspeth's *ekele* was not that far from Starblade's. She wasn't going to like being awakened out of a sound sleep—but then, who did? *She took the oath,* he told himself a little smugly as he pulled on his boots. He splashed water from the basin Sathen had left onto his face to wake himself up. *She might as well find out what it means.*

Besides, being shaken awake in the middle of the night might also shake up that attitude problem of hers. And once she saw a basilisk for herself, he had a shrewd notion that she might start paying better attention to him when he told her something. Particularly about the dangers that lurked out in the Uncleansed Lands, and how you couldn't always deal with them combatively.

This would be a good exercise in patience for her, as well; now that he thought about it, he realized he couldn't have *planned* this encounter more effectively.

Other than staging it by daylight instead of darkness.

For a basilisk could not be moved by magic power—it grounded attacks out on itself, sent the power out into the earth, and ignored the attackers. And it could not be moved by force.

It could *only* be dealt with by persuasion. And a great deal of patience, as Elspeth would likely discover the hard way.

He took the gracefully curved stairs down to the ground, jumping them two at a time, suppressing the urge to whistle.

This promised to be very, very entertaining.

It was not just any basilisk. It was a basilisk with a belly full of eggs.

Snowstar held his torch steady, no doubt trusting in the cold to keep the creature torpid. It blinked at them from the hollow it had carved for itself in the rocky bank of the stream, but remained where it was. Torchlight flickering over the thing's head and parts of its body did nothing to conceal how hideous the poor creature was.

"Havens, that thing is ugly," Elspeth said in a fascinated whisper. Basilisks came in many colors—all the colors of mud, from the dull red-brown of Plains-mud, to the dull brown-black of forest-loam mud, and every muddy variation in between. This one was the muddy gray-green of clay. With the face of a toad, no neck to speak of, the body of an enormous lizard, a dull ash-gray frill running down the head and the length of the spine and tail, a mouth full of poisonous half-rotted teeth, and a slack jaw that continuously leaked greenish drool, it was definitely not going to appeal to anything outside of its own kind. And when you added to that the sanitary habits of a maggot, and breath that would make an enraged bull keel over a hundred paces away, you did not have anything that could be considered a good neighbor.

And that was when it was torpid. As soon as the sun arose, and warmed the thing's sluggish blood, it would go looking for food. It wasn't fussy. Anything would do, living or dead, so long as it was meat.

But as soon as the blood warmed up, the brain would warm up, too—and when that happened, nothing nearby would be safe. Not that the basilisk was clever; it wasn't—it wasn't fast either, or a crafty hunter. It didn't have to be. It simply had to feel hunger and look around for food, and everything within line-of-sight would freeze, held in place by the peculiar mental compulsion it emitted.

Then it could simply stroll up to its chosen dinner, and eat it.

As Snowstar explained this to Elspeth, Darkwind created a heatless mage-light and sent it into the basilisk's shelter, so he could get a better idea of how big it was. Elspeth shuddered in revulsion as the light revealed just how phenomenally hideous the creature was.

"Are we going to kill it now?" she asked; Darkwind had the feeling that she wanted to get this over with quickly. Well, he didn't blame her. Being downwind of a basilisk was a lot like being downwind of a charnel pit.

Snowstar answered for him. "Gods of our fathers, no!" he exclaimed. "If you think it stinks *now*, you don't want to be within two days' ride of a dead one! That's assuming we *could* kill it. It has three hearts, that warty skin is tougher than twenty layers of boiled hide, and it can live for a long time with what we'd consider a fatal wound. It can live without two legs, both eyes, and half its face. Altogether. Assuming you could get near enough to it to take out an eye. Personally, I'd rather not try."

Elspeth shook her head, not in disbelief, but in amazement. "What about magic?"

"Magic doesn't work on them," Darkwind told her, as he reckoned up the length of the beast and judged it to be about the size of three horses, not counting the tail. "It just passes around them and goes straight into the ground. *We* should have shields like that! An amazing animal.''

"You sound like you admire it," Elspeth replied in surprise.

He shrugged, and walked around a little, to see if the basilisk noticed him, or if it had gone completely torpid. "In a way I do," he said, noting with satisfaction that the creature's eyes tracked on him. "It is said that they were created by one of the Great Mages, not as a weapon, but as a way of disposing of the carcasses of those creatures that *were* weapons, that even dead were too dangerous to touch and too deadly to leave about. Nothing else will eat a dead cold-drake, for instance." His brief survey complete, he returned to Elspeth's side. "They weren't supposed to be able to breed, but neither were a lot of other creatures. Most of their eggs are infertile, but there are one or two that are viable now and again."

He turned to Snowstar. The scout wiped the back of his hand across his watering eyes, and stood a little straighter. Snowstar was one of the youngest of the scouts; Darkwind was grateful that he had known enough to send for help and not attempt to move the basilisk himself. It *could* be done without magic, but the odds of success, especially in the uncertain weather of fall or spring, were not good. "Have you found any place for us to put her?" he asked.

"Yes, but it's not as secure as I'd like," the scout replied, wiping his eyes again. The wind had turned, and the fumes were—potent. Darkwind's eyes had started to burn a few moments ago, and Snowstar had been here for some time. Small wonder he had watering eyes. "I've got a rock-bottomed gully along this stream; the sides are too steep to climb and there's always lots of things falling into it to die. The only problem is that the mouth of the valley is open to the stream, and I couldn't see a way to close it off."

"Isn't there a swamp somewhere off that way?" Darkwind asked, waving vaguely in the direction where he thought he sensed water.

"Can you get the thing that far?" Snowstar asked, incredulously. "If you can, that would be perfect. There's plenty for it to eat, no *hertasi* like it because it's full of sulfur springs, and the sulfur's enough to make sure any eggs it lays won't hatch."

"If we can get it moving, we can get it that far," Darkwind told him. "The problem is going to be getting it moving without getting it worked up enough to think about being angry or frightened. If it's either, it'll start trying to fascinate everything within line of sight."

"Right." Snowstar spread his hands. "I'll leave that up to you. Get it moving and I'll guide you to the nearest finger of the swamp and make sure nothing interferes with you on the way."

"That will do." Darkwind studied the hideous beast, trying to determine whether it was better to lure it out of its rudimentary den, or force it out.

Force it out, he decided at last. He didn't think that the beast was going to take any kind of bait at the moment.

"Here's what we're going to do," he said, turning to Elspeth, who still watched the basilisk with a kind of repulsed fascination. "It's comfortable and it feels secure in that den. You and I are going to have to make it feel uncomfortable and insecure, and make it come out. Once it's out, it will try to go back in again; we'll have to prevent that. Then we'll have to herd it in the direction we want it to go."

Elspeth licked her lips and nodded, slowly. "We use magic, I presume?"

"That, or mind-magic, or a combination of the two," he told her. He yawned as he finished the sentence, and hoped he wasn't going to be too fuddled from lack of sleep to carry this off. Elspeth looked as if she felt about the same. "Got any ideas about what might drive it out?"

She leaned back against a tree trunk and frowned at the beast. "Well, what would drive you or me out of bed? Noise?"

Interesting idea. "That's one nobody I know of has tried." He thought for a moment. "If it were warmer, we could lure her out with an illusion of food, but she isn't hungry in the semi-hibernation she's in right now. Heat and cold in her cave—no, too hot and she'll just wake up more, and we don't want that. Too cold and she'll go torpid."

"How about rocks in her bed?" Elspeth hazarded. "Sharp, pointy ones. Maybe combine it with noise."

"Good. Good, I like that plan. It should irritate her without making her angry, and if we make her uncomfortable she won't want to go back in there." He scratched his head. "Now, which do you want? Rocks or noise?"

"Rocks," she said, surprising him. "I've got an idea."

Since he already had a notion about the noises that might irritate the basilisk, that suited him very well. He had been afraid that Elspeth wouldn't think herself capable of manifesting good-sized stones, but evidently she already had a solution in mind.

"Do it, then," he said, shortly, and concentrated all his attention on a point just behind the basilisk's body. The one thing he *didn't* want to do was frighten her—just make her leave her lair. If he frightened her, she might be aroused enough to set all her abilities working, and that would do them no good at all.

Fine thing if I met my end as a late-night snack for a foul-breathed, incredibly stupid monster.

He already knew how some pure, high-pitched sounds irritated wolves and birds; he reasoned the same might well be true of this beast. It just had to be loud enough and annoying enough.

Dissonance, he thought suddenly. That might work even better; two pure tones out of tune with each other.

He'd done this before as a kind of game, when he was just learning very fine control. He'd gotten good enough that he had been able to produce recognizable voices out of the air. Producing pure tones wasn't all that hard, it just took a lot of energy.

He started near the top of the human-audible scale, figuring to go up if he had to. It took him a moment to recall the trick of it, but when he got it, Snowstar jumped as a nerve-shattering squeal rang out from the basilisk's lair. The young scout clapped both hands over his ears, his expression pained. Darkwind wished he had that luxury. *He* had to listen to his creation in order to control it.

When he glanced out of the corner of his eye at Elspeth, he saw she had blocked both her ears with her fingers, and her brow was creased with concentration.

His sounds didn't seem to be having any effect, although already he noticed the basilisk shifting her weight, as if she found her position uncomfortable. He raised the notes another half step and waited to see the effect.

Another increment followed that, until he had gone up a full octave, and still he was not getting the reaction he wanted, although the monster turned occasionally to snap at the empty air, as if trying to rid her lair of its noisy visitor.

Finally, he took the sounds up past the range where even *he* could hear it, and he had one of the longest ranges in the Clan. Elspeth had taken her fingers out of her ears two steps earlier, and Snowstar had taken his hands down before that, with an expression of deep gratitude. This was the range that animals other than man could hear; he wasn't about to give up this plan until he'd passed the sounds that bats used.

And from the look on Elspeth's face, *she* wasn't going to give in until she had produced rocks the size of small ponies.

Neither of them had to go that far, although whether it was Darkwind's dissonant howls or Elspeth's stones that finally tipped the balance, he couldn't tell. The basilisk had been snapping and shifting uncomfortably for some time when he changed the tone again, and the basilisk came pouring out of her lair, burbling with anger and frustration.

She stood there for a moment, wavering between the discomfort of the lair, and the exposure of the outdoors. If she dove back in again, they might never get her out.

Before Darkwind could say anything, Elspeth solved the problem for him. He sensed her grabbing the underlying web of earth-energies at the mouth of the half-dug lair and yanking.

The lair collapsed in on itself, leaving the basilisk nowhere to go.

The monster rumbled deep in her chest, and turned, heading downstream and away from them, into the darkness. "That will do for a few furlongs, but then we're going to have to turn her out of this stream when it forks," Snowstar said, as the basilisk plodded out of the range of his torch and Darkwind's mage-light.

"Don't worry, I think we can deal with it," he said, breaking into a trot along the graveled streamside, sending his mage-light winging on ahead until it illuminated the unlovely rump of the basilisk. She was moving at a pretty fair pace; he'd had no idea they could move that fast. In fact—was he going to be able to keep up with her?

Elspeth supplied his answer, as she and the Companion trotted up alongside and she offered him a hand up. "Gwena can carry two for a while," she said. He took her at her word and got himself up behind her. "Are you going to use that sound of yours to drive that thing?" she asked once he was settled and Gwena was bounding after the tail of the monster.

"Yes," he said—shortly, as it was difficult to speak when bouncing along on the rump of a trotting mount. "That—was—the—idea—"

:I have another idea,: Elspeth said by Mindspeech. :It's a reptile, which means it can probably sense heat very well. Let's create a ball of warmth about her size, and lure her along with it. Keep it a couple of lengths ahead of her until she's where we want her, then dissipate it. What do you think?:

He switched to Mindspeech as well. :That is an excellent idea. This is going to be great news when we get back to the Vale,: he told her, and smiled at the glow of well-earned self-congratulation that met his words. :*You've helped uncover something entirely new, and very useful to us. The other forms of driving these monsters have all been much riskier. You are going to make your Clansibs quite happy with this news.*:

For that matter, she was making *him* quite happy. The basilisk responded to guidance-by-noise and the heat lure beautifully. They were going to be returning to the Vale much sooner than he had thought.

Much sooner, and flushed with success. Not a bad combination.

Not a bad combination at all.

Everyone wanted to hear about the basilisk drive. This was the first time that a basilisk had been moved with fewer than a dozen people and with no injuries. Small wonder that the Vale had been astir when they returned, and that the mages had all wanted to hear the story in detail. It seemed that if he and Elspeth hadn't used unorthodox tactics because there had only been two of them, they would never have budged the thing. And if Snowstar hadn't been so inexperienced in the ways of basilisks, he'd never have called for just a pair of mages.

"You weren't lucky," Iceshadow finally said. "Snowstar was relatively lucky because he got you. But you two—you were quite clever. Or am I being overly optimistic?"

Darkwind laughed tiredly, and drank another full beaker of cold water—the aftereffect of all that basilisk stench was incredible dehydration. He and Elspeth together had drained a small lake, it seemed, and they were still thirsty.

"No, we were bright enough that if we hadn't been able to budge the old girl with methods that wouldn't enrage her, we would have called for help," he assured the Adept. "I pledge you that. I don't trust anything that can entrance you to the point that you let yourself be swallowed whole."

When the others finally left them in peace, Darkwind realized that he was much too keyed up to sleep, at least not without a long soak in hot water to relax him.

He stood up abruptly, catching Elspeth by surprise; she jumped when he moved and looked up at him with round eyes.

"I need a bath and a soak," he said, "And the pool under your *ekele* is the nearest two-layered one I know of. Would it disturb you if I used it?"

"Would it disturb you if I joined you?" she asked.

At first, he thought she was making some kind of an overture, but a moment of reflection told him that she couldn't possibly be doing anything of the sort. She was just as tired as he was—even if she wasn't bruised from riding for furlongs on the sharp and protruding hipbones of her Companion. Even if the two of them had been ready to tear one another's clothes off in a fit of unbridled lust, neither of them would have had the energy to do so. No, she was just being polite.

But at least she wasn't as shy as she had been. And she was still an attractive woman. There might be some hope after all.

"It surely won't disturb me," he told her, and offered her a polite hand to help her rise. "In fact, I doubt very much if it would disturb me to share a pool with—"

He stopped himself before he said "with that basilisk"; realizing at the last moment that the comment could be construed as saying that he did not find her attractive. Which was not the case, at all.

"—half the Clan," he concluded. "All I want is to get this stink off and soak my muscles until I can sleep."

"Good plan," she said, and smiled. "I'll make you a bargain. If you find some of that fruit drink, I'll get soap, robes and towels from my treehouse."

"I'll take that," he said instantly. Elspeth disappeared into the greenery while he sought one of the storage areas, and dug out a tiny keg of a peculiar, mineral-rich drink Elspeth had gotten very fond of. Normally he didn't care much for the stuff, but when he was as parched and exhausted as he was now, he downed it with the same enthusiasm as she did.

Keg under one arm and a pair of turned wooden mugs in the other hand, he retraced his path and followed in Elspeth's wake. When he arrived at the pool, he found that she had been as good at keeping her word as he. There was strongly herb-scented soap beside the lower of the two heated pools, and towels and robes hanging nearby on a couple of branches, with one small mage-light over each pool providing just enough light to see by.

Elspeth was already in the upper soaking pool. He left the keg and mugs beside it as she waved at him indolently from the steam, then he stripped and plunged straight into the lower pool.

It took three full soapings before the last of the stench was gone and he felt clean again. By then he was more than ready for a mug and a long, soothing soak.

"I think I took all my skin off," Elspeth complained languidly from her end of the pool as he slipped across the barrier between the pools and into the hotter water of the second. "I scrubbed and scrubbed—every time I thought I was clean, I could still smell that thing."

"Worse than skunk or polecat," he agreed. She seemed very relaxed for the first time since he had met her. "Did you see how much Ice-shadow liked that idea of yours, moving the basilisk with noise?"

"But it was your idea to use pure-tones in dissonance," she said immediately. "I had just thought of using volume, or maybe make it sound like the cave was falling in."

He allowed himself to feel pleased about that part of it. "Well, I guess that I'm going to have to admit that you *are* right about trying new things even in magic. Just because they aren't the way we've always done something, that doesn't mean new ideas aren't going to work. Change comes to the Vales; quite a concept."

She laughed heartily. "I thought I'd never hear you say that! But I have to make a confession to you, though. I *have* been pushing you, just because you were being such a—mud-turtle about things. Not wanting to try *anything* new. But—well, now I know that there's good reasons why some things aren't done in the Vales and in this one in particular. Hydona's been explaining things to me. . . ."

Her voice trailed off, and he thought she was finished, until she spoke up again. "You know, Hydona reminds me a great deal of Talia."

That old friend of hers. The one that's some kind of aide to her mother, and not the one that's the weapons teacher.

"In what way?" he asked.

She waved steam away from her face. "She made me give her a promise back when I was a child—that I would never simply dismiss anything she told me just because I didn't want to hear it, or that I was angry at her or anything else. That I would always go away and think about it for a day. Then if I couldn't agree with *any* of it, I had the right to be angry, but if I could see that she was right in at least some of what she'd said, I would have to come back to her and we'd talk about it as calmly as we could."

Well, if that isn't an opening chance to talk about her attitude—

"I know we don't know one another as well as you and Talia do," he said tentatively, "but could you grant me that same promise as a Wing-sib?"

"Oh, dear," she said, her voice full of ironic chagrin. "Been a bitch, have I?"

He wanted to laugh, and decided against it. Still, he smiled. "Not exactly a bitch. But your attitude hasn't been helping me teach you. That was one reason why, when the gryphons volunteered to help, I agreed."

"Attitude?" she asked; her voice was carefully controlled to the point of being expressionless. Not a good sign.

"Attitude," he repeated, getting ready for an outburst. "You're very self-important, Elspeth. Very aware of your own importance, and making sure everyone else is aware of it, too. Take what you just said, about being a bitch. You laughed about it; deep down, you thought it was funny. You think you are so important it doesn't matter if you're offending those around you. You just make some perfunctory apology, smile and laugh, and that's that. But nothing has really changed."

She was quite silent over there in the steam, but he wondered if he'd just felt the temperature of the water rise by a bit. That silence was not a good sign, either.

"The truth is, Elspeth, right now you're an enormously talented liability." She wasn't going to like *that*, one bit. "I never heard of your land, outside of something vague from the old histories. You could be a bondslave from Valdemar, and we would be treating you the same as we are now. Your title doesn't matter, your country doesn't matter, and your people don't matter. Not to us."

Little waves lapped against him as she shifted, but she remained silent.

"What does matter is that you did help us; for that, we made you a Wingsib. Because we made you a Wingsister, you became entitled to training. *Not* because of a crown, and not because of a title. Not even because you asked us. Because you are part of the Clan. And what's more, the only ones willing to train you were myself and the gryphons. Everyone else has more important matters to attend to."

That wasn't precisely the truth, but it was close enough that it might shake her up a bit.

"So." No doubt about it, she was angry. "I don't matter, is that it?"

"No, that's not it. You matter; your title doesn't." He hoped she could see the difference. "So you might as well stop walking around as if there was a crown on your head. Kings don't mean much, out here. Anyone can call himself a king. Having the power to *enforce* authority—

that's something else again. Until you have that, you'd best pay a little closer attention to the way you treat those around you because we are not impressed.''

"Oh, really?'' He sensed an angry retort building.

But then, she said nothing. Nothing at all. He tensed, waiting for an outburst that never came. He wondered what she was thinking.

Finally she yawned and stretched, water dribbling from her arms.

"I'm tired,'' she said, yawning again. "Too tired to think or react sensibly. I'll sleep on what you just said.''

"Please do, and carefully, Elspeth. More could depend on it than amiable learning conditions.'' He looked down and sighed. "I do like you, and would prefer not to spend my time with you deciphering what you really mean under the royal posturing.''

She rose, surprising him, and hoisted herself out of the pool, wrapping a towel around her wet hair, then bundling one of the thick, heavy robes around herself. She turned and looked down at him.

"You've said quite a bit,'' she told him quietly. "And I'm not sure what to think. Except that I'm certain you weren't being malicious. So— good night, Darkwind. If there's anything to say, I'll say it tomorrow.''

She gathered her dignity about her like the robe, and walked off into the darkness, leaving him alone.

The Heartstone

Chapter
Ten

Twice Darkwind tried to wake up; twice he turned over to climb out of
bed. Twice he closed his eyes again, and fell right back to sleep. And
since no one came to fetch him, and there was hardly ever any noise
around Starblade's *ekele*, he slept until well past midmorning unaware
of how long he'd been dreaming.

When he finally awakened and *stayed* awake, he lay quietly for a moment, feeling confused and a bit disoriented. The light shouldn't have
been coming in at that angle. . . .

Then it finally occurred to him why it was doing so.

I haven't overslept like this in I can't think how long.

Feeling very much as if he'd done something overly self-indulgent, he
snatched his newly-cleaned clothing from a shelf and hastily donned it.
There was no one in the *ekele* except Vree, who was still dozing. He
vaulted the stairs to the ground and hurried down to Elspeth's *ekele* only
to find her gone.

He was both embarrassed and annoyed. Annoyed that she had left
without him; embarrassed because she'd needed to. She had at least left
a note.

It looked like gibberish, until he realized that she had apparently spelled things the way they sounded to her.

Takt tu Starblaad n Winrlit sins we r not owt. Taa sed tu werk on bordr majik wit grifons. We r al waading fer u wen u waak up.

It took him a moment to puzzle out that she had checked with Starblade and Winterlight about what she and he should do since they weren't on patrol. He surmised that they had both asked her to work on border protections under the gryphons' tutelage. All three of them were expecting Darkwind whenever he got there. She hadn't even told him *where* they were working. They could be anywhere.

Once again, as with everything Elspeth did, he had mixed feelings. Pleased that she had taken it upon herself to find something useful to do; miffed that she hadn't consulted him.

He snatched a quick meal, and wondered if he should try to find Winterlight. Presumably the scout leader would know where they were.

Then it occurred to him that he hadn't bothered to ask the most obvious "person." Vree. The forestgyre was still back at Starblade's *ekele*. Undoubtedly, recovering from the way he'd stuffed himself yesterday.

He sent out a mental call, and was rewarded within a few moments by a flash of white through the high branches. He held out his arm, and Vree winged in, diving down to the ground and pulling up with spread wings in a head-high stall. He dropped delicately down onto Darkwind's wrist.

The gyre chirped at him, and inclined his head for a scratch. *:Messages?:* he asked.

:From Horse,: Vree replied. Horse—with the mental emphasis of importance—could only mean the Companion.

Vree's intelligence was limited; he had to get messages in pieces. *:Who is the message from Horse about?:*

:Female and Big Ones.: Vree leaned into the scratch, his eyes half-closed in pleasure.

:What is the message?: He had long ago given up being impatient with this slow method of finding things out. It was simply the way Vree and every other bondbird worked.

:At magic-place,: Vree replied.

Well, he *wouldn't* have to ask Vree to track them down. Good thing, too, since Vree was still drowsy from a long night of digestion. He'd be so fat Darkwind wouldn't be able to find his keelbone if he was fed that way all the time. Interesting, though, that the Companion could talk to Darkwind's bird. He wasn't surprised, but it wasn't something that Gwena had shown she could do—or wanted to do—before this.

And he wasn't going to have to leave the Vale, which was a bit of a relief. His backside was still a little sore and stiff from the ride yesterday.

:Do you need to leave the Vale?: he asked Vree. After all, the poor bird had been in here for more than a day. The gyre turned his head upside down as he considered the question and his bondmate.

:No,: Vree decided. *:Head not itch.:* That was how he had described the way that rogue powers of the Heartstone had affected him; that his head had itched. It had taken Darkwind a while before he had figured out that the bird meant *inside* his head, not outside.

:Go back to Starblade's, then,: Darkwind told him. *:Or hunt, if you want—just don't go too far from the Vale. I'm going to the magic-place and I don't want you in there. Your head would* really *itch.:*

:Yes,: Vree agreed, and half-spread his wings, waiting for Darkwind to launch him. The scout gave him a toss, and the gyre gained height rapidly, disappearing into the branches above.

No need to guess what the "magic-place" was: the Practice Ground. It was entirely possible to direct the border defenses from in there, although it would require great patience and careful shielding to keep the Heartstone from affecting whatever the three of them did in there.

Maybe that was the idea.

It'll certainly test the integrity of my shielding. And if I can shield against the Stone and work at the same time—I just might be ready to help handle the Stone myself. The gods only know that there'll be no peace for k'Sheyna until I do.

Well, if they were waiting for him, they were probably wondering if he'd fallen down a well or something. He'd better go prove he was still alive.

He had heard a mutter of conversation before he crossed the pass-through in the barrier that divided the rest of the Vale from the Practice Ground. The sudden silence that descended as he appeared told him that *he* had been the topic of discussion between Elspeth and the gryphons. He suppressed a surge of irritation at being talked *about*.

"Sorry I slept so late," he said, trying not to let his irritation show. "What are we doing?"

"Consssstructing ward-off ssspellsss," Hydona said mildly, as if she hadn't snapped her beak shut in mid-syllable the moment he came into view. "Elssspeth had one of the *hertasssi* look in on you, but you were sssleeping ssso deeply we decsssided you musssst need the ressst."

His irritation faded a little. At least they had checked on him before doing anything on their own. This particular task was not something he would have expected for the four of them. Ward-offs were simple things, but they had to be constructed and set carefully, another task of patience. Intended to discourage rather than hurt, ward-offs were the first line of defense on the border; the more intelligent the creature that encountered one, the more likely it was to be affected by it. A basilisk, for instance, would not be deterred by one, but a Changewolf probably would, unless it happened to be very hungry. Humans certainly would be; especially wanderers, peddlers, and the like—people who had crossed into Tayledras lands by accident.

Treyvan roused his golden-edged crest and refolded his wings with the characteristic rasp of feathers sliding across feathers. "You and I arrre not to make ward-offsss. Ssstarblade hasss a tasssk forrr usss; to move ley-linessss," he said. "We work while Elsspeth watchesss. We are to diverrrt them to the node beneath the lairrr, sssevering them from the Heartssstone."

Darkwind frowned. That came under the heading of "tedious and necessary," as well. But anything to do with the Heartstone had its own share of danger involved. Certainly this was *not* beneath his abilities. It was along the lines of doing his share to work with the imbalanced Stone.

"Do you have any idea why we're doing this?" he asked.

"Thessse are minorrr linesss," Treyvan told him. "Ssstarrblade wantsss all the minorrr linesss rrremoved, to sssee if they can be, and to sssee if thisss weakensss the Ssstone."

"Hmm. It could well be that once the minors are removed, the majors could be split into minors, and diverted in the same manner to other nodes, perhaps other Heartstones if there were any near."

Treyvan gave him one of those enigmatic, purely-gryphonish expressions of his, the one that always looked to Darkwind like "I know something you would dearly like to know." He spoke slowly. "It isss not imposssible."

Darkwind nodded, watching Elspeth with his Othersight; taking note of how she built the ward-off layer by layer, with the deft and delicate touch of a jeweler.

Showing no signs of impatience. And no signs of Attitude, either.

And that irritated him all over again. Why couldn't she just have been reasonable in the first place?

Because no one put things to her in a way she understood, he reminded himself. *She's as much an alien here as the gryphons, no matter how comfortable she looks or how well she seems to fit in.*

And she did look as if she fit in, wearing the clothing he'd had made for her instead of those glaring white uniforms or the barbarian getup she'd had in her packs. She didn't quite look Tayledras, not with that hair—but until she spoke, no one would know she was not one of the Tayledras allies.

Get your mind on the task, Darkwind, and off the female.

"Hasn't anyone tried this line-diverting with the Stone before?" He couldn't believe that they hadn't. It seemed like the logical sort of thing to do.

"Yesss," the gryphon said, switching his tail restlessly. "But it did not worrk. And not asss we will be worrrking. Parrrtially the Sstone ressissted having the linesss taken; and parrrtially it rrreclaimed them within a day. We will give the linesss a new anchorrr, fixing them in place, rrrather than letting them find theirr own anchorrr. Beforrre, they werrre allowed to drrrift, and the Sstone rrreclaimed them."

Elspeth put the final lock on the ward-off, and sent it away to settle into its place on the border. In his mind's eye it drifted away like a gossamer scarf blown by a purposeful wind—or a drift of fog with a mind of its own.

"I'm done," she announced, dusting off her hands. "Your turn." She took a seat nearby, her face alight with interest. "I thought these lines were like rivers or something. I didn't know you could change where they went."

"Generally only the little ones," Darkwind told her as he stretched. "At least, the major lines take all the mages of a Clan to reroute. That's something we do when we start a Vale; we find a node or make one, then relocate all the nearest big lines to it, so that we can drain the wild magic of an area into the Heartstone."

"It isss much like crrreating a riverrrrbed before therrre isss a rrriver," Hydona said. "When the waterrr comess, it will follow the courssse laid forrr it. Ssso isss the wild magic to the grrreaterrr linesss. The grrreaterrr

linesss have theirrr bankssss widened. The unsssettled magicsss join
theirrr flow.''

"I can see how that would make sense. And when you leave, you
drain the magic from the Stone—along a new-made set of 'riverbeds,' I
assume,'' Elspeth said, with a measure of surety in her voice.

"That, or a series of reservoirs are made temporarily.''

"Then what?'' she asked Darkwind.

"Then we sever the lines and let them drift back into natural patterns,
and physically remove the Stone,'' he told her as he concentrated more
of his attention on the complex of shields and probes he would need to
handle his task. Shields against the Heartstone, some set to deflect energy away, some to resist, sensory probes to know what it was doing.
Heartstones were not precisely *aware*, they certainly weren't thinking
creatures, yet they were alive in a sense and normally tractable. But this
one was no longer normal.

"But didn't you redirect the greater ley-lines in the first place to get
rid of wild magic?'' she asked, puzzled. "Or am I missing something?''

At least this time she didn't phrase it in a way that made me sound like I
didn't know what I was talking about.

"We did—'' This juggling of preparations and explanations was going
to get him into trouble if he wasn't very careful, which, again, was
probably Treyvan's intention. In a job like this, "trouble'' had the potential of being very serious indeed. The gryphons were merciless in
their testing. "We do. And by the time we leave, it's gone, changed into
a stable form. The magic we're draining . . . isn't in its natural state.''

Set the shield just—so—got to be able to sense through it without getting
blinded if the Stone surges— "It doesn't belong here, and certainly not in
a random state. Once we finish, the only thing left is the natural magic
flow.''

"Ah, so you take down the Stone and leave, and everything goes back
to the way it was before the Mage Wars.'' Both he and Hydona had
already explained the natural flow of magic energy to her; how it was
created by living things, how it collected in ley-lines and reservoirs in
the same way that water collected in streams and lakes.

"Probably not exactly, but at least a human can live here without fear
that his children will have claws or two heads. And there won't be any
other Changecreatures there either, unless they manage to get past our
lands somehow.'' *I'll need a secondary shield to slap between the end of the*
severed line and the Stone. . . . "And when we leave, we take the inno-

cent or harmless mage-created creatures with us, so *they* don't have to fear the full-humans who inevitably arrive."

Her face changed subtly at that, as if it was something that hadn't occurred to her until that moment. He would have liked to know what she was thinking.

Well, time enough for that, later.

"I would like you behind as many shields as you can put up," he told her. "I do not know what is likely to happen; there has been so much work with the Stone that it may have changed the way it is likely to react. Can you watch through my 'eyes,' or Treyvan's?"

She nodded and extended a tentative "hand" to him, waiting for him to take it.

Well, that's promising. She didn't just fling a link at me without asking. He took her up; making certain that everything including surface thoughts was well-shielded against casual probes. He didn't *think* she would intrude, but there were always accidents. Some of his personal thoughts were less than flattering to her; most he would rather not share with anyone.

Treyvan indicated his readiness to act with a nod and a "hand" of his own. He settled into partnership with the gryphon with the same ease that one half of an acrobatic team has with the other.

But Treyvan waited for *him* to initiate the action. The gryphon's intention was clear; he meant to observe the act as a backup in case of trouble but to otherwise let Darkwind take the lead. The Heartstone glowered before them, sullen red, pulsing irregularly, with odd cracklings of random energy discharge flowing over and through it. The lines were anchored firmly in its base, concentrated amidst the major lines like roots from a crystalline tree of lightning, their rainbow-patterned raw power transformed by the stone itself.

Was he ready?

He would have to find out sooner or later. Might as well get it over with.

:All right, old friend,: he Mindsent. *:Let's make this one clean and quick.:*

Clean it was; quick, it was not.

The Stone resisted their attempts to sever the lines, as Treyvan predicted; he was not prepared for the uncanny way in which it reacted when he severed the first of them, though.

He formed his own power into a thin, sharp-edged "blade," sliding it into the join of Stone and line, intending to excise the line as if cleaning a rabbit hide. To his surprise, though, it Felt precisely like trying to cut the leg from an old, tough, and overcooked gamebird; he encountered a flexible resistance that was at once yielding and entangling.

He changed his tactic; changed from trying to cut his way through the join, to burning his way through. It resisted that as well, so he changed to a mental image of wielding bitter cold at the join, to make it brittle, then breaking it away. That worked, but it was a good thing he had secondary shields ready to protect the raw "ends," because the moment he got the line loose and held in one of his "hands," he Sensed movement from the Stone.

He passed the line to Treyvan, protected the end with an expanding shield. Just in time. The Stone itself created tiny tentacles of seeking power, probing after the lines it had lost. Thin, waving strands of sullen red energy groped toward him, lengthening as they searched. The hair on the back of his neck rose as they came to him, then ignored him, and sought after the line. For one frightening moment, he thought they were coming after him, that the Stone *knew* he had taken the line and wanted retribution. They reminded him of the filaments of energy cast out in the creation of a Gate, the filaments that sought for and found the terminus at the other end and drew the two "together." They found the line—and slid along the surface of the shield protecting the severed end. Before they could seek further, perhaps touch past the sides of the shield, Treyvan hauled the line out of reach.

He shivered, watching the red fingers weaving and groping after the line. There was something very *wrong* about this. In all of his training, in all of the tales he had ever heard, there had been nothing like this behavior noted in a Heartstone.

Fortunately, these tentacles were neither as powerful nor as persistent as the Gate-energies; they receded into the seething chaos of the Stone moments after they pulled the line out of reach. But he certainly remained aware of them—and aware that the Stone might have more surprises.

He did not like the feeling that it knew exactly what he had done, and was angry with him.

With one "eye" on the Stone, he and Treyvan put their strength into relocating the line and, to some extent, the pathway it would take in the future. Moving the line was a great deal like pulling one end of a very heavy, very long rope—a rope that was, perhaps, as thick as his waist. The line resisted being moved from its accustomed course, just by pure inertia. By the time he got the severed end within easy distance of the new node, he felt as if he had run a long uphill race.

Treyvan's mind was focused on his and Hydona's home. He manipulated the node beneath the lair; that was appropriate, since he was the most familiar with it. He created a kind of "sticky," or "rough-surfaced" place on it, at least that was the analogy Darkwind used for himself. Whatever he did, it made the raw end of the line seek it as soon as Darkwind removed the shield; they joined, jumping together as a thread will jump to a silk-rubbed amber bead, or a bit of iron to a magnet. Then he ran magical pressure along the line, to straighten and broaden it slightly, so it would seat in place easier.

Darkwind studied the join for a moment, and mentally shook his head. :I don't want to take any chances, this time,: he said to Treyvan, feeling Elspeth in the back of his mind, watching with interest. :I didn't like what the Stone did back there, and I don't want it to recapture these lines. Let's armor and shield the joining.:

:A good plan,: Treyvan agreed.

It was probably not necessary. They were probably doing far more work than they needed to. But Darkwind could not get those seeking tentacles of power out of his mind—

—and the more I weaken the Stone, the less chance it has of turning the tables on us when we finally drain it. Or whatever we do when we finally take it down.

He was aware that he was thinking of the Stone as if it was a living, sentient creature. A discomforting fact of magic, also, was that often thinking about something made it happen, especially with skilled Adepts. Magery was not a matter of spell components and rituals at Adept level, it involved a high measure of subconscious skill and influencing of the physical world.

He had no doubt that there were others among the Hawkbrothers who thought of the Stone as having a mind—a half-mad, malicious one, to be sure. Personifying a problem was also not unheard of among people of all ages and races, much less mages. It might, by now, have a kind of mind. That might even be the root cause of its behavior back there. If it did, the last thing he wanted to do was underestimate it.

So he and Treyvan spent some time in ensuring that the Stone would *not* be able to get that particular ley-line back. And the next. And the next.

Four lines later, and he was quite ready to call an end to the exercise. So, he surmised, was Treyvan. When he disengaged his attention from Othersight and glanced over at the gryphon, poor Treyvan's crest drooped, and his neck-ruff had a decidedly wilted look about it.

:That's enough,: he said. *:We know this will hold. And even weakened, my father could do this alone. In fact, if I can do this, any pair of the Adepts should be able to. I think I'll advise that they work in pairs, though. I don't think anyone should ever turn an unguarded back on that Stone from now on.:*

Treyvan acknowledged his decision with a weary nod, and broke the link. As Darkwind brought all of his attention and concentration back to his physical body, the gryphon slumped over his foreclaws and sighed.

"That Sstone isss *mossst* sstubborn, Darrkwind," the gryphon complained, his crest-feathers slowly rising. "I have neverrr ssseen anything like it."

"Let's get out of here," Darkwind urged. "I'm too tired to really trust my shields."

"I agrreee," Hydona rumbled, and turned to lead the way across the pass-through. On the other side of the barrier, Treyvan resumed his interrupted observation.

"I have neverrr ssseen anything like the way the Ssstone behaved," he repeated, his voice troubled, and his crest rising and falling a little with his agitation.

"You mean the way it tried to reach after the line once we severed it?" Darkwind asked. "By the way," he added in an aside to Elspeth, "Treyvan is right in that what you Saw wasn't normal behavior for a Heartstone. It's not supposed to reach out after things like that on its own."

The gryphon shuddered. "It acted asss if it werre alive and thinking. It issss jussst a *node*. Nodesss arrre not sssupposssed to be alive!"

"Yes and no," Darkwind replied, "Although this is sheer speculation on my part, I must remind you. But I have seen another kind of magic-imbued object act like that; when you build a Gate, the energy integrated into the portal does the same thing."

"Yesss, but *not* on itsss own," Treyvan corrected. "You make it do sssso!"

"Initially, perhaps," Darkwind argued, "but eventually, a mage can work parts of the spell without consciously thinking on it. After a while the process proceeds without direction—"

A flash of white in the branches up above should have warned him, but he was too tired to think of more than one thing at a time, and his mind was already occupied with the problem of the Heartstone. So it wasn't until Vree had made three-fourths of his dive at Treyvan's crest that he realized what was about to happen. And by then it was too late.

"NO!"

This time, Treyvan was tired, irritable—

Vree reached out claws to snatch and encountered something he had not expected.

Treyvan had suffered the bondbird's behavior enough.

Vree found himself flying straight for Treyvan's enormous beak; easily large enough to engulf the bird.

Darkwind reached out his hand in a useless gesture. He didn't even have time to *think*. It was all happening too fast. Vree frantically tried to pull up out of the dive.

Too late.

Crack.

The sound of Treyvan's beak snapping shut echoed across the Vale like nothing that had ever been heard there before. Like the sound of an enormous branch snapping in two, perhaps, or the jaws of a huge steel trap closing.

Or the hands of a giant slapping together. Clouds of songbirds took wing in alarm.

Vree screamed in pain and dove for the safety of Darkwind's wrist. Treyvan spat out the single tail-feather he'd bitten off with an air of aggrieved triumph.

Darkwind heaved a sigh of relief. Treyvan was a carnivore, as much a raptor as Vree was; something *he* never forgot. Vree was lucky; incredibly lucky—

Because Treyvan hadn't missed. He'd snapped off exactly what he intended to. The gryphons' reflexes were as swift and sure as the fastest goshawk, and if Treyvan had chosen, it would have been Vree's neck that was broken, not a tail-feather.

:*I warned you*,: Darkwind said, as Elspeth hovered between sympathy for the badly-frightened bird and the laughter she was obviously trying to repress. :*I warned you, and you wouldn't listen!*:

Treyvan fixed the trembling, terrified bondbird with a single glaring eye. "You arrre jussst forrrtunate that I wasss not hungerrred," he hissed, and Darkwind "heard" him echoing his words in simple thought-images the bondbird would have no difficulty understanding. "You may not farrrre so well a sssecond time."

Vree cowered against Darkwind's chest, making tiny sounds of acute distress and pain.

:Now you're going to be minus that feather until you molt, unless I can imp it back in.:

:Hurts,: Vree wailed. *:Scared!:*

:I know it hurts. You should be glad he didn't pull it out, or bite your tail off.: Darkwind caressed the gyre until he stopped trembling, as Elspeth bent to pick up the feather and offered it to him.

He took the gesture at face value, and not for the one implied by Hawkbrother custom. *:Tell Treyvan you're sorry,:* he told Vree sternly, holding the bondbird out to the gryphon's face, within easy reach of that enormous beak.

Maybe this will impress him enough that he won't try the game again. He sighed. *I certainly hope so.*

The gyre looked up into the huge amber eyes as Darkwind held him up to the gryphon's face. *:S-s-s-sorry,:* the bird stuttered—no mean feat, mentally. *:S-s-s-sorry!:*

He certainly sounded sincere.

:Promise you won't do it again,: Darkwind ordered.

Vree shook, and slicked down all his feathers with unhappiness. *:Not snatch again,:* he agreed. *:Not ever. Never, never, never, never.:*

Darkwind transferred the bird from his wrist to the padded shoulder of his jerkin, where Vree huddled against his hair, actually pushing himself into the hair so that it partially covered him, hiding. Darkwind examined the feather carefully, hoping that it hadn't been too badly damaged. Vree depended on his tail for steering; the loss of one feather might not seem like a great deal, but it would make a difference in his maneuverability.

"You did a good job," he remarked to Treyvan, whose crest was rising slowly again. "It's a nice clean cut, only cracked the shaft a little. I won't need to use one of last year's set. I should be able to imp this one back in with no problems."

The gryphon chuckled. "It isss in parrt Vree'sss doing. If he had not turrned, I ssshould not have been able to catch the tail featherssss. If he did not turrrn, I wasss going to catch him and hold him, then let him go.''

''He'd have been frightened to death. Well, I think you've finally made an impression on him,'' Darkwind replied—*not* chuckling, though he wanted to, for fear of hurting the bird's feelings. ''He finally sees you as a bigger, hungrier, meaner version of a bondbird, and not something like a glorified firebird. To tell you the truth, I think he's just fascinated by beautiful feathers, like your crest and the firebirds' tails. He snatches *their* feathers all the time.''

Treyvan's crest rose completely, with mock indignation. ''I ssshould hope we arrre not *glorrrified firrrebirds*,'' he snorted. ''I am a vain birrrd, and I appreciate that he findsss my cresssst ssso attrrractive, but we arrre not anything like firrrrebirrrdsssss.''

''What are you, though?'' Elspeth asked, suddenly. ''I mean, you don't really look like anything I know of—other than vaguely like hawk-eagles and falcons.''

''Oh, well, we arrre not anything you know,'' Hydona replied, vaguely. ''Not hawk, not falcon. It isss not asss if sssomeone took bitsss and piecesss of birrrd and cat and patched usss togetherrr, afterrr all!''

''Yes, but there *are* supposed to be gryphons north and west of Valdemar,'' Elspeth persisted. ''But there aren't any in any of the inhabited lands I know—so where do you two come from?''

''Wessst.'' Hydona shrugged. ''You would not know the place. Even the Hawkbrotherrsss had not hearrrd of it.''

Elspeth wasn't giving up that easily. ''Well, is that where your kind comes from? Is that why there aren't any gryphons in Valdemar?''

Treyvan gave her a droll look out of the corner of his eye. ''If you arrre asssking if we arrre a kind of Changechild orrrr Pelagirrr monsssterrrr,'' he replied, ''I can tell you that we arrre not, and thanksss be to Sssskandrrranon forrr that. We werrrre crreated by one of the Grreat Magessss, the Mage of Ssssilence, whom we knew asss Urrrtho. That wasss a long time ago, beforrre the Mage Warrrs. He crrrreated the *herrrtasssi* asss well, and otherssss. That wasss hisss grrreat powerrr and joy, to crrreate new crrreaturessss. Ssso they sssay.''

Before Elspeth could leap in with another question, Hydona yawned hugely and looked up at the sky. ''It isss late,'' she said abruptly, ''and I am hungerrred, even if Trrreyvan isss not.''

''Not hungerrred enough forrr falcon,'' Treyvan chuckled. ''But a nicsse clawful of geesssse, now—orrr a young deerr. . . .''

Hydona parted her beak in a gryphonic smile. "I think we will leave you now, Darrrkwind."

"Until tomorrow, then," he said, smoothing Vree's feathers with one hand. "Sleep well, and pass my affections on to Lytha and Jerven."

"Mine, too," Elspeth piped up, to Darkwind's surprise.

"Tomorrrrow," Treyvan agreed. The two gryphons moved off down a side path that would take them to the entrance of the Vale; they couldn't possibly take off from within it, for the interlacing branches of the great trees would make it too difficult for them to fly without damage to themselves or the trees.

Elspeth looked after them for a moment, then made a little shrug and turned back to Darkwind. From her expression, there was a lot going on behind her eyes.

"Is there something bothering you?" he asked, thinking she might have questions about the lesson just past.

But her observations had nothing to do with magic. "They are certainly very good at avoiding questions they don't care to answer," she pointed out dryly. "This isn't the first time I've tried to pin them down about where they come from and what they are, and their answers have always been pretty evasive."

"You can trust them," he felt moved to protest.

"Oh, I have no doubt of that; after all, Need trusted them, and she's about the most suspicious thing in the universe. But they seem to have as many secrets as a Companion!" This, with a glance at Gwena, who shook her head and mane and snorted. "I had the feeling that they hadn't told the Tayledras much more than they've told me."

He nodded slowly. She was absolutely right about that, anyway. He hadn't quite realized how little he knew about them, really. The fact that they had been his friends for so long had obscured the fact that what he knew about them was only what they had chosen to reveal.

There had been any number of surprises from them, lately. The fact that they were fluent in the ancient *Kaled'a'in* tongue, for instance, and just how much of a mage Treyvan really was. That they spoke of Urtho as if *they* knew the lost history of the Mage Wars in much greater detail than any Tayledras did.

As if that history hadn't been lost to their people, whoever and wherever those people were.

Interesting. Very interesting. But it was so *frustrating!* They didn't even work at being mysterious, the way Elspeth's friend Skif did. They just *were*.

It gave him enough food for thought that he remained silent all the way back to Elspeth's *ekele*, and from the expression on her face, she found plenty of room for speculation there herself.

Chapter Eleven

Skif packed the new supplies he had gotten from the *hertasi* carefully; Cymry needed to be able to move with the same agility she had without packs once they got back on the trail. Lumpy and unbalanced packs would not make either of them very happy.

"You look like a Hawkbrother," Elspeth observed from the rock beside him; like everything in the Vale, it had been made to look natural, while being placed in the perfect position to be used as a seat, and had been carefully sculpted to serve that very purpose. She sat cross-legged with a patch of sun just touching her hair. There were already a few white threads in it; he wondered how long it would be before she was completely silver. Wintermoon had confided that Elspeth was handling more of the powerful energies of node-magic in her first few months than most Tayledras Adepts touched in a year or more. And she spent a great deal of time in the unshielded presence of the Heartstone. While Wintermoon was quite certain that none of this would harm her, he did warn Skif that her training and the discipline needed to handle such powers might cause some changes in his friend, and not just physical ones.

Indeed, there were some changes since he had left the Vale. Elspeth seemed a little calmer, and considerably more in control of her temper. She no longer reminded him of Kero, or her mother . . . she was only, purely, Elspeth. His very dear friend—but no more. He could not imagine anyone having a romantic attachment to this cool, contemplative person; it would be like having a fixation on a statue.

He glanced up at her and smiled. "So do you," he said. "It suits you."

She really did look like a Hawkbrother; she was growing her hair longer, and although it wasn't yet the stark white of a mage, or the mottled camouflage colors of a scout, she had somehow learned the Tayledras tricks of braiding it so that it stayed out of the way without looking severe. And the tunic and trews she wore—flowing silk in deep burgundy, cut so that the tunic fastened up the side with little antler-tips— well, it suited her much better than anything she'd ever worn at home.

"What happened to your Whites?" he asked.

She laughed. "They disappeared, and I have the feeling I won't see them again until we're ready to leave. I have the feeling that the *hertasi* disapprove of uniforms on principle. Whenever I ask about them, the *hertasi* give me this *look*, and say 'they're being cleaned.' It's been weeks now, and they're still being cleaned."

"Mine are probably with yours," Skif said. "Wintermoon wouldn't let me bring them; he said they weren't even suited to winter work. He made me get scouts' gear."

She chuckled a little. "I'm beginning to agree with Kerowyn about Whites," she told him. "At least, about the way they're made. You get tired of them. They can't have changed in hundreds of years—you know, we really could stand to have a style choice, at least."

He shrugged. "Probably nobody ever thought much about it." He lifted the pack experimentally. It was about as heavy as he wanted Cymry to carry, and after all, it wasn't as if they were cut off from k'Sheyna and more provisions. "That's going to do it, I think."

Elspeth measured the pack with her eyes. "What's that—two weeks' rations at the most?"

"About. We'll be back in by then." He fastened both packs to Cymry's saddle, and turned back to Elspeth. "I'm sorry I didn't have any news for you."

She shrugged. "I'll tell you the truth, big brother—I really don't think it's all that important for me to get Need back, even assuming she'd be willing to return to me, which I doubt. I think it *is* important for you to find Nyara, for both your sakes."

He flushed but didn't reply to that directly. Another change; she was either much improved at reading body language or she had picked up an uncanny ability to intuit things. "I don't know how much you're aware of the weather in here, but we're just about on to winter out there," he said. "We won't be able to cover as much ground once it starts snowing."

She didn't seem concerned. "Take as much time as you need. Our orders haven't changed; no one needs us back home, and I need training as complete as I can get. Gwena says that things haven't deteriorated with Ancar and Hardorn any more than they had the last time we got word. It might simply be the weather. They're already into winter up there."

"And no one, sane or insane, attacks in winter." He nodded. "With luck, you'll be ready by spring."

He had other, unspoken thoughts. *And with more luck, your Darkwind will be willing to come along when we leave.* He smiled, but only to himself. Elspeth wasn't the only one good at reading body language.

Elspeth shifted her position a little. "Well, we've also got the possibility of some new allies. According to Gwena, there's some indication that Talia, Dirk, and Alberich are getting somewhere in negotiating with the Karsites."

"The—what?" He felt his eyebrows flying up into his hairline with astonishment. Last thing *he* had heard, people were simply grateful that the Karsites were too embroiled with Ancar and their own internal politics to harass the Border they shared with Valdemar. "When did all this start?"

"Early fall—about when we reached here," she said. "Sorry; I forgot that I didn't hear about it until after you left." She looked up and frowned a little. "Let me see if I can tell you this all straight; I've been getting it in bits and pieces. Alberich got some tentative contacts with someone supposedly official in the Karsite army through a really roundabout path. It was supposed to be someone he knew and tentatively trusted."

"From Karse?" He could hardly believe it. "How did anything get out of Karse?"

"Convolutedly, of course; Gwena said the pathway involved traders and the renegade faction of the Sunlord that keeps allegiance with Valdemar." She raised an eyebrow. "Not the most secure line of communication, and the message was pretty vague. Sort of—'we might be willing to talk to you people if you happened to show up at this place and time'; he wasn't sure he trusted it at all, but it was the first positive gesture we've had from those people in hundreds of years, so he didn't want to dismiss it out of hand."

"He wouldn't, and he'd be right," Skif agreed. "But it could have been a trap, counting on the idea that he might be homesick."

She snickered. "Surely. Anybody who'd think that doesn't know Alberich. Anyway, that was about a month ago; he and Eldan and Kero checked the stories out, and they seemed to be genuine. Two weeks ago, they were actually approached officially. Then a week ago Mother arranged for Talia and Dirk to go down to the Border, the Holderkin lands, and meet an envoy from the Karsite government."

"Which means the Sun-priests." He tried the thought out in his mind. "Any idea what started all this?"

Elspeth started to chuckle. He gave her a quizzical glance.

"If Gwena is relaying what Rolan told her correctly—it's as convoluted as the Karsites are. The infighting settled this fall—and the Priest-King suddenly seems to be a Queen now. The envoys are half women, and Talia had picked up a kind of grim 'we're all women together' kind of feeling from them, though whether that's their feeling about her, or the Priest-Queen's feeling about Selenay, I don't know."

"Interesting," Skif said absently. In either case, the chances of coming to an agreement were much better.

"That's only the first factor. Ancar has been harassing them much more than he has us, probably because they don't have that anti-magic defense we do. That, it seems, was bad enough, but now he's stealing the Sun-priests' pet demons, and that was absolutely the last straw." She grinned like a horse trader who's just sold an ill-tempered Plains-pony as a Shin'a'in stud. "That must have doubly stuck in their throats— not only to have to come to *us*, the unholy users-of-magic, but to have to admit that *they* were using magic themselves!"

"Ah, if I know Talia, she was very careful about not rubbing their noses in the fact." He shook his head and chuckled. "That's something I would have had a hard time doing."

"You and me both," she admitted. "Anyway, that's where things stand at home. With luck, we can at least get them to promise not to harry our borders until Ancar is dealt with once and for all."

Skif rubbed the back of his neck, and stared off into the distance. North and east. "I'd like to be there," he said, more than half to himself. "I really would. Peace with our old enemy . . . Havens, wouldn't that be something!"

"I'll believe it when it happens," she replied. "For now, it's enough to know we aren't the only ones that Ancar's been hurting. That at least opens up the possibility of uniting against a common enemy."

He shook off his reverie. "Amazing. But I have my own job to take care of. Standing here and biting my nails over something happening hundreds of leagues away is not going to accomplish much of anything."

"I have patrol with Darkwind," she told him. "We're taking an evening shift, with one of the scouts that flies an owl. He's got some beasties hanging about at night that he wants a mage to have a look at."

"Gryphons, too?" he asked with interest. He liked Treyvan and Hydona a great deal, and his sole regret in going out with Wintermoon was that he was unable to learn more about them.

"No, they're going to stay with the little ones; we monopolize enough of their time as it is." She started to chuckle.

"What's so funny?" Skif wanted to know.

"Oh, just their *kyree*-friend, Rris. The *kyree* are usually so dignified; Torrl is, anyway. But Rris is like—like a big puppy. All bounce and friendliness. But what's funniest is that he's just *full* of stories about 'my famous cousin, Warrl.' "

That sounded familiar, somehow. "Warrl. That—that can't be the same *kyree* that was Kero's teacher's bondmate, is it?"

She nodded vigorously. "The same. And hearing the same stories Kero used to tell us told from the *kyree* point of view is an absolute stitch!"

He sighed. Another thing he was missing. Well, he couldn't be here and out there at the same time, and on the whole, he was doing better and more productive work out there. There had been an encounter with another pack of *wyrsa*—this time on their terms, and he and Wintermoon had destroyed them. There'd been more of those *gandels* that they'd had to lure into a pit-trap—and some smaller, but still nasty, encounters.

All of which meant hazards no k'Sheyna scout would have to face, something that Winterlight, the new scout-leader, had been quick to point out to the Council. Permission to return to the search had been readily given.

Though several of Wintermoon's friends told him he was crazy, staying out in the winter-bound forest when he could be warm and comfortable in the Vale, in his off-duty hours, anyway.

Skif still wasn't quite certain of Wintermoon's motivation, but the scout had told him repeatedly that even if he had been running patrols, he would have continued to live in his *ekele* outside the Vale. That to him, winter camping was no great hardship.

If that was the way he felt, Skif would take his words at face value.

"We'd better get going, then," he said. "Wintermoon should have gotten the cold-weather gear together by now." Already he wanted to be back on the hunt. . . .

"Darkwind and Gwena are probably waiting for me. I'd better go get my scout gear on." She bounced to her feet and planted a kiss on his cheek. "See you in about two weeks?"

"Right." He patted her on the head as if she were a very small child; she mock-snarled at him. "Don't get into too much trouble, all right?"

"Hah! Me?" With a wave, she was gone.

The first snow of the season was going to be a substantial one. "Does winter always start so—enthusiastically?" Skif asked his guide, as they arranged things in the shelter they had rigged beneath the overhanging limbs of a huge pine. It was a very small shelter, compared to the way-stations the Heralds used, but it was big enough for two if no one moved much. Skif couldn't begin to guess what it was made of; some kind of waterproof silk, perhaps. Wintermoon had taken it from a pouch scarcely bigger than a rolled-up shirt. Light for now came from a tiny lantern holding a single candle suspended from the roof; not much, and not very bright.

Wintermoon shrugged. "Sometimes yes, sometimes no," he replied. "Often it depends upon what the mages have done. Great fluxes in the energy-flow of magic can change the weather significantly, usually to make it worse."

"Now he tells me," Skif said to the roof of the tent. "Havens, if I'd known that, I'd have kept everyone out of that to-do with Falconsbane!"

"Oh, that was not significant," the Hawkbrother replied carelessly. "Not enough to make any real difference. Building a Gate, now—one has to make certain that the weather is going to hold clear for several days, if one has a choice, or any storm will worsen. If they manage to drain the Heartstone—that would be significant, very much so. That is why we try always to work the greater magics in stable times of the year."

"For a nonmage you certainly know a lot," Skif observed. Winter-moon only laughed.

"One must, if one is Tayledras. As one must know horses, even if one is a musician or weaver, if one is also Shin'a'in. Magic is so much a part of what we do that we *all* of us are affected by it, if only in the bleaching of hair and eyes." He completed rigging his own sleeping place, and eyed Skif's pad of pine boughs dubiously. "Are you certain that you wish to sleep upon that? It looks very cold and stiff, and I brought a second hammock."

"I'm used to it," Skif replied. "I'm not used to being suspended like a bat."

"Well, it is warmer so." Wintermoon looked out of the flap of the tent, and resecured it. "This will be a heavy storm. I think we will be here until well past midmorning at the least. Nothing is like to be mov-ing this night, not even a cold-drake."

"Comforting. At least nothing can wrap us up in our tent and carry us away." The two owls, Corwith and K'Tathi, had perches in one corner of the shelter; packs took up the remaining space, including be-neath Wintermoon's hammock, making the area very crowded. Cymry and the *dyheli* had a lean-to rigged against the side of the shelter, and were huddled together under blankets.

:*Are you all right?*: he asked his Companion. :*If you're too cold, we'll find some other way—*:

:*No worse than if I'd been up north,*: she told him. :*Better, in fact. The snow may be heavy, but it isn't that cold, really. And the* dyheli *are warm, and good company.*:

Well, if she wasn't going to complain, he wasn't going to worry.

Hawkbrother winter gear was a lot better than his own; lighter, for one thing. Instead of relying on layers of wool, fur and leather for their bedrolls and heavy-weather coats, they had something light and fluffy sandwiched between layers of what he knew to be waterproof spider silk, because the *hertasi* had told him so. No cloaks for them, either. Cloaks were all very well if you were spending most of your time on horseback, but not if you were trying to make your way through a pathless forest. Cloaks caught on every outstretched twig; the slick-finished coats did not.

"Would we were mages," Wintermoon observed wistfully. "We could make lights, heat—I have a brazier, but it needs a smoke hole, and that lets in as much cold as the brazier supplies heat in any kind of wind.''

"According to Elspeth, an Adept doesn't need to make heat; he can ignore the cold.'' Skif shook his head. "I don't know about that.''

"Oh, that is possible, but there is a price in weariness,'' Wintermoon told him. "Keeping warm requires some kind of power, whether it be the power of the fire, or the power of magic. If she has not learned that yet, she will.''

"Ah.'' He felt a bit better. "I thought that sounded a bit too much like—well—magic.''

"Tayledras magic is no more than work with tools other than hands,'' Wintermoon laughed. "Or so I keep telling my mage-friends. My brother said that. I think of all the mages I know, he is the most sensible, for he never relies on his power when his hands will do.''

It occurred to Skif that, given that philosophy, Darkwind was probably the best teacher Elspeth could have. She tended to fall prey to enthusiasm about anything new, and look to it as the solution for every problem. Darkwind should keep her from falling prey to that fault. "Are you changing our tactics now that we've had heavy snow?'' he asked.

"Actually, it will be easier.'' Wintermoon slid into his hammock with a sigh; bundled up to the neck as he was, he looked like a human-headed cocoon. "The trees are leafless, snow covers the ground. Nyara will be hard put to hide the signs of her passing, of her living. The owls will most probably find her. We, though—we will be facing more of the hunters, and performing our secondary task for the Clan. The season of stupid young is over, the season of dying old not yet on us. This is the season of hunger for the hunters. This is when we truly prove our worth to k'Sheyna.''

Skif climbed into his own bedroll, and shivered as he waited for it to warm around his body. The hot springs and summerlike atmosphere of the Vale seemed a world away. "The Clan means a lot to you, doesn't it? Even though—''

"Though my father rejected me, the Clan saw to it I was not left parentless,'' Wintermoon said firmly. "It is more than simple loyalty. K'Sheyna is my family in every way that matters. Can you understand that, who had no real family? I sometimes wonder.''

"Maybe if I hadn't been Chosen. . . .'' Skif listened to the soft ticking of snow falling on the fabric of the shelter, listened to the creaking of boughs in the forest beyond. "I do have a family, you know. More fathers and mothers, brothers and sisters than I can count. The Heralds gave me that, and they are *my* family in every way that counts."

"So—the Heralds are a kind of Clan?" Wintermoon asked curiously. "A Clan that is not related by blood, but by—purpose."

"I guess we are." It was an intriguing thought, one that had its own logic. Interesting. "I want my own family, though. Eventually. Well, I told you all about that."

"Where?" Wintermoon wanted to know. "Have you a place that has won your heart?"

His first thought was that farmhouse, so long ago. That was something he had to think about. "Back at Haven, I suppose, though it could be anywhere. Come to that, there's a lot of peace here. More than there is at home." Now that he thought about it, if there was any one place he'd seen in all of his travels that he felt called to him, it was here. "The Vale seems serene, tranquil. I don't really understand why you don't spend more time there."

"Appearances can be deceiving," Wintermoon replied dryly. "If you were at all sensitive to the currents of magic, you would find it less than peaceful, even if the Stone were intact. And every Vale is under a constant state of siege. When it isn't, it is time to move on to a new one. But you—how could *you* bear to leave the city? I should think you would miss the people and all the doings. There must be much to keep you busy there."

"Not that much." He considered the question. "It's just as easy to be lonely in a city as out in the wilderness. Easier, really. It's harder to get to know someone when you meet in a crowded place. People can freely ignore you in the city; they can assume they don't have any responsibility for you. When there are fewer people, I think they begin assuming some kind of responsibility, simply because you naturally do the same."

"Perhaps. But let me show you how a Vale appears to me, before you assume that it is a kind of wonderland." There was silence for a moment. "Take the Vale itself; there is the constant undercurrent of magic, even in a Vale with an intact Heartstone, because magic is how the place is maintained. It is as if there were always bees droning somewhere nearby, or something humming in a note so low it is felt more than heard. Then there are ever the *hertasi* underfoot." Wintermoon sighed. "They mean well, but they are so social they are nearly hive-minded. They cannot understand that one might wish to be without company."

"I'd noticed that," Skif chuckled. "If I'm not asleep, there always seemed to be a *hertasi* around wanting to know if I needed anything."

"And if you are asleep, they are there still. It can get tiresome," Wintermoon said with resignation. "They also do not see that some of us can live without certain luxuries. For instance—did they steal your clothing?"

Skif blinked with surprise. "Why—yes—"

"They do not approve of it," Wintermoon told him. "I am certain of that. It is too plain, too severe. You will not see it again until you are ready to leave. And even then, I fear they will have made alterations to it."

Skif choked on a laugh.

"Oh, no doubt this is amusing, but what if one *prefers* simpler clothing? What if one *prefers* to make one's own food? What if one would rather his quarters were left undisturbed? Then there is the matter of my Clansfolk."

"What about them?" Skif asked.

"Several matters. The one which concerns both of us is the attitude that those with little magic are less important." Wintermoon's voice conveyed faint bitterness. "It matters not that someone must do the hunting, must keep the borders secure, must meet with the Shin'a'in and arrange for those few things we cannot make. There are a hundred things each day that must be done that need no magic. Yet those of us whose magic is only in the realm of thought and not of power, are, at least in this Clan, often discounted."

"That might only be because of Starblade," Skif pointed out. "It could change."

"Indeed. It may, and I hope it will. But if it does not—you, Wingsib, will, soon or late, find yourself accounted of less worth than your friend Elspeth."

The bedroll warmed, and Skif relaxed into it. "That wouldn't be anything new," he replied drowsily. "Back home, after all, she's the Queen's daughter, and I'm nobody important."

"Ah." The tiny candle dimmed and died, leaving them in the darkness. On the other side of the tent wall, one of the *dyheli* snored gently, a purring sound like a sleepy cat. "They also do not much care for Changecreatures."

"You mean Nyara." Skif forced himself to think of her dispassionately. "Well, we'll worry about that when we find her. No point in getting worked up over something that hasn't happened yet."

"They have other prejudices," Wintermoon warned. "Outsiders in general tend to be met with arrows and killing-bolts. And that is not the k'Sheyna way only; that holds for all Clans. Only your acceptance by the Shin'a'in and the presence of your Companions kept you from gaining a similar welcome."

Skif yawned. "I'm sorry, Wintermoon, but I'm drifting off. I wish I could concentrate on what you're saying, but I can't."

The Tayledras sighed. "I suppose it is just as well," he admitted. "I am losing track of my thoughts."

Skif gave up trying to fight off sleep. "We can take this up in the morning, maybe," he muttered after a while. And he never heard Wintermoon's answer.

There was too much light coming in the tower window.

Nyara unwrapped herself from her furs and winced as cold air struck her. She wrapped a single wolfskin about her shoulders, and moved cautiously to the narrow slit in the eastern wall. She looked out of her tower window on a world transformed, and panicked.

Snow. The forest is covered in snow!

It was at least knee-deep; deeper in some places. The wall below her glittered with patches of ice—predictably, wherever there were hand- and foot-holds.

What am I going to do?

She wasn't ready for this. She still hadn't worked out a way of getting up and down her wall in snow and ice, she wasn't nearly good enough a hunter yet.

All the game must have gone into hiding, or worse, into hibernation; it will see me coming long before I'm in range, and I can't run or leap as fast, it'll be like trying to run in soft sand, but so cold.

Her mind ran around in little circles, like a frightened mouse—and it was that image that enabled her to get hold of herself.

Stop that, she told herself sternly. She forced herself to sit and *think,* as Need had taught her; to use all that energy that was going into panic for coming up with answers.

The first, and most immediate problem, was how she was going to get down out of the tower to hunt in the first place.

And she had already come up with one possibility; she just hadn't done anything about it yet. Well, now she was going to have to.

We have plenty of rope, and no one is going to cross all that snow without leaving tracks a baby rabbit could see, so there's no harm in using a rope to get up and down with. No one will get in here to use it without my knowing. I can just secure one end of the rope up here and climb down that way. That isn't perfect, but then, what is?

And as for game, well, whatever hampered her would also hamper the game. In fact, as cold as it was, she could even think about creating a hoard for emergencies; if she hung the carcasses just inside the tower, they'd stay frozen. If she put them high enough, they'd be out of reach of what scavengers were brave enough to venture inside with her scent all over everything. She could even take deer, now, and not worry about spoilage.

And since she hadn't bothered the deer yet, they did not yet regard her as a predator. Snow would be at least as hard on them as it was on her.

I can pull the carcasses easier through the snow, too; I won't have to try to cut them up to carry them back. . . .

With a plan in mind, at least for getting into and out of her shelter, and the possibility of new game to augment the old, she looked down on the forest with curiosity rather than fear.

She had never seen snow before, not like this. Falconsbane had copied the Tayledras, whether he admitted it or not, keeping the grounds of his stronghold free of ice and snow, and warmed to summer heat. He had hated winter; hated snow and ice, and spent most of the wintry days locked up inside his domain, whiling away the hours in magery or pleasure. The only time she had ever seen snow was when she had ventured to the gates, and had looked out on a thin slice of winter woods and trampled roadway from the tiny and heavily-barred windows. She was not permitted on the tower tops, lest she attempt to climb down and escape, and the windows in wintertime were kept shuttered and locked against the season.

She had always dreaded the coming of winter, for during the winter months her father often became bored. It was difficult for his creatures to move through the snow; even more difficult for them to slip into the Hawkbrothers' lands unseen. And of course, Falconsbane would not venture outside unless it was an absolute emergency, so his own activities were greatly curtailed. Humans tended to keep to their dwellings in winter, and the intelligent creatures to band together, so the opportunities for acquiring victims were also reduced. He dared not be too spendthrift with the lives of his servants, for there were only so many of them, and fewer opportunities to get more. They were trapped within the walls, too, and if he pushed them too far, they might become desperate enough to revolt. Even he knew that. So Falconsbane's entertainments had to be of his own devising.

When he grew bored, he often designed changes he wished to make in his own appearance, and worked them out on her, an activity that, often as not, ranged from mildly to horribly painful. And when that palled, there were other amusements in which she became his plaything, the old games she now hated, but had then both loathed and desired.

No, until now, winter had not been her favorite season. Spring and fall had been best—spring, because her father was out of the stronghold as often as possible, eager to escape the too-familiar walls, and fall, because he was seizing his last opportunities to get away before winter fell.

But this year, the coming of winter had not induced the fear that it had in the past.

Odd. I wonder why?

Then she realized that all the signs of winter that she had learned to fear were things Falconsbane had created; the increasing number of mage-lights to compensate for the shortening days, the rising temperature in the stronghold, and the shuttering of the windows against the gray sky.

Any mage might do those things—there were other signs in Falconsbane's stronghold that marked the season of fear.

Forced-growth of strange plants brought in to flower in odd corners, creating tiny, often dangerous, mage-lit gardens. Many of those plants were poisonous, some had envenomed thorns, or deadly perfumes. It was one of her father's pleasures to see who would be foolish enough to be entrapped by them.

More slaves in the quarters reserved for those Falconsbane intended to use up, slaves usually young and attractive, but not terribly bright. Her father tended to save the intelligent, warping their minds to suit his purposes, keeping them for two or even three years before pique or a fit of temper brought their twisted lives to a close.

Strained expressions on the faces of those who hoped to survive the winter and feared they might not. Sometimes, usually in the darkest hours of the winter, her father's temper exceeded even his formidable control—though most of the victims were those former "favorite" slaves. . . .

There had been none of that this year. The shortening of the days had not signaled anything to her, and she had simply reacted to the long nights by sleeping more. There had been no blazing of lights in every corner to wake old memories, merely the flickering of her own friendly fire. There was no tropic heat to awaken painful unease, only the need to move everything closer to the firepit, and to build up a good supply of wood.

This place that she lived in could be called squalid, compared to the lush extravagancies of an Adept's lair, but it was *hers*. She had made it so with pride, the first place she could truly call her own, unfettered by her father's will. The wood and rope and furs were placed by her desires alone, with the advice and help of Need, who had become a trusted friend. Taken as a sum of goods, it was insignificant; taken in its context, it was delightful.

The view from her window surprised her with unexpected beauty; the ugliest tangles of brush and tumbled rock had been softened by the thick blanket of snow.

It was astonishing; it took her breath away. She simply admired it for many long moments before turning her thoughts back to the reality that it represented.

It could also be deadly to one who had no real experience in dealing with it.

For a moment, a feeling of helplessness threatened to overwhelm her with panic again.

She quelled it. *No point in getting upset—I have Need. She can always help me solve any problems that come up. If we have to, she can deal with them with magic.*

She turned her mind to her sword—

And met only blankness.

She never quite remembered the first few hours; hours when she had huddled in her furs, alternately weeping and howling. It was a good thing nothing dangerous had come upon her then; she would have been easy prey.

When she exhausted herself completely, she fell asleep, doing so despite her fears, despite her despair, she had drained herself that badly.

When she woke again, in the mid-afternoon, the sheer, unthinking panic was gone, although the fear remained. Somehow she managed; that day, and the next, and the next.

She found game, building a blind beside the pond where the ducks and geese came to feed, and covering it with snow. She caught a goose that very night, and not content with that, hung it in her improvised larder to freeze and scoured the forest for rabbits. She didn't catch any of those, but she discovered a way to fish in the ice-covered ponds, using a bit of metal found in the tower, scuffed until shiny, as bait.

She hauled wood up to her shelter, and kept it reasonably warm and dry; made plans for a blind up in one of the trees above a deer-trail, so that she could lie in ambush for one.

Somehow she kept panic from overwhelming her at the thought that the sword was no longer protecting her from detection.

For if something had happened to Need, she would have to protect herself. She had no choice, not if she wanted to live. Sooner or later, something would come seeking her.

She spent hours crouched beside the fire, bringing up everything Need had ever told her about shielding, about her own magic. Then she spent more hours constructing layer after layer of shields, tapping into the sluggish power of the sleeping forest and into her own energies. But to tap into her own power, she needed a great deal of rest and food—which brought her right back to the problem of provisions. She decided that she *must* start hunting deer; that there was no choice, that it was the only way to buy her the necessary days of rest and recovery when she built up her shielding.

The rest of the time—the hours of darkness before sleep finally came— she spent bent over the sword, begging, pleading with it to come back to life. Prodding and prying at it, to try and discover what had gone wrong. Something must have; there was no reason for the blade to simply fall silent like that, not without warning.

And all with no result. The blade was a sword now; no more, no less. A weapon that she could not even use properly, for without Need's skill guiding her, she was as clumsy as a child in wielding it.

Finally, after trying so hard on the evening of the third day that she worked herself into a reaction-headache, she gave up, falling into an exhausted sleep, a sleep so deep that not even her despair penetrated it. A dreamless sleep, so far as she knew.

When she woke again, quite late on the morning of the fourth day, the clouds had vanished overnight, and sun blazed down through the windows of her tower with cold, clear beams. When she looked out of her window, she had to pull back with her eyes watering. It was *too* bright out there; too bright to see. The sun reflected from every surface, and although there were shadows under the trees, they were not dark enough to give her eyes any rest.

Now she knew what her father's men had meant when they spoke of "snow blindness."

There was no way she was going to be able to see out there without getting a headache, unless she found some way to shade her eyes.

Shading her eyes probably wouldn't do that much good; there would still be all the light reflecting up from the snow.

Wait, though, she could *change* her eyes. After all of Need's lessons, she had a little control over her body; she might be able to make her eyes a little less sensitive, temporarily . . . perhaps darken them to let less light through. . . .

:It's about time you started looking inside yourself for answers,: came the raspy, familiar mind-voice.

She whirled, turning away from the light, peering through shadows that were near-black in contrast with the intense sunlight. "You're back!" she cried, staring at the vague shape of the sword leaning against the firepit where she had left it the night before.

:I never left,: Need said smugly. *:I just decided to let you see you could manage completely on your own for a while.:*

Anger flared; she took a deep breath and fought it down. Anger served no purpose unless it was channeled. Anger only weakened her and could be used as a weapon against her. She reminded herself that Need never did anything without a good reason.

Anger faded enough so that she was in control, not the emotion. She tried not to think of the fear, the first hours of desperation—of all the endless hours when she had been certain that she would not live through this season. That would only make her angry again.

"Why?" she asked bluntly. "Why did you *do* that to me? I didn't do anything to warrant being punished, did I?"

The sword didn't answer directly. *:Look around you. What do you see? The game stocked away, the firewood, all the defenses you constructed.:*

She didn't have to look, she knew what was there. "Get to the point," she snapped. "Why did you leave me alone like that? Why did you leave me defenseless?"

:Did I do any of that, any of the things you've accomplished in the last

few days? Did I hunt the game, catch the fish, rig that hidden ladder to the top?: There was a certain quality in Need's words that overrode Nyara's anger completely.

"No," Nyara admitted slowly. She had done quite a bit, now that she thought about it. Without any help at all.

:Did I rig all these shields?: the sword persisted. *:Did I figure out the way to make them cascade, so that the only one under power is the first one unless something contacts it?:*

"No," Nyara replied, this time with a bit of pride. "I did that." Given that her magic was pathetically weak compared to Need's, or even the least of the mages that her father controlled, she really hadn't done too badly.

:If I really was destroyed tomorrow, would you be able to get away, to hide, to keep yourself alive?: The sword waited patiently for an answer, and the answer Nyara had for her was a very different one than the one she would have had a few days ago.

"I think so," she said, nodding to herself. "Yes, I think so. Was that the point?"

:It was. Four days ago if I had asked that question, you would have said you couldn't do without me. Now you know that you can.: Need's mind-voice conveyed a hint of pride. Nyara smiled a little, despite the remains of her anger.

Need chuckled at her smile. *:It wouldn't be easy for you to do without me, and any number of creatures could take you in a heartbeat, but I would give you even odds of being able to hide and stay hidden if you chose that route over fighting. You were coming to depend on me too much, and I am not invincible, dear. I can be hurt, or even destroyed. Your father could have done it, if he'd known how. Any of the Tayledras Adepts could. You needed to know you could survive if I was not here.:*

Nyara considered that for a moment and let her anger cool. Another of Need's ongoing lessons—anger used to make her incoherent; now, once it was under control, it made her think with a little more focus. That *could* be a problem, too; being too focused meant that you could miss something, but it was better than being paralyzed and unable to think at all.

"What about what you've been doing to fix what Father did to me?" she asked. "I can't do *that*. And it isn't finished—"

:It may never be finished,: Need told her frankly. *:It could take a Healing Adept—which I am not—years to change all the things that were done to*

you. But you are *doing some of that for yourself. If you didn't recognize the problems and want the changes, if you weren't consciously helping me, there wouldn't be any changes. I can't work against resistance, my dear.:*

"Oh." Nyara couldn't think of anything else to say.

:There's something else I want you to consider.:

A breath of chill breeze came in the window. Nyara shivered and moved away from it, returning to the warmth of her furs. She wrapped up in them, cuddling down into their warmth, and let her eyes readjust to the darkness of her tower room. "What?" she asked, expecting something more along the same theme—perhaps something about using her own magic more effectively.

:What do you want?: asked the voice in her mind.

The question took her completely by surprise. "Wh–what do you mean by that?" she stammered.

:It's a question no one has ever asked you before—and one that you were never in a position to decide, anyway,: Need said patiently. *:But you are out here in the wilderness. No one knows where you are yet. You are in a position to decide* exactly *what is going to happen to your life because there's no one here to affect you, to do things you don't expect and haven't planned for. So what do you want? Assume all the power in the world—because, my dear, you have many powerful people who consider you a friend worthy of helping, and they might just do that if you came to them and asked it of them.:* The sword's voice warmed. *:You are quite worthy of being helped, child, though I don't want you to come to depend on it.:*

What *did* she want? To be left alone was the first thing that sprang to her mind—

To be left alone . . . there were no complications out here. Nothing to get in the way of simply living. No emotional pain—that is, when Need wasn't deserting her! This was the first time in her life that she had been in a position of control over her own actions and reactions. There was something very attractive about that.

But—no. It was lonely out here. She was often too busy to think about the isolation, but in the dark of the night, sometimes, she felt lonely enough that she had to fight back tears. At first, she had been too busy to think about it, and then Need had been enough company, but now she wished there was someone else to talk to, now and again. Someone who wasn't a teacher, who was just a friend.

Or . . . maybe a little more than a friend? The frequent urges of her body had not gone away, they had simply become less compulsory, and more under her own control.

But if she didn't want to be left alone, that meant rejoining some portion of the outside world. North meant other Birdkin Clans, and she had been warned they were far less tolerant of Changechildren. South was Dhorisha. There were only two real directions for her, east to the *real* "outside" world, or west, back to the k'Sheyna Vale.

There were problems with both directions. Should she leave the area entirely, and try to find someplace in the east where she could go?

But then what could she do? She would have to find some way to support herself. She had to eat—there was little or no hunting in lands that were farmed. She would have to have clothing, and a place to live, and in civilized lands, one couldn't wear rough-tanned furs or live in a cave. Even assuming there were caves about to live in.

"I could go to the lands where the Outsiders came from. When I am there, I can track and hunt," she said aloud. "I could hire out as a hunter or a guide . . . or maybe as some kind of protector."

Need indicated tentative agreement. *:True, but what are the drawbacks of running off like that, into places you know nothing about and where you have no friends? Remember, out there, no one has ever seen anything quite like you. They might not treat you well, they might greet you with fear or hatred, and you would be one against many if it came to hostility.:*

There was another option—one in which her alien appearance might be of some use. "I could . . . hire out as a bed-partner." There. She didn't like the idea, but it was a viable one. It was one thing she was well-trained in. Skif had certainly been pleased.

Again, Need indicated tentative agreement, but with reservations. *:You could do that, and you would probably do very well. But is that what you want? I thought that was the point of this discussion.:*

She sighed. "No, it isn't what I want. It would be a choice, but not a good one. I suppose—if I had to, it would be better than starving. But I don't have to go east, do I?" If she didn't go east—

Then she went west. Back to k'Sheyna. Back to where the Outland strangers were. . . .

No point in avoiding it. The one person in the whole world that she thought of with longing was that stranger. The young man called Skif— who was with k'Sheyna. And the only Hawkbrothers in the world who *might* look upon her with a certain amount of kindness were the k'Sheyna. She had helped them, after all—fought against her father's controls. *She* was the reason they had known that one of their own was Falconsbane's slave. In a sense, they did owe her a debt. . . .

In more than a sense, so did Skif. She had saved his life at the risk of her own.

And they had shared so much in such a relatively short period of time, enough that the intensity of her feelings had frightened her. That was more than half the reason why she had run away from him. She did not want him near her while her father's directives still ruled her so closely.

Not while she wanted him so very badly. . . .

:I rather thought so,: Need said, following her thoughts, with a feeling of wry humor. *:I rather thought that your Skif would be in the equation somewhere.:*

"Is there anything wrong with that?" she asked defensively, a little apprehensive that Need would not approve. After all, when she had been a woman, she had been celibate. And now that she was a sword, did she still understand feelings?

:No, child, there is absolutely nothing wrong with that. I think your emotions are quite healthy. I think it's just as well that you feel this way, especially since he's out here looking for you.:

She held quite still, rigid with surprise. *What?*

Nyara had never experienced such mixed emotions in her life, all of them painfully intense. Elation and fear. Joy and dismay. She hugged her furs to herself and trembled.

:I rather imagined you'd react this way.: The sword all but sighed, but there was an undercurrent of satisfied humor. *:I suppose I have seen true love often enough to recognize it when it smacks me between the quillions. From at least a dozen of my bearers. And lately—first that sorceress who went into repopulating the Plains all by herself, then that Kerowyn child, and now you. I am beginning to feel like a matchmaker. Perhaps I should give up my current calling and set up as a marriage broker. Very well.:*

Nyara fought all of her emotions down enough to get some kind of answer out. "Very well, what?" she asked.

:We know what you want. So. Now we get you ready for it. That young man needs and wants a partner, *youngster—not a little girl, not just a bedmate, not someone he has to drag about like an anchor and rescue at regular intervals. So, we'd better start building you in that direction. If,:* the sword finished, with a hint of dry sarcasm, *:that suits you.:*

She sat up straighter. A partner. Someone who could stand alone, but chose to stay with another. Someone who just might come rescue *him* once in a while.

"Yes," she said, quietly, calmly, with her chin up. "That suits me very well."

Tre'valen

Chapter Twelve

Tre'valen closed his eyes and narrowed his consciousness, pulling his concentration within himself until he was aware of nothing but himself. A moment only, he paused, finding his balance and center, and from deep within—he stepped out. Onto the Moonpaths, into the spirit realms.

By virtue of their close bond with the Star-Eyed, any Shin'a'in could walk the Moonpaths; provided that it was at night, under the full moon, and he sought the place with unselfish intent and enough concentration. Any Swordsworn could walk the Moonpaths on any night; and call and be answered by the *leshy'a Kal'enedral,* the spirit-warriors sworn to the martial aspect of the Goddess.

A shaman could walk the Moonpaths into the spirit world at any time he chose, and call and be answered by any spirit that lingered there, if the spirit he sought was willing. . . .

That knowledge brought no comfort, only doubt and trepidation. *And that is the question, indeed. Is Dawnfire willing?*

Dawnfire. Of Tale'edras, but called by the Shin'a'in Aspect of the Goddess, to serve in a form a Shin'a'in would recognize—the emblem of one of the four First Clans. He had called and spoken with her on several occasions now, but each time he called, it was with questioning and fear deep in his heart. Fear that this time she would not answer.

Questioning his own motives.

Kra'heera had ordered him to remain at k'Sheyna Vale to learn the Star-Eyed's motive and purpose in creating a Shin'a'in Avatar out of one of the Hawkbrothers. Never had She created an Avatar before, much less one from a child of the Sundered Kin, the magic-users. If Kra'heera had speculations, he kept them to himself. Tre'valen had no guesses at all.

He had learned nothing of Her motivation in all the time he had dwelt here. He had, however, learned far too much of his own heart, a heart that ached with loss, and yearned for one that he could not touch. Ironic that he should discover the love of his life and his soulmate only after she was—technically at least—dead. But was that not like the Goddess, to create such ironies for Her shaman?

Keep to the journey, traveler. The Moonpaths are peril enough without your wandering off them. He walked the Moonpaths, dream-hunting in the spirit world; keeping safely on the trails meant for the living, and sending his call out into the golden mist beyond where lingering spirits lived. Golden mist, for he hunted by daylight; at night, the mist would be silver. This was not wearisome for a shaman, though one who was not so trained returned to his body weary and drained if he dared to venture here. And as a shaman, he knew that time meant very little in this realm, so he walked onward with patience, waiting for the sign that would tell him that Dawnfire was coming—or not.

One moment he was alone; then she was there, before him, in her hawk-form, hovering above the pathway on sun-bright wings. A great vorcel-hawk, glowing with a fierce inner light, so full of energy that the mist about her crackled.

But this time, instead of coming to rest upon the path as she always had before, she spoke one word into his mind.

:*Follow.*:

Then she was gone, diving out of the spirit realm with speed he could not match—but leaving behind a glowing trail that he followed back, back, back to his body, to the material world. He sank into himself; feeling crept back to arms and legs, he put on the shell of himself as a comfortable garment.

He took a deep breath, then opened his eyes to find the Hawk that was Dawnfire poised before him. She watched him; before he could blink his eyes twice, the Hawk shimmered, a trembling like a heat haze passing over her, intensifying the glow of her inner fire. Soon she glowed like a tiny sun, as she had when she first transformed.

He looked away for a moment, his eyes watering with the brightness. When he looked back, the Hawk no longer perched there.

In its place was the transparent and radiant form of the woman. He had never seen her this way in the real world, only in the spirit realm. *A woman made of glowing, liquid glass. . . .*

He took a deep breath of surprise, as she examined her hands and a smile crossed her lips. He rose from his cross-legged pose, and approached her; not certain that he should, but unable to keep at a distance. "I was not certain that I could do this, though my teachers assured me it is no great accomplishment for me now," she said, a little shyly. "I was never a mage; I am not really certain how I accomplish the half of what I do."

This was true speech, and not the stumbling, mind-to-mind talk he had gotten from her aforetimes. He willed his hands to still their trembling and nodded. "I think I can understand how you feel," he replied. "We are not mages, either, we Shin'a'in. That, we leave to Her."

She dropped her eyes from his hungry gaze. "I wanted—I wished to be with you, in as real a way as I could," she said, slowly. Then she looked up, and there was no mistaking the expression she wore, even though her "face" was little more than air and power. It showed a hunger and a desperation as great as his own. "I am *not* dead. I'm just— different, and I wanted to be like I was, for a while."

He had never wanted anything more in his life than to take her hand; he reached for her, shaking a little, stretching one hand across more than a gulf of physical distance—

And she reached toward him.

Their hands met—one of solid flesh, one of ephemeral energy. He felt a gentle pressure, warmth—and it was enough, almost. So, they could touch, for just a moment, letting touch and eyes say what words could not.

He withdrew first; she brought her own hand back and set her face in a mask of calm, although longing still stood nakedly in her eyes.

He did not know what to say to her. "I am not only here with you for my own sake," she said after a moment of strained silence. "I am here—my teachers tell me that I must speak with you, telling you what I have learned because I can see things anew, being what I am now.

Things they did not know, and could not see. Maybe that is *why* I became what I am—not quite in the spirit world and not quite in the material world.''

He nodded and set his own feelings aside; this was the first time she had said anything like this, the first time that she had given any hint of what Kra'heera wanted to know. Not that he had not asked her questions, for he had. Until now she had shown great distress when he had asked her those questions about her current state, so he had stopped asking them. He feared she might stop coming to him; he was afraid he might have frightened her with all his queries.

Apparently not. But then, she was a brave woman, and I do not think that she has ever run from what frightened her.

"When you started asking me questions—I didn't want to think about them, but I had to anyway," she told him slowly. "Like this, there is no sleep, no dreams to run to. Once I started thinking, I started asking questions myself. . . .''

She stared off somewhere above his head for a moment, and he held his breath, as much to try and still the pain in his heart as in anticipation of what she might say next. She could say she had to go, leave him forever, for the Goddess willed it so.

This was far from easy for him. He had dreamed of this woman for years, ever since becoming a man. Since he had been initiated as a shaman, the dreams had more power. He had known in the way of the shaman even then that this woman was his soul-partner, and yet he had never seen her. When Kra'heera had asked him to stay and learn of her, he had thought no more of it than any task the Elder Shaman had set him.

Until she had first come to him on the Moonpaths, this Dawnfire, this transformed Tale'edras. Until he had seen *her* face, and not the hawk-mask of the Avatar.

Now he knew who and what she was, and after the initial joy of discovery, the knowledge was a burden and an agony to his soul, for she was untouchable—out of reach—not truly dead, but assuredly not "alive" in the conventional sense. There was no way in which she could become the partner his dreams had painted her as. How could his dreams, the dreams of a shaman, which were supposed to be accurate to within a hair, have been so very wrong?

"There are threats and changes on the winds," she said, finally, bringing his attention back to something besides his own pain. "Terrible changes, some of them—or they have the potential to bring terror, if they are not met and mastered. One is a lost man of your own people, whom we have faced once already. No Shin'a'in, no Tayledras, no Out-lander has the answer to these changes, only pieces of the answers."

He groped after the answers that her words implied. "Are you saying that the time for isolation to end is at hand?" That in itself was a frightening thought, and a change few Shin'a'in would care for.

"In part." She did not breathe, so she could not sigh, but he had the impression that she did. "It is easy for me to see, but hard to describe. All peoples face a grave threat from the same source, but three stand to lose the most; the Shin'a'in—"

"For what we guard," he completed. *That* was a truism, and always had been.

She nodded emphatically. "Yes. The Tayledras, also, for what we know—and the Outlanders of Valdemar, for what they *are*. And somehow those threats are as woven together as the lives of the Outlanders and the Sundered Kin have become in these last few days." She shook her head in frustration. "I cannot *show* you, and I do not have the words that I need; that is the closest that I can come."

But Tre'valen understood; what she said only crystalized things he had half-felt for some time now. "This is no accident, no coincidence, that things have fallen out as they have," he said firmly.

"It is less even than you guess," she responded immediately. And that confirmed another half-formed guess—that it had been the careful hands of the gods that had worked to bring them all here together. Him—and the Outlanders. "This path that we are all on was begun farther back than even our enemies know. I can see it stretching back to the time of the Mage Wars. There were cataclysms then that are only now echoing back to us."

A cold hand of fear gripped his throat at that, driving out other thoughts. "What do you mean?" he asked, carefully.

She searched visibly for words, her gaze unfocused as though she were watching something that she tried to describe for him, like a sighted woman describing the stars to a blind man. "Neither Urtho nor his enemy were truly aware of what they unleashed upon the world. It is as if what they did has created a *real* echo, except that this echo, rather than being fainter than the original catastrophe, has lost none of its strength as it moved across time and the face of the world. And now—it returns, it sweeps across our world back to its origin."

"But what has this to do with us?" Tre'valen cried. "Those were mages of awesome power—what has this to do with us and what we can do? Surely *we* cannot counter their magics! It is all we can do to hold them away from those who would use them!"

She shook her head dumbly, at a complete loss for an answer. "I can only tell you what I see," she replied, slowly, unhappily. "You asked me of the past and present, and this is what I see. The future is closed to me."

He was at as much of a loss as she, and slowly lowered himself to a stone within arm's reach of her translucent form.

They sat together for a long and painful moment, as he tried to think of words to give her; something with a bit of meaning to it.

"This, I think, must be what Kra'heera sensed when he charged me with remaining here," he said, finally. "He is my senior in much. Perhaps he can give us an answer; perhaps Kethra can, or one of your own people. I shall speak with Kethra and my teachers; I shall relay this to the Kal'enedral. . . ."

"When you do this, speak of the need to speak to one another, Hawkbrothers, Shin'a'in, and Outlanders all," she said, interrupting him. "That much I do see. There has been overmuch of sundering, of the keeping of secrets. It is time for some of this to end."

"Secrets. . . ." He looked up at her, and he knew that longing and pain were plain upon his face, plain enough that any child would see and know them and the cause.

"I must go," she said abruptly; she did not "stand up," so much as gather her energies about her and rise. Her form began to fluctuate and waver, and he held back frustration that she was so near, and yet untouchable except for a moment or two. Despite all that she had told him, his heart cried out for her—his own pain eclipsing the importance of her words.

She turned toward him; held out her hand. "I—" she said falteringly. He had not expected to hear her speak again, and the sound of her voice made him start in surprise.

She was in a kind of intermediate form; womanly, with her human face, but a suggestion of great wings. Again, the power in her made her difficult to look at as she wore the glory of the noon sun on her like a garment, but he would not look away, though his eyes streamed tears.

"I have seen your true heart, and I see your pain, Tre'valen," she said. "I—I share it. Beloved."

Then she was gone, leaving him with a heart torn in pieces, and a mind and soul gone numb.

Darkwind waited for his brother at the edge of the Vale, packs in his hand, and shivered as he looked out on the snow. He was not hardened to this weather, not as he would have been at this time last winter. Then he had sheltered outside the protection of the Vale, and most time not spent in sleeping had been spent in the snow.

He had not gone back to his old *ekele* except to gather his things and bring them back to the Vale with the help of several friends. He had been one of the first to do so, but now that the Vale no longer troubled the bondbirds, most of the scouts had followed his example and returned to the shelter and safety of the rocky walls and enclosing shields. Probably even Wintermoon would join them when his search was over. Darkwind's brother was stubborn but not foolish.

Shelter and safety the Vales held indeed—and comfort, which was something only someone who had never been without comfort scorned. This was going to be a hard winter; it had begun that way, and all signs pointed to the weather worsening before spring. The Vale was warm, with *hertasi* to take care of everyday tasks . . . difficult to resist such comforts, when the winter winds howled around one's windows and drafts seeped in at every seam. Especially when the *ekeles* of those within the Vale needed no protections from the cold; when hot springs waited to soak away aches and bruises, when windows could stand open to the breeze—

Well, they could if one lived on a lower level, at any rate. The *ekeles* near the tops of the trees tended to find themselves whipped by wilder winds than those near the ground. He smiled through his shivers at recalling when Nightsky had left her windows ajar—and came back after a lesson to find belongings strewn about the room. She had learned quickly that it was as well to leave the windows closed.

Few lived in those upper levels, in k'Sheyna. With the population so reduced, there was little competition for dwellings nearer the Vale floor. One or two still preferred heights, but never scouts. After returning from a long day on patrol the very last thing anyone cared to do was to climb a ladder for several stories just to get home to rest.

Darkwind was no different in that respect from any of the rest of the scouts, once the general consensus was reached that a move back to the Vale would be a good thing for all. He had stayed with his father for a brief while, in part to help Kethra at night, then moved into an *ekele* in the lowest branches. His tree stood near the waterfall end of the Vale, so that both the cool water of the waterfall pools and a nearby hot spring were available. He ran his patrols with Elspeth and her Companion as he had since the coming of autumn, but now he returned with gratitude to the warmth and the comfort of the Vale. And he pitied Wintermoon for his self-chosen exile to the winter-bound forest.

On the other hand, we can't seem to track down Nyara from within the Vale. I've tried Looking for her, but she—or that sword—have shielded themselves too well to spot. I am glad it isn't me out there.

K'Tathi had flown in just before he and Elspeth went out on patrol, carrying a message; a written one, since it was fairly complicated. Wintermoon and Skif had given a good portion of food to a *tervardi* temporarily disabled by an encounter with Changelions. Rather than lose any great amount of time, Wintermoon was leaving Skif with the bird-man, and coming in to fetch replacements and enough food over to keep the *tervardi* fed while he healed. So would Darkwind be so good as to put together thus-and-so, and meet him and his *dyheli* friends at the mouth of the Vale at sunset?

Darkwind not only *would*, he was glad to. It often seemed to him that there was never a great deal he could do for Wintermoon; he and his brother had very little in common, and Wintermoon's position as elder often led to him being the one to lend aid to the younger brother. Wintermoon seldom asked favors of anyone; he was as much a bachelor falcon as Darkwind, if not more so.

With that in mind, Darkwind went out of his way to root through some of the old storehouses and uncover the last few cold-lights, mage-cloaks, and a fireless stove left from the days when mages in k'Sheyna could lend their powers to making aids to the scouts. It had been a very long time since scouts of k'Sheyna made overnight patrols—and a very long time since any of them had been willing to use mage-made things, for fear that the creatures of the Uncleansed Lands might sense them. He thought that Skif and Wintermoon might well be willing to chance that, since they were between k'Sheyna and the Cleansed Outland. The cloaks kept the wearer warm and dry; there were five, enough for both humans and the Companion and *dyheli* to sleep beneath. The stove should be good for several weeks of use, or so his testing had confirmed—and should heat the tiny tent his brother and the Outlander shared quite cozily.

When he asked for permission to take the things, Iceshadow had queried with a lifted eyebrow whether they needed it—or were keeping warm some other way. He had answered the same way that the notion was wildly unlikely. He still was not certain about Outlander prejudices in that regard, but he knew his brother well enough to be certain that young Skif was *not* likely to become Wintermoon's bedmate unless they encountered some wild magic on the borders that wrought a complete change of sex in either of them.

The last gray light of afternoon faded and died away, creeping from the forest by imperceptible degrees, and deepening the shadows beneath the trees. He shivered in a breath of cold air that crept across the Veil and hoped that Wintermoon would arrive soon. It had been a very long day, and he was bone weary. He and Elspeth had tracked and driven off a pair of Changelions—perhaps even the same ones that injured that *tervardi*, in fact—and it had not been an easy task in knee-deep snow. Even Elspeth's Companion had been of little help, not with the snow so deep and soft. The cats, with their snowshoelike paws, had a definite advantage in weather like this.

It had been snow with ice beneath; they had slipped and slid so often that he reckoned they were both black and blue in a fair number of places. He wanted to get back to his *ekele*, to the hot pool beneath it. He thought, briefly, about seeking one of the other scouts for company, then dismissed the idea. There were several women of k'Sheyna who were friends, willing and attractive, but none of them were Elspeth. . . .

Stupid. Don't be an idiot. Don't complicate matters. She's your friend, sometimes your student; be wise enough to leave it at that. You aren't living a romance-tale, you have work enough and more to do.

Still—she was a competent partner now as well; *he* felt more confident in his magic, and so did she. As a team, they were efficient and effective. Working with the gryphons had been a stroke of genius.

A white shape flickered through the branches ahead, ghosting just under the branches in silence; a breath of snow-fog, with a twin coming in right behind it.

Vree cried a greeting; not the challenge scream, but the whistling call no outsider ever heard. A long, deep *Hooo, hoo-hooo*, answered him, and one of the two owls swooped up across the Veil and onto a branch just above Darkwind's head.

The second followed his brother, and as he flew up to land above,

Darkwind made out the distant figure of someone riding through the barren bushes and charcoal-gray tree trunks of the unprotected forest.

The *dyheli* waded through the soft snow easily, his thin legs having no trouble with drifts a man would be caught in, his sharp, cleft hooves cutting footholds in the ice beneath. Astride him was Wintermoon. Behind the first *dyheli* came the second, unladen, his breath puffing frostily out of his nostrils.

Wintermoon waved as soon as he saw Darkwind, grinning broadly. Since he was not normally given to such things as broad grins, Darkwind was a bit surprised.

Being with that Outlander has done him some good, then. Loosened him up.

It occurred to him that Wintermoon might have found himself a real friend—rarer still, a close friend—in the Outlander Herald. Could it be mutual? Perhaps they had learned that they had a lot in common; Skif had struck him as rather a loner himself. A close friend was something, so far as Darkwind knew, his brother had never had before.

About time, too.

Wintermoon and the *dyheli* crossed the Veil and the scout slid from the *dyheli's* back to land beside his brother. "Darkwind!" he said, obviously pleased. "Thank you for doing this yourself, and thank you for fetching the supplies for me at all. What's all this?" Wintermoon briefly embraced his brother and indicated "this" with a toe to one of the extra bundles. "I did not ask you for nearly so much."

"And it doesn't look like provisions, I know." Briefly, Darkwind told his brother what he had put together for the little expedition.

Wintermoon frowned at that. "I don't know. I hesitate to use anything magic made out there."

"I've shielded it as best I can," Darkwind pointed out, "We have been using magic without attracting trouble for many weeks now. And if I were the one doing the scouting, I would weight the benefits of warmth and light very heavily in any decisions I made. Winter is only just upon us, and already it has the Vale locked around with ice and snow. It will be worse out there."

"It already is worse." Wintermoon eyed the bundle dubiously, but then heaved it onto his mount's back. "You were the first of us to object to using magic on the border; if you say it is probably worth the risk, I will believe you. I have very little to return you for your gift, I am afraid."

"No sign of Nyara?" Darkwind asked, expecting a negative.

"Very little sign, and old," Wintermoon replied, as he helped his brother tie the bundles securely to the *dyheli* backs. "But there are things that tell me she passed the way we are going. I have some hope that we will find her, though I have not told this to Skif, for I do not wish to raise his hopes with nothing more substantial than old sign. It is a difficult secret to keep, though."

"That is probably wise," Darkwind said carefully, balancing the first *dyheli's* load.

His brother looked up at him from the other side of the stag's back. "He is a man who has had many disappointments," the scout said suddenly. "I would not add to them, if I can avoid it. He is Wingsib; more than that, he does not deserve it."

"We seldom deserve disappointment," Darkwind observed dryly. "But I do agree with you."

He fastened the last of the bundles to the second *dyheli*, and straightened from tightening the cinch. "If you are worried about losing time and need someone to meet you with supplies, send K'Tathi again," he said. "It's no trouble, and perhaps I can find you something else useful, rummaging around in the old stores."

"You might indeed, and thank you." Wintermoon peered out into the growing darkness beyond the Veil. "I had best get on the trail; it will take some time getting back with all these supplies."

Darkwind nodded, and Wintermoon mounted the second stag, so that the work of bearing him could be shared between the two. With a wave of farewell, Wintermoon urged his mount and its brother out of the Vale and into the night; vanishing into the darkness beneath the trees, followed by two silver shadows, ghosting out and above.

Darkwind turned his own face back toward the Vale, figuring to find some dinner, soak himself in hot water, and go to bed. A headache was coming on, and he assumed it was from fatigue. It had been a very long day. Bed, even one with no one in it but himself, had never seemed so welcome.

So when he passed his father's *ekele* and saw the Council of Elders, even old Rainlance, huddled in conference with most of the mages of k'Sheyna, including Elspeth, he was tempted to retrace his steps before anyone saw him. Such a gathering could only mean trouble. Surely he had done enough for one day. Surely he deserved a rest.

But—

Damn. This looks important. I can do without food and sleep a little longer. I've done it before.

The mage-lights above them were few and dim, and if he had gone another way, they would never have known he was there, now that the shadows of night had descended. Elspeth was the first to spot him, but as soon as the rest realized she was looking at someone and not staring off into the darkness, they glanced his way. Their glances sharpened as soon as their eyes fell on him, and with a resigned sigh, he joined them.

I guess I was right. It is important.

The very first thing he noticed, once he joined their circle, was that they were all, barring the few scouts among them, drained and demoralized. They slumped in postures of exhaustion, faces pale and lined with pain, white hair lying lank against their shoulders.

All? There was only one thing that would affect them all.

"The Heartstone," he said flatly. Iceshadow nodded, and licked dry lips.

"The Heartstone," the Elder replied in agreement. He passed his hand over his eyes for a moment. "Precisely. We have failed in our attempt to stabilize it. And there will be no more such attempts."

"The spell not only did not drain the Stone," one of the others whispered wearily, "It enabled the Stone to drain *us*. We will be days, perhaps even a week, in recovering."

So that's why Iceshadow said there would be no more tries . . . if it could do that once, it will do so again. Thank the gods that the mages worked within shields, or we would likely all be in the same condition.

"K'Sheyna will not be defenseless, thanks to good planning," Iceshadow sighed. "The mages that are also scouts were not involved in the spellcasting, nor you and Wingsister Elspeth. But it is only thanks to that caution that we still have magical defenders."

There was one face missing from the group, one who *should* have been there. "My father?" he asked sharply.

Iceshadow winced. "A side effect we had not reckoned on," he replied, averting his eyes from Darkwind's. "Starblade's life is bound to the Stone in some way that we do not understand and did not sense until too late. When our spell backlashed, it struck him as well."

Darkwind tensed. "What happened to him?"

Iceshadow said nothing. Rainlance spoke softly. "It nearly killed him, despite the shaman Kethra throwing herself into the link to protect him."

"He lives, and he will recover," someone else said hastily, as he felt blood drain from his face. "But he and the Healer are weak and in shock. The shaman, Tre'valen, is tending them."

They are in the best hands in the Vale. If I have regained him only to lose him— "Is this a Council meeting, then?" he asked, keeping back all the bitter things he wanted to say. They were of no use, anyway. How could anyone have known the deep plans that had been laid against them, all the things that had been done to Starblade? They severed his links to Mornelithe Falconsbane, but there had been no reason to look for any others. *Even gone, Falconsbane's influence lies heavily upon us. Even gone, he left behind his poison in our veins.*

"A meeting of the Council and of all the mages," Iceshadow replied. "We have determined that we have tried every means to neutralize the Heartstone at our disposal, and all have failed. There is no other way. We must look outside, to other Clans, for help."

The faces in the dim light showed how they felt about it; that it was an admission of dependence, of guilt, of failure. Darkwind had urged them all for years to seek help from outside, and swallow that pride. Bitter and sweet; victory at last was his, but it had nearly cost the life of his father. Caught between two conflicting sets of emotions, he could only stare at the leader of the Council.

"You must send the call," Iceshadow said, finally. "You, the Wing-sister, and the gryphons. Elspeth has already agreed, as have Treyvan and Hydona. You are the only ones that we can turn to now, you and Elspeth. You remember the way of constructing a seeking-spell strong enough to reach who and what we need."

He nodded numbly, still caught in a web of surprise and dismay.

"You look ready to drop," Elspeth said firmly into the silence. "You're tired—I'm tired—we aren't going to get anything done to-night." She stood up and nodded to Iceshadow. "With respect, Elder, we have had a long day, and we need to rest. We'll see what we can do tomorrow."

"It has waited until now, it can certainly wait another night," Iceshadow agreed wearily. "And there is no sense in exhausting you two as well. Tomorrow, then."

"Tomorrow," she agreed, and signaled Darkwind to follow her down the path.

"I had the *hertasi* bring food and that mineral drink to the pool near your treehouse," she said as soon as they were out of sight and sound of the circle of exhausted mages. "I thought you would probably need both. And a good soak."

"You were right." He rubbed his temple, as a headache began to throb behind his eyes. "When did all this happen?"

"Just at sunset," she told him. "That was when they had timed the drainage to begin, and that was when the spell backlashed. I didn't feel it, and neither did anyone else outside of the Working area except Starblade; I first knew something was wrong when two of them staggered out the pass-through looking for help, and I happened to be nearby. Some of them had to be carried out."

"Gods." He shook his head. "So there are only four of us to work this seeking-spell."

:Five,: corrected a voice in his head.

He had not noticed Gwena's presence until that moment; she moved so quietly behind them that she might have been just another shadow. "Five?" he repeated. "But lady, I did not know you were Mage-Gifted."

Elspeth's glare could have peeled bark from the trees. "Neither did I," she said flatly, her voice so devoid of expression that the lack alone was a sign of her anger. She stopped; so did he and the Companion.

Before Gwena could jerk her head away, Elspeth had her by the bottom of the hackamore. "Look," she said tightly, "You *know* how important strategy is. That, and tactics. Especially here and now."

Gwena tried to look away; Elspeth wouldn't let her. :Yes,: she agreed faintly.

"*You* have been withholding information," Elspeth continued, her voice still dangerously flat and calm. "Information that I—*we* need to have to plan intelligently. What would you do to someone who had deliberately withheld information that vital?"

Gwena shook her head slightly, as much as Elspeth's hold on her hackamore would permit.

"*I. Have. Had. Enough.*" Elspeth punctuated each word with a little shake of the halter. "If you haven't worked *that* into your 'great plan,' you'd better start thinking about it. No more holding back. Do you understand?"

Gwena rolled her eyes and started to pull away. Elspeth wouldn't let her, and Gwena was obviously not going to exert her considerable strength in something that might harm her Herald. But from the look of shock in her bright blue eyes, she had not expected this reaction from Elspeth.

"I said, *do you understand me?*" Elspeth pulled her head down and stared directly into her eyes.

Darkwind stood with his arms crossed, jaw set in a stern expression. He was trying his best to give the impression he supported Elspeth's actions completely. In fact, he did.

:*Yes,:* Gwena managed.

"Are you going to *stop* holding back information?"

Gwena pawed the ground unhappily, but clearly Elspeth was not going to let her go until she got an answer she liked.

:*Yes,:* she said, meekly, obviously unable to see any other way out of the confrontation.

"Good." Elspeth let go of the halter. She straightened, put her hands on her hips, and gave Gwena a look that Darkwind could not read. "Remember. You just gave your word."

Darkwind did not think that Gwena was going to forget.

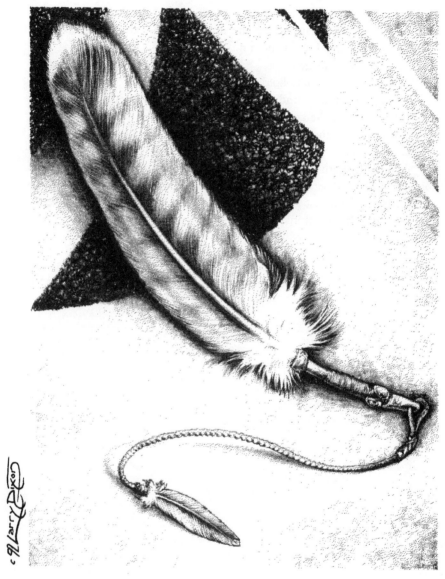

Chapter Thirteen

A gray sky gave no clue as to the time, but Darkwind thought it was not long after dawn. He had spent a restless night, haunted by the exhausted faces of the k'Sheyna mages. He had not been expecting anyone so early and the first words out of Darkwind's mouth when Elspeth appeared at his *ekele* were, "We cannot do it here."

He had been thinking hard about what they were to do; all during his meal, the long soak before bed (in the midst of which he had fallen asleep until a *hertasi* woke him), and into the night before sleep took him. And he had decided on certain provisions as he dressed. *What* they were to do was no problem; thanks to Elspeth and Treyvan he was accustomed now to improvising on existing spells. This would be a variation on the seeking-spell. But *where*—that was different. It could not be done within the confines of the Vale, even outside the shielded Practice ground. He knew that with deep certainty that had only hardened during sleep. Every instinct revolted when he even considered the idea.

Something was happening to the Heartstone, or possibly within it. He had no notion of what was going on, but now he did not want to do anything that affected it while within its reach. It was not just that the

Stone had drained k'Sheyna mages, it was the way it had happened. It had waited, or seemed to, until they were certain of success and off their guard.

Perhaps that had been accident, but what if it was not? He did not know. It didn't seem likely, but less likely things had been happening with dismaying regularity. These were strange times indeed.

He realized as soon as he said the words that Elspeth would have no idea what had been going through his mind since the meeting. He felt like a fool as soon as he closed his mouth.

She's going to think I've gone crazy, that I'm babbling.

But instead of confusion, Elspeth met the statement with a nod of understanding. "Absolutely," she replied, as if she had been talking to him about the problems all along. "Too much interference from shields and set-spells, plus the Heartstone's proximity itself. I've been thinking about that since last night. That Heartstone of yours is acting altogether too clever for *my* comfort. I don't want to do something it might not like when I'm anywhere around it. It might decide that since I'm an Outlander, it'll do more than just drain me."

"It is not a thinking being," he protested, but without conviction.

"Maybe not, but it acts like it is." She glanced back over her shoulder, in the direction of the Stone. "Maybe it's all coincidence, or maybe it's something that Falconsbane set up a long time ago. But when it acts like it can think, I'm going to assume that it *is* thinking and act accordingly." She grinned crookedly. "As my Shin'a'in-trained teacher would say, 'Just because you feel certain an enemy is lurking behind every bush, it doesn't follow that you are wrong.' "

Shin'a'in proverbs from an Outlander. God help me. But he couldn't help but smile ruefully in reply. "The trouble with proverbs is that they're truisms," he agreed. "You make me think that you are reading my thoughts, though."

It was a half-serious accusation, although he made it with a smile. It was no secret that these Heralds had mind-magic—but did they use it without warning?

She laughed. "Not a chance. I don't eavesdrop, I promise. No Herald would. It was just a case of parallel worries. So, where are we going to go to work?"

No Herald would. Perhaps the Companion might . . . but I suspect she knows that. He wasn't worried about her Companion reading his thoughts. It was not likely that there was anything he would think that a Guardian Spirit had not seen before.

"Have you eaten yet?" he asked instead. When she shook her head, he went back into his *ekele* and rummaged about in his belongings and what the *hertasi* had left him. He brought out two coats draped over his arm, and fruit and bread, handing her a share of the food. She took it with a nod of thanks. "I thought," he said after she had settled beside him on the steps, "that we might work from the ruins."

"The gryphon's lair?" She tipped her head to one side. "There *is* a node underneath it. And we're likely to need one. But what about—well—attracting things when we do the magic?"

"We won't have the shields of the Vale, and that's a problem," he admitted, biting into a ripe *pomera*. "I don't know how to get around that."

She considered that for a moment, then shrugged. "We'll deal with it, I suppose," she replied. "Gwena can't think of any way around it either, but she's in agreement with both of us on not working near the Heartstone." She finished the last of her bread and stood up, dusting her hands off. "So, what, exactly, are we doing?"

He licked juice from his fingers and followed her example, handed her a coat, then led the way down the stairs to the path below. "Well, we can't do a wide open Mindcall," he began.

"Obviously," she said dryly. "Since we don't want every nasty thing in the area to know that k'Sheyna is in trouble. I wouldn't imagine we'd want to do a focused Mindcall either; something still might pick it up, even though we meant it only for Tayledras. There might even be something *watching* for a Mindcall like that, for all we know."

"And what's the point in wasting all the energy needed for a focused Mindcall to all the Clans when there may not be more than one or two Adepts that can help us?" he concluded. "No, what I'd thought that we should do is to send a specific message-spell; that is a complicated message that can be carried by a single bird." He smiled to himself; she wouldn't believe what kind of bird would carry the incorporeal message, but it was the most logical.

"To whom?" she asked in surprise, as Gwena joined them, following a polite ten paces behind. "I thought—" she stopped in confusion.

"I don't know *who* to send it to, but I know *what*," he explained, brushing aside a branch that overhung the path. "Somewhere in the Clans is a Healing Adept of a high enough level that he either knows or can figure out what we need to do. Now I know that no one here can, so I send out a message to the nearest Clan, aimed at any Adept that's of our ability or higher. In this case, the nearest Clan is k'Treva. And I'm pretty sure they have someone better equipped to deal with this than we are. They offered their help a while back, and Father refused it.''

"And if no one there can help us after all?" she asked, darkly.

He shrugged. "Then I ask them to pass on the word to the others. *They* don't have a flawed Heartstone in their midst. *They* can send out to any Clan Council. To tell you the truth, our biggest problem with getting the Stone taken care of has been isolation. Solve that, and we can solve the rest.''

The Vale was unusually silent, with all the mages abed and recovering. Their steps were the only sounds besides the faint stirring of leaves in the breeze and the bird songs that always circulated through the Vale. She was quiet all the way to the entrance and the Veil that guarded it. Beyond the protections, another winter snowstorm dropped fat flakes through the bare branches of the trees.

They shared a look of resignation; wrapped themselves in their coats and crossed the invisible barrier between summer and winter. The first sound outside was of their boots splashing into the puddles of water made by snow melted from the ambient heat of the Vale's entrance.

There was no wind, and snow buried their feet to the calf with every step they took. Flakes drifted down slowly through air that felt humid on Darkwind's face, and not as cold as he had expected. Above the gray branches, a white sky stretched featurelessly from horizon to horizon; Darkwind got the oddest impression, as if the snowflakes were bits of the sky, chipped off and slowly falling. Beneath the branches, the gray columns of the tree trunks loomed through the curtaining snow, and more snow carpeted the forest floor and mounded in the twigs of every bush. There were no evergreens in this part of the woods, so there was nothing to break the landscape of gray and white.

Snow creaked under their feet, and the cold crept into his boots. Their feet would be half frozen by the time they reached the ruins.

Darkwind didn't mind the lack of color. After the riot of colors and verdant greens within the Vale, the subdued grays and gray-browns were restful, refreshing. He wished, though, that he had time and the proper surroundings to enjoy them.

This is a good day for bundling up beside a fire, watching the snow fall and not thinking of anything in particular.

"This is the kind of day when I used to curl up in a blanket in a window and read," Elspeth said quietly, barely breaking the silence. "When I'd just sit, listen to the fire, watch the snow pile up on the window ledge, and think about how nice it was to be warm and inside."

He chuckled, and she glanced at him. Gwena moved around them to walk in front, breaking the trail for them.

"I was just thinking the same thing," he explained. "If we only had the time. I used to do much the same."

"Ah." She nodded. "I'd forgotten you used to live outside that glorified greenhouse. I like it, the Vale, I mean—but sometimes I miss weather when I'm in there. It's hard to tell what time of day it is, much less what season."

"Well, I imagine Wintermoon and Skif would be willing to trade places with us right now," he replied thoughtfully. "This is good weather to be inside—but not for camping. Snow this damp is heavy when it collects on a tent. Oh, if you're wondering, I sent Vree on ahead with a message about what we want to do; I expect Treyvan and Hydona will be waiting for us."

"I was wondering." She glanced at him again, but this time she half-smiled as she tucked her hair more securely inside the hood of her coat. "Not that I expected them to object, but it is considered good manners to let people know that you are planning on setting off fireworks from the roof of their house—and you plan to have their help in doing it."

He laughed; this was a very pleasant change from the Elspeth of several weeks ago. Reasonable, communicative. And showing a good sense of humor. "Yes it is," he agreed. "My message to them was that if they objected to the idea, to let me know immediately. That was when I first woke; since Vree didn't come back, I assume they don't mind."

"Either that, or he forgot his promise and made a snatch at a crest-feather again," she said with mock solemnity. "In that case, you'll have to find yourself another bondbird."

Elspeth enjoyed the walk, for with Gwena breaking the trail for them, the trip to the lair was something like a pleasant morning's hike. They had to keep a watch for unexpected trouble, of course, but nothing more threatening appeared than a crow scolding them for being in his part of the forest.

This is the most relaxed I've been since I got here, she thought. Perhaps it was because the waiting was finally over. She'd had the feeling all along that the mages of k'Sheyna would never be able to solve the problem by themselves. Darkwind felt the same, she knew, but he never discussed it. He was relieved, too—but too conscientious to feel pleased with the failure of his Clan's mages, even though it proved that he was right. He wasn't a shallow man.

The ruins were cloaked in snow, which gave some portions an air of utter desolation, and others an uncanny resemblance to complete buildings. Passage of the gryphons in and around their territory kept the pathways they used relatively free of snow. It was easier to move here, but with the last of the trees out of sight, the place felt like a desert.

Vree was on his best behavior, it seemed, for when they approached the gryphons' lair, they found him up on the "rafters" of the nest, pulling bits from a fresh-killed quail with great gusto.

He didn't have time to do more than call a greeting to Darkwind, though. The gryphlets tumbled out of the nest and overran all three of them, knocking Darkwind off his feet and rolling him in the snow, wrestling with him as if they were kittens and he was a kind of superior cat-toy.

Elspeth laughed until her sides hurt; every time he started to get up, one of the youngsters knocked him over again. He was matted with snow; he looked like an animated snowman, and was laughing so hard she wondered how he caught his breath.

Gwena watched the melee wistfully, obviously wishing she could join in.

Elspeth decided that Darkwind could use a rescue. She waded in and started pulling tails, which turned the gryphlets on *her.* Within a heartbeat, she found herself going rump-over-tail into a snowdrift, with a squealing Jerven on top of her, flailing with his short, stubby wings and kicking up clouds of the soft snow in all directions.

That was when Gwena joined the fun; making short charges and shouldering the youngsters aside so that she tumbled them into the snow the way they had knocked Darkwind and Elspeth over. The gryphlets loved that; Gwena was big enough to hold her own with them, and provided they kept their foreclaws fisted, they didn't have to hold back with her in a rough-and-tumble.

In a few moments, their parents appeared, and rather than calling a halt to the game, they joined it. Now the odds were clearly against the gryphlets, and first Darkwind, then Elspeth switched sides, coming to the youngsters' defense while Gwena sided with the parents. In moments, snow flew everywhere. It looked like a blizzard from the ground up.

The best strategy seemed to be seizing the tail of an adult, hampering movement, while the young one batted away at the front end with blows of their wings and with their claws held tightly into a fist to avoid injury.

That wouldn't work for long, however.

Just as Elspeth was getting winded, Hydona turned the tables on them. The gryphon whirled, dragging Elspeth along with her and bringing her into the range of the huge wings. Suddenly she went tumbling, buffeted into another snowbank by a carefully controlled sweep of a wing; landing right beside Jerven who had gotten the same treatment. Before either of them could scramble to their feet, Hydona was upon them, pinning each of them down with a foreclaw.

"Trrruce?" the gryphon asked, her head cocked to one side, her beak slightly open as she panted. Steam rose in puffs from her half-open beak. Elspeth sensed the controlled power in the claw pinning her carefully into the drift, and marveled at it, even as she signaled her defeat laughingly. Hydona let both of them up, extending the claw again to help Elspeth to her feet.

"Thanks," she said, looking for Gwena, and finding that Darkwind and Lytha had taken Gwena hostage, holding her against Treyvan's continued good behavior. The Companion's blue eyes sparkled like sapphires, and her ears were up and tail flagged—

In short, they only *thought* they had her.

Elspeth kept her mouth shut, waiting for Gwena to make her move.

Treyvan feinted, and Darkwind turned just a little too far to block him. For one moment, he took his eyes off the Companion.

That was when Gwena grabbed his collar in her teeth, and, whipping her head around on her long, graceful neck, jerked him off his feet and flung him sideways into Lytha.

Darkwind *whuffed* with surprise; Lytha squealed. They both went down in a tangle of legs and wings.

Elspeth giggled uncontrollably, then took a huge double handful of snow, packed it tight, and lobbed it at Gwena. It impacted against Gwena's rump, and she whirled to glare at her Chosen indignantly. Darkwind howled with laughter, and the gryphlets joined in.

"I was afraid you were going to break the game up," Elspeth told the female gryphon, as Darkwind and his partner surrendered to her mate.

Hydona shook her head to rid it of snow. "No," she replied. "The little onesss werrre resstlessss. Now they will sssettle, and let usss worrk in peace."

Elspeth stretched and began beating the snow out of her cloak, feeling vertebrae pop as her muscles loosened. "I feel like I've worked off a bit of nerves, too," she began, when another creature popped its head out of the gryphon's lair, ears pricked forward and eyes wide with interest.

:Is the battle over?: the *kyree* asked. *:Or is this a temporary truce?:*

"I think we've been defeated too soundly to make another attempt," Darkwind said cheerfully. "Despite Gwena's indignation. Am I right, my shieldbrother?" he asked, turning to Lytha.

The gryphlet nodded vigorously, and sneezed a clump of melting snow from her cere and crown. "Wet," she complained. "Got sssnow in my feathersss."

"If you fight in sssnow, you mussst expect sssome in your feathersss," Hydona told her, with a twinkle.

:My famous cousin Warrl used to say, "You cannot have a battle without getting your fur in a mess.": The *kyree* scratched meditatively at one ear. *:He used to say, "You know how fierce the fighting was by how long after it takes to clean up." If you two want to come inside, I can start a mage-fire for you to lie beside, and tell you a story.:* The *kyree's* head vanished into the lair again.

Jerven beat Lytha inside by less than half a length.

"I take it that was Rris?" Elspeth said, trying not to laugh.

"Yesss," sighed Hydona. She looked at Treyvan, and the two of them said, in chorus, "That wasss Rrisss Let-me-tell-you-of-my-famousss-cousssin-Warrl of Hyrrrull Pack."

"The childrrren love him," Treyvan added. "I think I can bearrr with hisss famousss cousssin sstorriess sssince he doesss not repeat them."

"Only the proverbsss and advice." Hydona shrugged. "It isss no worsssse than living with a Ssshin'a'in."

"Surely, but what could be?" Darkwind agreed, and squinted at the sky. "We have all of the afternoon and some of the morning left. Do you want to start now?"

"I thought it might be wisssse," Treyvan replied. "The lair isss not dirrrectly above the node. When I found the place that wasss, I built it into a ssshelter asss well. Would you follow?"

Darkwind waved him ahead; he and Hydona took up the lead, with the two humans following, Gwena between them. Elspeth laid a hand on her shoulder.

:*Did you enjoy yourself?*: she asked. :*You looked like you were having a wonderful time.*:

:*Very much,*: Gwena replied, her breath steaming from her nostrils, her eyes still bright and merry. :*That was fun! I'd nearly forgotten how much fun it is to be a child. Or to be with a child. No matter how serious things are, they can always play.*:

:*A good thing, too,*: Elspeth chuckled, patting her on the neck. :*They can remind us grownups that there's a time to forget how serious things are. I miss the twins.*:

:*So do I.*: Gwena sighed gustily. :*I miss a lot of things.*:

Elspeth realized Gwena must feel rather alone. *She* at least had other humans around, however alien they were. With Skif out on the hunt for Nyara, Gwena didn't even have Cymry to talk to.

Gwena must have guessed the direction her thoughts were taking. :*Oh, don't feel too sorry for me,*: she said, poking Elspeth in the shoulder with her nose. :*I can do that well enough on my own!*:

Elspeth made a face at her, relieved. :*I'm sure you can,*: she teased. :*And I wouldn't even have to encourage you.*:

:*Too true.*: Gwena's ears pricked forward and she brought her head up. :*I do believe we have arrived.*:

Before them loomed another rough building-shape, much like the lair, but cruder. Where the lair was clearly a dwelling, this was no more than a simple shelter; the most basic of walls and a roof. But it was fully large enough for the gryphons and their guests, with room to spare.

It was clear that Treyvan and his mate had constructed this place before the first snow fell. Elspeth wondered why they had built it. Had they always intended to work magic here in their ruins? Or had they some other purpose in mind?

They entered, to find that Treyvan had already started a mage-fire inside; the glowing ball gave them both heat and light. The interior of the crude building was appreciably warmer than the outside, although an occasional draft whipped by at ankle height. Elspeth decided to leave her coat on; it wasn't *that* warm inside.

"What, exactly, arrre we doing?" Treyvan asked, settling down on his haunches. "I know of one kind of messsage-ssspell, but I do not know that it isss like the one you ussse."

"Ours requires a carrier," Darkwind explained carefully. He looked around and found a block of stone to sit on. "We generally use a bird of some kind. There are a lot of advantages to that. The spell itself weighs nothing, and it can't be detected unless a mage is quite close to the bird. The bird doesn't need to remember anything, so it doesn't have to be a bondbird. The spell is in two parts; one is the message, and the other will identify the target. That part will tell the bird when it has found either the specific person that the message is for, or in our case, the *kind* of person the spell is for."

"Interesssting." Hydona nodded. "Better than oursss; lesss inclined to be detected. What bird arrre you usssing?"

"This one." He pointed to the hood of his coat; a tiny head peeked out from beneath his hair. Very tiny; mostly bright black eyes, and a long, sharp beak. Elspeth blinked, and looked again.

"A *hummingbird?*" she said incredulously. "Where did that come from?"

"The Vale," Darkwind grinned. "He was in my cloak hood until just before the children ran at us. He went up to shelter with Vree while we played; Vree knows better than to molest a hummingbird, since we use them for message-spells all the time. He ducked back inside my hood when I told him it was safe, and that was how I brought him here."

"But a hummingbird?" She frowned; it was not the choice she would have made. The tiny birds were pretty enough, and certainly they did very well in the artificial world of the Vale, but it seemed to be a poor choice for carrying a message for what might well be hundreds of leagues. "Isn't he going to freeze to death in this weather? What's he going to eat? And how is he going to defend himself?"

Darkwind held his hand up to his hood; the bird flew out and hovered for a moment before settling on his finger. It was no larger than the first joint of his thumb. "As long as he keeps moving, he'll be fine; he won't have any trouble with the cold. He won't have to stop to eat, because I will have given him a tiny store of mage-energy that will carry him as far as k'Treva. And look at him."

Elspeth kept her reservations to herself and took the time to examine the tiny bird closely. It was not one of the little flying jewels she was used to seeing; the bird was black, with only a hint of dull purple at his throat.

"This little fellow doesn't need to defend himself because very few creatures or birds will be able to see him," Darkwind continued. "The fact that you didn't see him fly out of my hood or back in is proof of that. His speed is his defense; that and his size. He's so small that even if something sees him, it isn't likely to catch him. And if something is foolish enough to try to catch him, it is going to discover that it's nearly impossible to try and catch a hummingbird in full flight."

"Hmm." Treyvan bent his head to examine the bird at short range. It looked right back at him, completely without fear, despite the fact that the gryphon could have inhaled the tiny creature and never noticed he had done so. "Ssso you will create a pocket of mage-enerrgy to feed the birrd? That ssshould make no morrre ssstirr than the ssspell it-ssself."

"Exactly." Darkwind looked very pleased. "These little fellows move so quickly that even if someone detected a spell, by the time they got to the place where they'd first detected it, the bird would be a hundred furlongs gone."

"From the maps I've seen, it's an awful long way to k'Treva," Elspeth said doubtfully.

"Wild hummingbirds migrate so far to the south in the winter that we don't even know where they go," Darkwind replied.

:He's right,: Gwena put in. :One of Kero's men, the black fellow—I listened to him tell stories once to some of the trainees. He said that hummingbirds spent the winter in his land. And we have no notion of how far north he came.:

Well, if hummingbirds really traveled that far—

"He can do it, don't worry," Darkwind replied firmly. "These little ones have carried messages like this one before, even in winter. And once he gets to k'Treva and finds our Adept, someone will see to it that he gets the best honey-nectar and will find a territory for him in their Vale."

Once again she was struck by the care the Tayledras had for the creatures that they shared their lives with—even a tiny hummingbird that was in no way the kind of partner that their bondbirds were.

Darkwind shook his head. "The little fellow is ready and eager to go. Let's get to this, so that he doesn't have to wait."

Elspeth couldn't imagine how he would know that, but she agreed. This was likely to take a fair amount of time.

"Indeed," Hydona said, nodding. "Rrrisss cannot keep the little onesss quiet forever."

★ ★ ★

Elspeth was very glad Gwena had come along and even happier that the Companion wasn't as tired as she was.

The walk back to the Vale, which had been so pleasant on the way out, was a daunting prospect now.

:Neither of you are heavy,: Gwena said, as the three of them followed the gryphons out into the snow. *:The Vale is not that far. I can carry both of you, or you can lean against me, if you like.:*

The sun was faintly visible through the thick clouds; there was perhaps a candlemark until sunset. "What do you think?" Elspeth asked the Hawkbrother. "Walk, or ride?"

:I can get you there by sunset,: Gwena said, coaxingly.

"Ride," Darkwind replied decisively. "If you have no objection."

"None at all." In fact, this might prove to be an intriguing opportunity. . . .

Darkwind was possibly the single most attractive man she had ever met, and not just because he was so exotic. And once she had figured out that he wasn't being obtuse in his lessons just to aggravate her, she found him even more attractive.

Admittedly, most of the Tayledras were attractive, either physically, mentally, or both. But Darkwind drew her as no one else had. She wanted to know more about him—and she wanted him to know more about her. It was one thing to be attracted to some one. It was another thing entirely to act on that attraction.

Especially if it proved to be only one-sided.

Horrible thought. But possible.

And her pride would not permit her to go panting after him like a puppy. Skif's example of slavish infatuation was enough to decide her on that. She would never put herself in the position to be humiliated the way he had been.

She mounted first; Darkwind, less experienced, used a handy chunk of fallen rock to mount up behind her.

:I promise I'll be gentle,: Gwena teased, reminding them both of the uncomfortable jog Darkwind had taken, perched behind Elspeth over Gwena's hipbones, as they hurried to the aid of another scout. *:Nothing more than a fast, smooth walk.:*

"Thank you," Darkwind said fervently.

The gryphons had already made their weary farewells; as custodians of this node, they had used the most strength in linking into it and feeding the power to Darkwind, Gwena, and Elspeth. The hummingbird was on his way, shooting into the sky like a slung stone. There was nothing holding them here.

Snow continued to fall, but the light was fading, and the ruins had a haunted look to them that made Elspeth's skin crawl. Gwena responded to her uneasiness by heading out by the most direct route, one that would skirt the *hertasi* swamp but would not go in. That was no place to be in weather like this.

"What happens to the *hertasi* in the winter?" she asked, suddenly. "The ones that live out in the marsh, I mean?"

"They don't precisely hibernate, but they do not leave their caves much," Darkwind said into her left ear, while Gwena waded through the soft snow at a fairly brisk pace. His hands felt good on her hips. "They seal themselves into their caves; sleep much, and eat little, stay close to fires. What time they spend awake, they use in making small things. Carvings, mostly. Everything they own is carved or ornamented, at least a little."

"I gathered they had a fondness for that sort of thing," Elspeth replied. "You know, they don't approve of my uniforms. Too plain, I suppose."

"Precisely." He chuckled. "That is one reason why they enjoy working with us. They have a number of traditional designs they use, but we are quicker at creating new ones than they are. Or perhaps it is simply that we are more uninhibited. That is part of the trade they have with us; when one of them wants a new design for something, he goes to one of us craftsmen, and we create it for him. That, and protection and shelter, and we earn their service."

"Us craftsmen?" she said, puzzled. "I didn't know you were a craftsman."

"I do clothing design, or I did. I am no great artist like Ravenwing," he replied, and she had the impression that he was a little uncomfortable, perhaps embarrassed. "Odd as it may seem, when they are at leisure, the *hertasi* of the Vale enjoy having elaborate clothing to wear."

She considered teasing him and decided against it. She recalled the festival clothing that he and Starblade had worn; clothing that seemed to have been created by the same hand. Now she knew it probably had been. His hand. Had that been a kind of silent signal of reconciliation? What other signals was she missing?

"You know," she said slowly, "Back at home there's an entire set of codes in the flowers people wear, that they give to one another. It's even more elaborate at Court. People have carried on entire conversations, wordlessly, with the flowers they have worn during the course of a day.''

''Really?'' He seemed amused and relieved that she had turned the topic to something else. ''Here there is only one meaning to a gift of a flower.''

''And what is that?'' she asked.

''The same as a gift of a feather—that one wishes intimacy.'' She blinked, now understanding a number of exchanges she had seen but hadn't understood.

''If the feather is from any bird, the relationship is casual,'' he continued. ''If it is from one's bondbird, however, the meaning is that it is to be one of deeper intentions.''

A sudden image flashed from memory, of the shaman Kethra, a string of feathers braided into her hair when she had never seen the Shin'a'in wear feathers before.

''Is that why Kethra—'' she exclaimed, then stopped, blushing at her own rudeness.

But Darkwind didn't seem to think it was rude. ''Yes,'' he said simply. ''Those were feathers from the birds he bonded to before that raven—a gray owl, and a falcon called a perlin. When our birds molt, we save the feathers. Those we do not need to use for repair when a bird breaks a feather, we keep for special purposes, and for gifts.''

''He needs another bird,'' she said, thinking out loud. ''You know, watching you and the others with your birds—it isn't like a Herald with a Companion, but it's an important relationship. He needs a bird, and I don't think either he or Kethra realize how much, or the good it would do him to have one.''

Silence then, as Gwena continued to push her way through the snow beneath the barren, gray branches of the forest, as the light slowly leached from the sky and the shapes of trees far away lost their definition, blurring into charcoal shadows. She wondered if she had broken some unspoken taboo among the Hawkbrothers. Or if, perhaps, she had sounded arrogant, as if she thought that she knew it all.

''Odd,'' he said, finally. ''That is precisely what I have been thinking. Father lost his last bird to Falconsbane, and may hesitate to ask someone to help him find another. Kethra knows nothing of the bond of Tayledras and bird, how important it is to us. *All* of us have a bird of one sort or another, Elspeth. The mages often bond to a small owl, or to one of the corbies, but all of us have birds, and all of enhanced breeding.''

"It seems to me that the birds you have are more like—well—house-cats. They have that kind of independence of thought, but willingness to *be* somewhat dependent." She shook her head, at a loss to explain what she meant. "They're not like dogs—well, mostly they aren't. But they sure as fire are *not* like the falcons and accipitors *I* know! The best you can get from them is tolerance, unless you can Mindspeak with animals."

"You are very observant. That is very true. They have that capacity for real affection that most of the true raptors lack; they are social, and they are intelligent enough to work together instead of preying on one another. Because of that capacity, the bond between us is as much of friendship as dependence. The only trouble is, this is not breeding season, and all the adult birds within the Vale are already bonded."

Perhaps the waning light had made her other senses sharper; perhaps it was just that she had become accustomed to listening for nuances in the way Darkwind spoke. "Within the Vale?" she repeated. "Are there birds of Vale lineage outside the Vale?"

"Many. All those that are not claimed by someone as an eyas are left free to follow their own will." He was silent for a moment. "But without the bond, their wild instincts come to the fore, and aside from size, it is difficult to tell them from their wild cousins. We could trap a passage bird, perhaps. But that would be a poor way to begin a relationship that is based in trust."

"I see your point." And she did. A wild-bred bird never connected the trap with the human that took him from it. In fact, a wild-bred bird often woke to his surroundings when securely mewed, and the falconer began the careful process of manning him. But a bird as intelligent as one of bondbird stock would make the immediate connection between trap and trapper. And he would not be pleased, however good their intentions. "Have you asked Vree what he thinks we should do?"

"Actually, no." She could tell by the tone of his voice that she had surprised him, probably by saying something one of his people wouldn't have thought of. But she was used to asking Gwena's advice, and while she wouldn't have considered posing a complicated question to the bondbird, this was something he could realistically handle.

The gyre dropped down ahead of them out of the trees, circled about beneath the branches, and chirped at Darkwind before regaining the height he preferred with a few strong wingbeats.

Darkwind laughed aloud. "You pleased him, Wingsib," he said. "He was very flattered by being asked his opinion. And in his own very direct way, he has the perfect answer. He says that we must wait for one of the birds of the proper lineage to be injured. It is winter; first-year birds are injured all the time, trying for difficult kills. In the normal way of things, they will heal upon their own; sometimes other birds of Tayledras breeding, even their parents, will feed them while they heal. And in the way of things, if they do not heal properly and there is none to feed them, they die. But if the other birds of the Vale know we are looking for an injured bird, they will watch for one such, and we may play rescuer.''

"Giving us a grateful bird instead of an angry one." She smiled; it was the best kind of solution. "I take it that he's going to speak to the other birds?"

"Once again, you guess correctly." Darkwind's voice was as warm as the gathering night was chill. "Elspeth, if it will not offend you, I would like to say that you are a much easier person to be around now."

She flushed. "Well . . . Darkwind, some of what you didn't like was something I *have* to do when I am around my own people. They expect me to lead; they expect me to act in certain ways. That 'attitude' you accused me of having is a big part of that. I'm sorry it had become a habit that I wasn't conscious of. I think some of it was associated with a kind of reflex; if the person I was with wasn't wearing a white uniform, then I acted a certain way without even considering what I was doing." Would he understand? Would he even try? "I *am* royalty, Darkwind. No matter that my land matters less to you than one of Vree's broken feathers, I still am royal, I am expected to act in a certain way, and I can't escape that. I've been bred and raised to it."

"Ah." She hoped that what she read into the tone of that single syllable was dawning understanding.

She sighed. "There's something else," she said, through painful shyness. "I'm rather the plain-plumaged bird of my family. Everyone else is so handsome it's like—like living among Hawkbrothers. So the only reason *I* can think of for a young man to be attracted to me is because of my rank. And there have been those. I try to keep them at a distance."

"I can understand that," he said after a moment, in which the sound of Gwena's breathing and the muffled sounds of her hooves in the snow filled the twilight forest and defined the borders of their little private universe. "But, Elspeth, those young men who were blinded by your rank were fools. Or else they failed to see the quiet beauty inside the showy. Or—"

She sensed, rather than saw, the grin behind her.

"Or perhaps they were dazzled by the stark white attire."

She groaned. "Don't tell me *you're* in on the conspiracy to steal my Whites!"

"Only a little." She waited for him to continue. "I will admit to advising Lursten on a choice of substitute wardrobe."

She chuckled, and they passed the rest of the journey in silence, as the twilight darkened to true night and the air chilled further. Before it became too dark for him to see to fly, Vree came winging in to land on Darkwind's wrist. He held the bird between them, keeping him warmed with the combined heat of their bodies, something *no* raptor of Elspeth's acquaintance would have tolerated, much less enjoyed.

True to her promise, Gwena brought them to within sight of the Vale just as the last of the dull light of sunset faded from the western sky.

Darkwind slid from her back as soon as they passed the entrance to the Vale, Vree balancing carefully on his wrist. "I am for sleep," he said with a smile. "Do not take this amiss, Wingsib, but take it as a compliment, please. I have wished to offer you a feather since the days of our first acquaintance, for *I* find you a very attractive woman. More so when you smile, rather than frowning on me so formidably!"

She blinked at him in shock, then tentatively smiled in return.

"Thank you," she said simply, blushing. "Ah—Darkwind, if I wasn't so tired—oh, that sounds like such a transparent excuse but—"

"But it is, sadly, true. Elspeth, even if you were not weary, I feel that I am like to fall asleep even as I walk to my *ekele*. Shall we take it as true and not an excuse?"

Something warmed deep inside her. "I think that's reasonable."

:And I think you should both go to bed. To sleep,: Gwena chided gently.

"All right, little mother," Darkwind said, amused. "We shall. Tomorrow we will be dealing with all the creatures our magics attracted, at any rate. We will need a good rest."

She couldn't be disappointed, she thought. Not after all that. But no, that would not do. It was not enough.

She dismounted and went to him, wrapping her arms around his waist. With an inner flush, she looked up into his clear eyes.

Darkwind held Vree a little further from his body, inviting her in closer. She smiled, not knowing how well it could be seen, and felt Gwena send a quiet touch of approval.

Elspeth raised a hand to Darkwind's face, caressed the hair at his temple. He licked his lips as Vree spread his wings, and bent his neck down just a little, enough for one loving kiss, framed by the rich light and warmth of the Vale behind them.

Starblade & Hyllarr

Chapter
Fourteen

Darkwind woke to a cool, pebble-scaled hand shaking him awake. He raised his head from his pillow and blinked to clear his eyes.

It was still dark.

:Darkwind,: said the *hertasi* at his elbow, *:There is a disturbance.:*

He recognized the mind-voice as that of Suras, one of the three *hertasi* who had attached themselves to Darkwind when he moved back into the Vale. The lizard-folk did that; it was one of their many peculiarities. They simply decided who they wanted to serve and proceeded to do just that. One day, Darkwind was living in the clutter created by moving, and putting together his own meals; doing his own laundry and cleaning up after himself and Vree. Then, with no warning at all, he arrived home to find everything straightened, folded, and put away, and a meal waiting.

There were advantages and disadvantages to being back in the Vale. He'd felt a pang of displeasure at his loss of autonomy. However, with *hertasi* serving him, it was much easier for people to find him when he was needed. That, too, could be a disadvantage, especially when he was trying to sleep off the last time he'd been needed.

Suras patted his arm again. *:Disturbance, Darkwind. You are needed, please.:*

"What kind of trouble is it this time?" he asked—or rather, mumbled into his pillow—hoping it was something he could get someone else to take care of.

:Magical,: Suras said curtly. His tone told Darkwind everything he needed to know. He was not getting out of this one. *:A magical disturbance between here and the ruins.:*

No doubt about this; he, Gwena, and Elspeth were responsible for dealing with it. "I'll be right there."

Suras lit a lantern and vanished. Darkwind clenched his eyes closed, opened them reluctantly, and dragged himself out of bed. Vree roused and blinked sleepily, then yawned widely. *:Awake again? Rather sleep.:*

Darkwind yawned in response. "You and I both, beloved. I'll go on ahead, and call on you if you're needed. Fair enough?"

:You go. I sleep. Fair deal.:

Vree settled and tucked his beak under feathers again while Darkwind felt around for the clothing Suras would have laid out before waking him. *I can't say I wasn't expecting this,* he thought glumly. *But I wish it had waited until after sunrise to start. Maybe we should have just stayed with the gryphons.*

He had known that when they worked a spell requiring that much power and concentration, things would be attracted. There were too many power-hungry creatures in the Pelagirs for any educated mage to think that magical workings of any scale could go unnoticed. Odd how much had gone into so simple and tiny a package as that hummingbird messenger, though.

Well, tiny, yes. Simple, no. There had been all manner of enhancements on that little bird, for speed, for endurance, plus the pocket of energy it would use to feed. Then all the spells needed to hold the message, to deliver it, to recognize the right kind of person to unlock it. . . .

We did what we could to shield, everything we could spare from the spells themselves, without harming the little thing itself, he told himself. *We did everything we knew how to do, but I suppose the bleedoff was noticed. There hasn't been anything really troublesome around since the basilisk. If luck is with us, these things will be small. Something we can run off, rather than killing.*

He dressed carefully, knowing that he would probably be spending the whole day out in the cold, wrapping his joints and neck in brushed-cotton and insulation. It was still dark by the time he descended the steps to the Vale floor, and he had no idea how long it would be until dawn.

It was going to be a very long day indeed.

Another messenger *dyheli* came galloping closer just as they ran the younger of the *lodella* pair off with its fuzzy tail tucked down between its legs, all its dorsal spines flat, and its hairless head ducked low. The elder had already flagged its surrender with its retreating back, but the younger one had less sense and more bravado. They'd actually had to pound it a bit with hammer-spells before it gave up.

Darkwind waved to his partners, who came up beside him just as the stag neared. "Now what?" Elspeth asked, as she propped herself against her Companion's neck, then shifted toward the saddle to avoid being caught in Gwena's steaming breath.

Elspeth hadn't spent a lot of time in the saddle; the Companion had been far more effective helping as a third herder when they met with creatures that were willing to be shepherded away. It wasn't just her size; she also seemed to be able to project a "presence" that played a factor in discouraging hostilities from the less-intelligent creatures.

These "disturbances" had actually included a fair percentage of "browsers"; creatures that meant no real harm, but could not be allowed close to habitations. But the rest—

The rest of the beasts facing them would have been only too happy to work some harm, but the beasts faced the three of them, plus the two gryphons, and Falconsbane was no longer there to support his creatures with magic.

The gryphons had tackled the first real problem; the half-dozen *gandels* that tried to force their way into the ruins. But without Falconsbane's will driving them, they were inclined to fold at the first show of resistance. A few feints of Hydona's claws and a stooping dive by Treyvan convinced them elsewhere would be far safer.

That set the tone for the day; to frighten the creatures away rather than actually closing to fight with them.

Illusions proved as effective as real threats; after the *gandels*, they had sent a pack of Changewolves running with the illusion of a bigger, stronger pack downwind facing them to claim the territory. Illusions were exhausting, though; they took more magical energy from the caster than actually fighting, but certainly left the user less winded, and less likely to strike at shadows. After a full day of active casting, though, illusions could deaden even the most ardent of mages.

On the other hand, one generally doesn't get wounded casting illusions. Or bitten, gored, horned, or worse. As Vree would say, "Fair deal."

It actually had a certain entertainment value, as he and Elspeth got into an impromptu contest over which of the two of them could create the most imaginative counter to the problem at hand. He'd conceded defeat when Elspeth began dropping huge illusionary clay pots on the dumber creatures' heads, or sending blizzards of wildflowers in their faces. They'd both found themselves laughing after that.

So far, they had been incredibly lucky; the illusions hadn't failed yet to drive away their targets, though once or twice they'd needed to reinforce the illusion with a bit of magical force.

The *dyheli* stopped and pawed at the snow, a signal for attention. Was their luck about to run out?

:You are called to the ruins,: the *dyheli* said, before Darkwind could ask him why he had been sent. *:The gryphons say there is a message waiting for you there. Three of the Vale mages are following me, to take your place.:*

Darkwind slumped against a tree in relief. He had completely forgotten that the mages of k'Sheyna would recover from their draining eventually. He had been so used to depending on himself and no one else, used to the idea that there was no one to relieve him. It had literally never occurred to him that someone would be along to take their places.

"So what is it?" Elspeth asked. "Who are we going to have to rescue this time?"

"No one," he said, mentally thanking the messenger at the same time. "Believe it or not, no one. We've had a reply to our call for help. It came to the ruins, since that was where the hummingbird started from. Keyed to us, of course, so no one else can break into it."

:Would that be the kind of personally keyed message we would have sent if we'd been able?: Gwena asked, her tiredness fading as her interest was caught. *:But it hasn't been more than a day—I had no idea that little bird could fly that fast or far!:*

"I hoped he would find a good carrying wind somewhere up above the clouds," Darkwind told her. "That, and the enhancement spells we put on him would have made all the difference. Once k'Treva got the message, of course, it wouldn't take them very long to reply—they knew where to send it and who to send it to; it takes a little longer than straight Mindspeech, but not much."

"Then the bird probably reached them just as we tackled the wolves," Elspeth replied thoughtfully. "It hardly seems possible, but I suppose that if a falcon can be carried off for hundreds of leagues by a high wind, there's no reason why a hummingbird couldn't have that happen to him, too."

She straightened, and looked around. "We're going to have to walk," she told Darkwind. "Gwena is in no shape to carry us."

She bent down and scooped up a little snow, and rubbed Gwena's forehead with it. When Gwena didn't protest that she was *fine*, thank you, Darkwind figured that Elspeth was right. While the Companion hadn't been working any direct magic, she had been acting as an energy source for both of them, plus giving the more timid creatures a good scare when she charged them. She must be as exhausted as they were.

"That's all right," he said. "It isn't that far." He oriented himself, recognizing a clump of mingled evergreen and goldenoak, stand of willows, and a rock formation. "We've been working in circles, actually. We're hardly more than a dozen furlongs from the edge of the ruins."

"Then what are we waiting for?" Elspeth asked.

"For me to get my second wind," he told her. "I haven't your youthful resilience." She chuckled. He closed his eyes for a moment, drew up reserves of energy, then pushed away from the tree he had been leaning on. "Let's go see what the news is."

The visible component of the message was a tiny, incandescent spark that danced in the air above the exact center of the crude building in the ruins. It brightened as soon as they entered the building, and the moment they were both in place, with Darkwind to the east of the node and Elspeth beside him, the spark flared suddenly.

Then it—unfolded, was the only word Darkwind could think of. It stretched down in a line that just touched the ground, then the line opened up on either side, until it formed a soft-edged mirror that hung in the air between them.

For a moment, Darkwind saw only his own reflection. Then the mirror dimmed and darkened to blue starlight, and the face of another Tayledras, this one a contemporary of his father at a guess, looked solemnly out at him.

It was hard to remember that this was only a message, that he could not actually speak to the one in the mirror, any more than he could hold a conversation with a piece of parchment. The illusion was so complete that it took an effort of will to keep from greeting the stranger.

:*K'Treva has heard the need of k'Sheyna,*: came the mind-voice of the stranger. :*While we are grieved by your situation we are relieved that you came at last to us. We feared for you but saw no way to help you without acting like tyrants or well-meaning but intrusive siblings.*:

Darkwind nodded; that made sense. No Clan interfered in the affairs of another without some kind of truly catastrophic emergency involved.

:*We have the help you need,*: the other continued, :*A Healing Adept, strong and well-versed in his craft, and who is one of the most creative mages this Clan has ever held.*: The other smiled, briefly. :*Such praise may seem excessive, but as the Shin'a'in saying goes, "It is no boast when it is fact." I will build him a Gate to a place I know within your territory, one that I hope will be far enough away that it will not disturb your Stone. From the Gate terminus, I believe it will be about a half day's ride to your Vale under good conditions, and certainly no more than a full day. Expect him within that time once you feel the perturbations of the Gate. If Firesong cannot help you, no one of k'Treva can. Be of good cheer, brothers.*:

With that, the entire construction sparkled and winked out. Darkwind stared across the room at Elspeth, unable to believe their good fortune.

"You look like a stunned bird," she observed.

"I feel like a stunned bird," he admitted. "It's incredible."

"I have to tell you," she said, shaking off her daze, "I was standing here waiting for the ax to fall. I never thought there'd be anyone in the first Clan we sought help from powerful enough—and willing—to handle this mess. Especially not after what it did to our mages."

"Nor did I," he admitted. "I thought that surely even if there was a Healing Adept within k'Treva that we would have to convince him to come here. And then we would have to convince his Clan to permit him to put himself at risk. They must have been convinced already that we needed their help and were just waiting for us to ask for it."

Elspeth crossed the room to stand closer to him. "Was I missing something, or did he imply that he was here after the Stone shattered and that his Clan was worried about yours?"

Darkwind winced, but felt comfortable enough with her now not to bother covering it. "You are correct. He said—or implied—exactly that."

Memories, though dimmed with time, still had the power to hurt him. *Heart and mind in agony, as well as body—the dim shapes of strangers in his sickroom. Shock holding him silent in the face of their gentle question-*

ing. Then the voice of his father, harshly telling them to leave the boy alone. . . .

"Right after the Stone shattered, I was told that k'Treva sent mages to discover what had happened and to volunteer their help," he told her. "I was—still in shock, hurt, and I do not recall most of it. But they went away without doing much except to help treat some of the worst wounded. I suppose that Father must have sent them away as soon as he could."

"Evidently if he tried to cover things up, he didn't manage as well as he thought he had," she replied, dryly. "Not if they were still concerned after all this time."

"Or he managed to let them see enough that there were still doubts; kept from completely covering things up, despite Falconsbane's control." That seemed the more likely, given what else Starblade had done. *Like protecting his son by driving him away. . . .*

Elspeth shook her head. "I wonder sometimes if you realize just how strong your father is. When you think what that kind of attempt must have cost him . . . I can't imagine doing half that much. It took some kind of cleverness, too, to get around Falconsbane's compulsions. Starblade's a strong man."

"It is a brittle strength," he replied, sadly. "And like a bit of metal that has been bent too often, he is apt to break if he is stressed again." He shook his head. "Ah, this is gloomy thinking and poorly suited to our good news. Who knows? It may speed Father's recovery."

"It might at that." It seemed to him when she stood up that she moved with a bit more energy; certainly he felt that way. A great burden had been taken from his shoulders. K'Sheyna would have the help it needed. The long nightmare would soon be over.

He refused to think beyond that. There would be time enough for plans later. Let the Stone be dealt with first, and worry about what followed that when the time came.

He stopped at the gryphons' lair long enough to give them the good news, then they trudged back to the Vale through the snow, though it was nowhere near the job it was yesterday. They had been this way so often they were making a trail between the ruins and the Vale. A few months ago he would have worried about that, but not now. There wasn't any real reason to worry about leaving signs of where they had been. He sighed with relieved contentment, and relaxed a bit more, feeling muscles unknot all over his back. Shortly this would all be true Tayledras land again, and things like the Changewolves would not get past the borders—

:Up! Help!:

His head snapped up to a call only he heard. Vree!

He froze where he stood and linked with the gyre, fearing the worst. Dawnfire and her redshouldered all over again. Elspeth and Gwena stared at him for a half-heartbeat, then went into defensive postures. He prepared to break the link with Vree if he had to, to save himself—

—but caught no pain, no feeling of imminent danger. Vree felt him link and welcomed him in, his mind seething with agitation but not pain. He had given a distress call, but the bondbird himself was uninjured.

:Here! Help! Look-look-look!: the bird Mindcalled again, and this time gave Darkwind a look through his eyes.

A disorienting look; for Vree circled and twisted wildly, but Darkwind was used to looking through his bird' eyes. He recognized the spot immediately; on the edge of the swamp, but he did not recognize the man that was the source of Vree's anger and distress, a man laying out what could only be a *hertasi* trap. The view dipped and swung, as Vree circled, his silent rage burning in Darkwind's mind, making the Tayledras clench his fists and longed with the bird to screech out a battle-cry. Then with another turn, Darkwind saw what must have triggered that rage.

The man had three pack-mules with him, and on the third was a raptor, a big one, bound on its back and hooded. From the little he could see, it looked to be a crested hawk-eagle; from the size of it, it could only be of bondbird breeding.

He had no idea that he was running until he saw Elspeth pounding beside him, already astride her Companion, and offering him a hand up. He seized it, and scrambled behind her. Then they were off, plunging through the thick snow. This was not like the last wild ride he'd made, for Gwena could not run or trot in the heavy snow. Her progress was a series of lunges or leaps; it was harder for him to keep his balance on her back, but easier on his bones.

Their quarry knew they were coming, for they made no effort to hide the noise of their passage. But their quarry did not know two very pertinent facts.

He was nearer the *hertasi* village than he knew. And while they were sluggish in the cold, they were by no means impotent. Anger alone was enough to keep their blood warm in the snow and give them the same agility they had in the high heat of summer. They, too, could dress for the cold and preserve some body heat when action outside was needed.

And although the encroaching mage had prevented the bondbird he had caught from calling its distress, Vree was under no such handicap. Nor was Darkwind; while he was nowhere near as adept at Mindspeaking with other creatures as his brother Wintermoon, he was still one of the best in the Clan. The soundless cry went out for assistance.

While Vree was calling his fellow bondbirds, Darkwind was rousing the *hertasi* village, starting with old Nera. The attack was conceived and coordinated in a matter of moments. The three forces converged on their target at nearly the same instant.

If the mage—for mage he was; he had a lightning-flare ready for them the moment they plunged over the top of the hill and began the sliding descent toward him—had only had to face Darkwind and Elspeth, he might have won. They were tired, and he was fresh. If he had only faced the *hertasi*, with their simple fishing spears, he *would* have won. And he had already proven he was capable of felling bondbirds from the sky.

But, since only Darkwind's party was making any noise, he had no idea that the others were on the way until it was too late to do anything about them.

Darkwind flung a shield up before them to deflect the first bolt. The second went awry as Vree dove, his claws ripping through the cloth of the man's hood, narrowly missing the scalp. Behind Vree came another forestgyre, in the same stooping dive, then a gyrkin, then a trio of perlins, all of them slashing at head and face with their long, sharp talons. They struck to hurt, not to bind; the perlins in fact struck close-fisted, as if they were trying to knock a duck out of the sky. The mage screamed in pain as the talons scored deep gashes in his scalp; staggered under the blows of the perlins, any of which would have been hard enough to stun him had they hit the temple.

He tried to protect himself with his arms. Apparently, like most Pelagir-wilds mages, there were severe gaps in his education. He seemed unable to summon any physical shields.

The birds retreated to the protection of the skies, gaining altitude as one. The mage stood, one hand on his bleeding scalp. From behind him, a thicket of spears boiled up out of the half-frozen swamp.

Darkwind struck then, gesturing behind Elspeth's back with two clenching fists. Gray and green stripes of a binding spell tangled the mage's hands and his magic for a moment. That moment was all that was needed. The *hertasi* did the rest.

They swarmed about the mage, casting their fishing spears and pulling on the lines. He tried to run, then slipped and floundered in the heavy snow. He scrambled to his feet again, and fell for the last time. The *hertasi* overran him, and he writhed to avoid the wicked points of the spears.

In moments, he looked like nothing so much as a hedgehog. In heartbeats, he was dead.

Gwena skidded to a halt in the snow beside the man's string of pack animals, a trio of tired mules who gazed at them with absolute indifference. Darkwind slid down off her back and hurried to the last one, the one bearing the bird like just another bundle of forest gleanings.

This much the man had known; he had bound the talons into fists, tied them together, bound the wings to the body so that it would not injure itself, then hooded the bird so that it could not see and would not struggle. The hood was strung to the bound feet by a cord, to prevent further movement, and from the cord dangled a carved bead.

As Darkwind's hands touched the bundle, he felt—something. It was akin to the draining effect of the Heartstone, and was centered in that bead, and spread throughout the bindings.

He drew back and examined the bird with mage-sight—and swore. Small wonder he had not Heard the thoughts of this bird; it was bound by magic as well as by bands of fabric, a binding that linked its life-force to the spell that held it. And that could only have been for one purpose.

Elspeth bit her lower lip and peered at the bindings on the captured hawk-eagle. Her face looked as it did when she was hearing news she didn't like.

"He was going to use this bird as some kind of sacrifice, wasn't he?" Elspeth said, her own voice tight with anger. She put a hand toward the hawk-eagle. "That's not all, Darkwind, this bird is in pain. He hurt it when he caught it."

She had been quicker than he; though she could not sense the bird's thoughts, she had felt its pain. He was glad he hadn't touched the poor thing; he could only have hurt it worse, unknowingly.

First things first; destroy the mage-bindings so that the bird's mind could roam free and it could hear his Mindspeech. Until then, it would struggle against him, thinking he was an enemy, hurting itself further.

The man had been a Master, but no Adept; Darkwind snapped the shackles of magic with a single savage pull but left the physical bindings in place. With a carefully-placed dagger cut, he removed the carved bead. Beneath the bindings, the bird was in a state near to shock, but not actually suffering from that ailment. Darkwind could still touch its mind, talk to it sensibly, and know he would be heard.

He stretched out his thoughts—carefully, gently, with a sure, but light touch.

:*Friend,*: he said, soothingly.

The hawk-eagle tossed up its head as far as it could and struggled fruitlessly against the bindings. :*NOT!*: it Screamed.

:*Friend,*: Darkwind repeated firmly, showing it a mental picture of its former captor lying in the stained snow. :*The Enemy is dead.*:

The bird struggled a moment more, then stopped. Its head came up again, but this time slowly, as fear ebbed and the bird's courage returned. It considered his words for a moment, and the image he had Sent; considered the sound of his mind-voice.

:*See!*: it demanded imperiously.

"I'm going to unhood him," Darkwind warned. The *hertasi* backed off, but both Elspeth and her Companion stayed. "I don't know what he might do. He's bondbird stock, and right now he's sensible, but he may go wild once he can see again."

Elspeth reached forward with gloved hands. "You need four hands to undo those wrappings. I'll take my chances."

"Don't say I didn't warn you." No matter how intelligent, bondbirds were raptors, and likely to do unexpected things when injured and in pain, even one like Vree, brought up from an eyas and bonded before he was hard-penned. And this bird had never bonded to anyone. Still, she was right, and the sooner they got the bird untied, the more likely it was to listen.

The bird had been hooded with an oversize falcon's hood; a little too small; uncomfortable, certainly, and it would have been impossible for the bird to eat or cast through the hood. But Darkwind doubted that this man had made any plans to feed his catch, through the hood or otherwise. He got the end of one of the ties in his teeth, and the other in his free hand, and pulled, continuing the motion with his hand to slip the hood off the magnificent hawk-eagle's head.

It blinked for a moment, as the feathers of its crest rose to their full, aggressive height, the pupils of its golden eyes dilating to pinpoints as it got used to the light. Then it swiveled its head and saw for itself what Darkwind had shown it.

It opened its beak in a hiss of anger and satisfaction, then turned those intelligent golden eyes back to Darkwind. *:Out,:* it demanded, flexing bound wings once in a way that left no room for doubt about what it meant. *:Out!:*

It seemed calm enough, if still in pain. *:Let me get your feet free first,:* he replied. *:Then you can stand while I get the rest of this mess off of you.:*

Once again, the bird gave careful consideration to what he had said, weighing his reply against what it wanted. Darkwind marveled at the bird's intelligence; even Vree seldom *thought* about what Darkwind told him.

:Good,: the hawk-eagle said shortly, and stopped any effort to free itself. It held itself completely still, and while Elspeth held the huge creature, Darkwind picked delicately at the mess of rags and string muffling the hawk-eagle's talons and tying them into fisted balls.

Finally he got them free, and Elspeth placed the bird on the saddle-pack. Its talons closed convulsively on the leather, and it flexed its claws once or twice to assure itself of its balance.

The hawk-eagle stood on the saddlepack and looked Darkwind straight in the eyes. *:Good,:* it said. *:Out now!:*

It waited while they picked the wrappings from its bound wings, talons digging deeply into the leather covering of the pack. Those talons were as long as Darkwind's fingers, and the cruel, hooked bill would have had no trouble biting through the spine of a deer. Darkwind wondered at the temerity of the dead man who had caught the bird, mage though he was. Vree could kill a man, with enough precision—and had done so in the past. This bird was nearly double Vree's size, and not only could kill a man, he could do it as easily as Vree killed a rabbit.

If the hawk-eagle hadn't been of bondbird stock—and hadn't Mindspoken with such clarity and relative calm, given the situation—Darkwind would never have dared to unhood him. It would have been suicide. The bird could have seriously hurt him, even bound, with a swift stroke of that terrible hooked beak.

When the last binding had been cut, the magnificent hawk-eagle spread wide, brown-banded wings to the fullest—and winced, dropping the left one immediately. The wing continued to droop a little, after he had folded the right and tucked it up over his back.

He looked at Darkwind demandingly. *:Hurts,:* he said. *:Chest hurts, wing hurts. Hurt when fell.:*

Darkwind ran careful hands over the bird's breast, and quickly found the problem. A cracked wishbone. There was only one cure for that injury; resting quietly, while the bone set and mended. It would take weeks to heal properly, for bone Healing did not work well on birds, and the great hawk-eagle might never fly with the same ease and freedom again. Winter would bring special problems; cold would make the old injury ache, and the stiffness in the wing would make it harder to catch swift prey.

A tragedy—if he continued to live wild. No special problem—if he lived in the Vale.

But a bondbird, when not bonded as a fledgling or even an eyas, was traditionally given a choice. Freedom, or the bond.

Darkwind explained it to the hawk-eagle in simple terms. If he would come and live in the Vale, his life would be thus. He would bond to Starblade, who was himself wounded and in need of healing. . . .

It was not his imagination; the bird's interest, dulled by the pain he was in, sharpened at that.

:Show,: he demanded. Darkwind obeyed, showing him mental images of Starblade as he was now—and one of Starblade and his cherished perlin Karry.

:Yes,: the bird said, thoughtfully. *:Ye-es.:* He dropped his head for a moment, and it seemed to Darkwind that he was thinking. Then his head came up again, and he stared directly into Darkwind's eyes. *:I go— we go to that one,:* he ordered, *:To warm place, to wounded one. We belong, him, me. Need, him, me.:*

And although Darkwind dutifully offered him his continued freedom after healing, the bird refused to consider it. *:We go,:* he insisted, and Darkwind gave in gladly to him, but with no little wonder. He had never had a bondbird speak so clearly to him—nor had he ever seen one exhibit genuine abstract thought before. There was no doubt in his mind that the bird was quite certain Starblade *needed* him. And there was no doubt that the bird had responded to that need.

He had heard that the crested hawk-eagles were different, that way— that they had a greater capacity for bonds of affection than any other breed. They often hunted in family groups and shared kills in the wild, something most other raptors never did. But no one in k'Sheyna had one of their kind, so he had only hearsay to go on.

Until now, that is. And he wondered; since no one in k'Sheyna had ever flown the crested hawk-eagles, where had this one come from?

"I was following that, a little," Elspeth said as she dumped the packs from the mules, leaving them for the *hertasi* to paw over. "So he does want to come with us?"

"So it would seem," Darkwind replied, a bit amazed by how readily the bird had fallen in with their idea. Could it be a trap of some kind?

:Stupid,: Vree said contemptuously, from his perch in the tree above. *:Hyllarr goes to Vale. Gets good food, warm place, safe place, hunts only when he wants. Gets good friend. Hyllarr wants good friend, mind-friend. Hyllarr flies, he gets winter snow, summer storms, has to hunt, get hurt again, dies alone.:*

Darkwind laughed, and so did Elspeth, though she looked a little surprised that she could hear the gyre's "voice." "Put that way, it makes all the sense in the world, doesn't it," she said, with a bright sparkle in her eyes. "Here—" she offered her leather-clad arm. "I'll take him for a moment while you get up on one of those mules. Then I'll pass him back when you're mounted."

Hyllarr looked at her arm for a moment, then directly into her face— and with a delicate care that in no way hid the fact that his talons could pierce through her arm if he chose, he stepped onto her forearm and balanced there while Darkwind hoisted himself onto a mule's back. Elspeth blanched and inhaled abruptly when Hyllarr dug in while balancing himself.

No point in doing anything with the others. He would leave them to wander or follow as they chose; if they followed his mount to the Vale, someone there could always put them to good use. If they didn't, they would survive—or not—as their fate and wits decreed.

Elspeth held the hawk-eagle—*Hyllarr,* she reminded herself—steadily, despite the fact that it was a heavy weight, there on her wrist. But once he got himself settled, and before he could reach out his own wrist to take the bird back, Hyllarr half-spread his wings and hopped from Elspeth's arm to Darkwind's shoulder.

He tensed, expecting the talons to close through his leather coat and into the flesh beneath. But Hyllarr shifted a little, getting his balance, and then closed his feet slowly, carefully.

:Hurt?: he asked Darkwind, increasing the pressure a little more.

:No—no—there.: As the claws just pricked his skin, he warned the

bird, and Hyllarr eased off just that trifle needed to pull the talons back through the leather.

:Good,: the bird replied with satisfaction. *:No hurt. Good. Go to warm place now.:*

That was an order, if Darkwind had ever heard one. He turned to Elspeth, to see her own eyes alight with laughter and a little wonder. "I heard him that time!" she exclaimed. "I think—maybe—I've got the knack of talking to the bondbirds now. They're kind of—pitched higher than human mind-voices."

"Yes, exactly," he replied, as pleased by her accomplishment as she was. "That's excellent! Well, then, you heard. We've gotten our marching orders."

She eyed the long, sharp talons—the fierce beak—and grinned. "You know, given where he's perched right now, I wouldn't argue with those orders if I were you."

"I don't intend to," he assured her, and kicked the mule into a reluctant walk toward the Vale, Elspeth and Gwena following.

When Darkwind turned the mule over to the *hertasi,* he got them to find a stout branch that he could brace across his shoulder and hold with one hand. That gave Hyllarr a much more secure perch, and one that eased Darkwind's aching shoulder quite a bit. He was going to be very glad when he delivered the bird to his father. After that, Starblade could figure a way to carry him; it would no longer be Darkwind's problem.

The hawk-eagle reveled in the heat of the Vale, rousing his feathers with a careful shake and raising his crest fully. Darkwind had decided on a tentative approach to his father on the slow ride to the Vale; now it only remained to convince the bird to cooperate.

He got Hyllarr's attention with a little mental touch, the kind he used with Vree.

:?: Hyllarr replied, definite feelings of relaxation and satisfaction coming along with the reply.

:Starblade is hurt,: he said, hoping he could convey the complex idea in a way the bird would understand.

:Hurt,: Hyllarr agreed. And waited.

That was encouraging. *:Starblade is proud,:* he continued, showing the bird an image of Hyllarr himself, hurt, but refusing all aid, trying to fly and unable to.

:Proud,: the bird said, agreeing again. Then, *:Stupid. Like first year. Try too much.:*

:Exactly!: Darkwind said, astonished that the bird understood so much. He was to have an even bigger surprise.

For suddenly, Hyllarr drooped on his shoulder, dropping the injured wing even further. *:Hurts,:* the bird moaned, making little chirps of distress. *:Oh, huuuurts. Need Starblade! Need Starblade, make better!:*

Then the bird straightened again, a distinct gleam of humor in the eye nearest Darkwind. *:Good?:* he asked. *:Good for proud Starblade?:*

Darkwind wanted to laugh, both at the bird's astonishing ability to *act* and at Elspeth's expression. "I'm as surprised as you are," he grinned, then returned his attention to the bird.

:Very good!: he replied. *:Exactly right!:*

The bird roused again with satisfaction. *:Hyllarr plays hurt-wing-eyas, Starblade feels good, Hyllarr gets many good eatings, tender eatings, tasty prey, make Hyllarr better. All good.:*

"You," he said, shaking an admonitory finger at the bird, "are going to wind up too fat to fly."

Hyllarr bobbed his head to follow Darkwind's fingertip, then blinked in mock drowsiness. Darkwind felt his amusement. He turned his head to look at Elspeth, who was fairly bursting with laughter. "Don't you dare give this away," he warned. "I don't know how Hyllarr managed to grasp it, but Father really *does* need him. This is going to make all the difference in his recovery, if we don't ruin everything."

She nodded. Darkwind smiled his thanks to her.

As soon as they were within sight of Starblade's *ekele*, he gave a silent cue to the hawk-eagle, who immediately went into full droop, complete with weak, pathetic chirps.

Weak they might have been, but Starblade heard them readily enough. He appeared at the door of the *ekele*, leaning against it heavily, with Kethra supporting him from behind, his face full of concern. "Darkwind?" he said, peering down at them in the gloom of late afternoon, "What is wrong with—"

His eyes widened. "That is *not* Vree!"

Darkwind gave his father a brief version of the rescue. "Hyllarr needs quiet, and someone to care for him, Father. He's in a lot of pain. I don't have the time to coax him to eat or keep an eye on that injury—and Kethra's a Healer, I thought she might be able to help him a little."

Hyllarr chose just that moment to raise his head and look directly into the elder Hawkbrother's eyes. :*Hurts,*: he said plaintively. :*Oh, huuuuurts.*:

Darkwind suspected that he himself might have worn that stunned expression a time or two. The first time Vree spoke directly into his mind, perhaps. But it was more than he had expected to see it on Starblade's face.

It was only there for a moment; then it was replaced by concern and something else. A fierce protectiveness—and the unmistakable look of the bondmate for *his* bird. "Bring him up," Starblade ordered, turning to go back inside.

Darkwind struggled up the stairs as best he could with the weight of the bird on his shoulders, overbalancing him. He managed to make it to the door of the *ekele* without mishap, but he had a feeling that the next time Hyllarr went from ground to door, it would be under his own power. Starblade was not going to be up to carrying Hyllarr any time in the near future.

One of the *hertasi* squeezed by him as he moved inside, and Kethra met him at the door itself. He tensed himself for her disapproval, for Starblade was moving about the room, putting things aside, readying a corner of the place for the "invalid." But her eyes were twinkling as she asked, "Will he let me touch him?"

"Yes, I think so," Darkwind replied, and as Kethra placed a gentle hand on the hawk-eagle's breast-feathers, she leaned in to whisper in Darkwind's ear.

"You just gave him the best medicine he could have had," she said softly, "Something to think about beside himself. Something stronger and prouder than he was, that is hurt as badly and needs as much help. Thank you."

He flushed, and was glad that it wasn't visible in the darkness of the room.

"He has a cracked keel and wishbone, *ke'chara*," Kethra said to Starblade, who had taken spare cushions from beneath the sand pan all Tayledras kept under their birds' perches, and in the case of Starblade's *ekele*, for guests' bondbirds. "He must be in tremendous pain. It will take a great deal of care for him to fly again."

"He'll have it, never fear," Starblade said, with some of his old strength. "You brought him to the right place, son."

His eyes met Darkwind's and once again Darkwind flushed, but this time with pleasure. Starblade actually *smiled* with no signs of pain, age, or fatigue. Darkwind's heart leapt. *That* was his father!

Before he could say anything, the *hertasi* returned, with two of his fellows. Two of them bore bags of sand for the tray; the third had an enormous block-perch, as tall as the lizard, and very nearly as heavy. The perch went into the tray, and the other two *hertasi* poured their bags of clean sand all around it, filling it and covering the base of the perch for added stability. Kethra stood aside and watched it all, a calculating but caring expression on her face, curling a length of hair between her fingers.

Darkwind took Hyllarr over to his new perch; the bird made a great show of stepping painfully onto it, but once there, settled in with a sigh; a sigh that Darkwind echoed, as the weight left him. He put a hand to his shoulder and massaged it as he headed toward the exit; Kethra nodded to him with approval.

Starblade took his place beside the perch. The look of rapt attention on his father's face was all Darkwind could have hoped for, and the look of bliss in the bird's eyes as Starblade gently stroked under his breast-feathers was very nearly its match.

Darkwind & Elspeth

Chapter
Fifteen

His partner and her Companion had waited below while he presented Starblade with *his* new partner. "Well?" Elspeth asked as soon as he got within whispering distance, her face full of pent-up inquiry.

"It worked beautifully," Darkwind told her. He permitted himself a moment of self-congratulation and a brief embrace, then gestured for her to follow so that there would be no chance of Starblade overhearing them. "He's already up out of bed and fussing around Hyllarr—it's a definite match. I don't think either of them have any idea how well they mesh, but I've seen a hundred bondings and this is one of the best."

"Is Hyllarr going to heal up all right?" she asked, dubiously.

He shrugged. "As long as he isn't in pain, it doesn't really matter how completely he heals. Even if the bird never flies again, it won't make any real difference to Father. Starblade isn't a scout; he doesn't need a particularly mobile bondbird. Hyllarr will be able to get by quite well with the kind of short flights a permanently injured bird can manage."

Elspeth considered that. Gwena nodded. :*I see. Injuries that would doom a free bird wouldn't matter to one that is never likely to leave the Vale. It is relief of pain that matters, not mobility.*:

He chuckled his agreement. "In fact, I remember one of the mages from my childhood who had a broken-winged crow that couldn't fly at all, and *walked* all over the Vale. If it came to it, Hyllarr could do the same. And be just as pampered."

Gwena snorted delicately. :*That makes an amusing picture; Starblade with the bird following him afoot or, more likely, carried by a* hertasi. *Well, Hyllarr isn't going to get fat if he finds himself walking. I doubt that anyone as frail as your father is right now* could *carry that great hulk.*:

"*I* couldn't carry him for long," Darkwind admitted. "I have no idea how scouts bonded to hawk-eagles manage. I thought my shoulders were going to collapse."

"The important thing is Starblade," Elspeth pointed out, "and it sounds like having Hyllarr around is going to make the difference for him."

Darkwind nodded, and then the insistent demands of his stomach reminded him that they were both long overdue for a meal.

Both? No, all. Surely Gwena was just as ravenous.

Unless she and Elspeth, too, were suffering from something that often happened with young mages; where the body was so unused to carrying the energies of magic that basic needs like hunger and thirst were ignored until the mage collapsed. Just as the impetus of fear or anger made the body override hunger and thirst, so did the use of magic—at least until the mage learned to compensate and the body grew used to the energies and no longer confused them.

"If you two aren't hungry, you should be," he told them. "Elspeth, I warned you about that happening, but I don't think I told Gwena; it never occurred to me that she might be susceptible."

Gwena paused, her eyes soft and thoughtful for a moment. :*I should be starving. Hmm. I think I shall find a* hertasi, *and have a good grain ration. If you'll excuse me?*:

With a bow of her head, she trotted up the trail, leaving them alone.

"A wise lady," he observed. "Let's drop by Iceshadow's *ekele* long enough to give him the good news from k'Treva, and then take this conversation to somewhere there's food for us."

Elspeth grinned. "I think I'm used to magic enough now because my stomach is wrapping around my backbone and complaining bitterly. Let's go!"

Iceshadow was overjoyed at the good news from k'Treva and almost as pleased with the news about Starblade. They left him full of plans to inform the rest of the mages, and with unspoken agreement, reversed their course, back to the mouth of the Vale.

There were "kitchens" on the way, but somehow, that "somewhere" wound up being Darkwind's *ekele*, where his *hertasi* had left a warm meal waiting. The *hertasi* information network was amazing; word must have gotten around the moment they'd crossed into the Vale. Before them were crisp finger vegetables and small, broiled gamehens; bread and cheese, fruit, and hot *chava* with beaten cream for two for desert. Darkwind dearly loved *chava*, a hot, sweet drink with a rich taste like nothing else in the world. Sometimes the *hertasi* could be coaxed into making a kind of thick cookie with *chava*, and the two together were enough to put any sweet lover into spasms of ecstasy.

And while he had a moment of suspicion over the fact that the *hertasi* had left food and drink for two, he had to admit that they had done so before. And given his past, perhaps the preparation was not unwarranted. Until Elspeth had entered his life, he had certainly eaten and slept in company more often than not. This was a lovers' meal, though. And they knew very well that he had not had any lovers since they had begun serving him. Was this an expression of hope on their part? Or something else?

Well, the *chava* could be used as bait to tempt Elspeth into his bed, that was certain. He knew any number of folk who would do astonishing things for—even with—the reward of *chava*.

It was Elspeth's first encounter with *chava*, and Darkwind took great glee in her expression of bliss the moment she tasted it. Once again, another devotee was created. They took their mugs over to the pile of cushions in the corner that served as seating and lounging area.

"You look just like Hyllarr when Starblade started scratching him," he told her, chuckling. "All half-closed eyes and about to fall over with pleasure."

"No doubt," she replied, easing back against the cushions with the mug cradled carefully in her hand, so as not to spill a single drop. "Complete with raptorial beak, predator's eyes, and unruly crest."

She spoke lightly, but Darkwind sensed hurt beneath the words. That was the same hurt he had sensed when she spoke of being afraid that most men were interested only in her rank, not in her. "Why do you say that?" he asked.

She snorted, and shook her head. "Darkwind, I thought we were

going to be honest with each other. I've mentioned this before, I know
I have. Can you honestly say that I am *not* as plain as a board?''

He studied her carefully before he answered; the spare, sculptured
face, the expressive eyes, the athletic figure, none of which were set off
to advantage by unadorned, white, plain-edged clothing—or, for that
matter, the drab scout gear she wore now. The thick, dark hair—which
he had never see styled into anything other than an untamed tumble or
pulled back into a tail. ''I think,'' he replied, after a moment, ''that you
have been doing yourself a disservice in the way you dress. With your
white uniform washing out your color and no ornaments, you look very
functional, certainly quite competent and efficient, but severe.''

''What I said: plain as a board.'' She sipped her *chava,* hiding her
face in her cup. ''I like the colored things the *hertasi* have been leaving
out for me, but they don't make much difference that I can see.''

''No,'' he corrected. ''Not 'plain as a board.' Improperly adorned.
Scout gear is still too severe to display you properly. You should try
mage-robes. Mages need not consider impediments such as strolls
through bramble tangles.''

Many Tayledras costumes were suited to either sex; Elspeth, with her
lean figure, would not distort the lines of some of his own clothing.
There were a number of costumes he had designed and made, long ago,
that he had never worn, or worn only once or twice. When Songwind
became Darkwind, and the mage became the scout, those outfits had
been put away in storage as inappropriate to the scout's life. They were
memories that could be hidden.

And, truthfully, he had not wanted to see them again. They belonged
to someone else, another life, another time. Their cheerful colors had
been ill-suited to his grief and his anger. He had not, in fact, even worn
them now that he was a mage again and in the Vale, though he had
brought them out of storage, with the vague notion that he might want
them.

They were here, now, in this new *ekele,* in chests in one of the upper
rooms. He studied her for a moment, considering which of those half-
remembered robes would suit her best.

The ruby-firebird first, he decided. *The amber silk, the peacock-blue, the
sapphire, and the emerald. Perhaps the tawny shirt and fawn breeches—no,
too light, they will wash her out. Hmm. I should go and see what is there; I
can't recall the half of them.*

"Wait here," he said, and before she could answer, ran up the ladderlike stair to the storage room at the top of the *ekele*.

Maybe the tawny with a black high-necked undergarment for contrast. . . .

He returned with his arms full of clothing; robes and half-robes, shirts and flowing breeches in the Shin'a'in style, vests and wrap-shirts, all in jewel-bright colors, made of soft silks and supple leathers, and scented with the cedar of the chests. Light clothing, all of it, made for the gentle warmth of the Vale. There were other mage-robes, heavier, made to be worn outside the Vale, but none of those were as extravagant as these outfits. Tayledras mages did not advertise their powers in outrageous costumes when outside the confines of their homes, unless meeting someone they knew, or knew would be impressed.

"Here—" he said, shaking out the ruby-colored silk half-robe and matching Shin'a'in breeches, cut as full as a skirt, and bound at the ankles with ribbon ties. The half-robe had huge, winglike sleeves with scalloped edges, and an asymmetric hem. "Try this one on, while I find some hair ornaments."

She stared at him, at the clothing, and back again, as if he had gone quite mad. "But—"

He grinned at her. "Indulge me. This is my art, if you will, and it has been long since I was able to spare a moment for it. Go on, go on— if you're modest, there's a screen over there you can stand behind to dress."

He turned to his collection of feathers and beads, crystals and silver chains, all hung like the works of art they were, on the walls. By the *hertasi*, of course; when he'd lived outside the Vale he'd had no time to sort through the things and hang them up properly. They winked and gleamed in the light from his lamps and candles as he considered them. Some of them he had made, but most had been created by other Tayledras. Most of them, sadly, were either dead or with the exiles. But the delicate works of their hands remained, to remind him that not every hour need be spent in war and defense.

After a moment he heard Elspeth rise and take the clothing behind the screen; heard cloth sliding against cloth and flesh as she undressed, then the softer, hissing sounds of silk against that same flesh. He closed his eyes for a moment, reflecting on how good it felt to be doing this again—after all that had happened, that there was still a skill he could use without thought of what it meant tactically.

A moment later, she slipped from behind the screen, and he heard her bare footfalls against the boards of the *ekele* floor. "I hope I have this stuff on right," she said dubiously, as he selected three strands of hair ornaments from among those on the wall.

He turned, his hands full of beaded firebird feathers, and smiled with pleasure at the sight of her.

She made a sour face, and twisted awkwardly. "I look that silly, do I?"

"On the contrary, you look wonderful." She pursed her lips, then smiled reluctantly. He admired her for a moment; as he had thought, the variegated, rich rubies and wines of the half-robe heightened her otherwise dull coloring. With her face tanned by the wind and sun, and her dark brown hair, without the help of color reflected up from her clothing, it was no surprise that she thought herself plain. But now, she glowed, and her hair picked up auburn highlights from the ruby-red silks. And with her hair braided and ornamented instead of being simply pulled back from her face—

She is going to look magnificent when her hair turns white, he thought admiringly. *But now—no, this severe style is not going to work. Color's a bit too strong. It looks wrong now.*

Before she could move, or even protest, he had his hands buried in her hair, braiding the beaded cords of feathers into one side. Then he created a browband with another cord, pulling some of the rest of her hair with it across her forehead to join the braid on the other side. It didn't take long; her hair was ridiculously short by mage-standards, and even many of the scouts wore theirs far longer than hers. But when released from that severe tail, it had a soft, gentle wave that went well with the braids and beaded feathers.

"There," he said, turning her to face the mirror that had been left covered, as was customary, with an embroidered cloth. He whisked the cloth away, revealing her new image to her eyes. "I defy you to call yourself plain now."

Her mouth formed into a silent "Oh," of surprise as she stared at the exotic stranger in the mirror. She flushed, then paled, then flushed again, and her whole posture relaxed and softened.

"I would give a great deal to see you appear in your Court dressed this way," he said, a little smugly. He was rather proud of the way she looked in his handiwork. Better than he had imagined, in fact. "I think that you would set entirely new fashions."

She moved carefully, holding out her arms to see the fall of the sleeves, twirling to watch the material slip about her legs and hips, her eyes sparkling with unexpected pleasure. "I had no idea. The last time I wore anything like this, it was for Talia's wedding. I was a cute little girl, but, well, cuteness wears off. I never thought I could look like this." She shook her head, her eyes still riveted to the mirror. "I thought that the clothing the *hertasi* had been leaving for me was nice, but compared to this—"

"Scout's clothing, it was, really," he said, with a shrug. "Quite as practical as your Herald uniforms. Mages tend to prefer more fanciful garb, and certainly more comfortable. *These* are for delight. Showing off. Dancing. Display, as our birds do, for the sheer joy of doing so, or for—" Before she could respond to that, he had picked out a full robe in monochrome intensities of vivid blue. "Come," he said, coaxingly. "Let us try another. I wish to see you in all of these."

"Me? What about you?"

"What about me?" he repeated, puzzled. "What have I to do with this?"

"You're a mage, aren't you? And aren't these *your* costumes?" She folded her arms stubbornly across her chest. "I'd like to see what *you* look like in these things!"

Try as he would, he could not dissuade her. Before she would consent, she insisted that if *she* was going to prance about in bright feathers, he would have to do the same. So nothing would have it but that he must don a set of dancing gear before she would change her costume for another. The evening hours passed, the two of them playing among the costumes like a pair of children at dress-up, laughing and admiring together.

Some time later, he had draped her in a swath of amber-gold that brought sunlike highlights to her hair and a Tayledras-sheen to her skin. Any of the vivid colors suited her, but she glowed in the warm colors, he had decided. This particular robe, though he did not tell her so, was a lounging robe—a dalliance robe, in fact. A lover's robe. Meant for display to one person, not to many. He had made it for himself, but had not liked the color once he had tried it on—one of the few times he had misjudged color for himself.

But on her—

"You must keep that," he whispered, as she turned and twisted, plainly taking sensuous pleasure in the soft slip of the silk against her skin. "No, indeed, you must," he insisted, as she turned to protest. "It was never suited to me, but I think I must have somehow designed it with you in mind.''

The words had been meant to come out teasingly, but somehow, they turned in his mouth and hung in the air between them with more meaning in them than he had intended. He reached delicately to a glass box and opened it, and before he knew what he was doing, he reached toward her, his hand holding a single brightly beaded feather.

Not one of Vree's—though at this moment, he would have offered her that, if he had thought she might take it. But he dared not. He hardly believed that he dared this.

She knew what that meant now—and as she stared at it and at him with her expression gone quiet and unreadable, he feared that he had just undone all that had been built between them.

But her hand reached for his—and gently took the feather.

And carefully, as if it, or she, might break, she braided it into her hair, then took a deep breath, her eyes wide and dark, waiting.

They both stepped forward at the same moment; he reached up with both hands and cupped her face between them, as carefully as he would grasp a downy day-old falcon. Her skin was as soft as the washed silk she wore, and very warm beneath his hands, as if she was flushed or feverish. It occurred to him then that she might—no, must—be shy, of him, and of what was to come; with a last, weary exercise of his magic, he dimmed the mage-lights.

The comparison and the contrast was inevitable; this was no Dawnfire. Elspeth, for all her courage elsewhere, all her eagerness, was trembling and half-frightened with him. It came to him in a rush how far away from her home she was—all the trials she had faced, and now this—it was up to him to take the lead. She was unsure of herself and not certain what he wanted of her, but there was desire there.

So, he would go as gently with her as he would with caring for a frightened wild bird. She was not likely a virgin, but it did not necessarily follow that she was experienced in lovemaking; he could by accident frighten her with a technique she had never experienced. With all sincerity, he hoped there would be ample times in the future to explore.

He kissed her, once, then dropped his hands, catching hers, and led her back to the bower of cushions on the floor. He slowly drew her down beside him, and there they stayed while he caressed her, letting the silk slide over her body beneath his hands. He touched her gently; shoulders, back, breasts, neck—let the silk carry the movement of his hands. She shivered again, but now it was not from half-formed fear, but from anticipation.

Her lips parted in a gentle moan of pleasure, and she lay her head back with a visible expression of delight.

After a moment, she returned his caresses, hesitantly at first, then with more boldness. Her hands wandered as freely as his, and he kept careful control over himself, lest he move too quickly with her.

But it had been a very long time since his last lover . . . a very long time. Controlling himself was as difficult as any magic he had ever attempted.

Now they drew closer, and her lips met his.

If he had any thoughts until that moment that she might regret having accepted his feather, they were dismissed by the eagerness with which she returned his kiss. He allowed his mind to brush hers for a moment, as his mouth opened for her. He garnered two important things from that brief contact; she was by no means as experienced a lover as he, but she was as perfectly willing to be his pupil in this as in the other subjects he had taught her. She had confidence in his skill abed.

So; take things slowly. The greater her desire, the calmer at first, the more fully she felt their bodies, the better the experience.

He slid his hands under the silk of the robe, and continued his slow, sensual caresses; continued until any thought of fear was a long-forgotten triviality. Then he joined his mind to hers, very lightly, and showed her wordlessly what would pleasure him, as he noted what pleasured her. She was soft silk in his hands, and warm honey in his mouth; feather-caress and nectar. Her scent was of sandalwood, cinnamon, and herbs. His was of musk and rich *chava*. Her skin tasted salty-sweet, and where their bodies touched, liquid fire poured between them.

When their minds were so entwined that there was no telling where one ended and the other began, only then did he join his body into hers.

A pair of hawks spiraling slowly up a thermal, talons entwined, they rose together, and soared into the sun. . . .

Elspeth lay in silk and warmth, and thought of absolutely nothing, content to savor the warm glow that bathed every pore. Content to listen to Darkwind breathing beside her. Content, for the moment, to forget everything she was, and simply be.

Darkwind lay quietly beside her, his breathing slow and even. She listened to him, thinking that sleep could not be far off for her, either, but hoping to hold it away a little longer, and savor the moment.

"I trust I achieved your expectations."

She started; he laid a calming hand on her shoulder, and she laughed, breathlessly, willing her heart to calm. "I thought you were asleep," she said. "I mean, you sounded like you were."

"That would be unforgivably crude," Darkwind replied, with just a hint of laughter in his voice. "At least, it would be by our customs."

She thought of the few—to be honest, three—lovers she had taken to her bed, not counting the almost-lover whose tryst Talia had interrupted so long ago. Skif had never been one of them—which might have accounted for the way he had overreacted when they were alone on the road together. They were all friends, she and her lovers, but never more than that, and they had trysted with the understanding that it would remain that way. Heralds, all of them, of course; Talia had been right about that. Only a Herald could be trusted to be completely discreet about making love with the Heir. Two of them had always fallen asleep immediately afterward, and she had slipped out of *their* rooms to return to her own.

Oh, they were always tired, she thought, in their defense. *And no sooner were they rested than they were haring off again, out on circuit. They couldn't help it. And it would have been an awful scandal for me to act openly as their lover.*

Neave never fell asleep, but then he never *ever* fell asleep with anyone else in his bed. He couldn't. Not after what he'd been through. He was healing, but sometimes she wondered if he would ever really be *healed.* Perhaps not. And her times with him had been as much comfort for him as lovemaking. Oh, he was skilled; he'd had no choice but to learn skill . . . poor child. How anyone could make a child into an *object* like that; to use a child, an unconsenting, terrified *child*—

She deliberately turned her thoughts away from the past. "I think I could learn to like your customs," she said, keeping her tone light. "It seems a bit more civilized than to simply roll over and forget one's partner when the moment is gone."

"Well, but it is no jest, not really," he replied, with a finger-brush along her cheek. "Wait a moment—"

He gently disentangled himself from her, and with a whisper of cloth, faded into the darkness. Her ears strained to hear what he was doing, but she could not make anything out except some vague sounds of moving about.

He returned in a moment, and took his place beside her again; felt for her hand, and pressed a cool cup into it. She sipped, and found that it was delightfully cold and sweet water. Before she knew it, she had drained the cup; and feeling for a secure place to put it, set it down on a table beside her with a sigh.

"Sometimes I suspect the *hertasi* of prescience," he said, after a moment. "A meal for two waiting, *chava* for two to inflame the senses, with cool water waiting with two cups to quench the thirst—"

She chuckled. "Maybe. Is that one of your customs? Pampering your partner?"

"Oh, the custom is simpler than that," he replied, setting his cup down somewhere with a faint *tick*. "It is that one does not simply fall asleep without expressing one's delight in one's partner." His voice was warm with approval, and she found herself blushing.

"That is a most civilized custom," she replied, after a moment. "And," she groped for something to say that would not make her blush even harder, "consider it expressed."

"Would you care to accept my feather in the future, Wingsib?" he persisted.

She couldn't help it; she flushed so hotly that she feared she must be glowing in the dark. "I—would very much like it," she stammered.

"Ah, now I embarrass you, forgive me," he said quickly. "We are a forward people, we Tayledras. The Shin'a'in claim that like kestrels, we have no shame. But I hope you will not take it amiss that I am very glad to hear your reply."

"No—no, not at all." Oh, she must sound like a schoolchild in the throes of infatuation!

"Thank you, bright lady." That gentle hand touched her cheek again, and this time, he did not withdraw. "Are you rested?" he asked, his finger tracing a line down her cheek, then further down, along the line of her throat.

"I—think so—" she stammered again. What was he about?

"Well, then—there is another custom," he chuckled. "Which is why the Shin'a'in compare us to kestrels . . . in more than being shameless."

Then to her astonishment, he pressed gently against her, and began all over again.

At first she was too surprised to respond, but her astonishment did not outlive the realization that he was quite serious. And quite intent. And quite, quite splendid.

This time, she brought the water, with help from a tiny mage-light to find where the *hertasi* had left the pitcher. He accepted it with a sleepy smile, and a kiss in the palm of her hand.

She took her place beside him, quite certain that even if she had wanted to, her legs would not have carried her as far as her own *ekele*. And she didn't want to leave, not really. Her bed was cold and lonely, and Darkwind was warm and quite ready to cradle her in his arms.

Who would she outrage, anyway? Not Gwena. Not the *hertasi*. Not any of the Hawkbrothers, who partnered whomever they pleased. Even Skif could not take her to task. There were no Court gossips here. No word of this would get back to scandalize whatever potential bridegrooms there might be.

Not that there seemed to be any in the offing. *Nothing* would persuade her to wed Ancar, and it was not likely that Karse had any royal sons to wed to satisfy an alliance . . . her mother had satisfied any need for bonds with Rethwellan. Who would she wed? Some fur-covered hulk from the North? They didn't even *have* any government; they were a series of warring tribes.

Perhaps she *could* choose a partner to suit herself. . . .

"And now," Darkwind whispered, "custom satisfied—I fear—I *must* sleep—" A yawn punctuated the sentence, and she found herself echoing it.

"Custom satisfied—" she yawned again "—I agree—"

"Then, good night—" he whispered. *"Zhai'helleva—"*

Sleep had her by the shoulders and was dragging her down into darkness. But had she heard what she *thought* she heard?

Had he whispered, with the sigh of one drifting into slumber, *"Zhai'helleva, ashke?"*

Wind to thy wings—beloved?

The *hertasi* brought her clothing and laid it beside breakfast for two without so much as a single eyeblink to show that they considered her spending the night anything out of the ordinary. Gwena appeared shortly afterward, to tell them that they had been relieved of the duty of chasing away what had been attracted by their profligate use of power. And even her Companion had nothing to say on her choice of sleeping places and partners.

:*Iceshadow approved of your choice of nonweaponry,*: she told them. :*Illusions make a less-visible use of power. He has some other mages out there doing what you did—with backups, of course, in case the beasties don't frighten away. Right now he wants you to meet with him and the Elders and anyone else that is free—he's holding a Clanwide general meeting.*:

"I assume he wants us to tell them all exactly what the message said?" Darkwind replied after a moment of thought, as he braided his hair away from his face.

:*Probably. He didn't tell me.*: She tossed her head with feigned indignation, but Elspeth could tell that she didn't mean it. :*I told him that it was my opinion that you two needed a day of rest, anyway. He seemed inclined to agree. His exact words were "as much rest as the Clan can afford them, at any rate."*:

Darkwind chuckled. "Meaning that we are still on call. Ah, well. It is better than being out in the snow!"

They ate slowly, Elspeth being very aware of Darkwind's eyes lingering on her, and being unable to resist taking a few, long, lingering glances herself.

He certainly provided a pleasant place to rest the eyes. He no longer seemed so exotic—although he did look a bit odd, with white showing at the roots of his hair; she couldn't help but think of certain "blonde" ladies whose hair often showed the opposite coloration at its roots. It no longer seemed strange to have the bondbird sitting beside them, taking bits of raw meat from Darkwind's fingers. For that matter, it no longer seemed revolting to eat her breakfast and watch the bird bolting his tidbits. . . .

She remembered, then, that she had been able to hear the bird yesterday. Was that still true?

Well, why not test it?

:*Vree?*: she called, tentatively, pitching her mind-voice up high, trying to reach the same place she had Heard him.

The bird looked up, startled, and immediately turned his head upside down to look at her.

:*?*: he Sent. :*!*:

"Yes, she's speaking to you, silly bird," Darkwind said lightly, with an approving glance at her that warmed her all the way down to her toes. "It's considered polite to answer."

:Ye-es?: Vree replied, cautiously, righting his head again.

:How is Hyllarr?: she asked, figuring that was an innocent enough question, and one the bird should be able to answer easily enough.

:Hungry. Healing. Happy.: Vree roused all his feathers, evidently tickled by his own alliteration. *:Very good. Is good bonding.:*

:Thank you,: she told him, and he bobbed his head at her before turning his attention back to Darkwind's tidbits.

"Why can I talk to him now when I couldn't before?" she asked, hoping he knew the answer.

"I think—mostly because you know now that he Mindspeaks, so you began listening unconsciously for where he was Speaking," Darkwind hazarded. "The gryphons Speak high, but in the ranges you were listening in already—but listening to them made you ready to listen even higher. I think. I don't *think* that you are developing a new Gift."

"Good," she replied, a little relieved. "One at a time is enough."

He laughed, and fed Vree the last bit of meat. "Shall we go?" he asked, standing up and offering her his hand.

The meeting was relatively uneventful, until Starblade put in an appearance. He leaned heavily on Kethra and a walkingstick, and sat down immediately, but it was already obvious that despite his physical weakness there was new life in his eyes, and new hope in his spirit.

He listened to both of them recount what they remembered of the message, and waited for the buzz of conversation to die down, before clearing his throat to speak.

He got immediate silence.

"Before any of you speculate," he said, carefully, "Yes—k'Treva *did* send mages to see if we needed help immediately after the Stone shattered. And I did turn them away, with protests that we were fully capable of dealing with the situation ourselves. You all know why I did that. I am sorry. But this may have been all to the good, in some ways. When they offered help, the healing Adept of which they speak had only just come into his power. Now he is at full strength. Had he tried to deal with the Stone as it was, it might have killed him and the rest of us as well. Certainly it would have damaged him, and our great enemy would have had a way into the power of a Healing Adept as a result. And that would have been even more of a catastrophe."

Murmurs around the circle showed that most of the Clan agreed with him. Elspeth didn't even want to *think* about Mornelithe Falconsbane having that much power. The little that she had seen of him had convinced her that he had been far too powerful as it was.

"Now—" Starblade continued, "I believe that with the help of Darkwind, Wingsib Elspeth, honored Gwena, and our gryphon allies, all will be well. But I am only one. I think that every voice should be heard in this. It is the fate of our entire Clan that we are discussing."

Elspeth followed as much as she could, but the Hawkbrothers were more than a bit agitated, and as a result, spoke a little faster than she preferred. She gathered that they were, on the whole, inclined to agree with Starblade, but they had been deceived before and were determined to do what they could to see that it did not happen again.

As the meeting went on, Starblade wilted visibly—yet seemed stubbornly determined to remain and prove that he was no longer acting against the good of the Clan. Finally Elspeth couldn't stand it any more. She stood up.

All eyes focused on her, and the babble of speech cut off, abruptly, leaving her standing in silence.

"I haven't endured what you have," she said, slowly. "And I haven't been a mage for very long. I've certainly never seen a Healing Adept, so I have no idea what they can or can't do. But we took a lot of time preparing that message; we told k'Treva everything we knew, in as much detail as we could. *Surely,* since they were already worried about us, this Adept they are sending has had time to prepare for trouble! Surely he comes not only armed but armored!"

She sat down again, wondering if she'd managed to insult all of them, or if she'd made some sense.

Evidently the latter, since she saw Iceshadow smiling, slowly, and there was very little muttering and much nodding of heads.

"Has everyone said what is needed?" Iceshadow asked, once the last of the muttering died down. He looked about, but no one seemed inclined to jump to his or her feet. "Very well, then, I—"

The bottom dropped out of Elspeth's stomach, and although she hadn't moved, it felt as if she had suddenly plummeted about five feet.

What in— She looked wildly about. Was it an attack? Had something gone wrong with the Stone?

But no one else seemed alarmed, and she calmed her pounding heart. Iceshadow actually grinned at the expression on her face, whatever it was.

It probably looks like someone hit me in the back of the head with a board.

"That, I think, makes the rest of the arguments moot," Iceshadow said. "So, if no one has any objection, I will declare the meeting closed."

Under cover of the rest standing up and moving off in twos and threes or more, Elspeth leaned over to Darkwind and asked, "And just what *was* that? Was that an earthquake? I've heard of them, but—"

"Not an earthquake, no, although I am told that the feeling is very similar, save that the earth itself does not move," Darkwind replied. "No, that was the establishing and closing of a long-ranging Gate that you just felt. Very abrupt—probably to keep from disrupting the Stone too much. Normally the flux is much more gradual and less noticeable."

"You mean—"

He took her hand and squeezed it, his smile inviting her to share in his triumph. "Yes. At last. There is very little that is likely to stop him. And there is no more chance for argument. Our help is on the way. We have won."

Firesong

Chapter
Sixteen

Darkwind took nothing about Elspeth for granted, but when she returned with him to his *ekele*, he thought it reasonable to assume that she was not displeased with him in the clear light of day. He had not been certain; she was so self-possessed, she rarely revealed what was in her mind. As important as her mind, he was not certain what the reaction of her Companion would be to their assignation, despite the fact that Gwena had left them alone together.

But there were inevitable awkward moments to come. The early moments of a new liaison were always full of such things . . . when neither knows quite what to say or do, and neither is familiar enough with the other to read body and voice. Trying not to appear too distant, yet not wanting to seem possessive, making the dance moves of courtship and trying not to stumble through them—all of this was universal.

He paused at the foot of the stairs and cleared his throat at the same time that she said "Darkwind—"

They looked at each other and laughed self-consciously.

"I was about to suggest that we take advantage of our temporary freedom to soak away some bruises," he said, offering a neutral occupation which had the potential to become something else entirely. In this, at least, he had more experience than she. He had sky-danced through a fair number of courtships. "The *hertasi* are skilled at massage, if you like. They use carved wooden rollers instead of claws, and thick oils."

She stretched in a way that suggested that she might well be suffering from sore muscles, stiffly, and with a little wince of pain, rather than coyly or provocatively. "I would like that," she replied. Then she smiled, wryly. "Now the pertinent question—were you thinking of soaking in the same pool as me, or going off on your own? I would enjoy your company, but I won't be upset if you'd like to have some time to yourself." Her smile became a grin. "Astera knows you've seen quite enough of me and my over-sharp tongue. I wouldn't blame you if you'd like a respite!"

"Actually, I was hoping you'd join me, but in the pool near *your* tree," he said, relieved at her words, and even more so at the touch of self-deprecating humor. "Yours is the warmest pool in the Vale. I will ask my *hertasi* to bring oils, once I find them. They haven't established a summoning method yet."

"Shall I meet you there?" she suggested gracefully. "You've got things to do—and I'm still something of an appendage to the Clan."

It didn't take him too long to find the two lizard-folk; it took him even less time to make his way to the pool he now thought of as "Elspeth's." But by the time he got there, she was already chin-deep in hot water, her hair piled up on the top of her head and her eyes half-closed in pleasure.

"We must have slipped and fallen in the snow a hundred times. I have bruises in places I didn't even guess at. I have got to find some way to reproduce these pools once I get back home," she said, as he shed clothing and joined her. "A hot bath is no substitute for this."

The two lizard-folk busied themselves in setting up cushions and towels beside the pool; once they were ready, he and Elspeth could go to their skillful hands with their muscles warm and pliant. *Much* easier to take the knots out of muscles that were relaxed and warmed than those that were stiff and tense.

"Have you no hot springs in your homeland?" he asked lazily, slipping into the hot water with a sigh of pleasure. "I would find that very strange."

"You would find a lot of things about my land very strange," she said. "At least as strange as Skif and I find the Vale. And speaking of Skif—"

He felt a chill in spite of the heat of the water. Was she about to reveal that she and Skif were betrothed, or something of the sort? While he had no claims on her, nor had any right to think of such things—the idea disturbed him in a way that he did not want to examine too closely.

But she was continuing, and there was nothing in her tone to give him any kind of clue to her feelings about the other Herald. "Speaking of Skif—Darkwind, what should I do about Nyara? If—when he finds her. Should I worry? Should I even try to do anything?"

"I do not know," he said, carefully, choosing his words in the hopes that they would not turn to stones and bruise his already shaken pride. "First I must ask you this—what is Skif to you?"

"To me?" She opened her eyes and looked him full in the face, and he was relieved to see that there was nothing hiding there. No hitherto undisclosed passions. No pain. Only simple concern. "My very good friend. My blood-brother. My—Wingsib, if you will, for the Heralds are the closest thing to a Tayledras Clan that my people know. He *has* no other kin but the Heralds, and I'm one of the closest friends he has among them. I'm *worried* about him, Darkwind."

There was something she hadn't told him yet. "Why should you worry?" he asked. "He seems perfectly capable to me."

She sighed, and chewed her lower lip. "I've known him a long time, and the Skif you know isn't the Skif I first made my brother. I haven't talked to anyone about this, but something happened to him a couple of years ago, something to do with the war with Hardorn, and it changed him. He hasn't been the same since. But he never said anything to me about it, and I don't feel that I should press him on the subject. I mean, he values his privacy."

He considered her words for a moment, hoping that the relief he felt on learning that Skif was no more than a brother to her did not show too clearly. But changes in a personality—oh, he was all too familiar with that. Though this was not likely to be the kind of sinister change that had overcome Starblade.

No, more like the change of shock that had made Songwind become Darkwind.

"I think that if it was something he felt comfortable about revealing to you, he would have done so," he said carefully. "That may have been because he considered you to be too sheltered to reveal it, because he was ashamed of it, or even because you are female and he is male. Do I take it that this experience—whatever it was—damaged him in some way?''

''Not physically, but he was never as—carefree afterward,'' she replied thoughtfully. ''Yes, I would say that it damaged him. Probably all three reasons have something to do with why he has never told me about it.''

''In that case, he might well reveal it to Wintermoon,'' Darkwind mused aloud. ''That would be a good thing. My brother is a remarkable man and has his own burdens he might be pleased to reveal. That would be a good thing as well.''

She gave him a glance filled with hope and speculation. ''Do you think so? He's been so—I don't know. Before, he was always eager for the next adventure. Now it seems as if adventure has soured for him, and all he's looking for is peace. And I think that Nyara just *might* be able to ease some of what is hurting him. *If* she doesn't hurt him further.''

''A good point. I do not think that she would do so a-purpose,'' he said, raising a dripping hand from the water to rub his temple. ''She has been both cause and receiver of too much harm to wish to work further such, I think.'' Nyara . . . oh, *there* was a potential to become the lash of a whip if not carefully dealt with. ''But there is pain waiting for him, with that one, be she ever so well-intentioned.''

Elspeth nodded. ''You're thinking what I'm thinking. If he—no, when he finds her, if she is not in love with him, he's going to be hurt.''

''Would it were only as simple as that. You know that if she *does* love him and ran to save him before for that reason, he is destined for even greater hurt.'' Darkwind raised himself a little higher in the water, rested his arms on the ledge around the pool, and propped his head on one hand. ''You must know that, Elspeth. Think on it. Suppose she loves him truly. Suppose she *accepts* his love. *My* people would have trouble in accepting a Changechild as the lover of one of their kin. But yours? To them, will she not seem a monster?''

She groaned, and rubbed her eyes. ''I wish I could tell you no, but I can't. Gods, Darkwind, the Shin'a'in are looked at askance when a rare one comes to Valdemar. The Hawkbrothers are legends only. They'd try to put *her* in a menagerie!'' She shook her head. ''No matter what we did, how we tried to disguise her, I doubt it would hold for long.''

''Soon or late, any disguise is unmade, any illusion is broken,'' he agreed. ''Nor is that the only problem with Nyara. She is utterly, totally foreign. Her ways could never be yours. Gods of my fathers, her ways are utterly alien to *my* people! Among yours, she would be like unto a plains-cat given a collar and called a pet!''

Elspeth groaned. "And that—that aura of sexuality she has—that isn't going to win her any converts, I can tell you that. Havens, she even made *me* annoyed, sometimes, and there was nothing for me to be irritated with her over!''

"Except that every male eye must ever be on her," he said ruefully. "Be he ever so faithful to his lover, he *still* must react to her like a male beast in season! Even I—well, I entertained fantasies, and I knew well the danger she implied. You say that Skif seems to seek only peace. Well, he will not find it with *that* one on his arm! Every male with no manners will be trying to have her for himself. Every female will react as you—or more strongly.''

"And she can't help herself.'' Elspeth's mouth quirked in a half smile at his confession, but she quickly sobered. "Darkwind, what should I do?''

"Should you do anything?'' he countered. "Can you do anything? Is there even any advice that you could give him that he would heed?''

She shook her head sadly. "Probably not. I guess there's only one thing I can do—to be ready for whatever decision he and she make.''

"That is all that a friend can do, Elspeth,'' he agreed. "And I think perhaps that is all that a friend *should* do. But you know, there is another course that he might take that you do not seem to have considered. What would you and your people think if he should choose to stay here—with her?''

"If he—'' She stared at him now as if the very idea were so alien that she couldn't quite grasp it. "But he's a Herald!''

"He is also a human—and a man. And he is very much in love.'' Darkwind had a fleeting feeling of disorientation, as if he were not talking only about the Herald Skif. "Would your people make him choose between his love and his land? Would this cause his Companion to abandon him?''

"I don't know,'' she said helplessly. "The subject has never come up.''

"Interesting.'' He leaned back into the water again. "Perhaps you and Gwena should discuss this at length. I have the feeling that it may be important.''

"So do I,'' she replied, slowly. "So do I . . .''

* * *

The Adept from k'Treva did not appear by nightfall, at which point Darkwind felt that he had most probably taken the wise course of finding a secure place to rest for the night. When he and Elspeth sought out Iceshadow just after dusk, the Elder said words to that same effect.

"I do not think our Clansbrother is likely to arrive on our doorstep until the morning," Iceshadow predicted, as the three of them strolled back to the Elder's *ekele*. "Were I he, I would find a *tervardi* and share his shelter for the night. I have sensed nothing amiss, and I think if he were in trouble, we would certainly *know* it."

Darkwind nodded. Very few Tayledras traveled by night by choice. Even fewer did so in unknown and possibly dangerous territory. "He knows that our borders are shrunken, and that the land within them is not certain. The heavy snows of the past few days have probably slowed him down. I doubt the one who replied took the difficulties of winter riding into account when he sent the message and told you the Adept would arrive in half a day. Even on *dyheli* I would not undertake to go anywhere in this snow in half a day."

They reached Iceshadow's home at that moment; the Elder stretched, and paused with one hand on the railing. "I would not worry, were I you. *I* am not concerned. We will see this marvel when he arrives and not before, and the matter of one or two days more is not going to make a great deal of difference to our situation. True?"

When they agreed, he chuckled, and bid them a pleasant evening, a certain twinkle in his eyes as he looked from Elspeth to Darkwind and back.

Not that Darkwind minded the delay. Once the Healing Adept arrived, he and Elspeth would start on a round of magic-use that would leave them quite exhausted at day's end. He knew *that* from experience. Sadly, heavy magic-use tended to leave one too weary for dalliance.

They would have one more night together, at least—

Or so he hoped.

This time, since they were so near, she had invited him to her *ekele* for supper, while the *hertasi* turned them both into limp yarn dolls. At the time he had thought he saw Faras, the one working on her back, smile a little when she made the invitation. He said nothing, though, then or now; she knew that the lizard-folk used Mindspeech as easily as humans used their voices. Though what she might not know was the way the little folk like to play at matchmaking. . . .

They took a second soak in the pool, then slipped into a pair of thick robes that the *hertasi* had left there for them, leaving the pool when dusk was only a memory and full darkness shrouded the Vale. Darkwind was not certain how Elspeth felt, but *he* had not been so relaxed or content for a very long time. He followed her up to her *ekele*, pretty well certain of what he would find there.

He was not disappointed. The robe of amber silk, clean again, was waiting for her—and his favorite, of deep blue, lay beside it across the cushions. And on the table there waited another intimate supper for two. This one was a bit different, though.

He recognized it, though she would not have. This was a lover's supper, a trysting meal. Sensual delights. Things to tease the palate and the four senses. Light foods, the kind found at festivals, arranged in single bite-sized pieces. Food made to be eaten with the fingers—

—or fed to another.

Oddly modest, she caught up the robe and carried it into the next room to change into it, although she had not seemed so shy at the pool. He would have enjoyed seeing the soft silk slip over her young, supple body. Well, that would come in time as she lost her shyness with him.

If they had the time. . . .

He pushed the thought from his mind. He would enjoy what they had, and not seek to shape their future. He slipped into his own robe as she returned, the amber silk caressing her and enveloping her like a cloud of golden smoke. She made a circuit of the room, lighting scented candles to perfume the air; he watched her with pleasure, and wondered a little at her grace. Had she always moved like that? Or had he only now begun to notice?

He waited until she had made herself comfortable before moving toward her. She patted a place beside her and he settled next to her. His most urgent appetite was not for food, but he contented himself with nibbling on a slice of quince as she hesitantly took a piece of cheese.

"What do you think he'll be like?" she asked abruptly, proving that whatever his thoughts were, hers were elsewhere.

The question took him by surprise, and he had to drag his thoughts away from contemplating *her*, and apply them to something a bit more abstract.

"The Healing Adept, you mean?" he hazarded. That was the only "he" the question seemed apt for. "The one from k'Treva?"

She nodded, and he made a half shrug. He hadn't thought about it; he was far more interested in the Adept's skills than in anything else.

"It usually takes a Healing Adept years to come into his full power, so I suppose that he is probably about the age of my father," he said, after a moment. "Probably very serious, very deliberate. Although—" he frowned, trying to recall the message's exact words. "—they did say that he was a kind of experimenter. That is an interesting point. He might be more like Kra'heera than my father."

"What, that funny kind of trickster?" She nibbled at a piece of fruit. "But powerful."

"Oh, that, at the least," he agreed. "He would have to be, to be willing to ride alone across uncertain land. I think that he will definitely have that kind of air about him that Iceshadow has when he is truly certain of himself. Except that he will have it all the time."

"You have that air sometimes," she said suddenly.

"No—" Now that startled him. "I do?"

"Yes." She licked juice from her fingers and gave him a sidelong glance. "You did last night. Sometimes I think you don't give yourself enough credit."

He shook his head. "I think you are being flattering, but—"

"I'm not really hungry," she interrupted him. "Are you?"

He laughed, now knowing where the pathway was leading. "Not for this sort of food," he said.

Bondbirds carried the message in midmorning that the k'Treva Adept was less than a league away. Those of the Clan that were not otherwise engaged in Clan duties gathered at the entrance of the Vale to await his arrival. Although the snow was knee-deep beyond the Veil, it would not have been a proper welcome to greet him within.

Elspeth and Darkwind were among them, and she thought privately that this mysterious mage could not have contrived a more perfect backdrop for his first appearance. The clouds of the past few days had cleared away by dawn, and the sun shone down out of a flawless blue sky, filling the snow-bedecked woods outside the entrance of the Vale with pure white light. There wasn't even a breath of wind, and the woods were completely silent except for a few calls of birds off in the distance. As they waited in the snow, straining their ears for the sound of hoofbeats, Elspeth fretted a little beneath the suspense of the moment. Even Gwena seemed tense with anticipation.

Finally, the sound they had been waiting for echoed beneath the trees; the muffled thud of hooves pounding through snow. From the cadence, Elspeth knew that he had urged his mount into a gallop. Not that *dyheli* had any objection to galloping, but he could not possibly have kept up that pace all the way here. Only a Companion had the stamina to gallop for hours at a time.

Either he's impatient for the end of the trip, or he wants to make an impressive entrance, she thought with amusement.

And then the object of their anticipation came pounding in, sprays of snow flying all about him, and a magnificent, snow-white firebird skimmed just beneath the branches precisely over his head, its tail streaming behind it as the Adept's long hair streamed behind him.

The firebird was the biggest one she had ever seen—and never had she ever heard of anyone using one for a bondbird. It threw off the little false-sparks of golden light as it flew, glittering, a creature of myth or tales.

From the murmurs of surprise, she surmised that no one among the Hawkbrothers had ever seen a firebird bondbird before, either.

It was at least as large as Darkwind's forest-gyre. It seemed to be larger, because of the length of its magnificent tail. The head, with its huge, ice-blue eyes, was just as large as any bondbird's head, which meant it could be as intelligent as the rest.

But the firebirds were seed and fruit eaters. Not carnivores or hunters. . . .

Well, why not? He's a mage. He doesn't need *a combative bird to help him, the way the scouts do.*

The Adept pulled up before the entrance to the Vale in a shower of snow and a flurry of hooves, like some kind of young god of winter, or an ice-storm personified. Even his mount gave Elspeth pause for a moment, until she saw the curving horns over the two ice-blue eyes, for he rode a *dyheli* bleached to snowy white just as the bondbirds were.

He *posed* for a moment, and she realized that he was doing it deliberately. Not that she blamed him. She smiled, but kept it to herself.

Oh, what a vain creature he is! And how he basks in the admiration he's getting. Rightfully.

They had expected a venerable wise man; another Iceshadow with more presence, perhaps. What they had gotten was something else entirely.

He swept his arm out and the firebird drifted down to rest on his snow-white leather gauntlet, alighting as silently as one of its own feathers would fall. Only then was it clear that the firebird was fully as large as any of the greater hawks, and approached the size of the hawk-eagle. Its tail trailed down gracefully to within a hand's breadth of the snow, and it, too, posed, as if perfectly well aware of its unearthly beauty.

He was dressed all in white; white furs and leathers, long white hair with white feathers in a braid to one side, white coat draped over the rump of his white *dyheli*. Three sets of ice-blue eyes looked over the assembled Clansfolk dispassionately; the eyes of the *dyheli* and the firebird held only curiosity, but the eyes of the Adept held more than a touch of a self-confidence that was surely forgivable—both for his Adept status (and indeed, he could never have achieved that complete bleaching of hair and eyes and bird if he had *not* been controlling node-magic since he could toddle) and for his absolute physical perfection.

Never in all her life had Elspeth seen anyone so beautiful. That was the only word for him. He was beautiful in a way that transcended sexuality and yet was bound up with it.

So some arrogance and self-assurance could certainly be forgiven, even if he was no older than Darkwind.

Gwena was staring at him intently, much more intently than Elspeth expected.

:What's wrong?: she asked the Companion quietly. *:Is there anything wrong?:*

:Nothing wrong, exactly,: she said slowly. *:No, that's not true. There's nothing* wrong *at all. But it almost seems like I've seen him before, though I can't imagine how I ever could have. But there certainly is something familiar about him—:*

:Of course there is, my dear,: a deep, masculine mind-voice interrupted. And the k'Treva Adept winked at the Companion, slowly, and unmistakably.

Elspeth was left floundering in surprise—and as for Gwena, clearly, if the Companion's jaw could have dropped in shock, it would have. Gwena stepped backwards.

"Greetings, Clansibs," the Adept called to them all, as calmly as if he had not just utterly flabbergasted Gwena. "I am Firesong k'Treva, and I trust I have not made you wait for too long for my arrival."

With that, he dismounted, sliding from the back of the *dyheli* so smoothly that the firebird was not in the least disturbed. There was a pack on his back—also of white leather—which had been hidden until he dismounted. The *dyheli* paced beside him as he walked forward to the Veil and the Tayledras waiting to greet him, one hand still on the *dyheli's* shoulder, a half-smile on his handsome face. Iceshadow and the other Elders greeted him first, as was only proper, but when he had done clasping arms with them, he turned immediately to Elspeth and Darkwind.

"And here are those whose message summoned me," he said, tossing his head to send his braid over his shoulder, his lips curved in an enigmatic smile. "I see one Clansib—and two Outlanders. A fascinating combination."

"This is Wingsister Elspeth k'Sheyna k'Valdemar, and her Companion Gwena k'Valdemar," Darkwind said carefully. A little too carefully, Elspeth thought. "I am Darkwind."

"K'Valdemar, hmm?" Firesong repeated, his smile increasing by just a hair. "*And* a Companion. *Zhai'helleva*, Wingsibs. The tale of your coming here must be a fascinating one indeed."

"Elspeth is a Herald of Valdemar, if you have heard of such things." Darkwind's voice was carefully neutral. "There is another Herald out on the borders of k'Sheyna who was also made Wingsib, one Skif k'Sheyna k'Valdemar—but it is pressing business that keeps him there, and at any rate, he is no mage."

"Which you, bright falcon, most certainly are." Firesong's handclasp was warm and firm as he took Elspeth's hand in greeting. "And as it happens I have heard of Heralds before. It is something of a k'Treva legend, the visits of Heralds. But then, k'Treva has always been considered—hmm—unconventional." He glanced aside at Iceshadow, who coughed politely.

"But here I am keeping you out in the snow and cold, when we could be in the welcoming warmth of the Vale!" he exclaimed, turning swiftly in a graceful swirl of snowy hair, feathers, and clothing. "Come, Clansibs! Let us continue these greetings in comfort."

Darkwind struggled against annoyance. This Firesong—this *young* Firesong—displayed a body-language that flaunted his arrogance. And a confidence that implied a competence fully as great as the arrogance.

Well, the firebird resting on his shoulder said something of his competence. It had been generations since one of the Tayledras had thought to breed up a new species of bondbird—and to do so from firebird stock was doubly amazing. Firebirds were shy, highly territorial, easily startled—none of those being traits that augured well for their potential as bondbirds. Yet here he was, this Firesong, bearing a snow-white firebird that sat his shoulder as calmly as ever a forest-gyre sat a scout's.

Small wonder that his Clan described him as an experimenter.

He *could* be older than he looked; it often took an Adept up to sixty years to show any signs of aging. But Darkwind doubted that. The arrogance that Firesong flaunted was that of youth, not age; Darkwind reckoned that he *might* even be a year or two younger than *he* was.

Just as annoying was Elspeth's obvious fascination with the newcomer.

He is as beautiful as a god, a traitorous whisper said in the back of his mind. *How could she not be attracted to him? How could anyone?*

He took small comfort in the fact that Firesong chose an *ekele* near the opposite end of the Vale from Elspeth's. Right beside Starblade's in fact, a little higher in the same tree. But no sooner had the Adept tossed his white pack carelessly up into the open door, sent his white firebird to a perch, and shed his heavy outer garments, than he turned and looked down at Darkwind with that annoying half-smile on his face.

"I should like to see your father Starblade, if I may," he said without preamble. "If you will excuse me."

And with that, he ran lightly down the stairs and tapped upon the doorpost of Starblade's *ekele* as if he were expected.

Perhaps he was, for Kethra beckoned him inside, leaving Darkwind *outside*. She did not beckon him in, although she clearly saw him standing there.

He felt like a fool, and only felt like less of one because there was no one there to witness his exclusion from what was obviously a private conference.

He gritted his teeth, and went off to find something marginally useful to do, before he did something decidedly the opposite.

"Ho, Darkwind!"

The unfamiliar voice hailing him could only be Firesong's. Darkwind stopped, put a pleasant expression on his face with an effort of will, and turned to face the young Adept.

Firesong had changed his costume, from the winter whites he had ridden in wearing, to something more appropriate to the warmth of the Vale. A half-robe and trousers of fine silk—and if Darkwind had not

seen it, he would not have believed that it was possible to create a costume that was *more* flamboyant than that of his arrival.

Firebird gold, white, and flame-blue were the colors, and they matched
the blue of his eyes, the silver of his hair, and the gold of his skin to
perfection. Someone—*hertasi*, probably—had taken great pains with his
hair. Darkwind felt positively plain beside him.

"Darkwind," Firesong said, cheerfully, as he strode up beside him.
"I have had speech of Starblade and Kethra, of the Elders, and also of
the Shin'a'in shaman Tre'valen. What they have told me has confirmed
the impression your message gave to me. We can do nothing about the
Heartstone for a brace of days; I must study it at close hand."

Well, at least he has that much sense.

"I trust I don't need to warn you to be careful about it," Darkwind
said.

Firesong nodded, for once, seeming entirely serious. "There is no
doubt in my mind that the Stone is treacherous," he stated. "It has
behaved in a way that no such Stone in the history of either of our Clans
has ever done before. I shall take *no* chances with it."

That much gave Darkwind a feeling of relief. However arrogant this
young man was, he was at least no fool.

"There is something else, however," Firesong continued. "Something I think you have probably anticipated. There are only two among
the humans of the Vale who are of a power and an ability to aid me in
dealing with this Stone. Yourself, and the Outland Wingsister. But you
are not yet tested and confirmed as Adepts."

Darkwind grimaced, and began walking back toward his *ekele*, the
direction in which he had been going when Firesong hailed him. "That
is true. Although we have Adepts among us, there were none who felt
strong enough to do so."

"I have seen that, and I think it was wise of them to work within
their strength," Firesong replied, keeping pace with him easily. "But
that must end now. I shall complete your training, and Els-peth's, and
confirm you, for I shall need you at full ability to aid me." He stared
ahead, down the trail, as Darkwind glanced at him out of the corner of
his eye. "I shall be accomplishing something with your father as well,
but it is nothing you need to concern yourself over."

*No, of course not. He's only my father. Why should I worry about what
you are going to do with him?*

But Darkwind kept his thoughts and his comments to himself, simply nodding shortly. "When do you want to see us, then? And do you want to work with us singly, or together?"

"Oh, together," Firesong replied, carelessly, as if it did not matter to him. "Since I shall need you to work as partners, that is best, I think. And, tomorrow. But not *too* early." He yawned, and smiled slyly. "I am weary. And the *hertasi* have pledged me a massage. It was a cold and fatiguing journey; I believe I shall go and rest from it."

And with that, he turned abruptly off on a sidepath, one that would take him back to his own *ekele*.

And Starblade's.

Of course he already has hertasi, Darkwind thought with irritation. *They flock to beauty and power, and he has both in astonishing measure. He probably had a half dozen begging to serve him within moments of his arrival. If he walked by the swamp village, they would follow him in hordes, for all that they consider that they are independent. Nera would probably lead them.*

He turned his steps toward Elspeth's dwelling to give her the news of their new tutor.

And how was *she* reacting to this arrogant youngster, he wondered. This powerful, breathtaking youngster. . . .

And he was surprised by the stab of jealousy he felt at the memory of the open admiration he had caught in her eyes.

Mornelithe Falconsbane

Chapter Seventeen

Nyara woke to the thunder of great wings above her tower, and the sound of something heavy landing on her roof. She slipped out of bed, hastily snatching up the cloak she had made from the skin of a winter-killed bear.

Before she had a chance to panic, or even to shake herself out of the confusion of interrupted sleep, Need spoke in her mind. *:It's the gryphons. Tell them hello for me,:* Need said casually, as she stood, blinking, and trying to shake her dreams off.

The gryphons? She wrapped the cloak around her narrow shoulders and slipped up the steep stone stairs to the rooftop.

The gryphons? But—why have they come here?

"Brrright Grrreeetingsss little one!" Treyvan called, as she poked her head cautiously over the edge of the stair opening. "How goesss the lessssoning?" He looked as cheerful—and as friendly—as she had ever seen him, his wings shining in the sunlight, his head and crest up. As if she had never betrayed his little ones, his trust. As if she had never fled his lair with a stolen sword. As if nothing had ever happened between them but friendship.

She tried not to show her surprise, and ventured the rest of the way onto the rooftop. "Well, I think," she said shyly, bobbing a greeting to Hydona, who had landed behind her mate. "Or at least Need says that I do well. She says to tell you hello. How did you find me?"

"Ssstand, and let me look at you," Hydona demanded, turning her head from one side to the other, like a huge bird surveying something that intrigued it. Nyara obeyed, instantly.

"Good," Hydona pronounced. "The taint isss gone, and you arrre looking lesss—ferrral. We knew wherrre you werrre becaussse Need told usss, of courssse."

"Of course," she said faintly.

"Sssomeone had to know," Treyvan admonished with a flick of his tail. "What if you encounterrred sssomething you could not deal with? What if crrreaturresss of yourrr fatherrr found you? Need judged usss able to defend you, and otherrrwisssse likely to leave you in peace."

"Morrre sso than the Hawkbrrotherrrsss," Hydona said. "But that isss why we arrre herrre. Becaussse of Ssskif and Winterrrmoon."

She inadvertently brought her hand to her throat. "Are they near?" She had not thought she would have to deal with Skif so soon. . . .

"Verry," Treyvan said shortly. "The trrrail isss hot. You will not brrreak passst Winterrrmoon without him ssstriking yourrr esscape trrrail. The owlsss will find thisss place tonight or tomorrrrow night."

Hydona nipped at her mate. "And we mussst leave, if we arrre not to brring dissscovery on herrr soonerrr." She hesitated a moment. "Nyarrra, we have all forrrgiven you. You did yourrrr bessst. We wisssh you verrry well. And Ssskif would make a fine mate. But I think you know that alrrready."

With that, she launched herself from the tower like a sea-eagle, in a dive that ended with a great *snap* as she opened her wings and turned the dive into a climb. Treyvan only nodded, then turned and did the same.

Within moments, they were far out of sight. Nyara stared after them—comforted, and yet tormented.

She descended the stairs to her living quarters slowly, still not certain what to do. Should she wait for him to find her? Should she hide somewhere, so that he found only her empty lair? Should she hide *here* and pretend that she was not here?

:Go find him, girl,: Need replied. *:You heard Hydona; now you have a second opinion. A little stronger than mine, really—but then Hydona has a mate of her own. She tends to favor matings.:*

"But—" Nyara began.

:*But nothing. Don't let the opinion of someone who never had a man get in your way.*: Need actually chuckled. :*Look, girl, I never, ever, put my bearers between a boulder and a rock, making them choose between me and a man. Just because I have always chosen to* defend *women, that doesn't mean I* despise *men. Demons take it—that would be as blind as the opposite! I am not about to go copy the behavior of some woman-hating man! Now go on out there and* deal *with your feelings. Meet them, instead of waiting for them to trap you.*:

"I still don't know," Nyara said, feeling as helpless as a kitten in a flood.

:*You don't need to know. Get it over with one way or another. If you don't—girl, don't you know that's something your father will use against you? Make it into a strength, and not a weakness! It worked before. Remember?*:

Yes, she remembered. Remembered attacking her father with tooth and claw, for striking at Skif. Recalled the surprise on his face before he struck her.

:*The beast just does not understand the strength of true feelings, and he never will. It makes you unpredictable to him. Use that.*:

Nyara sighed and moved to her window, looking out over the peaceful countryside that up until this morning had been only hers—full of light—

And now seeing the shadows. They had been there all along, but she had chosen not to see them. "I suppose I should be grateful that he has been sulking and licking his wounds for so long, and has not come looking for me."

:*You're waking up, girl. The gryphons were my hedge against Skif or Mornelithe finding you. Well, Skif showed up before the beast did; I suppose we should be grateful for that, too. Skif's a good one, as young men go.*:

"So." She settled her cloak firmly about her shoulders. "If he is hunting with Wintermoon and the owls, he hunts by night."

:*True enough.*:

"He will be sleeping now," she said, thinking out loud. "I should be able to approach without Cymry rousing him, and be there when he wakes. Yes, I think that now is the time to go and meet him."

:*Good girl.*:

She turned to face the sword. "So," she said, feeling a kind of ironic amusement after all, "since I am sure that you know—or can find out—where is he?"

★ ★ ★

Mornelithe Falconsbane reclined on a soft couch in his darkened study, and brooded on revenge, like some half-mad, wounded beast. He had not left the room since his return, sore in body and spirit, depleted, but refusing to show any weakness. Weakness could be fatal to someone in his position. A show of weakness would give underlings . . . ideas. He had learned that decades ago.

His own people hardly dared approach him; they ordered slaves to bring him food and drink, silently, leaving it beside the door. The slaves obeyed out of immediate fear of the lash, fear of pain even overcoming their fear of Falconsbane, praying that he would not notice them. For sometimes, the slave in question would find those glowing golden eyes upon him, shining out of the darkness of the study-corner where he lay. . . .

And when that happened, more slaves were summoned later, to take the remains away. The remains were not pretty. Usually, there were pieces missing. No one looked into the study to find them.

He had used his own blood to open the great Gate in the ruins; had wrenched that Gate from its set destination to a portal of *his* choosing. He had done so out of desperation, not knowing if the thing would work, not knowing if he had the strength left to make it work. Not knowing if it would take him where he willed, or somewhere unknown. He chose to risk it anyway, preferring to die fighting rather than be taken by the cursed Horse-Lovers and the Bird-Fools.

In the end, he stumbled from the mouth of a cave at the very edge of his own realm, fell to the ground, and lay in a stupor for over a day. Only the strength he had cultivated, the stamina he had spelled into himself, had saved him. A lesser being would have died there. A lesser Adept would have been stranded in the nothingness between Gates, trapped, unless and until some accident spewed him forth—perhaps dead, perhaps mad, certainly tortured and drained. But he was not a lesser Adept, and it would take more than a day of exposure to kill him.

He woke, finally, ravenous and in pain from wounds within and without. His mage-channels had been scorched by the unrestricted torrent of energies he had used. The first thing he had needed was food.

He had caught and killed a tree-hare with his bare hands; eaten it skin and bones and all.

He had chosen his exit point well; once he had strength to move, he turned his attention to his next need, shelter. That was not a problem, for wherever he had established a possible Gate-anchor, he had always built a shelter nearby. That was a habit so ingrained he never even thought about it, centuries old, but this time it had saved his life.

He had staggered to the hunting shelter, a small building of two rooms, but well-stocked with food, wood, and healing herbs. He spent over a moon-cycle in recovering from the worst effects of wounds and spells. His own slaves and servants had not known whether he lived or not, until he had limped home. Only their fear of him had kept them at their posts. Only sure knowledge of his retribution when he recovered completely kept them there once he returned.

Fortunately, obedience was a habit with them. He was at a reasonable fraction of his strength once fear and habit weakened, and someone thought they might try for freedom.

Since he had neither the strength nor the time for finesse, he simply killed the offenders.

Fear of what he was now continued to keep them here.

He reinforced that fear, periodically, by killing one of the slaves. Reminding them what he had done; what he could do. Reminding them all that their lives rested in his hands.

It was a diversion, anyway.

There was an ache inside him that no herb and no rest could touch—a hunger for retribution. That was what drove him to killing the slaves. The deaths themselves did nothing to ease the pent-up rage that smoldered in his soul. There were only three things that would slake his thirst for blood.

Nyara.

He flexed his claws into the leather of his couch, and considered what he would do to her once he found her. She would die, of course, but not for a very long time. First he would ease his lust in her, repeatedly. He might share her; it depended on his own strength and how deeply he wished to wound her spirit. Then he would flay her mind with the whip of his power until she was nothing more than a quivering, weeping heap of nothingness—until the *person* that had dared to defy him was utterly destroyed. Then, only then, would he carefully, delicately, flay the physical skin from her body—leaving her still alive. Then he would see that what was left was placed in a cage and hung over his towers for the carrion crows to pick at. An example for those who considered treachery. His magic would see to it that she lived for a very long time.

Perhaps he would make a rug of that skin, or wear it.

K'Sheyna.

That was the second cause for his anger and hate. Only the destruction of the entire Clan would do. He had held back his power until now, enjoying the challenge, but now he would take them, one by one. First the scouts. Then the mages. Then, last of all, Starblade and his sons, plucking them from the heart of the Vale and bringing them to grovel at his feet before they died. The others he would kill however he could, but those three—those three he would deliver to the same fate as his treacherous daughter. Then, when the Vale was empty of all but the hangers-on, he would suck the power from the Heartstone and blast it back again, turning the Vale into an inferno of melting stone and boiling water.

Then the last—and greatest—cause for rage. *The gryphons.*

Oh, the gryphons. Creatures that he had thought long gone. Returning to these lands, after all these many centuries. Returning to live here once again. Returning to the home of Skandranon. . . .

The gryphons. My hated ancient adversaries. Something very . . . special . . . for them.

He brooded in the hot darkness of his study, and never quite knew the moment when his brooding slipped over the edge into dreaming.

He watched himself through other eyes and knew that he was An'desha shena Jor'ethan, Shin'a'in of the Clan of the Bear, an offshoot of Wolf-Clan. A young almost-man, in his early teens. He stood on the edge of all that he had known, and shivered.

He was not yet a warrior, this youngling of the Plains. Only—he was Shin'a'in no more. He could no longer hold place in the Clans, for he had the power of magic, and yet he had not joined the shamans. The Goddess had declared that no one but Her shamans could work magics within the bowl of the Plains, for the task of the Shin'a'in was to keep magic from their home-land. He had felt no calling for such a life-task, and no liking for it, either.

For such a one, one with the gift of magery, yet unwilling to go to Her hands, there was only one choice. Exile, to the Kin-Cousins, the Tale'edras, the Hawkbrothers. They had magic; they were permitted—nay, encouraged— by the Goddess to use it. They would freely adopt any of their magic-bearing Kindred into their ranks, so it was said, to teach the use of such a gift.

So he had come, to the edge of Hawkbrother lands. Yet he had come without the knowledge of the rest of his kin, nor the guidance of the shaman, for no one else in his Clan knew of this secret power. He had feared to disclose it, for he was not a strong-willed young man, and he knew only too well what such a disclosure would bring to his lot.

And now, as he stood in the silent forest, he wondered. Should he have confided in Vor'kela, the shaman? Should he have confessed his fatal gift before the rest of the Clan? Should he not have claimed his rights, and been given guidance to the nearest of the Tale'edras?

Yet even as he wondered, he knew that he could not have born the weight of Vor'kela's insistence that he take up the shaman's staff and drum. No one in all of the Clan would have been willing to let him go to the Kin-Cousins without great outcry and argument. There would have been those who said that his gift was unclean, and the result of his father's liaison with the Outlands woman at Kata'shin'a'in, even as he was the result of that liaison. There would have been those who would have said he should take vows of celibacy, that this gift not be passed to others of the Clan. There would not have been a single one of his Kin willing to let him pass out of their hands without long argument and contention.

And he—he would have folded beneath the weight of their words. He would have taken up a place at the shaman's side. And there he would have been utterly miserable. He trembled at the thought of all the years of sacrifice the place as shaman's apprentice would cost him. He was revolted at the idea of being forced to serve at Vor'kela's side and bear the brunt of the shaman's humor.

Better that he had done what he had done; to creep away in the dead of night, and seek out a new life among the Kin-Cousins. He had taken only what was his by right. He had violated no laws.

Because of this, he had no guide. He had never been outside the Plains. As he stood at the top of the path that led from the bottom of the great bowl of the Plains to the top of the rim, he wondered at the forest before him. Huge trees, more trees than he had ever seen in his life, towered before him, and marched endlessly to the horizon. Only there was no horizon, only trees, trees, endlessly trees.

Trees were a rarity on the Plains, and never grew to the height of these. He could not see their tops, only their interweaving branches.

Trees that bent over him, as if watching. Trees that murmured on all sides of him, as if whispering. Trees that had a secret life of their own.

With a bravery born of desperation, he shouldered his pack—for he had left his horse at the base of the path, to find her way back to the Clan—and marched into the cool shadow of the endless trees. Always he had heard how *jealously the Hawkbrothers guarded their lands. Surely he would be found and challenged before long.*

Before midday, he was lost. By nightfall, he was lost, cold, and terribly afraid. He had heard all too many tales of the strange beasts that lived beneath these trees—the beasts that the Tale'edras fought and penned. Strange mage-created creatures that no arrow could harm. Beasts with the cunning minds of men. He knew none of the sounds of the forest around him; he could not tell if they were the voices of harmless things, or terrible predators, or even demon-spawn.

If only he had a fire—but he had left his fire-making tools behind, for they did not belong to him only, but to all of his family. He was so cold—and all men knew that true beasts feared fire. If he had a fire, it would shine through the darkness of this forest like a beacon, drawing the Tale'edras to him. If only he had a fire. . . .

But wait—had he not heard that a mage could call *fire? Even so untutored a one such as himself? He knew where the currents of power ran; he felt them beneath his very feet. He had felt them, even stronger and wilder, on the Plains. Why could he not use them to bring a spark to waiting tinder?*

No sooner thought, than he hurried about in the gathering gloom, scraping a dirt hollow in the moss, gathering twigs, dried pine-needles, bits of dry bark; laying larger branches close to hand. When he had his tinder going, he would soon have his fire built as high as he needed.

He closed his eyes, reached for the power, and thought of the springing flames—

And got what he had not expected.

YES!

He *came with a roar, filling the boy's body, thundering out of his hiding place, into the body of the blood of* his *blood,* his *coming triggered by the moment of Fire-Calling. As it had always been. Once again* he *took and lived. From the time when Ma'ar, Mage of Dark Flames, had fought and conquered Urtho and had learned of a way to preserve* himself *down through the ages. . . .*

Using the power of the death of his body to hide himself *in a tiny pocket of the nothingness between the Gates, he preserved his own person, sealed himself there with spell upon carefully-wrought spell. And when one with a trace of the blood of great Ma'ar in his veins learned to make Fire, he came, and overwhelmed the boy's fledgling personality with his own. So he lived again. And when the time came for the death of that body, he moved again into hiding. . . .*

Hiding to live again.

So it had gone, down through the centuries, taking new bodies and taking on other names. Krawlven. Renthorn. Geslaken. Leareth. Zendak.

And now, a new rebirth, a new body, a new name. As the young spirit struggled beneath his talons with fear and hopelessness, as the spirit grew quiet, then disappeared altogether, he baptized himself in the blood and flesh of a new incarnation.

Mornelithe. I am Mornelithe! And I live again!

The sound of his laughter rang beneath the branches of the pines, and shocked the forest into sudden stillness.

Then he gathered his powers about himself and vanished into the night, to build his empire anew.

Mornelithe woke with a sudden start. He had not thought of that moment in . . . decades. Why now?

And why had he first felt the long-vanished spirit of the Horse-Loving halfbreed whose body he had taken?

Never mind, he told himself impatiently. *It matters not at all. Or if it matters, it was to remind myself that I have lived more lives than this, and I am surely wiser for all of that living. And stronger. Wiser by far than the Bird-Fools. It is the gryphons that should concern me. The gryphons. K'Sheyna. Nyara.*

He stretched and sat up on his couch. Discontent weighted his shoulders like a too-heavy garment. In the days that he was Ma'ar, he would merely have had to stretch out his hand to have them all—

But the power that was so rich and free in his day as Ma'ar was a poor thing now. Shattered and scattered, dust in the storm. Like his power, his empire was a small thing. He was constrained to harbor allies he would never have suffered in the old days.

For a moment, he felt a kind of shame, that he should be reduced to this meager existence. Yet what had worked in the long-ago days could work now, if only on a smaller scale.

The gryphons. The gryphons. Why is *it that they do not fade, but prosper?* In his mind's eye the male gryphon took on the black-dyed elegance of Skandranon, and his lip lifted in a snarl. There was no mistaking the beast's lineage. And that should not have been. The gryphons of Urtho's pride should not have survived him.

Nor should those too-faithful servants, the beast-breeding Kaled'a'in. They should have perished, they should all have perished in the cataclysm that destroyed his kingdom *and* Urtho's. There should have been nothing left but a pair of smoking holes. Every trace of Urtho's handiwork and Urtho's allies should have been erased for all time.

Yet, here they were. The Kaled'a'in, Urtho's faithful servants, still prancing about in the guise of the Bird-Fools and the Horse-Lovers. Sundered, yet still prospering. Half of them guarding what remained of the old magics, half of them removing the scars and taint of the destruction. Both halves working beneath the eye of that wretched Goddess who took so deep an interest in their doings.

And the gryphons—thriving! Clearly established in the west, and moving eastward!

How? How did this happen?

He flung himself off of his couch, and began to pace the room, like a restless, caged lion. He had been brooding here for too long. He needed to act! He needed to stir his blood, to exact some token of vengeance before his followers lost their fear and began to desert him.

He needed a show of strength that would convince them that he was still as all-powerful as ever. And he needed the sweet taste of revenge to completely heal him.

Nyara. She was the weakest, the most vulnerable—and the most personal target. Yet she was inexplicably out of his reach. He had sought for her ever since he returned to his stronghold, and yet it had been in vain. He searched as far as his strength was able to take him. There was no trace of her.

Or rather—something was hiding her. He would have known if she had perished, for the power he had invested in her would have come rushing back to him. There was someone, or some power, hiding her.

K'Sheyna, perhaps?

A possible, if surprising, thought. He had thought the Bird-Fools of k'Sheyna too bound up by long custom to change. *Could* the Bird-Lovers have lost their hatred of Changechildren enough to shelter her? Was it possible?

After the way she had fought at cursed Darkwind's side—after the way that she had defended the gryphons—yes. It was possible. In fact, now that he gave it consideration, it was likely.

The gryphons—

The target he longed to strike.

No, the time was not right to exact his revenge upon them. Besides, they too lay under the shelter of k'Sheyna. He might ambush them, but he had no major mages at his disposal now. The last of them had vanished during a hunt for spell-components. He would have to go in person to deal the blow. That was too risky; there was too much he did not know about them.

That left—*k'Sheyna*.

The most logical choice, if he was to impress his followers with his still-vital power.

He would have to do something to hurt the Clan, and hurt it badly. But it would have to be something swift and decisive, and something they had not guarded themselves against.

If he struck at the Clan, his followers would see that he was strong again, and fear to desert him. In striking at the Clan, he might persuade the Bird-Fools to give up the shelter of all those not of their blood. If he were clever enough, he could make it look as if the blow had come through them. K'Sheyna would never shelter them, then. That would put not only Nyara within his reach, but the Outlanders and the gryphons.

The gryphons.

Yes, then he would gather in his dearest daughter—and her winged friends. . . .

And the Outlanders as well, the strange ones. The girl, now—she had all the potential for an Adept. When he saw her last, she had but the most rudimentary of tutelage. It was unlikely anyone in k'Sheyna could be persuaded to give her lessons, and the half-taught were the most vulnerable. He would need a plaything when Nyara was dead.

Yes, he would slay the Outland man, but keep the Outland woman. She might do well to carry his seed for the next generation, since Nyara had proved barren, and turned traitor in the bargain. He might even make the transfer without waiting for the death of his body. Yes. That was a good plan. An excellent plan. It would be good to have a young, strong body again, full of vigor and energy.

That left only one question to be answered.

If I am to hurt k'Sheyna, where must I strike?

His lips twisted in a feral smile.

Where else, but at the weakest bird in the flock, the broken-winged, broken-souled Starblade? He will no longer be mewed up away from my power. They surely think me dead. They must be getting very careless at this point.

An attack on Starblade in and of itself would not hurt the Clan as a whole. But if he used Starblade's link to the Heartstone, and completed the work that he had begun there—

Yes, if I shatter the Heartstone—it might not destroy everything in the Vale, but it will surely destroy most of what is important, and at least half of the mages will die in the backlash of power.

It went against the grain to loose all that power.

But if I cannot control it, then I shall destroy with it.

If he were truly fortunate—although his revenge would be a little less— the gryphons would be destroyed with the rest.

Or better, far better, the gryphons would be *hurt* when the Stone shattered completely. Leaving them weak, and vulnerable.

Yes, that would be the best of all.

He flung himself back down upon his couch, chewed the last pain-spiced flesh from a former servant's thighbone, and began to plan.

Firesong deemed most of the Vale too near the Heartstone to work in, and although Darkwind agreed with him, this tiny clearing at the far end was a damned awkward spot to get to. It had been made as a trysting-spot, but had gotten overgrown. To reach it, they had to wind their way through tangles of vines and bushes, only to discover when they got there that most of the clearing itself had been eaten up by encroaching vegetation. "So, clear it." Firesong said casually, and sat down on a stone to await the completion of their task. Darkwind seethed with resentment that he held closely, permitting none of it to slip. He had thought that Elspeth tested his temper; he had never thought that one of his own people would bring it so close to the snapping point.

Except, perhaps, his father.

The Adept did not even watch them; he called in his snow-white fire-bird and fed it flowers and bits of fruit while they worked, clearing the vegetation by hand since using magic would have been fairly stupid for so simple a task. "Good enough," Firesong said at last, when the earth of the clearing had been laid bare, and all the seats were free of vines and overhanging bushes. "Now, we return to basics. Darkwind, you will tap into the ley-line beneath us."

Back to basics? For what? Or doesn't he trust our training?

"Stop," Firesong said, with calm self-assurance, as Darkwind obeyed him; he grounded himself carefully, centered his personal power, and prepared himself to grasp for the power of the ley-lines. "What are you doing?"

"I am grounding myself," Darkwind told him, not adding, *as any fool could see*, for it was obvious that Firesong had some deeper intention in mind. Sunlight trickled through the leaves above them, making patches of brilliance in the Adept's hair. This morning Firesong wore blue, the same blue as his eyes. He looked good enough to have his will of any female in the Vale, and no few of the males.

"Why?" the Healing Adept asked, flicking his hair over his shoulder with one hand. "Why are you grounding yourself and your shields?"

"Because—because that is the way that I was taught. That—" he groped after long-forgotten lessons "—if I am not grounded when I reach for the ley-line power, it will fling me away by the force of its current." His resentment continued to seethe at being forced to dredge up those long-ago lessons. What difference did it make? It was something you *did*.

"All well and good," Firesong replied, with that same maddening calm, and a smile that said volumes. "But what if you release your ground *after* you have the power? What, then? And *why* must you always sink your ground into the earth below you? Why not elsewhere?"

Darkwind only gaped at him, unable to answer questions that ran counter to everything he had ever been taught.

"I will show you." The young Adept centered and grounded faster than Darkwind could blink; seized upon the ley-line beneath them as if he owned the deed to it. He made the energies his own, feeding them into his shields with an ease that called up raw envy in Darkwind's heart.

Then cast loose the ground. "Now, strike me. Full force, Darkwind, trust me." The shields stayed where they were, contrary to everything Darkwind supposed would happen.

Darkwind struck—with more force than he had consciously intended, all of his pent-up frustration going into the blow. All of his fury and bruised pride combined to make the blow one that *would* have done harm if it had properly connected. It should have completely shattered Firesong's shields, the outer one, at least.

But instead of meeting the blow, the shields, no longer anchored by the ground, slid aside. Darkwind watched in complete shock as his angry blast did no more than to bow the shields slightly. The energy of his strike was neither absorbed, nor reflected; it was deflected, routed around the outside, skittering away in bright eddies of flame. Nothing touched the mage inside.

"This *is* dangerous, cousin," Firesong warned, smugly cradled within his untouched shields. "A clever mage will see at once that without the ground protecting the essential flow of magic energy from the line to myself, that tie is vulnerable. A clever mage could also force the shields toward me, then instead of striking a blow, could lance through them at the nearest, thinnest, weakest point. But until he does that, I sit untouched, allowing all his force to spend itself uselessly. I need not even fear the contamination of his magic, for it never touches me or my shields."

To Darkwind's great chagrin, Elspeth nodded, her face aglow with admiration. "A clever mage could also create a whirlwind of edged magebolts around you," she pointed out. "Those things can shred a shield in next to no time. And although they can't touch you physically, that would leave you open to attack."

"Ah, but that whirlwind would have no effect, Wingsib," he said, turning a dazzling smile upon her that caused a shaft of jealousy to stab his "cousin." Darkwind chewed his lip and looked away, at the tangle of vines behind one of the empty seats. "A whirlwind that would erode a grounded shield would only cause this one to spin with it. It would find purchase but spin freely. Since 'I' am not connected to the shield, it would have no effect on me."

"I see." She prodded the shield with a bit of power, experimentally, and Darkwind saw for himself how the shield simply bent away from it. "Interesting. So if the enemy doesn't know that this is possible, you can let him wear himself out against you."

Firesong imploded the shield and collapsed it down around himself. "Aye, and a bit of acting, and he'd continue to do so, as I looked 'worried.' Now—this is the trickier task. Grounding in something other than the earth." His face sobered for a moment. "Take heed, cousin. This is something only a powerful Adept can attempt, and never with impunity. I think that you can do this, but it is very dangerous."

Once again, Firesong centered, grounded, and shielded, all within the blink of an eye. To Darkwind, he looked perfectly "normal," insofar as a mage of his power could ever look "normal." But then he took a closer look.

"Where is your ground?" he asked, perplexed.

"You'd like to know, wouldn't you?" the young mage taunted, "Find it! You already know it is not sunk into the earth at my feet. Look elsewhere! Have I somehow grounded into the air? Perhaps I have only created an illusion of being grounded."

Elspeth only shook her head, baffled. Darkwind was not prepared to give up so easily. He studied Firesong carefully, ignoring the mage's mocking smile. Finally he acted on a hunch, and moved his Mage-Sight out of the real world and onto the Planes of Power. There he saw it—and a cold sweat broke out all over him at the Adept's audacity.

He stared at Firesong and could not believe that the mage simply stood there, calm and unmoved. As if he did this sort of thing every day.

Maybe he did. If so, he was the bravest man that Darkwind had ever seen. Or the most foolhardy. Or even both, at the same time.

"You grounded it—in the place between Gates!" he managed to get out, after a moment. "I can't believe you did that! You could call a deadly storm that way—or find yourself drained to the dregs!"

Firesong shrugged, and dismissed the shield, ground and all. "I told you, no mage does that with impunity. I would not attempt it while someone else held a Gate near me, or during a thunderstorm. But that Place makes an energy-sink that is second to none. If you wish to drain an enemy, ground yourself in the Place, tie your shields to the ground as always, and let him pour all of his power out upon you. It will drain into the Place and be swallowed up, exhausting him and costing you no more than an ordinary shield."

He held out a long, graceful hand to Darkwind. "Touch it," he ordered. Darkwind did so. The hand was as cold as ice. "Therein lies the danger there. The Place is an energy-sink. It will steal your energies as well, and there is no way to keep it from doing so. You had best hope that you can outlast your enemy, if you ground there; work him into an irrational fury before trying it."

He turned to Elspeth, who was again visibly impressed. "Take nothing for granted, Wingsib. No matter what you have been told, most anything in magery *can* be done, despite the 'laws' that you have been taught. The question is only whether the result is worth it."

It galled him to see the admiration on her face. Oh, Firesong had undoubtedly earned the right to arrogance; his Clansfolk had not exaggerated when they said that they considered him a powerful experimenter. He was, without a doubt, a genius as well.

But none of that meant that Darkwind had to like it.

At the end of the day, when he was exhausted, and Firesong was still as outwardly cool and poised as he had been that morning, Darkwind was ready to call a halt to the entire thing.

But Firesong didn't give him that opportunity.

"You'll do," he said, with cool approval. "At least, you aren't hopeless. I'll have a different course of action for you two tomorrow."

And with that, he simply turned on his heel and left, he and his bird together, melting into the greenery.

Trevalen & Dawnfire

Chapter
Eighteen

Darkwind and Elspeth walked together to her *ekele*. They were going to hers, because it was nearer; Darkwind was so drained that he didn't think he could go any further without a rest and something to drink. He was glad that it was still mid-afternoon. If it had been dark enough he'd had to conjure a mage-light, he'd have fallen over; he felt that tired.

"So what do you think of Firesong?" Elspeth asked as they crested the gentle curving path between six massive flowering bushes. The flicking tail of a *hertasi* ducked under a trellis, distracting him for just a moment.

He cast her a suspicious glance, gauging the import of her question, but her expression, like her voice, remained carefully neutral. "Well, he's certainly brilliant," he admitted grudgingly. "And unconventional. But I don't think I've ever met anyone so arrogant in all my life."

"He's earned the right to be," Elspeth replied, to his increased annoyance. "I mean, there are a lot of people who think Weaponsmaster Alberich is arrogant—or Kero. And they're right, but there's a point where you're so good that you've earned a certain amount of—hmm—attitude."

He didn't reply. He couldn't. Not and maintain his own calm. In a certain sense, Elspeth was completely correct. In fact, if he mentioned Firesong's arrogance to Iceshadow or his father, he would probably be told that it *wasn't* arrogance at all, it was simply self-assurance, and a pardonable pride.

Firesong was the best mage Darkwind had ever seen in his life; perhaps the best living mage that there was. Not just a Healing Adept, but an innovator; a brilliant creative genius. Not fearless—at the levels at which Firesong was working, being fearless could get him killed quite quickly—but so knowledgeable that he was able to judge risks to within a hair.

He was worlds away better than Darkwind was now, and what was more, he was better than Darkwind, or anyone known to the Vales, would ever be. And that did not come as a comfortable revelation.

Darkwind was not used to seeing himself as second-best. It stung his pride, even as Firesong's attitude made him angry. And then, on top of it all, for the cocky mage to be so cursed *handsome!*

Elspeth openly admired him. That was just as difficult to take. How short a step was it from admiration to something else more personal—more physical?

It was only then, when he caught himself seething with completely unwarranted jealousy, that he realized the trend his thoughts were taking. *All right. Stop right there. Think whatever you like, but be careful about anything you say. Right now it would be the easiest thing in the world to say something that would completely alienate her—to make accusations that you have no right to make.*

Elspeth wouldn't react well to that. And never mind that it galled that Firesong's power and beauty were enough to make anyone inclined to throw themselves at his feet. If Elspeth chose to join the crowd, Darkwind had no say in the matter.

You don't own her. She consented to share pleasure with you. That gives you no rights, remember that. She can continue to share your bed and Firesong's and you have no right to demand that she cleave only to you. She can throw you over for Firesong if she wants. That is up to her.

"You're thinking very hard," Elspeth said, glancing at him.

"I'm thinking that—I am likely to be very irrational about Firesong." That was all the warning he could bear to give her. But hopefully, it would be enough. "He is right when it comes to magic, anyway. I've never seen anyone as skilled or as powerful as he is, except maybe Falconsbane."

"He's going to try something different with the Stone, no one even guessed could be done," she said. "We knew he was going to be doing *something* like that, but I honestly didn't think he was going to include us in it." She gave him a lopsided smile. "I guess we must be good for something after all."

Darkwind suddenly saw a way to get some of his own pride back, especially if the Adept planned on training the two of them together. Firesong wasn't the only one who could be innovative.

Gwena joined them a moment later, and Darkwind swallowed down some of the things he wanted to ask Elspeth. *Is she attracted to him? Just how attracted is she? Is she thinking of asking* him *to continue her teaching? And if he's teaching her magic, does that mean she goes to k'Treva after the Stone is dealt with?*

He shouldn't care, and he couldn't help himself. He had no holds on her. She shared his bed sometimes. He shared hers. She was not truly of the Vales; she was an Outlander. All the arguments against Skif and Nyara's success together held true for the two of them, too.

Tayledras simply didn't leave their Vales. How could he continue the work he had sworn to do, if he left the Vale? He was a Hawkbrother; a Pelagirs healer of ruined lands. He could never leave the Vale, the Pelagirs—it was impossible. She was the Heir to a throne, vital to the safety and government of her land. She couldn't stay here. *That* was impossible.

She would go, and he would stay, no matter what happened here. He began building himself a kind of emotional bulwark to save what was left of his pride and heart. He would have to watch his tongue, and not *drive* her away—she would be leaving soon enough. He would deal with that when it came. He would fight back the tears that he knew, somehow, would come when his Wingsib Elspeth left.

There was little enough in his life now. No need to act like his namesake—Darkwind, an approaching storm-cloud. It made no sense to ruin what there was, least of all by voicing his own foolishness.

"Elspeth," he said, with cheerfulness that didn't sound *too* forced, "Once we recover from being run like rabbits, did you have any plans for this afternoon?"

Starblade eased himself down onto the couch beside the huge block-perch Hyllarr had taken for his own, and scratched beneath the hawk-eagle's breast-feathers. Hyllarr all but purred, pulling one foot up in complete contentment.

In this alone, Hyllarr was like Karry, but in no other way. Starblade was grateful for that. There were no poses, no lifts of the head, nothing to haunt him. Hyllarr was Hyllarr, and unique. Uniquely intelligent, uniquely calm, uniquely charming. He had succeeded in charming Kethra, who had been immune to the blandishments even of Darkwind's flirt-of-a-bird, Vree. Hyllarr had her securely enchanted.

Kethra settled beside him, with an amused glance at the bird. "I have no idea how you're going to carry him around once he's well, *ashke*," she said. "He'd be a burden even for someone like Wintermoon. I can't even begin to think how you're going to have him with you."

"I shall worry about that when the time comes," he told her serenely. He already had some notions on the subject. Perhaps a staff across the shoulders. . . . "Is your kinsman coming?"

"He should be here at any moment," she began, when footsteps on the staircase heralded their visitor. And, as Starblade had expected, it was Tre'valen who appeared at the doorway—a Tre'valen who, to Starblade's pained but keen eyes, was a young man in serious emotional turmoil.

Starblade had been seeing the signs of trouble in Tre'valen's face for some time now, but it had never been as obvious as it was now. So, he had been right to ask the shaman here. There was something going on, and the Clan needed to know what it was.

"Sit, please, shaman," he said mildly.

Tre'valen obeyed, but with a glance at Starblade that told the Hawk-brother that this shaman was quite well aware Starblade had not asked him here to exchange pleasantries.

Good. In these times, it was no longer possible to hide behind a veil of politeness. Some of the others of the Clan had relaxed, thinking that now that the Adept was here, all their troubles would be over. They had not stopped to consider the fact that Firesong was here to solve only *one* of the Clan's problems. When he had dealt with the Stone, he would be gone. Then there would remain the rest of the puzzle-box. How to safely reunite the Clan. What to do about Dawnfire. What to do about this Territory. How to deal with Falconsbane's daughter, who was a danger—and *in* danger—as long as there was any chance her father was still alive.

How to discover Falconsbane's fate. What to do about him if he still lived. . . .

"There was a time," he began, "when I could afford to hint, to be indirect. I no longer have the strength for such diplomacy. Tre'valen, your Wingsibs of the Clan know why Kethra is here, why Kra'heera asked us to allow her to stay. She was already a Wingsister, and there was obviously a great need for her help."

Kethra's left hand found his right, and she squeezed it, but said nothing.

Starblade smiled at her, and took strength and heart from her support. "Kra'heera asked us to grant the same status to you, and the same hospitality, but with no explanations. I had not pressed you for such an explanation, but I think the time has come for one."

Tre'valen looked very uncomfortable and glanced at Kethra.

"You need not look to me for aid, Clanbrother," she replied to his unspoken question. "I am in agreement with Starblade."

Tre'valen sighed. "It is because of Dawnfire," he said, awkwardly.

Starblade nodded. "I had already surmised that," he said dryly. "I should like to hear what the reasons are."

Tre'valen was clearly uncomfortable, more so than Starblade thought the situation warranted. "Kra'heera wished me to seek her out—if I could find a way to bring her to me—and speak with her as much as I might. It seemed to him quite clear that she has become some kind of avatar of the Star-Eyed, but it is not an avatar we recognize. But it also does not seem to be anything your people had seen before, either. He wanted me to discover what the meaning of this was, if I could. This is a new thing, an entirely new thing. We have had no direction upon it. Kra'heera does not know what to think."

He paused, and rubbed the side of his nose, averting his eyes from Starblade's unflinching gaze.

"New things simply do not occur often in the Plains, *ashke*," Kethra put in. "The Star-Eyed has been a Lady more inclined to foster the way things *are* rather than bring on changes."

But Starblade was watching Tre'valen very closely, and there was more, much more, that Tre'valen had not told them. For a moment he was at a loss as to what it could be.

Then the memory of the young shaman's face, gazing up at a bird that *might* have been Dawnfire, suddenly intruded. He had not seen that particular expression of desire very often, but when he had, it always meant the same thing.

"You long for her, do you not?" Starblade asked quietly, and to his own satisfaction, he watched Tre'valen start, and begin to stammer something about emotions and proper detachment.

"Enough," Kethra interrupted her younger colleague. "Starblade is right, and I should have recognized this when I saw it. You *have* become fascinated—enamored. With Dawnfire. I think perhaps you may have fallen in love with her."

"I—have—" Tre'valen looked from one to the other of them, and capitulated, all at once. "Yes," he replied, in a low, unhappy voice. "I have. I tried to tell myself that I was simply bedazzled, but it is not simple, nor it is bedazzlement. I—do not know what 'love' is, but if it means that one is concerned for the other above one's own self—I must be in love with her, with that part of her that is still human in spirit. And I know not what to do. There is no precedent."

It was one thing to suspect something like that. It was quite another to hear confirmation of it from Tre'valen's own mouth. Starblade looked to his beloved for some kind of an answer, and got only a tight-lipped shrug. *She* did not know what to make of this, either.

A nasty little tangle they had gotten into . . . a worse thing still to offend a deity. If indeed, they were doing so.

"Do I take it that the Star-Eyed has offered you no signs?" Starblade said delicately. "No hint as to how *Her* feelings run in this matter?"

Tre'valen shook his head. "Only that She has permitted us to continue to meet, either in this world or in the spirit realms. And she has granted Dawnfire the visions that I told you, the ones I do not understand, about ancient magic returning. And about the need for peoples to unite and change in some way."

Starblade closed his eyes for a moment, but no answers came to him, so he analyzed the few facts in the matter. Dawnfire was not dead, at least not in the accepted sense. But she was no longer anything like a human being. Mornelithe Falconsbane had destroyed her body, but left her spirit—her soul—alive and in her bondbird. Such a tragedy would have meant a slow fading until at last there was nothing of the human left, leaving a mentally crippled raptor to live as long as it could. But in this, there was a powerful being that had shown Her interest in the situation by creating some kind of different creature out of Dawnfire. Dawnfire was not like the *leshy'a* Kal'enedral, who were entirely of the spirit-world, yet could, on occasion, intervene in the physical realm. And not like a mage, who could on occasion intervene in the spirit world. She seemed to dwell in both worlds at once, and yet truly touched neither.

The Shin'a'in face of the Goddess—her Warrior face, in fact—seemed to have created her, then abandoned her. It was most unwise to second-guess a deity; what appeared to have been abandoned may have, in fact, been left to mature.

"All that I can say is that I warn you to be careful," he said at last. "These are strange waters that you swim in, and I know not what lurks beneath the surface. Whatever it is, is fearsome, shaman."

"I know," Tre'valen said at last, after a long pause. "I know this. The Star-Eyed marked Dawnfire for her own, but to what purpose, She has not revealed. She might not approve of my—inclinations and intentions."

"Starblade could only shrug. "I am not a shaman," he pointed out. "You are. I say only—be careful and consider first what is best for Dawnfire and those you have sworn to serve."

"I shall." Tre'valen stood, and moved toward the door. "I will keep you closely informed from this moment of what I see. And—of what I feel."

He bowed, turned, and descended the stairs quickly, but the air of trouble he had brought with him remained. Kethra held Starblade's hands wordlessly for a long time afterward.

Darkwind tossed his head, and sent his soaking-wet hair whipping over his shoulder. Sweat poured down his forehead and stung his eyes, but external vision did not matter. *Internal* vision did.

No matter that he had picked a quarrel with Elspeth not half a candlemark before they joined Firesong in the glade that he had made into their Working Place. No matter that he had left her without a reply to the hurtful words he had not truly meant, but said anyway. Once across the invisible boundary, he and Elspeth were two halves of a working whole, and there was no quarrel dividing them.

He frankly had not expected that of her. He had been faintly surprised when her power joined to his with no hesitation. But he could not be less than she, his pride would not permit it.

But he wondered, in a tiny, unoccupied section of his mind, if he had deliberately quarreled with her in hopes that she would storm off, making it impossible for them to practice with Firesong driving them?

Firesong lived up to his use-name; his power-signature crackled with illusory flames, and he used music, drumbeats, to focus it. That made it easier, rather than harder, for Darkwind to follow him; all of his training as a dancer came to the fore, guiding him where he might otherwise have stumbled blindly. So Darkwind had gone Firesong one better; now in the circle he *danced* his magic, eyes closed, moving in place.

I am going to be much leaner before this is all over . . . and a better dancer.

Elspeth, interestingly enough, chose to follow his dancing with a manifestation of power he had heard of, but had never seen; lightweaving. She created patterns of energy that matched his dancing and Firesong's drums, uniting them, in a way that he didn't understand, but fit well.

It seemed that Firesong didn't understand it either, for the first time Elspeth had woven her light-web he had been drilling them in the creation of a kind of containment vessel that was meant to contract down around something and hold it—

Firesong had been startled and had lost the beat—Darkwind had seen only the pattern and danced it—and the web contracted around *Firesong*.

The Adept had managed to extract himself from it before it closed convulsively and vanished with a little *pop*, but it had clearly been a near thing. They had afforded him a bit of a thrill. Ever since then he had guided them through a refinement of this technique; honing it down and making a weapon of it. Sometimes making a *real* weapon of it; Darkwind Felt something beginning to form before him. Firesong was about to create an enemy for them to face—a very real enemy, for all that it was made of mage-energy.

He changed his steps, and Felt the light above him weaving into a protection. And he sensed Firesong's surprise. He guessed that Firesong had intended Elspeth to weave a mage-blade, or even two, for them to fight with. But Elspeth had her own ideas. Perhaps the weariness of his dance steps had told her that defense would be better than offense. Whatever; he followed the pattern she sketched, and the power wove about them into an hourglass-shaped flow, a double-lobed shield, and the fire-creature Firesong had conjured hissed about the outside in frustration, unable to burn a way through. Since the walls of energy *flowed*, it could not focus its flames on any one place long enough to do any significant damage; the lances of energy dissipated and swirled, but did not burn through.

It sends out extensions of itself, as tongues of flame. Hmm. I think I can work with that.

The next time the creature attacked, Darkwind changed his steps. The protection suddenly became "sticky," if energy could be sticky.

An attractant, perhaps. Whatever the name of his defense might be, Darkwind caught the tongue of the creature's energy, and before Firesong had a chance to react, he spun the fire-shape into his shields, integrating it and making its power his.

The drumming stopped; Darkwind danced on for a moment, letting the power return into the flow of the ley-line beneath them, rather than permitting it to drain away into the air to hang like lightning threatening to strike. Then he stopped and opened his eyes, to gaze somewhat defiantly at their instructor.

"That was not at all a bad solution," Firesong said, calmly. "Not what I had in mind, but not at all bad."

"Darkwind couldn't have fought that thing off," Elspeth said flatly, with no inflection at all. "He was already exhausted from everything else you'd sent at us today."

"So you improvised a defense and solution in one; I like that." Firesong smiled at Elspeth, and Darkwind fought down a surge of irrational anger. "The Shin'a'in say—when you do not like the fight, change the rules. I have often found that to be a useful solution."

Firesong looked no more weary than if he had just taken a fast walk across the Vale. Not a hair was out of place, nor a thread of clothing, for all of his furious drumming.

I should have known. Perfect, as always.

As Darkwind had anticipated, Firesong had been—very popular among the k'Sheyna, human and non. Power and beauty are both powerful attractants, and Firesong had both in abundance. He, in return, accepted the attentions as only his due—and his devotees seemed to find his very insolence appealing.

Including Elspeth.

And as for the *hertasi*—well, his borrowed *ekele* swarmed with them. He would not even have had to dress, feed, or bathe himself if he had chosen otherwise. Perhaps he hadn't.

Now, Darkwind, your claws are showing.

But how could he have gone through this past training session without a hair out of place?

Because he's a greater mage, a greater Adept, than you or anyone in your

Clan has ever seen, that's how. He's likely enhanced his endurance for year upon year. Elspeth and the rest are perfectly right to admire him. And there is nothing wrong with him being proud of himself and what he can do. . . .

"I think that you are near to ready," Firesong said, standing up, and putting the drum away in the elaborate padded chest he used as a seat. "You work remarkably well together. We can begin planning what we will be doing with your rogue Stone tomorrow, hmm?"

Darkwind nodded, but Firesong wasn't done yet. Elspeth headed straight out of the clearing, going for the hot spring and a long soak, but Firesong caught Darkwind by the elbow before he had a chance to leave.

"There is trouble between you and the Outlander," he said, making it a statement rather than a question. Darkwind couldn't meet his eyes, nor could he say anything. "There are also thorns between you and me."

Darkwind faced him, resentment smoldering. "Nothing I cannot deal with," he said—keeping himself from snarling.

Firesong gave him a most peculiar look as he retook his position on the padded chest. He crossed his legs and intertwined his slender fingers across one knee.

Then he spoke.

"Darkwind, I have been working magery since I was barely able to walk," the Adept said slowly. "My hair was white by the time I was ten. I have ever had a fearsome example to live up to, for my great-great-many-times-great-grandfather was one Herald Vanyel Ashkevron out of Valdemar. Even as Elspeth's was, though she knows it not."

"But—" Darkwind was surprised he managed to get that much out, stunned as he was, "—how?"

"A long tale, which I shall make as short as I may." The Adept held up his hand, and his firebird came winging out of the tree cover above, a streak of white and gold lightning that alighted haughtily on his wrist. "This is the tradition, as it was handed down from Brightstar's foster-parents, Moondance and Starwind. One of k'Treva wished a child and there was no one in the Clan she favored. Moondance and Starwind also longed to be parents. Vanyel was well favored by all within the Clan, and consented to be father to twins, one of whom was my forefather, Brightstar. But in Valdemar, also longing for a child, was the King's Own and lover of the Monarch, Shavri. Vanyel obliged her in part so that it would seem that Randale was able to father children, which he was not. That child, Jisa, wedded the next Monarch, Treven, a cousin of the King, and from that line of descent springs yon Outlander."

Firesong chuckled at Darkwind's expression.

I must look like a stunned ox.

"Nay, cousin, we of k'Treva are not so well-versed in Outlander doings as you think. It is simply that Brightstar knew of his half-sister and her young suitor, and that the Ashkevron blood calls to blood; we know each other, though she does not know how." Now Firesong raised one winglike eyebrow. "That may be the source of the Outlander's fascination with my humble self."

Darkwind snorted. "As if *you* could ever be humble," he said sardonically.

"It has happened a time or two, but not recently." Firesong shrugged, and transferred his firebird to his shoulder. "I thought a word to you was appropriate. I have *much* more training than you, more thorough, and more consistent. I have never abandoned my magic. Considering all you have—experienced—you do far better than I had expected. Take that for what it is worth. There is more I would say when the time is appropriate."

He hung his head for a moment, then raised it again and brushed the moon-white hair from his forehead. Then he stood, an inscrutable expression on his face, and left by the trail Elspeth had taken, white-feathered firebird on his shoulder.

I should at least apologize to her, if he is not with her, Darkwind thought, finally. *Or even if he is with her . . . though I doubt I could.*

So eventually he, too, followed the pathway out of the clearing to the end of the Vale where Elspeth's *ekele* stood. He waited for a moment, listening at the entrance to the hot spring near her tree. There were splashing sounds; someone was definitely in there. There was no "in use" marker at the entrance. . . .

He hesitated a moment longer, then went in.

For a moment he thought he had made a terrible mistake, for Elspeth was lying beside the pool, wrapped in a lounging robe, head was pressed against another, crowned with flowing white—

:Oh, for Haven's sake, don't be more of a young fool than you are already,: Gwena snapped. He recognized, just before he backed out of the clearing, that it wasn't Firesong she was lying against, it was her Companion.

"Do you—mind if I use the pool?" he said awkwardly. She propped herself up on one elbow and gave him a long, penetrating look.

"I mind only if you plan on being as hateful as you were this morning," she said, levelly.

"I didn't exactly plan on being hateful," he replied weakly. "It just happened."

"Hmm," was all she said, and she laid herself back down again on the cushions.

:If you don't mind, I'm going to leave you two alone,: Gwena said, getting gracefully to her feet. *:I suggest whatever in the nine hells is bothering the two of you, that you get it dealt with before it shows up in the magic. That youngster and I agree on one thing, at least—that you'd better not bring your emotional upheavals into the reach of the Stone.:*

And with that, she melted into the undergrowth.

Darkwind stripped hastily, and slipped into the water. Elspeth stayed where she was, neither moving nor talking. He finally decided to break the silence before he got a headache from it.

"I'm sorry. I didn't mean to be nasty."

"I'm sure you didn't," Elspeth replied. Then she turned on her side and met his eyes. "Something occurred to Gwena, and she pointed it out to me. You're getting a dose of what your brother gets all the time, did you realize that?"

"What?" he said cleverly. "Wintermoon?"

"Certainly." Elspeth turned over onto her stomach, and pillowed her head on her arms. "Think about it. *You* were always the Adept, the one with all the power. The one who had anything he wanted, from Starblade's approval to his pick of lovers in the Clan. *He* was a lowly scout, no magic, and in a position of risk, so that even if someone had considered getting close to him, they were afraid to because he was as likely to die as return every patrol. Even when you gave up the magic and no longer were the darling of your father's eye, you still had high rank, a place in the Council, the friendship of the gryphons, and Dawnfire. Now you've taken the magic up again, and you have it all back. And there stands good old reliable Wintermoon, upstaged again."

"I never thought of it that way," he said, slowly. "It never occurred to me."

"I didn't think so. Ever wondered why he spends so much time outside the Vale—why he volunteered to go wandering about the countryside with Skif in tow?" She rubbed her forehead on her sleeve. "I did.

Gwena says she thinks he does it so that he won't get jealous of you. He really loves you, just as truly as any brother—but *hellfires*, Darkwind, it must be awful to stand around and watch you, and see everything you want just fall into your hand like a ripe fruit!"

"Oh," he replied, feeling very—odd. Very taken aback.

"So, now you're confronted with Firesong, and you're feeling the same way Wintermoon has since you started showing Mage-Gift." Her bright brown eyes regarded him soberly from beneath a lock of hair. "Doesn't feel very good, I'd imagine."

"No, it doesn't," he admitted. "But—you—"

"Oh, I'm used to not being the best." Elspeth shook her hair back. "Talia was better than me at classes, Jeri was better than me at swordsmanship, Mother is much prettier than me, Kero's better at strategy, Step-father at diplomacy, Skif at being sneaky—the only thing I was really good at was pottery, and I didn't deceive myself into thinking I was the best in the Kingdom." She spoke airily, but Darkwind sensed that old hurt under her words.

"Elspeth, I think the thing that bothers me the most is that Firesong has your admiration," he said, unhappily. "I *am* jealous of him. He is so much more my master at magic—I feel like a bare apprentice. But it is the fact that you admire him so that angers me, and I cannot help myself."

It truly cost him in pride to admit that, and she stared at him a moment longer. "You know, Kero told me something, once. She said—'you'd think being able to speak mind-to-mind would put an end to all the misunderstandings between people, but it doesn't.' She was right, too."

He shook his head ruefully. "I have often found that when there were misunderstandings, both parties found reasons not to share their thoughts."

"Exactly." She widened her eyes, and he felt the delicate touch of her mind on his. :*Firesong has Power. Firesong is too beautiful to be human. Firesong is worth admiring. But from a distance. He's not called Firesong for nothing—he breathes in the admiration and everything else around him. Fire can warm you from a distance, but it burns when you get too close to it.*:

There was no doubting the truth of the feelings behind the words. He ducked under the water for a moment, then emerged and hoisted himself up onto the bank beside her. "Then you forgive me for being a beast?"

She grinned. "I think you could persuade me to."

★ ★ ★

Tre'valen soared the spirit-skies in a new form; that of a vorcel-hawk. Smaller than Dawnfire—as was only appropriate for a tiercel—and with nowhere near her power, he still hoped that in this form she would see that he was trying to meet her halfway. She had avoided him for days now, and he was not certain if the reason was anything to do with him, or if it was something outside of both of them.

Surely the Goddess knew of his feelings toward Dawnfire. Could She not approve, to let him continue to pursue Dawnfire? It would take the barest blink on Her part to slap him to the ground, away from Her Avatar—yet Tre'valen sought Dawnfire still. Surely the Goddess knew that he was still devout, that he searched always mindful of serving Her people better. No matter how his heart might cry to him of how Dawnfire needed him, and he needed her—he was still a sworn shaman, and owed his loyalty to Her and Her purposes.

Hold, though—had he truly just *assumed* Dawnfire needed him? He did not know for certain if he read her emotions or his own. Her eyes were no longer human when he saw her. Could he believe the desire for companionship he saw in them? It was all so complex, and he had so few real facts to work with. He could only do the one thing a shaman ultimately must: trust in who he was and let his long-learned morals determine his actions.

He had always been bright-eyed and adventurous; the Goddess had not been displeased by it when She took him as Her shaman. It would be senseless to deny his nature—better to act on it.

He had walked the Moonpaths to no effect—so now he tried a desperation move. He left the Paths altogether, and turned his flight into the starry night between them.

Prudent Kra'heera had never left the Paths in all of his long life as a shaman. Tre'valen had heard of some—a very few—who had, and lived to do so again. They were not many, but their adventures had been in times calmer than these. There were new things happening, strange and promising and frightening at once, and risks were somehow more appropriate. The risk of leaving the Moonpaths paled before the danger of his courting the Goddess' own Avatar.

Still, if Dawnfire would not come to him, he must needs go to her.

He felt the lift in his "belly" as he lifted from the Paths, on wings made of glittering golden stardust and lit by his own life. A shiver as though from a cold wind, a knifelike wash through his sunlight-feathered body, and the Moonpaths dropped away below him.

Foolishness it might be—but glorious it certainly was.

He soared and wheeled above and under the Paths, able now to See the patterns upon patterns they coursed into, and the colors and layers as far as his spirit-eyes could discern.

But she was nowhere to be found.

Perhaps he was looking in the wrong place entirely? Well, there was nothing keeping him from using this form in the "real" world—and if she soared the physical skies in her hawk-form, she would *surely* see him in this guise.

He closed the eyes of the hawk, then turned within—sought the twist that brought him home—

And opened them again as warm sun flooded through him. Through, because as a spirit-hawk in the real world, he was slightly transparent. A tiercel-vorcel of golden glass. . . .

Was it not exactly like a lovesick tiercel to court a mate with fancy flying? Leaving the Moonpaths, diving from the starry soul-sea into the physical world—was that not the equivalent of skimming a cliff face to attract a lover's eye?

He couldn't help but laugh at himself over it all, still a little giddy from the feel of the soul-sea between the Paths. Should he continue with the analogy and hope that Dawnfire would be impressed? Could they be enough alike somehow that she would fly with him? So many mysteries, but then, there were few answers to begin with in his life's work. That was, he felt, part of its appeal—in searching for Truths, he'd found few absolute ones and thousands of personal ones. He'd follow his heart, wherever it led.

Perhaps his willingness to risk was only adaptability. He felt at home in this Vale of summer nestled amidst cruel winter, as he did wherever he traveled. So many times he'd been berated for his brashness by Kra'heera; perhaps his brashness was but unrefined bravery?

He increased his physical mass, steadied in the chilly breeze above his brothers' Vale. They, too, followed their hearts as certainly as they followed the Goddess' laws. He admired them. They fought for a goal that would come many centuries from their own lifetimes as though it would be enjoyed at day's end.

They were not so different from his own people, who guarded the Plains and the deadly things under it. The Hawkbrothers actively fought;

the Shin'a'in had the equally difficult tasks of unending vigilance and precise response. The Kal'enedral and the Hawkbrother Adepts were alike in some respects, were they not? Different but complimentary.

He had seen history drawn in tapestries in Kata'shin'a'in. Was it time now for a new tapestry to be woven?

Ah, if his thread and Dawnfire's could be woven together, it would be like the satisfying ending to a tale, and he would feel reborn. . . .

He angled over the Vale, careful of the sense of wonder that he felt. He couldn't let it blind him to his goal. The point of taking flight this way was to find Dawnfire, to speak with her. Tre'valen scanned the skies, widened his view—and saw something bright hurtling toward him and the Vale.

It was without physical form, a fiery spear of crackling magical energy, larger than two men. It came roaring toward him, rushing, unrelenting, like a storm-driven grass-fire across the Plains—and struck him full in the chest. A shower of splintered mage-energy burst around him and he screamed out.

He fell half a furlong, stunned; recovered; held himself in place with unsteady wingbeats. The next blow was coming, and he warded against it as best he could.

For one moment, he thought that his fears were coming to pass, that the Star-Eyed herself had decided to punish him for his audacity. But no—

No, he was not even the object of the attack. He had been in its bound-path, and it had diverted to him—and *through* him. He had only been in the way. The second strike was approaching differently; it struck at him, hurt him, but lost little of its power, continuing to its true target. That target was below him, in the Vale.

Starblade—

He Saw the Adept taking the force of the blow and falling to his knees while his bondbird screamed in anger and frustration; Saw him recover. Even as he folded his wings and dove to add his own small—and probably futile—strength, he Saw Kethra fling herself physically over the Adept, and magically join her power to his. Then he watched in astonishment as Starblade gave up control to Kethra, letting her spread the force of the attack over both of them.

It is Falconsbane!

A third blow came, and then a fourth; the pair sagged beneath the force of the brutal attack, their shields eroding. Kethra cried out, face toward the sky, fists clenched, transmuting the attack-energies into another form. A circle of intense cold spread out from her, covering everything it touched with a thick layer of frost. Furniture split and shattered as it was overcome; drinking vessels and pitchers burst; the very structure of the *ekele* was warping and cracking as it was engulfed in bitter cold.

Falconsbane—

Hyllarr shrieked in agitation and abandoned his perch, falling to the floor and backing against the wall of the *ekele* as the lethal white circle spread. Already, Tre'valen knew the victims were in pain from the deadly cold—which told him that withstanding the effects of the attack must have been worse even than its transmutation.

Even without ForeSight, the next few moments were writ clear for anyone to see. Help would not come from the rest of the Vale in time. Falconsbane had been merely testing their strength. The next blow would rip through their defenses, and surely channel through from Starblade inside the Vale, into the Vale—

And pour into the Heartstone, shattering it, and sear the country for leagues. The devastation would kill everyone, and unleash a score of wild ley-lines to tear through the landscape.

I must stop this—

He knew he would die.

It did not matter. Too many would be hurt—

:Here!:

He Looked up; Dawnfire was above him in her hawk-form, a blazing creature of glory. She had more than enough power to shield Starblade from the next attack. Whether he would survive the encounter, he could not know, but his brethren must be saved. And here, with him, was Dawnfire. . . .

She had the power. *He* had the knowledge.

:Now! Together!: he cried, and folded his wings to plummet down. She fell beside him, both of them rushing just ahead of the blast of power that they Felt hot on their necks. . . .

Firesong took up the drum and faced the Heartstone, his fingers pattering a little anticipatory run on the taut skin. Darkwind shook out his muscles, a chill of nervousness running down his spine. This was only to be an exploratory venture, a preliminary, to see what the three of them could do with the rogue Stone.

:Haiee!:

It was not so much a call, as a mental shriek of pain. And Darkwind knew immediately whose pain it was.

:Father!: He Reached for power, blindly.

But Firesong reacted first, reaching, clenching fists until his knuckles whitened, flinging the tightest shield Darkwind had ever seen around—

—the Heartstone.

What—

Darkwind had no time for anything other than a gasp of outrage. It was Starblade and Kethra who needed protection, not the damned Stone!

Firesong fell to his knees, hands spread wide, muscles straining as he built shield after shield around the Stone. The Stone flared and a dozen fire-red tendrils stabbed out toward Starblade's *ekele*, to be stopped short by Firesong's shields. They sought purchase in the inner shields, and half of them penetrated; Firesong built another layer and another, sucking in Power from all around him.

The tendrils were all reaching out to Starblade.

Darkwind's Sight clearly showed him the next huge fire-bolt coming in through the Vale's shields. Streaking down before it were two sun-bright vorcel-hawks. They dove wing to wing, turned as one above Starblade and Kethra's *ekele*—

—and caught the fire-bolt together. Power flared around his father and his lover, and then all was still, except for the hoarse protests of Hyllarr and a subsiding thrum from the Heartstone. Firesong constricted the shields, his eyes closed tightly in concentration. The tendrils receded.

Darkwind reached his power to Elspeth, without conscious thought of it—and found her doing the same toward him. They wove a counterattack, Lanced it up into the sky—and let it sputter off into nothing. The enemy—*Mornelithe Falconsbane,* he knew—had aborted his remaining attack and dispersed its power into a huge, flickering mantle over the Vale.

There was no path for a counterattack to follow.

Mornelithe Falconsbane had escaped again.

Nyara & Skif

Chapter Nineteen

"**T**hat was Falconsbane!" Elspeth gasped, climbing to her feet and swaying in her tracks with shock at Darkwind's side. "That was Falconsbane—I know it was! What stopped him?"

"I don't know," Darkwind replied. "I can't tell, Elspeth." His head rang with the echoes of power, and there was no reading anything subtle this close to the Stone. He stepped across the pass-through on the warded threshold that sealed the Stone away from the rest of the Vale, and sent out a fan of questing energy.

The trace was clear and clean, though quickly fading, and it ran back to a center that was not disturbed, but oddly empty.

No—more than empty—

When he realized what he felt, he recoiled and snapped up his own shields. Elspeth crossed the threshold, and Gwena appeared at her side. Both breathed hard from sprinting.

Vree, who had been sunning in the falls area of the Vale, shot overhead, alert for new danger. He abruptly sideslipped and landed in a tree outside the threshold, and sent a mental query, followed by a wordless message of support when he sensed how distraught his bondmate was.

Darkwind waved to warn Vree away, then began running toward a particular remote corner of the Vale—a place where he had sensed, not only the remains of burned-out power, but something more. The kind of emptiness only a Final Strike left behind.

Death.

Someone had died protecting Starblade, and given that it was a power-signature he didn't recognize, he was horribly certain he knew who that someone was.

Hoofbeats gained behind him and Gwena and Elspeth drew up just ahead of him. Elspeth's hand was open to him, and he grasped it and vaulted up onto Gwena's back. Together, they rode crouched, into the far reaches of the Vale. Gwena sprinted and stooped, dodging trees, limbs, and other obstacles. The lush, relaxing decorations of the Vale were now clinging distractions; Gwena could only make speed in clearings.

They were overtaken within moments. Gwena dove off the trail in time to avoid being trampled by Firesong's white *dyheli*, who streaked past them, lightning-fast and surefooted. The stag bore Firesong clinging bareback, and behind them flew the firebird, streaming controlled false-sparks of agitation along the flowing length of its tail.

By the time Darkwind, Gwena, and Elspeth reached their goal, Firesong was lifting the body of Tre'valen in his arms as if it weighed nothing, his face utterly blank and expressionless. Firesong's complexion had turned ashen; the firebird clutched at his shoulder and chittered angrily, then fixed its eyes on Tre'valen's lifeless face and went silent.

Firesong looked from Darkwind to Elspeth and back again, but said nothing. There was a chill in his eyes that made Darkwind reluctant to say anything. Elspeth stifled a sob behind her clenched fist; Gwena moved away, stepping backward very deliberately.

Firesong stalked carefully between them, eyes focused straight ahead. He carried his dreadful burden out of the clearing and into the depths of the Vale, without saying a single word to either of them.

Darkwind's thoughts seethed with anger. *He killed Tre'valen. He shielded the Stone and not my father, and Tre'valen died for it. And he knows it, the arrogant bastard. Why? Why did he shield the damned Stone? He saw the strike coming before I did—he knew what was going to happen!*

"Darkwind—your father," Elspeth said urgently, recalling to him the *other* casualties in this catastrophe.

"Gods—" he said, despairingly, and headed off at a run again, in the opposite direction that Firesong had taken. The *ekele* was not that far, but it seemed hundreds of leagues away as he hurtled through the foliage, taking a narrow shortcut. Branches whipped at his face, leaving places that stung until his eyes watered. His lungs ached, his legs felt as unsteady as willow twigs. But there was no time, no time—

Despite the fact that it seemed an eternity since the attack, he and Elspeth reached Starblade's home moments ahead of the rest of the mages of k'Sheyna. Hyllarr was shrieking alarm and outrage to the entire Vale. Darkwind pounded up the steps of the *ekele* and burst into the main room, and stepped back, shocked by the destruction.

Starblade was sprawled inelegantly across the floor, with Kethra lying atop him in an attitude of protection. He was awake, if dazed; she was not moving. Elspeth pushed past him and reached for Kethra, levering her off the k'Sheyna Adept so that Darkwind could get to his father. She slipped and steadied, after a floorboard shifted under her. All the wood in the room was splintered; moisture covered every part that was not patched in frost. Very little was intact within four arm's spans of Starblade and Kethra; the floor and walls were warped and cracked. This *ekele* could not possibly be livable again.

Hyllarr quieted as soon as they entered the room, though he continued to shift from one foot to the other, crooning anxiously and craning his neck to watch what they were doing. He came as far as the outer edge of the ice, then waited.

Starblade blinked up at his son, and tried to rise; Darkwind decided that it would be better to help him onto the couch than try to prevent him from moving. Starblade's fingers showed signs of frostbite.

"Falconsbane," Starblade murmured, bringing a trembling hand up to his eyes. "That touch again—filthy—"

He shuddered, and Darkwind got him lying back against a heap of pillows, then ran to fetch water and cups from the far side of the *ekele*. One cup he handed to Elspeth, who had managed to get Kethra into a sitting position. The other he handed to his father, who seized it in shaking hands and drained it as if it contained the water of life itself. Darkwind daubed his fingers into the pitcher and traced wet fingers across his father's brow and eyes and blew gently, an old mage's technique to help focus concentration.

"What happened?" he asked, as Starblade closed his eyes and lay back again, the lines of pain in his face even more pronounced than ever before.

"I am not certain," Starblade faltered. "It was Falconsbane—he tried my defenses.'' His face mirrored his confusion and his fear, the fear that he had once again betrayed his Clan.

"It seems he could not break them," Darkwind reminded him. "The beast *could not take you*, Father. His hold over you is gone forever—do you see?"

Starblade shook his head, though not in negation. "I—he attacked. Kethra tried to protect us both." He propped himself up onto one elbow, with obvious effort, and looked around.

"She's in shock," Elspeth said calmly. "She needs a lot of rest, and she needs her energies restored. But I'm sure she's going to be all right."

By now, they had an audience, but only Iceshadow pushed through to join them. He went first to Kethra, then to Starblade, and seeing that they were only badly shaken and depleted, shook his head.

"It is strange," Iceshadow said in puzzlement. "There was no time for *any* of us to have protected them. Yet someone did."

"There were hawks," Starblade whispered. "Two shining hawks with wings of fire. They dove from the sun, and sheltered us beneath their wings. That is what protected us."

"That was Tre'valen," said a new voice, flatly. Firesong stood just inside, keeping his face in shadow.

"That was Tre'valen, in spirit-form. And likely that one of k'Sheyna who was taken by the Shin'a'in Goddess." He seemed to be waiting for the name, and Darkwind supplied it, carefully controlling his own anger at the Adept's failure to shield his father.

"Dawnfire," he said, his own voice as expressionless as Firesong's.

Firesong did not even acknowledge that he had spoken. "Dawnfire. It was also Dawnfire. That was shamanic magic; it would have been the only thing this Falconsbane could not counter, for it is spirit-born, and he knows not how to use it, nor how to negate it." Firesong bent down for a moment, and laid his hand gently on Starblade's head, above his closed eyes. Starblade did not seem to even notice that he was there, so deep was his exhaustion. "He must have known he could not survive such a blow in spirit-form."

Darkwind kept a tight curb on his tongue, afraid to say *anything*, lest he lash out with words of challenge. But Firesong straightened, and looked into his eyes.

And the sheer agony Darkwind saw there killed whatever accusations had been forming in his mind. Firesong's ageless, smooth face, which bore only confidence scant hours ago, now showed creases of tension and grief.

"I could not shield your father and the Stone, both, Darkwind," Firesong said quietly, with unshed tears making his voice thick. "Tre'valen died because I was a fool. I did not think to look for your enemy; I did not ward the Stone against him. I had to make a choice; your father, or the Vale."

"Look," he said, and picked up a stoneware cup spiderwebbed with cracks from the cold. "Look here, how this is like the Stone. All the damage runs from this place, tied to Starblade. And a single blow *here*—channeled through Starblade—you see?" He dropped the cup, which shattered between his feet.

Indeed, Darkwind did see. That one blow, had Firesong not intervened, would have shattered the Heartstone completely; releasing all the pent-up energies at once.

It would not have created as large a crater as made the Dhorisha Plains, but it would have dug down to bedrock, and killed every living thing within the Vale, and far outside it.

"I am—sorry," Firesong said, and sighed heavily. "You will never know how sorry. I did what I had to. As did Tre'valen."

And with that, he retreated, with the rest of k'Sheyna parting before him.

It was a fair amount of time later when Darkwind left the *ekele*, having put Starblade and Kethra under the care of Iceshadow and the other mages. Iceshadow was confident that they would both be near recovery by morning; Elspeth had volunteered to stay with them, channeling energies through Gwena to renew what they had lost, helping the k'Sheyna Healers. Vree had wanted to stay with Elspeth.

Darkwind could think of no way to be of use. His own strength was not what it should have been; he had cast much of it into that fruitless counterattack on Falconsbane. And his mind was in a turmoil. He did not know what to do, or to think. He would have been of no use to the Healers, muddled as he was.

So he wandered the Vale instead, coming at last to the curtain of energies that hid the entrance. Snow was falling again. The last daylight dwindled beneath the trees. He reached the cleft in the hillside, and realized that the odd outcropping of snow there was not snow at all.

Firesong turned slowly, saw him, and nodded. It felt like an invitation. Darkwind stepped across the Veil and into the snow to stand beside him.

After a moment, Firesong spoke.

"He goes home now—" the Adept said dully. "—his body does."

Darkwind saw that one of the shadows at the limit of vision was moving; was not a shadow at all, but a black-clad rider on a ghost-gray horse, with a large bundle carried across the saddlebow. Moving away; toward that path that led down to the Plains.

"And what of the spirit?" Darkwind asked, finally.

"I am not a shaman. I cannot say."

Darkwind rubbed his arms as the residual heat of the Vale wisped away from his body into the silent snowfall.

"I want you to know, you did the right thing. In protecting the Heartstone. It would have killed us all."

Firesong stiffened, and looked up; white crystal flakes settled on his forehead and brows, laced his eyelashes and crown of white hair. "Knowing it was the better of two ills changes little." His hair rippled like silk in a breeze. "It makes Tre'valen's death hurt no less."

Darkwind nodded.

Firesong shifted his loose robes and lifted a long bone pipe to his lips. Thin, breathy notes fell softly upon the ear, mingled with the silence. Darkwind knew the tune, a Shin'a'in lament.

A second voice joined the flute's, though Darkwind could not have told what it was until he saw the white firebird perched in the tree branches above the Adept, its head and neck stretched out, its graceful bill open and its throat vibrating.

The scene etched itself into Darkwind's memory. After so many years in the company of Adepts, he knew the outward signs of self-induced trance; after a while, he realized that the Adept was paying no attention to anything but his music.

Darkwind turned and walked back into the Vale, leaving Firesong and his bondbird pouring out mournful notes into the dark and silence.

As he walked away, he thought he caught sight of something wet glittering on Firesong's cheek, though the notes never faltered, and the face remained utterly remote and as lifeless as a marble statue's. Perhaps it was only a melting snowflake.

Perhaps it wasn't.

★ ★ ★

A scream rang out and was cut short.

Falconsbane slashed, all claws extended, and the hapless slave fell to the stone floor, choking on his own blood. Falconsbane watched him with anger raging unappeased through his veins, as the boy gurgled and clutched desperately at his throat. Blood poured between his fingers and splattered against the cold gray marble as the slave twitched and gasped and finally died, his eyes glazing, his body twitching, then relaxing into the limpness of death.

Not enough. Falconsbane looked for something else to destroy, cast his eyes about the study, and found nothing that he could spare or did not need. He had already shattered the few breakable ornaments; the upholstery of his couch was slashed to ribbons. The table beside the couch was overturned, and he would not touch the books; they held knowledge too precious to waste.

So he turned back to his final victim, and proceeded to reduce the body to its fundamental parts, using only his hands.

When he was done, he was still full of burning rage. He kicked the door of the study open, hoping to find someone lurking in the hall, but they knew his temper by now, and had cleared out of the corridors. Likely they were all cowering behind locked doors and praying to whatever debased gods they worshiped—besides him—that he would appease his anger with the slave they had sent him. Cowards. He was surrounded by worthless, gutless cowards.

He growled deep in his chest. *Not as gutless as the slave is now.*

He stormed out into the corridors of his fortress, and ran upward, toward the rooftops. The place stifled him with its heat and luxury. He wanted to destroy it all, but instead, he went seeking the darkness of the night and the quiet of the snow to cool his temper.

He found a spot where he would not be tempted to destroy anything more because there was nothing to destroy—the top of one of the four corner towers.

It was open to the wind and weather, and since the quiet and cold did nothing to cool his anger, Falconsbane found another outlet for his rage. He reached out to the storm about him and whipped it from a simple snowstorm to a blinding, howling blizzard, taking fierce comfort in the shrieking wind. Wishing that it was the shrieks of dying Hawkbrothers he heard instead.

Thwarted. Again! It could not have happened. He'd posted sentries to spy upon them. They had done nothing out of the ordinary. They made no efforts at all to *use* the twisted power of their Stone. Instead, they had sought to drain power from it, and it, of course, had resisted as it had been trained to do. Their mages were exhausted; they had no reserves, no Great Adepts.

The timing could not have been better. And yet he had been thwarted.

First, his attempt to retake his pawn Starblade failed. All of the channels he had so carefully established into the Bird-Fool's heart and mind were *gone*. Not blocked, but gone completely, healed by some strange application of magics with a taste he could not even begin to sort out. Strongly female and laced with an acid protectiveness that made him flinch away.

That was bad enough, having to abandon his best tool, but when he tried to turn his controlling of Starblade into an attack on the k'Sheyna Heartstone as planned, he could not springboard to the Stone. Infuriating!

Not once, but *twice;* blocked at the Stone itself, by shields he could not penetrate, and blocked again at the channel he had tied to Starblade's life-force! *Where* had those fools gotten the Adept that had shielded the Stone? There had been no one, not even the Outland girl, with so much as the potential for power like that! And *what* had they used to block his death-strike on Starblade? Not only did he not recognize it, but his mind still reeled beneath the blinding counter it had made to his strike. What had intercepted his fire-bolt? It had taken all his power and transformed it into a force he could not even remotely name.

Either of those alone would have been bad enough. Together they awoke a killing rage in him that demanded an outlet. He had stormed out of his working-place and into his study, intending mayhem.

He discovered there was more—much more.

His outriders had been waiting for him; they had come in to him, all bearing the same story. Black-clad riders on black horses, haunting the edges of his domain. Riders who *did* nothing; simply appeared, watching for a moment, as if making certain that they had been seen, and vanished again. Riders who left no mark in the snow; whose faces could not be seen behind their veilings of black cloth.

His *mages* had come to him with more news of the same ilk, hundreds of tiny changes that had occurred while he was dealing that aborted attack to k'Sheyna. Along and inside all of his borders, there were tiny pinprick-upsettings of his magic. Traps had been sprung, but had caught nothing, and there was not even a hint of what had sprung them. Ley-lines that had been diverted to his purposes had returned to their courses, but they went *to* nothing specific nor any new power-poles. Areas that he had fouled to use for breeding his creatures had been cleansed. Yet there was no pattern to it, no plan. Some lines had been left alone; traps side-by-side showed one sprung, the other still set. Areas near to the Vale had been left fouled, while others, farther away, had been cleansed.

He snarled into the howling wind. He *hated* random things! He *hated* fools who worked with no plans in mind, and changes that occurred with no warning! And most of all, he hated, despised, things that happened for no apparent reason!

Every one of those pinpricks had taken away his order, interfered with his careful plans—and left chaos behind. And all to no purpose he could see!

He shouted into the night, and let the wind carry his anger away, let the cold chill his rage until it came within the proper, controllable bounds again. How long he stood there, he was not certain, only that after a time he knew that he could descend into his stronghold again, and be in no danger of destroying anything necessary.

He dismissed the stormwinds; without his will behind them, the winds faded and died away, leaving only the snow still falling from the darkened, cloud-covered night sky.

He opened the door into the warmth and light of the staircase and found one of his outriders waiting there for him.

He snarled and clenched his fists at his side; this was more of that *news*, he knew it, and he wanted so badly to maim the bearer of it that he shook with the effort to control himself.

The man's face was white as paper; he trembled with such fear that he was incapable of speech. He held out an intricately carved black box to his master, a box hardly bigger than the palm of his hand.

Falconsbane took it and waited for the man to force the words past his fear to tell his master where this trinket of carved wood had come from. But when the man failed utterly to get anything more than an incoherent hiss past his clenched teeth, Falconsbane ruthlessly seized control of his mind with yet another spell, and tore the story from him. It only took a moment to absorb, mind-to-mind, but what he learned quelled his anger far more effectively than the wind had.

His hand clutched convulsively on the box as the tale unfolded, and he left the man collapsed upon the stairs in a trembling heap, ignoring whatever damage he had done to the outrider's mind. He took the stairs two at a time back to the safety and security of his newly-cleaned study; there was no sign of where the dead slave had been except a wide wet spot. And only there, with all his protections about him, did he use a tiny spell to open the tiny box from arm's length.

If this was a rational, ordered universe, it would contain something meant to cripple or kill him.

He held his shields about him, waiting.

Nothing happened.

The box contained, cradled in black, padded suede, a tiny figurine carved of shiny, black onyx.

The figure of a perfectly formed black horse, rearing, and no bigger than his thumbnail.

There was no scent of magic upon it—no trace of who or what had made or sent it. Although he *knew* what had delivered it, if not who it was from.

One of the black riders.

He retreated to his newly-covered couch and held the delicate little carving to the light, pondering what he had ripped from his servant's mind.

This particular outrider had seen these black-clad riders three times before this, but always they had vanished into the forest as soon as they knew they had been seen, leaving not even hoofprints behind. But this time had been different. This time he had seen the rider cleave a tree with a sword blow, and leave something atop the stump. The rider sheathed the sword and slipped into the shadows, like another shadow himself. When the outrider had reached the spot, he discovered this box.

And it weighted down one other thing. A slip of paper, that had burned to ash in his hand as soon as he had read it. A slip of paper bearing the name of his Master, Mornelithe Falconsbane, in the careful curved letters of Tradespeech.

As if there had been any doubt whatsoever who this was meant for—

He turned the figurine over and over, staring at it. There was nothing here to identify it or the box, with its stylized geometric carvings, as coming from any particular land or culture. Was it a warning, or a gift? If a gift, what did it mean? If a warning—who were these riders, who had sent them, and what did they want?

★ ★ ★

Skif and Nyara talked idly about the chase; this rabbit they were dressing out had been far more trouble than it was worth, but Nyara's capture of it was as worthy of admiration as any hawk's stoop. Winter-moon was gently cleaning a deep scratch one of the *dyheli* had suffered, several feet from the two of them.

Nyara had reentered their lives by simply coming into camp and waiting to be discovered. They'd found her between the two *dyheli* when they awoke, sitting with her knees tucked up to her chest and the sword Need at her feet. She looked different now—more human, and with sharply-defined muscles. She also moved with purpose rather than slinking like a cat; she had visibly undergone many changes, all of which served to fascinate Skif further.

There was no sign of any trouble, but suddenly Cymry's head shot up, and her eyes went wide and wild, with the whites showing all around them. Her body went from relaxed to tense; she stood with all four legs braced, and there was no doubt in Skif's mind what she sensed.

Danger. Terrible danger. Something was happening.

Skif stood and put one hand on her shoulder to steady her, as Nyara's face went completely blank. Nyara leapt to her feet and stared off in the same direction as Cymry, her own eyes mirroring a fear that Skif recognized only too well.

He felt nothing, but then, if it was magic that alerted them, he wouldn't. But he recognized what direction they were both staring in.

The Vale—where Elspeth was.

He tried to Mindtouch his Companion, but all of her attention was on the danger she had sensed. It was Need's mind-voice that growled in the back of his head, as he tried to break through Cymry's preoccupation.

:*Leave her alone, boy. She's talking to Gwena. There's big trouble back with your bird-loving friends.*:

He dared a tentative thought in Need's direction, waiting for an instant rebuff. He still had no idea what Need thought of *him*, beyond the few things she had condescended to say to him. :*What kind of trouble? Something involving us?*:

The sword hesitated a moment. :*Hmm. I'd say so. Your kitten's sire just tried to flatten the whole Vale. And I think—yes. No doubt. There's been a death.*:

Before Skif could panic, the sword continued. :*Not Elspeth; not Dark-wind. More, I can't tell you. There's some shamanic magic mixed in with the rest, and damned if I can read it.*:

Wintermoon stared at all of them with the impatient air of a man ready to strangle someone if he didn't get an explanation soon. Skif didn't blame him, and he broke off communication with the blade to tell the Hawkbrother what little Need had been able to tell him. The name of Mornelithe Falconsbane got his immediate attention.

"Falconsbane! But I thought—"

"We all thought—or, we didn't think," Skif replied, trying to make his thoughts stop spinning in circles. "We just assumed. Not a good idea where magic is concerned." *Or where Falconsbane is concerned. Next time I won't believe he's dead until I burn the body myself and sow the ashes with salt.*

"If there is trouble, we *must* return, with all speed. And it must be with Nyara or without her, for we cannot delay to argue," Wintermoon said firmly. "I had rather it were 'with' but I shall not force her."

The mention of her name seemed to wake Nyara from her trance. "Of course we go, night-hunter," she replied. Her eyes still looked a little unfocused, but her voice was firm enough. "And I go with you. I know too much about my father to remain outside and watch your people struggle to match him again. I shall not hide while he tries to destroy your Clan, hoping he will miss me as he concentrates on you."

She shook her head, then, and hesitated, looking fully into Skif's eyes. "If I had a choice, I would tell you this when we are alone, *ashke*," she said softly. "But I think that Wintermoon must hear this so he can bear witness if need be."

Skif tensed, wondering what she was going to say to him. Things had seemed so promising a few moments ago.

"I care for you, Outlander," she said with quiet intensity. "More than I had ever realized when I saw your face this morn. I would like— many things—and most of all, to share my life with you. But you and I can do nothing until I come to terms with my father. There is much that I have not told you of him—and myself. It must be dealt with."

Skif had seen such looks as he saw in her eyes more than once, before he became a Herald—and after, among some of the refugees from Ancar's depredations. He saw it in the eyes of a woman who spoke of her father, and horrors between them.

He knew. He knew of many things that decent people would only think of as horrible nightmares, and deny that they truly happened. He knew the sordid tales that could be hidden behind those bleak eyes. She didn't even have to begin; he knew before she started. And he blamed her no more for what had been done to her than he would have blamed a tree sundered by lightning.

She was all the more beautiful for her strength.

Maybe it was just that he was too busy wanting to hold her and tell her that nothing in her past could make him want her any less. Falconsbane was dismissed from any redemption in his mind; to him he rated no more thoughts, not even hate—as his friend Wintermoon had taught him, such emotions can cloud purpose. Maybe that purpose was too important for him to have any room left for anger, now. That might change if he ever actually saw Falconsbane again, but that was the way he felt this moment.

All things could change. If he were the same person he was only a few years ago, he'd have already been sharpening knives, plotting revenge on Falconsbane; now, simply eliminating the Adept was more important. Revenge seemed foolish somehow, it would not help Nyara at all. How strange, that after a life like his, revenge seemed hollow compared to simple justice.

Nyara deserved far more consideration than her father.

He didn't even think about the sword's propensity to eavesdrop, until she spoke to him.

:Well, bless your heart, boy—I'm beginning to think there's hope for you yet.: Need's harsh mind-voice rattled in his head as she chuckled. :You are all right! Hellfires, I'd even be willing to nominate you as an honorary Sister!:

He felt his ears redden, as Nyara looked at him curiously. :Uh—thank you,: he said simply, not wanting to offend the blade by adding I think.

:Tell her, boy. Don't go into detail, keep it short and simple, but tell her. She needs to know.:

"Look, Nyara—" he said haltingly, wishing he could say half of what he wanted to. "I—I love you; I guess you've figured that out, but I thought I'd better say it. There. Nothing's going to change that. I'm not the picture of virtue—or innocence—I've seen more than you might think. I've spent time on Ancar's Border. I've seen girls—women—who've had pretty bad things happen to them. Who've been—I don't know. I guess you could say they've been betrayed by the parents who should have protected them. I know what you mean. You and I can't do anything about us until we get him out of our lives."

:A little confused, boy, but I think she got the gist of it. I'll have a little talk with her and lay things out for her later.: Again, that gravelly chuckle.

:I'll let her know you weren't just making pretty talk; you've seen things as rough as she's lived through. Who ever would have figured me for playing matchmaker. And at my age!:

Nyara only stared at him in dumb surprise, clutching the sword to her chest beneath her cloak of fur. But then one hand crept off the scabbard and moved down; searched for his and found it.

She gave him the ghost of a smile then. "Either you are lying, which Need says not—you are a saint, which she also says not—or you are as great a fool as I." She shook her head, but her eyes never left his.

"Well, then—let's be fools together," he whispered, staring down into her bottomless eyes. "I'm willing to work at it if you are."

Commotion at the entrance end of the Vale caught Darkwind's attention and broke into his brooding. Darkness had fallen some time ago, but he had not bothered to call any lights. Part of him still wanted to be angry with Firesong—angry at *someone*—but the rest of him knew that the Adept was punishing himself already. Anything he said or did would be superfluous, and likely cause much harm.

The disturbance was enough to let him know that a larger party than usual had crossed the Veil, and since the second shift of scouts had already gone out, this was not something expected. Something unexpected today could only mean trouble.

He sent a tentative inquiry to Vree, and the answer he received sent him shooting down the stairs of his *ekele* like a slung stone.

He met the tiny parade just past the first hot pool, and when he saw who had met Wintermoon's little troupe, as well as who was riding with it, he thought that he was dreaming.

The Outlander Skif rode his white Companion. Beside him to his right was Wintermoon on one of the two *dyheli* stags that had gone out with them. But on the left hand of the Herald was the second stag, who also bore a rider, and that was what caused him to stare and question his sanity. Nyara sat astride the *dyheli*, as if she had always known how to ride. She was clad in a rough bearskin cloak, carrying the blade she had taken across her lap.

Walking *beside* her, holding a mage-light to show the way and engaged in easy conversation with her, was Firesong.

Wintermoon held up his hand, and they stopped long enough to dismount. The *dyheli* walked off, into the side of the Vale, where the Clan kept grazing and water for their kind. Firesong stepped back to allow

Skif to aid Nyara from her mount, but then he fell in beside them, still deeply in conversation with both of them. Still more than a little stunned, Darkwind took his place beside his brother. Wintermoon thanked his mount and sent the stag on his way with a pat on the withers. Cymry walked ahead, but Darkwind had no doubt that she was following every word of Firesong's conversation.

"Who in the name of all gods is that?" Wintermoon asked, after hearty greetings between the two brothers.

"Firesong k'Treva. Healing Adept. The Council let us send for help," Darkwind replied. "He's—"

"Impressed by himself," Wintermoon completed. "But I'd guess that he must be something very special." He shook his head. "Brother, so much has happened to us since dawn this morning that I do not know where to begin."

"Then let me," Darkwind suggested. "After the last time you came in, Elspeth and I were permitted to call for aid. Firesong is what we received. He was more than we expected. And yes—he is of such power and ability that this arrogance of his is little more than pardonable pride, and almost a game to him."

Wintermoon only snorted. "Perhaps. I would like to see him in a situation where his pretty face means nothing, and he only frightens with his power. Take away the things he was born with, and I will be prepared to admire his accomplishments. But then, I am a crude man. Magic has never much impressed me."

Darkwind came so close to laughing that he choked, and gave his brother a quick embrace. "Nevertheless, he has been training me and the Outlanders."

"He has been training you, between attempting to impress the Outlander—"

"How am I to finish this tale?" Darkwind chided, then sobered. "Listen, there were ill things happened here, today. We were to attempt something small upon the Stone—when—"

"When Falconsbane raised his ugly head and attempted to foul the Vale," Wintermoon interrupted. "Do not fear to alarm me. That much we knew. Nyara felt the taint of her father, as did the Companion, and the sword knew where and that there had been a death. She said she did not think it was someone she knew. Whose death, then?"

"Tre'valen, the Shin'a'in shaman," Darkwind said, sorrow rising in him again. Wintermoon's eyes went wide with surprise. "He—the beast struck at our father, Wintermoon. Firesong shielded the Stone—no, do not interrupt me this time—had he not, none of us would be here to greet you. You would have returned to a smoking hole, and that I pledge you. I could do nothing, nor Elspeth; we were not quick enough.''

''But—Father obviously lives—was it Tre'valen that shielded him, then?'' Wintermoon shook his head, amazed. ''Surely though he is—was—a shaman, he could not have protected Father against the beast in his wrath!''

Darkwind nodded at everything his brother said, and was no little amazed at how much Wintermoon guessed correctly. ''Firesong thinks that he was not alone—that it was he and—and Dawnfire together who shielded Father.'' Now it was Darkwind's turn to shake his head. ''*He* does not know what happened to them, besides that Tre'valen is dead. I do not know what all this means. But there will be a little time to try to find meanings later. What is your tale?''

''Simple, compared to yours.'' Wintermoon took off his coat and slung it over one shoulder. ''I had struck signs of Nyara's presence and narrowed the search. I thought that we were within a day, perhaps two, of finding her. But instead, I woke to find her seated quite calmly in the midst of our camp.''

''Oh, so?'' He raised an eyebrow at that.

''The sword advised her to seek us out. Well, to seek Skif out, is closer to the truth. It was he that her eyes were upon, and it was he she wished to speak to, so I woke him. There was much sighing and exchanging of speaking looks.'' Wintermoon smiled, a smile tinged with sadness. ''I would be laughing if there were not so many things now that would make a laugh so greatly out of place. It was quite charming. A meeting out of a silly ballad, Darkwind, I could almost hear a harp a-playing. Skif would not thank me for telling you that. Well, I think I can safely say that the two are fairly smitten, absence from each other has only made the bond stronger, and that if I were a betting man, I would bet on them pairing as eagles. A true lovebond.''

Darkwind considered the two; considered what he and Elspeth had spoken of. ''I would not bet against you, but there are many obstacles in their way.'' *Not the least of which is her father—and what he will do to her if he finds her.*

''They know that. Which makes it—well—a better pairing, for my thinking. They know what they face, and face it together.'' Wintermoon gazed at the backs of those in front of him and smiled again. ''A good thing, to see some love in the midst of so much pain. But I should continue. Once we had gotten past the sighing and the looking and into the speaking, she would, I think, have spoken of those obstacles. But then came the attack upon the Vale." Wintermoon rubbed the back of his neck with one hand. "We decided to return. *She* determined to go with us, saying there was much she could tell us to aid against her father. I was not certain then of the wisdom of this, for she could be a breach in our defenses."

"Not with Need beside her," Darkwind said firmly. "I have spoken to Elspeth of the blade. Although she is not an Adept as we know them, she is very powerful, and has knowledge we do not."

Wintermoon nodded. "It did seem to me that Nyara was less feral and more human, but I only saw her once, and I thought I might have misremembered. Perhaps the sword is even able to change her. I knew, danger or no, that she must come here long enough to be given some kind of protection. If you have so powerful an Adept here, perhaps he can weave shieldings for her that will protect her. We cached the packs to make more speed, and returned as quickly as we could."

"When you arrived, was Firesong still at the entrance to the Vale?" Darkwind could not resist asking.

"That he was; quiet as an ice-statue, though he came to life quickly enough when he saw us." Wintermoon raised his eyebrows. "And that bird of his. It lit our way in. Is he always such a showman?"

Darkwind shrugged. "I cannot see how he could be anything less. I think it is part of his nature. But tell me, what did he make of the Changechild? I have heard that k'Treva is less forgiving of such creatures than we."

"If that is a trait of his Clan, he does not share it," Wintermoon said, a hint of speculation in his voice. "He did not even seem particularly startled, although if he viewed us from afar with the eyes of his bond-bird, he would have known what she was long before we rode through the Veil."

"And now he speaks with her." Darkwind ran a hand through his hair. "It is not what I would have expected of him."

:*Well, he's reserving judgment, boy,*: said a harsh mind-voice. :*He isn't terribly happy about having Falconsbane's daughter in his lap, but he thinks that he has some foolproof ways of telling if she's an enemy plant.*: A snort of laughter. :*As if I would leave any of the bastard's hooks in her!*:

Darkwind belatedly recognized the voice of the sword. :*I think you fully capable, warlady,:* he said carefully. *:Let me ask you this; is she ready to face her father?:*

:Alone? Hellfires, no. Not in a century. There's only so much I can do with the raw material. Only so much I can do. I'm no great Adept, just a mage-smith: The sword sounded surprisingly—humble? Darkwind found the changes in Need as interesting as the changes in Nyara. *:I'll promise you this, though; give that girl proper backing, and she'll defy her father. Though she hasn't quite figured it out yet, she's not his frightened slave anymore.:*

That was good news; the first of the day.

"Unless you have something planned—" Wintermoon began. Fire-song stopped, turned, and interrupted him.

"I think," the young Adept said, pitching his voice so that they all heard him clearly, "It is time to call a Council."

Iceshadow

Chapter
Twenty

It was a strange conference, held in a clearing below Firesong's borrowed *ekele*. Firesong's *hertasi* scrambled to bring food and drink for the participants, some of whom, like Firesong himself, Darkwind, and Elspeth, had not eaten for some time. Food had not seemed particularly important to Darkwind, but of course to the *hertasi*, it was a source of much disapproval that they had neglected themselves. The lizards hovered all over them, but paid particular attention to Firesong. There were, predictably, twice as many *hertasi* attending him as anyone else.

The conference was also a small one; Iceshadow, representing the Elders and mages, Darkwind, Firesong, Wintermoon for the scouts, Nyara, the blade Need. Kethra sent her regrets that she could not attend; she would not leave Starblade's bed. Elspeth had been reluctant to join in it, but at Firesong's urging, she too took her place in the circle. Skif presented himself at Nyara's side and would not be moved, and Darkwind urged the Companions to take places beside their Heralds as well.

The conference was interrupted immediateiy by yet another visitor, reminding them all that there was more at stake than just the Vale.

The *kyree* bounded into the group and planted himself right next to Nyara without even asking for permission. Darkwind recognized Rris immediately, by the jaunty tilt of his head and his alert eyes and ears. Firesong was somewhat taken aback by the *kyree's* brashness, and Darkwind was so amused to see his reaction that he insisted that Rris be allowed to speak.

:I am sent from Treyvan and Hydona,: the *kyree* said, holding his head up and refusing to be intimidated by Firesong's measuring glances. *:Those are the gryphons, young cub,:* he said then, with a kindly, patronizing tone to his mind-voice, turning to give Firesong a measuring glance of his own. *:They are the allies of this Vale, and they wish to know what has happened. Beyond the obvious, that is—the action of Mornelithe Falconsbane and the death of the shaman.:*

Darkwind hid his smile behind a cough. He himself had taken the time to send a message to the gryphons, but Rris had obviously been coached. And he had a shrewd idea by whom.

:They wish to know what you intend to do,: Rris continued blithely. *:They have taken steps; they have fortified their lair, which lies near to the node in the ruins. They have shielded that node, so that no one may use it but themselves. And they have found the old, buried Gate and have shielded it, so that Falconsbane may not use it to return. But they must know what their allies intend as well. And they wish the council to know that, with the sword Need, they vouch for the Changechild Nyara; that they feel she is trustworthy, for they have been aware of her movements and actions since she left their lair.:*

He lay down then, obviously very pleased with himself. Darkwind knew why; he had delivered Treyvan's message word for word with the proper tone, and no one had interrupted him. Darkwind hoped that Firesong was reading that pleasure as a taste of Rris' own self-conceit.

Young cub. I thought he was going to lose those eyebrows up into his hair.

But there was at least one surprise in all of that for him, as well; the gryphons had known where Nyara was and what she was doing. And they vouched for her.

Firesong might have lost the initial control of the council, but he regained it as soon as he stood up to speak.

"I have been lacking in forethought," he said, quietly. "I have not thought that Mornelithe Falconsbane could still be a danger, if he even lived. That was an error, and one that has cost a precious life. Perhaps two; I do not know if the one called Dawnfire also perished with Tre'valen. I think it is time that we deal with both our problems in a coordinated fashion. Our first problem is the Heartstone, for until we remove it as a threat, Falconsbane can use it against us, as he nearly did earlier. Then we must deal with Falconsbane himself."

He looked around the circle, and got nods of agreement from everyone. "To that end let each of us say what he knows, both of what happened this day, and what in the past may have been involved. Never mind that it has all been said before; there are going to be some of us that have not heard all the tale from all the participants."

He began, with his perception of the attack. The various stories took some time to complete, but in the end, even Darkwind was satisfied. Some of the pieces were beginning to make a whole.

"Now that we have built the proper picture, I see two different needs that must be addressed at the same time." Firesong shifted restlessly from foot to foot. "*I* know what must be done with the Stone, and those of you who are to help me should hear of this now, so that there is no more mystery. But what we are to do about Falconsbane, I do not know. I think that I would be of little aid there, for I am not well-versed in combative magics. I am not versed in combat, to speak of, at all, but I am not certain that direct combat, with magic or not, is the proper way to deal with him."

Darkwind must have looked a little surprised at Firesong's confession that there was something he did not know, for he caught the Adept's sardonic glance in his direction.

"So this is my suggestion. That we have two councils. I shall have Elspeth and Darkwind, the gryphons' representative—" he bowed ironically to Rris, who only bowed gravely back at him. "—and the Companion Gwena. If Iceshadow and Wintermoon would care to lead the other, I think that Nyara may know some ways of countering her father. She will certainly know more of his ways and his stronghold than any of the rest of us. And surely the sword Need knows combat by magic *and* blade far, far better than I."

:Thank you, youngster,: came Need's dry response, broadcast clearly to all. *:I do have a little experience there.:*

Firesong's eyebrows flew up into his hair again, but he did not comment. Wisely, Darkwind thought. One did not pick quarrels with edged wit or edged weapons. "When we have all reached some sort of conclusion, we will meet again as one, this time with the full k'Sheyna Council. Will that suit you all?"

"It suits me very well," Iceshadow said cautiously. Wintermoon and

Skif nodded. "Well, then, let us withdraw to my *ekele*, and leave this place to the others."

Firesong made some show of finding a place to sit while the others followed Iceshadow down one of the paths. Only when they were completely out of earshot, did the young Adept sigh, and look from Darkwind to Elspeth and back.

"Here is what I intend," he said, quietly. "Attend, sir *kyree;* you must carry this back to the gryphons as soon as I have done, for this is dangerous working that I propose, and I want—no, I need—them to participate."

Rris nodded, and pricked his ears forward eagerly.

Firesong took a deep breath.

"I intend to shatter the Heartstone."

At Darkwind's instinctive move of protest, he shook his head. "No, not as Falconsbane sought to—and not releasing the energy wildly. Faceting a precious stone is not the same as striking it with a mallet. No, I intend to do this under complete control. First, I wish to *prepare* the Stone as if it were to become a Gate. Call it a proto-Gate. I shall work only with the energy tied to the Stone, but never the Stone itself. That will anchor all of the energy but not in a physical anchor."

Darkwind nodded slowly. This made sense, but it was not something he would ever have considered. Everyone knew that creating a Gate anchored energy, but no one would have ever considered making a Stone into a Gate. It would entail circling the powers about the Stone from without; he did not even want to consider what would happen to someone who actually used such a Gate.

"K'Sheyna has prepared a new Stone in the new Vale—yes?" At Darkwind's nod, he continued. "Once *this* stone is shattered, the proto-Gate will be drawn to the point of greatest attraction and to the point that is nearest in type to the old Stone. It will seek, we shall push it gently in the proper direction. That should be the new Stone, for both were created by the same mages. It will carry the remaining ley-lines with it. We can guide its movement from here."

"That's not going to happen quickly," Darkwind put in.

"No. It will take several Adepts in relays to move it, and they will be working for several days to do so. But this should work." Firesong looked to Rris. "The shielding will be undertaken in pairs; like the shielding when a Heartstone is moved, but with double the mages. The pairs will be male-female, to enforce the balancing. I wish the gryphons to be in the West, if they would. Can you tell them that, as well as all else you have heard tonight? Can you remember?"

:*Surely*,: the *kyree* replied, with a lift of his head that signified slightly offended pride. :*I know every kyree history-song, every tale the Tayledras have shared with my clan, and all of the four-hundred and twenty-three tales of my famous cousin Warrl. Carrying what I have heard to Trevyan and Hydona is no great task at all.*:

Darkwind felt his lips twitching.

:*With your permission, I shall go to them*,: Rris finished. At Firesong's nod, he was off, leaping across the circle and into the underbrush, presumably on his way back to the ruins.

Gwena chose that moment to absent herself, leaving only Firesong, Darkwind, and Elspeth. Darkwind was about to take himself off as well, when Firesong put out a restraining hand.

"There is trouble between us, Darkwind," he said levelly. "That trouble has not been purged. There is trouble between you and the Wingsister, for you have not truly dealt with it. And there is trouble between Elspeth and myself, for there are some assumptions that she has made that I have not corrected."

Darkwind's stomach knotted with sudden tension. He would have liked to make an escape, but he did not dare.

"These must be dealt with, all, before we enter the circle together," Firesong said but instead of turning first to Darkwind, he faced Elspeth.

"You have not been honest with Darkwind," he said levelly.

"I—" She started to protest, but the protests died on her lips under his stern gaze.

"You have not told him your true feelings concerning me," the Adept continued. "He has sensed it, but you have avoided dealing with your own feelings, and with him. You have not told him the truth."

"I—suppose not. I am very attracted to Darkwind. Very. But—you—" She shrugged helplessly. "I can't help it, and it isn't just because you're so infernally beautiful. Firesong—" She blushed furiously, and hung her head. "I've never wanted anyone—physically—quite so much."

Darkwind felt his jealousy rising to eat him alive. Had she been fantasizing that her lover was Firesong every time that the two of them had. . . ?

"Well." Firesong nodded coolly, not in the least perturbed—or impressed. "You are not the first female to attempt to fling herself at me.

Let me tell you that you are a good student, Elspeth, and worthy of the praise that I have given you. But you must know this; I am not as you think.''

She shook her head, obviously not understanding. For that matter, Darkwind couldn't imagine what Firesong was getting at.

"I am," he said delicately, "the true descendant of your Herald Vanyel, on both sides of my family. It is from his blood that I have my power." Then, before Elspeth could register *that* surprise, he continued. "I inherited more than his power."

She shook her head; clearly she did not understand what he was trying to tell her.

He arched an eyebrow in Darkwind's direction. "Perhaps I should be a little more explicit. Elspeth, while I am sure you are a very attractive woman to some, it is Darkwind's hair that *I* would choose to braid feathers into if I could." He licked his lips. "In point of fact, I have been wishing that since I first laid eyes upon him. Had he not put his own feelings toward you out where anyone could see them, I should already have done so."

And Firesong actually *blushed.*

Elspeth had thought she had come to the end of the surprises that living with the Hawkbrothers brought, but this last series had caught her flatfooted.

First, of course—that the famous Vanyel had left *any* offspring. There was no record of that in any of the Chronicles, and no hint of it in any of the songs and ballads. Then came the revelation that Firesong was the descendant of that child—or children. There was no reason to doubt him; he had never lied before, and why lie about something so stupid, something that couldn't be proved or disproved here? Firesong already had plenty of status—and presumably fame—on his own; he surely didn't need to boast of a bloodline like some fading, failed highborn.

But the last surprise—

That he's—dear gods, what do they call it here? Shay'a'chern? Is that where we get shaych? Why am I thinking about where a word came from when—

When he wants Darkwind *and not me. . . .*

First came a rush of profound embarrassment. She hadn't been made a fool of. She'd made a fool of herself quite nicely on her own, with no help from Firesong, making assumptions she had no right to make. She just wanted to crawl away and hide somewhere.

But then she was overcome by a flood of jealousy. But not of Firesong's attraction to Darkwind. No, she was jealous—and afraid of—Darkwind's possible attraction to Firesong. She *knew* the Tayledras were a lot more flexible about sexual matters than the people of Valdemar, even the Heralds. What if, now that Firesong's preferences were out in the open, Darkwind preferred him to her?

She was so jealous she was literally sick. Her stomach and shoulders were in knots; her throat too tight to speak.

Firesong was watching both of them, wearing an unreadable little smile, and measuring them from beneath his long white lashes. What was he thinking? Did he know how she felt? Was he amused?

Once again, she was dizzy with embarrassment, sick with the emotions warring for control of her.

She flushed, then paled, feeling herself growing hot, then cold, then hot again. Her ears burned, and the back of her neck; her hands grew cold, and she fought dizziness as she looked up with defiance into Firesong's face.

There was no doubt that the Adept had at least some idea of her internal battling; Firesong's smile increased, just a trifle. He tossed his head, sending his hair whipping back over his shoulders, and deliberately, tauntingly, lifted his chin at her. Then he grinned insolently, and turned away, walking off into the darkness, leaving his mage-lights behind him.

She couldn't look at Darkwind. She couldn't *not* look at him. She tried to look at him out of the corner of her eye, but caught his eyes by accident and was forced either to meet his eyes or look quickly away. She chose the former.

He coughed, and she saw to her increased confusion—as if it *could* be increased any further—that he was flushed a little himself. No, more than a little; the peculiar illumination of the mage-lights tended to wash his color out. Her hands were cold, her face still flushed, but she no longer felt so sick.

"I feel like a fool," he said, just before the silence became unendurable. "I feel like a true and crowned fool."

"Well, imagine how *I* feel," she said sharply. "Especially when I realized that I didn't care a pin how he felt about me or *you*, but—"

"But?" he prompted, and she flushed again, feeling her ears, neck, and cheeks burning.

She didn't really want to answer him, but if she didn't, she'd never know what his feelings were in the matter. "It really made me very unhappy to think you—might—" She shook her head, and finally looked right at him. "All right!" she snapped, angrily. "I was *jealous*, if that's what you wanted to know! I was jealous, because you might be more interested in him than you are in me!"

He simply watched her, soberly, without so much as twitching a muscle. He didn't say a thing, and now she was sick with embarrassment again. And with humiliation.

She knew, now that Firesong had pressed the issue and humbled her by forcing her to reveal things she had kept only to herself, that her attraction to Firesong had been nothing more than simple infatuation. It had only been complicated because she had so admired his competence, his intelligence, as well as his stunning looks.

But Darkwind was competent and intelligent. And her attraction to him was something a great deal deeper. Deep enough to move her to jealousy; deep enough to make her willing to make a fool of herself, if it came to that.

"I have *been* a fool," Darkwind said quietly. "Even as you. Perhaps it was as much due to stress as anything else. We have been living a lifetime in the past few moons. We have both of us changed, sometimes profoundly. I can only take comfort in one of the Shin'a'in sayings— 'No one has lived who has not been a fool at least once.' And," he summoned up a ghost of a smile, "with luck, we have had our entire lifetime's foolery from this."

"Oh I hope so," she replied fervently.

"But there is one other thing. I think *that* one," he nodded after the departed Firesong, "brings trouble with him as easily and purposefully as he brings baggage. I think that no matter where he went, he would leave unsuspecting folk in some kind of tangle. And I do think that at some level he enjoys doing so."

Elspeth found herself smiling a little; the heat eased from her ears and neck, and her stomach calmed. "No doubt about it," she said wryly, as her flush faded. "He would just revel in having the entire Vale fussing over him the way the *hertasi* do. I doubt he'd be happy if he wasn't the center of attention."

"Oh, and he would enjoy having us at odds over him as well," Darkwind replied. "Make no mistake about it. He is aptly named. I suspect he leaves lovers strewn in his wake like old, dead leaves. He would take great pleasure in being the centerpiece of a quarrel, only to turn about and mend it. But he is too much the Healing Adept to allow that to happen now in a situation this important. In a quieter time, perhaps."

"Well, he isn't going to get another chance from me," she replied firmly. "Let him go play his games with someone else." She shook her head, and realized that the muscles of her neck and shoulders were aching with tenseness. "Look, after all that, I need a soak. Come with me?"

He smiled, and reached for her hand. She met him halfway. "A good notion," he replied clasping his warm hand around her cold one.

Moments later, they were side by side in the hot pool below her *ekele.* She sighed as the heat and her own deliberate attempt to relax her muscles took effect, easing the stiffness and some of the pain.

It was very dark under the tree, and neither of them put up a magelight to illuminate the shadows. He was a silent presence in the water beside her; not touching her, but there nevertheless. Above them the ever-present breezes of the Vale stirred the leaves of the tree; somewhere in the distance, a bird sang for a moment, then fell silent. Or perhaps it was someone playing a flute.

Darkwind lifted a hand out of the water, and the sound of drops falling from it to the pool seemed very loud. Elspeth emptied her mind and let it drift, full of nothing but the sounds around her.

"Do you think he meant that?" Darkwind said, finally.

"Do I think who meant what?" she asked, lazily.

"Firesong. Do you think he meant what he said about—" Darkwind hesitated. "—about me?"

"Why?" she asked, fiercely. "Because if you plan on taking him up on it, I'll—I'll—" She sought desperately for the most absurd thing she could say. "I'll *scratch* his big blue eyes out!"

Darkwind laughed, and she let relief wash over her again. "No, I do *not* plan on taking him up on it."

"Good," she replied. "Because in a cat-fight, I'd win."

"I believe you would," he said lazily.

"That's because I'd cheat," she continued.

"I *know* you would," he chuckled.

Then she reached toward him and found his hand catching hers, pulling her toward him. She decided not to fight and let her body drift to his.

"You would do that for me?" he asked. "Fight, cheat—"

"Well, fight, anyway. I'd only cheat if it was Firesong because he'd already be cheating." He put his arm around her, and suddenly it was good just to rest her head on his chest and listen to the night.

"He probably would." He took one or two deep breaths. "I do not think that you need to worry about Firesong, however." Another breath. "Or shall I show you that, so that you truly believe me?"

"Please," she said, surprising herself.

Then he surprised her.

Darkwind held Elspeth's hand, facing Iceshadow and Nightjewel across the circle, the Stone standing ominously in the middle, half-obscuring the other couple. To the right, Treyvan and Hydona faced the crazed surface of the Stone with no sign of trepidation; to the left, Starblade and Kethra stood, hand in hand, in a peculiar echo of Darkwind and Elspeth's own pose. In the middle of their carefully constructed circle was the Stone.

It *showed* its damage now, and not just to the inner eye. Trails of sullen red light crawled over its surface, strange little paths of lightning in miniature. Every line that could be severed from it, had been, and had been reattached to the node beneath the gryphons' lair. That had taken a full day, with a working team of the gryphons, Elspeth, and himself—and Firesong and Need.

He had been surprised when Firesong appeared with the blade in hand, he was amazed when the Adept actually *used* Need's powers. The two couples had held a warding about the circle, as the Adept and the blade together severed all but two of the remaining ley-lines and relocated them to the node beneath the lair. Firesong was not inclined to explain how he could use magics so openly feminine, and Need held her peace when Darkwind questioned the Adept. Elspeth was just as astonished. It was Nyara herself who had provided the answer, with an odd shyness, when he asked her.

"He is balanced," she had told Darkwind. "He is completely balanced between his masculine and feminine sides. So even as he can use man's magic, he can also use woman's magic, magic keyed only to females."

"Such as what Need holds?" he had asked.

She had nodded. "And since she is willing to do so, she can feed her power through his feminine side. She would not be able to do that, were he not so balanced.''

So although Nyara did not have the mage-strength to enter the circle and wield the blade effectively in this case, Need was there anyway, and lending her power to the isolating of the Stone.

Falconsbane, thank the gods, remained quiet during that day, and during the day that it took for Firesong—alone, completely unaided—to create the proto-Gate from the Stone's remaining power. He would permit no one else within the shielded area. It was too dangerous, he said, and something about his unusual grimness made Darkwind believe him completely. Darkwind and Elspeth took a patrol on the edge of the Vale, encountering nothing more dangerous than a lone *wyrsa*, and returned to linger outside the shielded area, waiting for Firesong to emerge.

That was when he finally realized just what it meant to be a mage as powerful as Firesong. What it meant to be a Healing Adept, in terms of personal cost.

As the sun set, Firesong staggered across the invisible pass-through at the boundary and fell into their arms. No longer the arrogant, self-assured young peacock; he was drained, shaking, drenched with sweat. His very hair hung lank and limp with exhaustion. He was hardly able to stand, much less walk.

They held him up, Darkwind's heart in his throat, until he told them in a hoarse voice that he was all right. "Just—tired," he had croaked. "Very—tired. I have—called help.''

The white *dyheli* that had brought him to the Vale appeared at that moment as if conjured, and Darkwind helped the Adept up onto the stag's back at his direction. "My *hertasi* are waiting,'' Firesong had whispered, from under a curtain of sweat-soaked hair. "I told them what to expect, what I would require. Thank you for helping me.''

"Shall I get some other help?'' Darkwind had asked, uncertainly.

The curtain of hair had shaken a faint negative. "They know what to do. It is their ancient function. I shall be well enough in a day or so.''

Darkwind had nodded and stepped back, letting the *dyheli* bear his burden away.

And Firesong *had* been well enough in a day, making a recovery that seemed little short of miraculous to anyone who had seen him the day before. It seemed he had recovery skills as remarkable as his other skills.

Darkwind and Elspeth had taken another turn as border guardians, with both of them expecting trouble from Falconsbane at any moment. But no trouble came, nothing more than some odd glimpses of shadow riders, who *could* have been little more than nerves and an overactive imagination. Certainly they left no traces on the fresh snow. At the end of that day, they had returned to find Firesong waiting for them, fully restored.

"Tomorrow," he had said. "It must be tomorrow. Starblade and Kethra are not as strong as I would like, but Nyara is afraid that with every passing day, it becomes more likely that her father will strike again. Need agrees, and I will not underestimate Falconsbane again if I can help it. I will go to instruct the gryphons this evening, and we shall gather on the morrow."

Darkwind still did not know exactly what passed between Firesong and the gryphons, but it must have been interesting. Hydona would surely have met his young arrogance with an arrogance of her own, and Treyvan would have deflated Firesong with a few well-chosen comments. Nevertheless, here they were, calmly prepared to do what they must.

And in the center of the circle, ready to strike when all was prepared—Firesong and Need.

The young Adept looked carefully at each one of his chosen pairs, meeting the eyes of each of them in turn. Darkwind brought his chin up and nodded in answer to that unspoken challenge, and Elspeth showed the ghost of a feral smile. What Firesong saw must have convinced him that they were ready, for he nodded.

"Let us begin," he said simply, with no elaborate speeches. There was no need for speeches, after all. They all knew what they were to do, they had drilled together as much as they could. If they were not ready now, nothing anyone could say would make any difference.

Darkwind already held Elspeth's physical hand; now he held out a mental hand, and felt her take it firmly, but without clutching. He let the power build between them for a moment, then he bent his attention (though not his eyes) to the left, where his father and Kethra stood. Elspeth turned hers to the right.

He sensed Kethra building the power between herself and Starblade; then having secured her ground, she bent her attention to him, and he held out another "hand" to her. She took it, fumbling a bit at first, then her "grip" firmed. It was the clasp of a warrior, for all that she was a Healer.

:But a Healer fights for the lives of her patients, does she not? As much a

warrior as a bladesman.: Kethra said lightly; then she braced herself to make their bond as strong as possible.

On the right, he sensed Treyvan catching Elspeth's extended "hand." At that moment, the circle trembled for a heartbeat, until all the powers within it found their balance points. Male and female, human and gryphon, old and young; earth, air, fire, and water; Tayledras, Valdemaran, Shin'a'in, far-traveler. . . .

Then the unexpected; when the balance came, it brought with it a sense of wholeness and astonished joy, a lift to his spirits like nothing he had felt since the Heartstone shattered. He saw his surprise mirrored in Kethra's eyes; felt it in the trembling of Elspeth's physical hand in his. He wanted to shout, to laugh, to sing—*this* was how magery should be! This marvelous feeling of rightness!

Movement at the center of the circle caught his attention, and he looked up for a moment at Firesong. The young Adept was smiling, his eyes alight—and somehow Darkwind knew that the wholeness, the joy, came from him.

Was *this* how Firesong felt every time he worked magic? No wonder it was effortless for him . . . no wonder he was willing to exhaust himself, drain himself to nothing, if this was his reward.

Somewhere in the back of his mind, Darkwind wondered if he would ever feel this way again—knew he never would—and at the same time, knew there would always be a little of this whenever he worked a spell. The touch of the Healer Adept had given that much to him.

The eight of them bound themselves ever closer, with Elspeth weaving their power around and about the circle until it was no longer a circle, but a shell of energy as precise as a porcelain egg, as strong as sword-steel.

Firesong began to tap his foot. He could not bring a drum into the circle, for he could not use it and Need at the same time—but standing just behind Starblade and well within the danger area was Nyara. She caught Firesong's rhythm, and began to drum with a skill Darkwind had not suspected of her. Darkwind picked up the rhythm within a few beats, moving his legs and loosening up; the others followed upon it. The stamping of his feet was enough like a dance that his own magic gained in strength; and where Elspeth's lightweaving gave their construct form, his dancing gave it movement, making it dance, so that there were no weak places, and no places holding still long enough to be weakened by an attack.

He closed his eyes and gave himself up to the rhythm; sensing Elspeth holding firm beside him. Sensing Firesong waiting, poised above the waiting Stone, choosing his moment—

Then, he *struck.*

Need rang as she impacted the Heartstone pointfirst, but instead of the shriek of agony that Darkwind had expected, there came a single bell-like tone.

The sound filled the air and filled his soul; carried all other sounds away, drowning them, and he sensed that they *must* contain it, or it would ring through the Vale and shatter everything in its path.

Nyara threw herself into the drumming, and though he could no longer hear it, he felt it. He threw all of his power and will into the effort of holding—holding—holding until he thought he must fall.

He felt himself faltering, felt the circle faltering. He steeled himself and poured more energy in. He sensed a change in the tone.

It was weakening, fading away.

That gave him his second wind and the strength to keep his place, to keep the power contained. As it faded, so did his strength, but always just a little behind the tone so that his ability to keep it contained was just enough to do so.

Finally it was gone, faded into an echo, then into nothing.

He opened his eyes, swaying on his feet, and looked around. Firesong leaned heavily on the blade, which was buried to the hilt in a pile of uneven, dull-gray shards. Starblade leaned on Kethra's shoulder, and even as he watched, Iceshadow and Nightjewel sank to the ground together. Even the gryphons' heads were hanging down with weariness. But when Treyvan finally raised his head with an effort, and looked into Darkwind's eyes, Darkwind saw satisfaction and triumph that mirrored his own there.

"Brothers," came the weary voice from the center of the circle. "Sisters. We have succeeded."

:Damn if we haven't,: Need said, and even the sword sounded exhausted. *:Damn if we haven't.:*

Firesong stood erect again, pulling himself up with an effort, and with a single gesture, banished the circle of power beyond them that had contained the rogue Stone for so long. He shared that power among them, equally, giving them all the strength to stand firmly again. Not much more than that, but at least they were no longer about to drop.

Darkwind did not need to close his eyes to sense the burning lens of power that had been the Stone and was now the proto-Gate. It hovered between this world and the world of Gates and ley-lines, affected by both—yet no longer the malignant, near-sentient thing it had been. Now it was only power. And now that the shields were down, the gryphons were able to draw safely on the clean power of their own node.

They lost their weariness, legs straightening, wings refolding with a *snap*, heads coming up.

Nyara entered the former circle quietly, and Firesong handed Need back to her with a little bow of courtesy before he turned back to the gryphons. "Well," he said, his voice already stronger, as he shared the power they were drawing from the node they had made their own. "And are you ready for the first stage of the move?"

"Lead on, featherrlesssss one," Treyvan said, cocking his head sideways. "And congratulationssss. That wasss *well* done."

Firesong had that arrogant little smile back, but this time Darkwind was not going to fault him for it. This had been the most brilliant, innovative piece of magic he had ever seen—and, he suspected, was ever likely to see.

"Thank you," Firesong replied with no show of humility at all, false or otherwise. "That was the hardest part. The rest, though it will be tedious, will be much easier."

"Hmm. Yesss. Perrhapsss. It isss not wissse to count the eyassess until they arrre fledged." Hydona roused her feathers with a shake, so much like Vree that Darkwind chuckled despite his weariness. "Ssstill, sssoonesst begun isss sssoonessst done. Let usss deal with thisss prrroto-Gate of yoursss before it getsss the notion to wanderrr on itsss own."

As the rest of them gathered themselves up and headed for the Council Oak, where the *hertasi* had assembled food and drink, Darkwind sighed with relief and squeezed Elspeth's hand. The worst, indeed, was over. No matter what else happened, Falconsbane would not be able to destroy the Vale and Stone together. So for now, at least, they were safe.

Or as safe as they were likely to get, with Falconsbane still out there. Still plotting. Still watching.

Still Falconsbane . . . a terrible and implacable foe.

The Black Riders

Chapter
Twenty-one

There was a peculiar feeling to the Featherless Fools' Vale today. Falconsbane could not quite put his finger on what it was, but he sensed that they had redoubled their shielding on the Stone again. They had also reduced the number of lines on the Stone to a bare two, but those were the most powerful of all. It would not have been possible to sever either of them—no matter how good that Adept thought he was.

He smiled to himself, fingering the tiny, carved horse—which was *not* onyx, nor obsidian, nor any other stone he knew. It could not be chipped nor marred in any way at all, no matter what he did to it. It should have been fragile. He had even ordered one of his artisans to strike it with a stone sledgehammer when nothing *he* had done had affected it in any way. It had chipped the hammer; obviously, it was anything but fragile.

A puzzle; like those who had sent it.

One he did not have time for, as matters stood. He needed to concentrate on his plan for k'Sheyna, a plan that required patience and vigilance, but would pay for that patience handsomely. The Bird Lovers could put all the shields they wanted to on that Stone of theirs; they still wouldn't be able to save it. And the moment they dropped the shielding, he would be waiting. He would not fail a second time.

Let them only drop the shield. He had been waiting for days now, buried in his study, gathering his strength, preparing a single, lightning strike that would overwhelm Starblade, burn away his mind, and burn *through* him to the Stone.

It was a new sort of action for him—and thus, he thought, it would be unexpected and unanticipated. There would be no testing, no struggling of wills. Just one single, quick, clean blow, spending all of his power in that strike and holding none in reserve. A reckless kind of action, audacious. Starblade would flare up like a stick of dry kindling, and a moment later, his home would follow, Adept and all. It was not the end he would have chosen for Starblade or his followers, but it would at least be revenge.

Only let them drop the shield—

He watched, as patient as a cat at a mousehole, as a lion above a salt lick, knowing that to reestablish those lines they would have to drop the shield—to use the power of the node in the ruins to try to heal the Stone, they would have to drop the shield. Sooner or later, it would have to come down. There was not enough untainted power within the Vale to even begin to heal the Stone.

Assuming it could be healed. He didn't think that was possible. He had hundreds of years of mage-craft behind him, and he would not have cared to try it.

He had caught his attention wandering for a moment and had redoubled his vigilance when a trembling of the shields alerted him to changes within the Vale.

LIGHT!

He fell back onto his couch with a cry of pain, squeezing his watering eyes shut, holding his ears, in a futile reaction to the blinding wall of "light" and "sound" that assaulted his Sight and Hearing.

If he had not been watching the Vale and the emanations of the Stone within it, he might have missed the death of the Stone itself. If he had been concentrating on something in the material world, he would never have noticed what had happened, for the only effect was in the nonmaterial plane. But since he was, and looking right at it with all of his powers—

For a moment it blinded his inner eye when it exploded in light and sound. A lesser mage would have been struck unconscious and possibly come away with his Senses damaged.

It *did* send him graying-out for a moment, and fighting his way back to consciousness. That was all that was possible; to hold tightly to reality and claw his way back—he couldn't think, couldn't do anything else.

When he came back to himself, the Stone was gone.

He could only sit and blink in dumbfounded shock.

At first he simply could not believe what had happened. It made no sense, it was simply not in the Tayledras to have done such a thing. He thought for a moment that he *had* been Headblinded; that his Senses had failed him.

Then shock gave way to anger. All his plans—destroyed in a single moment! How could he have so completely misjudged them? They should have tried to *save* their Stone, not destroy it! This was something those suicidal Shin'a'in might have tried, but never the Tayledras!

He shook his head, growling in bafflement and increasing rage. His head pounded with reaction-pain; his temples throbbed, and a sharp, hot jabbing at the base of his skull warned him that he was overstressing himself. The pain only increased his anger. How could they have done something so completely unexpected, so entirely out of character? More than that, how had they accomplished it, without destroying the Vale as he had intended to do?

His inner eyes were still dazzled, his outer eyes streamed burning tears in reaction, but he strained his Sight toward the Vale anyway, hoping for a glimpse of something that might give him a clue as to how this unknown Adept had worked the impossible.

Then, as the dazzle cleared under the pressure of his will, he got more than a clue. Far more.

Hanging in the between-world where Gates and ley-lines were born, was a lenticular form of pure, shining Power. It occupied the same not-space that the Stone had taken—or rather, that the Power the Stone contained had taken. For a long, stunned moment, he simply stared at it, wondering where it had come from and what it was. It didn't resemble anything that had been in or near the Vale before. It didn't resemble anything he had ever seen before, for that matter. And how had it gotten where the Power-form of the Stone had been? How had those two ley-lines gotten attached to it? He had never seen lines running to anything but nodes or Stones before.

He realized at that moment that it *was* the Stone—or rather, it was what had taken the place of the Stone. Whatever that Adept had done to the Stone, destroying it had purified the Power and allowed him to give it a new shape. There were only the two lines leading into it, and it was no longer anything he could use or control—or even touch, directly. It had become something that answered to one hand only, and that hand was not his. Power with monofocused purpose, and linked to a particular personality.

In fact, it was very like a Gate. Except that there could not be more than a handful of Adepts great enough to create a Gate with power that was *not* their own.

He nearly rejected that identification out of hand; even the Bird-Fools would not be so foolhardy as to make a Gate within a node, much less within a Stone! And why create a Gate with so much power in the first place? You couldn't use it; anything passing through a Gate like that stood a better-than-even chance of winding up annihilated.

But this was not a Gate, exactly. It was something like a Gate; something that could become a Gate with more shaping. But it was not, in and of itself, a Gate. In fact, the more he examined it, the less like a Gate it became. There was no terminus; it was entirely self-contained. There was no structure that it was linked to; it was linked to the half-world, a kind of Gate doubled back upon itself. That, in fact, was what gave it all the stability it had.

It was more like one of the little seeking tendrils of power a Gate would spin out, trying to reach its terminus.

As he thought that, he Saw it move, a little; watched it as it swung slightly to the west and north, seeking something—

Then he understood. It *was* seeking something, and that was why it had been made along the pattern of a Gate.

It was seeking the empty vessel that should have held it, the physical container that had been made by the same hands that had shaped its old vessel. The new Stone in the new Vale.

Unbelievable. Incredible. Something he would never have thought of doing, had he been in the same position.

For a moment, he could only blink at the astonishing audacity of it all. Bold, reckless—not only brilliant, but innovative.

A worthy foe. Not another Urtho, of course, but he was no longer Ma'ar. If he were going to be honest with himself—which he tried to avoid—he would have to admit that another Urtho would not find him much of a challenge these days. Or would he? They would both find themselves dealing with limited power . . . with magic that followed another set of laws, twisted by the end of their own warring.

Pah, I am woolgathering! No wonder the infant stole a march on me!

Infant? No—young, but no infant. Old in cunning and in skill—youthful only in years. I wonder . . . is he as beautiful as the rest of the Bird Lovers I have seen?

For another moment, he was overcome by a feeling of complete and overpowering *lust*. And not just for the power—but for the one who had created and conceived this plan. What would it be like to have such a one under *his* control, subject to his whims and fancies, placing his abilities at Mornelithe's call?

What would it be like to be under the control of such a one. . . ?

He shook the thoughts away angrily. Ridiculous! These Bird Lovers were *winning!* He could not permit that! Surely there was something he could do to wrench control of the thing out of their hands.

Wait; go at it backward. What would he do if he had it? What would it mean?

It would attract lines to itself; set in a neutral place, it would soon be the center of a web of lines as complete and complex as the old Stone had owned.

If I had this power-locus, I would have control of the entire energy-web of this area. I could pull all the lines to myself without effort, like a spider whose net spins itself. It would be like my present network of traps and wards, but with such power to tap. . . .

His thumb caressed the tiny horse as he chewed his lip, his mind running in furious thought. Then the image of the spider in the web came to him again. And with it, an idea.

So, little mage, we are going to try new magics, are we? He smiled, and his smile turned vicious. *Two can play that game. There was a time when I anchored a permanent Gate upon myself, after all.*

That had been far, far back in the past, before the so-clever Hawk-brothers had ever stretched their wings over this area. When it had been *his*, and he had fought to possess it against what seemed to be an endless supply of upstarts. He had been younger then, and willing to try things no one thought possible, for he had already sired a dozen children on as many mothers, human and Changechild, and he was secure in the continuance of his bloodline. And so long as there was someone with direct descent and Mage-Gifts alive, *he* was immortal. Wild chances had been worth the risk.

No one had ever tried to shift the focus of a permanent Gate from a place to a *person*. His advisors said it could not be done, that the power would destroy the person.

And yet, in the end, the temporary Gates were all partially anchored in a person, for the energy to create them came from that person. He had thought it worth trying. Permanent Gates had their own little webs of ley-lines, and acted much like small nodes—that was before he had learned of the Hawkbrains and their Heartstones, and had learned to lust after *real* power. It had seemed a reasonable thing, to try to make himself the center of a web of that kind of power.

So he had researched the magics, then added himself and his own energy-stores to the permanent Gate in his stronghold. He had truly been like a spider in a web then, for whatever he wished eventually came to him, falling into his threads of power. There had been a price to pay— a small one, he thought. After that, he had been unable to travel more than a league from his home, for his fragile body was not able to bear the stress of physical separation for long. On the other hand, he had only to will himself home, and the Gate pulled him through itself, without needing another terminus to step through. His innovation had worked, and then, as now, being home-bound had been a small price to pay for control of all the mage-energy as far as he could See.

He studied the situation, carefully, alert for any pitfalls. The most obvious was that the moment he touched the power-locus, his enemies would know what he was doing. The Adept was guiding it himself, with help from some other mages. How maddening to be able to See all of this and yet be unable to act on it!

So he would have to be subtle. Well, there were more ways of controlling the direction of the power-locus than by steering the thing itself. There were two lines on it still, and they could be used to bring it closer to him.

Carefully, he touched the line nearer himself, and pulled; slowly, gradually, changing the direction the power-locus was taking. No one seemed to notice.

Falconsbane's smile turned to a feral grin. The hunt was up, but the quarry did not yet know that the beast was on its trail.

Like all good hunters, he needed to rest from time to time. Falconsbane had pulled the power-locus as far out of line as he cared to for the moment. He had left his servants to themselves for a long while, perhaps too long; they needed to be reminded of his power over them. There were preparations he needed to make here, before he would be ready to make the Gate a part of himself and his stronghold. And before he undertook any of those preparations, or even interfered any more with the power-locus, he needed to rest, eat, refresh himself.

He left his study, and only then noticed that the air in his manor was thick with the heavy smell of incense and lamp oil, of rooms closed up too long and people sweating with fear. He shook his head at the dank taint of it in the back of his throat.

Before he got anything to eat or drink, he needed a breath of fresher air.

He turned around, and was on his way to the top of his tower when every blocked-up and shuttered door and window in his stronghold suddenly flew open with an ear-shattering crash.

Glass splintered and tinkled to the floor. Sunlight streamed in the windows, and a sudden shocked silence descended for a single heartbeat.

Then, with a wild howl, a violent wind tore through his fortress. It came from everywhere and nowhere, tearing curtains from their poles, sending papers flying, knocking over furniture, putting out fires in all the fireplaces, scattering ashes to the farthest corners of the rooms. It raced down the hallway toward him, whipping his hair and clothing into tangles, driving dust into his eyes so that he yelped with the unexpected pain.

Then, before he could react any further than that, it was gone, leaving only silence, chill, and the taste of snow behind.

That wild wind signaled the beginning of a series of inexplicable incidents. They invariably occurred at the least opportune moment. And they made no sense, followed no pattern.

They sometimes looked like attacks—yet did nothing substantial in the way of harm. They sometimes looked as if someone very powerful was *courting* him—yet no one appeared to follow through on the invitation.

Every time he set himself to work on pulling the power-locus nearer, one of those *incidents* would distract him.

The single window in his study was open to the sky since that wind had shattered both shutter and glass. A blood-red firebird—or something that looked like one—flew into his study window and dropped a black rose at his feet. It left the same way it had come and vanished into the sky before he could do anything about it.

A troop of black riders kept one of his messengers from reaching him, herding the man with no weapon but fear, running him until his horse foundered, then chasing him afoot until he was exhausted. Then they left him lying in the snow for Falconsbane's patrols to find. By then, it was too late; the man barely had a chance to gasp out what had happened to him before he died of heart failure, his message unspoken.

All of the broken glass in the windows of his stronghold was replaced somehow in a single hour—but not by clear glass, by blood-red glass, shading the entire fortress in sanguine gloom. *He* liked the effect, but his servants kept lighting lanterns to try and dispel it a little.

Every root vegetable in the storage cellar sprouted overnight, growing long, pallid roots and stems. The onions even blossomed. His cook had hysterics and collapsed, thinking Mornelithe would blame *him*.

Two hundred lengths of black velvet appeared in the forecourt, cut to cape-length.

All of the wine turned to vinegar, and all of the beer burst its kegs, leaving the liquor cellar a stinking, sodden mess.

Another black rider waylaid the cook's helper sent to requisition new stores and forced him to follow. There were wagonloads of wine- and beer-barrels, of sacks of roots, all in the middle of a pristine, untouched, snow-covered clearing. With no footprints or hoofprints anywhere about, and no sign of how all those provisions had gotten there.

All of the weather vanes were replaced overnight with new ones. The old weather vanes had featured the former owner's arms; these featured black iron horses.

A huge flock of blackbirds and starlings descended on the castle for half a day, leaving everything covered with whitewash.

Something invisible got into the stable in broad daylight, opened all the stalls and paddock gates, and spooked the horses. It took three days to find them all.

When the last horse—Falconsbane's own mount, on the few occasions he chose to ride—was found, it was wearing a magnificent new hand-tooled black saddle, black barding, black tack. And in the saddlebag was a scrying crystal double the size and clarity of the one he had shattered in a fit of pique.

He paced the length of his red-lit study, trying to make some sense of the senseless. It was driving him to distraction, for even those acts that could be interpreted as "attacks" could have been part of a courting pattern. He had done similar things in the past—sent a gift, then done something that said, "see how powerful I am, I can best you in your own home." The courting of mage-to-mage was sometimes an odd thing, as full of anger as desire . . . as full of hate as lust.

But if it *was* courting, who was doing it? It couldn't be Shin'a'in, for *they* avoided all forms of magic. It couldn't be Tayledras; they hated him as much as he hated them.

Who was it, then? He thought he had eliminated any possible rivals— and only rivals would think to court him.

He stopped stark still, as a thought occurred to him. There had been a time when he had fostered the illusion that the mage the Outlanders were so afraid of had been seeking to ally with him. What if *he* was the one behind all this? It would make sense—black riders to send against white ones—black horses instead of the Guardian Spirits.

Now that he thought about it, the idea made more and more sense. . . .

He called a servant, who appeared promptly, but showing less fear than usual. He had not blamed any of his servants for the bizarre events that had been occurring lately, and that had given them some relief. Besides, he had been getting tired of the smell of fear in his halls. Why, he hadn't even killed a slave in days. . . .

"I want you to find Dhashel, Toron, Flecker, and Quorn," he told the servant. "These are their orders, simple ones. There is a land to the north and east: Hardorn. Its king is one Ancar; he is a mage. He is also the sworn enemy of the two Outlanders with the k'Sheyna, and at war with *their* land of Valdemar. This much I know. I desire to know more. Much more." He blinked, slowly, and fixed the servant with his gaze. "Do you understand all of that?"

The servant nodded, and repeated the orders word-for-word. Falconsbane was pleased; he would remember never to kill or maim this one.

Good service deserved reward, after all.

"Now go, and tell them to hurry," he said, turning back to the couch and his new scrying crystal. "I am eager to hear what they can learn."

Darkwind rose unsteadily to his feet as Iceshadow tapped his shoulder in the signal that meant Iceshadow was there to relieve him. He staggered out of the former Stone clearing and up the path toward the *ekele* shared by Nyara and Skif. He was tired, but this couldn't wait.

Something or someone was diverting the path of the proto-Gate. Every moment spent in rapport with Firesong moving the proto-Gate toward the new Vale was a moment spent in constant battle to keep the Power-point on the right course.

They couldn't be sure who was doing it, of course, but for Darkwind, Falconsbane was high on the list. It *was* possible to anchor the proto-Gate temporarily, thank the gods, or they would all have been worn away to nothing, for what they had hoped would take only hours was taking days.

Firesong especially was under stress; since the proto-Gate was linked to him, personally, he had to be the one in charge of directing its path. Although the *hertasi* swarmed over him, bringing him virtually everything he needed, there was one thing they could not give him, and that was rest.

But since they had learned that the proto-Gate could be anchored, his helpers only needed to work in four-candlemark shifts, and he himself needed only to work for eight.

Darkwind had been very dubious about the wisdom of leaving the proto-Gate unguarded, but they really had no choice. Firesong would be helped into bed at the end of the day and sleep solidly until it was time to work again. So he had held his peace and had hoped that there was no way to interfere with the energy-point without Firesong knowing.

And once the proto-Gate was anchored for the night, it actually seemed that either there was something protecting it, or Falconsbane had not found a way to move it.

He paused for a moment, as that thought triggered a memory. *Protecting it. . . .*

He shook his head, and continued on his way. Had he seen what he *thought* he'd seen this morning, when he and Firesong and Elspeth took the first shift together? Had there been two shining, bright-winged vorcel-hawks flitting away silently through the gray mist of the not-world? And had they, a moment before, been standing guard over the proto-Gate?

In the end, it didn't matter—except, perhaps, to Firesong. If the Adept knew that Tre'valen had survived in some form, he would be much comforted. Although Firesong hid most of his deeper feelings beneath a cloak of arrogance and flippancy, Darkwind was better at reading him now. The young shaman's death still grieved him.

Then again, it could have been a trick of the not-world, a place where illusions were as substantial as reality, where nothing was to be trusted until you had tested it yourself. It could even have been a specter of his own half-formed hopes.

There was no denying the fact that someone was trying to steal the proto-Gate, however, and Darkwind was going to assume that it was Falconsbane until he learned otherwise. That meant that some of the nebulous plans the "war council" had discussed before and after the destruction of the Heartstone were going to have to be put into motion.

Darkwind was not certain what Falconsbane intended to do with the proto-Gate, or where he planned to anchor it, for that matter. Presumably on something *like* a Heartstone, somewhere deep in his own stronghold. If he did that, it would give him access to something that had the potential to become a full *permanent* Gate. If he knew how to effect the rest of the spell, that is. Firesong did, or at least Darkwind suspected he did. Not too many did, except for Healing Adepts—and not many of those. No one had had the secret in k'Sheyna for as long as Darkwind had been alive.

But even if Falconsbane didn't know the trick, having the proto-Gate in his control would give him access to a great deal of power.

Nor was that all; unless Firesong freed himself first, access to the proto-Gate meant access to the Adept.

Darkwind did not want to see Firesong—or anyone else, for that matter—in Falconsbane's hands. Firesong *might* be able to defeat Mornelithe in a head-to-head battle. He *might* be able to hold Falconsbane off long enough for someone to help to free him.

Darkwind was not prepared to bet on either of those possibilities. Dealing with Falconsbane had taught him this: it was much safer to overestimate the beast.

He could take over Firesong the way he took my father, and have the power of a Healing Adept to pervert. With that—he could undo anything any Vale has accomplished.

Horrible thought.

If he had a permanent Gate, he could bypass our shields and send his creatures straight into the mouth of the Vale at no cost to himself. That was another unpleasant scenario.

So it was time to consult Nyara who alone of all of them was an expert on her father.

Nyara had always liked Darkwind; now, with the pressures of her body and of her father reduced or gone altogether, she had discovered it was possible to simply be his friend. Over the past few days she had found him to be kind, courteous—and oddly protective, determined to keep his people from snubbing her or making her feel uncomfortable. That was not to be expected, particularly not with the pressures that were on him now.

She and Skif were actually working on sword practice; although Need had been putting her through exercises, this was the first time she had ever had an opponent to practice with. She welcomed the physical activity as a release from direct thinking. She did not want to consider what she would do when the time came that they both must leave the Vale. She wanted to go with him, but at the same time she was afraid to. It was much easier to lose herself in the hypnotic dance of steel and footwork.

Darkwind must have been standing at the edge of the practice circle for some time before she and Skif realized he was there. She spotted him first, and signaled a halt; only then did he enter the circle.

"You two look very good," he said quietly. "I hated to interrupt you, but I think we're going to have to figure out exactly where your f—Falconsbane is after all."

She wiped sweat from her forehead with her sleeve, and nodded. "Did you find those maps you were talking about?" Strange; not so long ago, even *thinking* of her father brought her to the verge of hysteria. Now—well, she was afraid, only a fool would *not* fear Falconsbane, but she could face that fear.

"They're in my *ekele*," Darkwind replied, with a nod. "Could you two join me there?"

His treehouse was not far, even by Vale standards. Together he and she and Skif took an old set of Shin'a'in maps out of their leather cases and bent over them with something more than mere interest. They worked backward from the spot where Darkwind had first encountered her; Darkwind pointed out landmarks that *he* knew, as she puzzled her way through the strange notation.

"This would be it, I think," she said at last, pointing to an otherwise unremarkable spot to the north and west. "I have not had much training in the reading of these things," she continued apologetically, "but I think this is the likeliest place for my father's fortress to be."

Darkwind nodded, marked the place, and rolled up the thick sheets of vellum. "That's the direction the proto-Gate is being pulled, so that rather confirms that your guess is correct," he said. "And it confirms *my* guess as to who is behind this. Firesong is trying to second-guess our would-be Gate-thief, but I don't think at this point that there could be much doubt about motivation. If it's Falconsbane, then there is only one real answer. He wants what he's always wanted; power."

"The proto-Gate would be irresistible to him," Nyara agreed, then widened her eyes as something occurred to her. "You know—it is rather odd, but he becomes more predictable under stress, had you noted that? I do not know why, but it is true. I have seen this over and over again, when I was still with him. The more he is forced to react to the surprises sprung upon him by others, the more likely he is to act as he has always acted, and think it is a clever new plan."

Darkwind nodded, as if what she had just told him confirmed something he had thought himself. "What do you think he's planning on doing with the proto-Gate when he captures it?"

"Oh, he will install it in his stronghold," she said immediately. With no effort at all, she could picture him gloating over his new-won prize as he had gloated over so many in the past. "That is predictable, too. Probably in his study; he is jealous of his things of power and often will not put them where other mages may even see them. He will want such a thing as near to him as may be."

"That would be a bad place to put a Gate," Darkwind observed. "A Gate works both ways—"

"No, I *suspect* he will try to anchor it in a stone or crystal of some kind, rather than as a Gate," she said, trying to remember if Falconsbane had ever indicated that he knew how to make the Greater Gates. "I am not sure. I believe he *knows* how to make a Gate but has not the strength. I think he would rather create something to use as a power-pole, to bring in more lines, if he can."

"What, use it to create his own kind of Heartstone?" Darkwind asked in surprise, and was even more surprised when she nodded. "Make a Heartstone like a Hawkbrother?"

"It seems amazing that he should imitate you," she told him earnestly, "but he has seen your success. He is *not* good at creating things. He is good at twisting them to his own ends, or warping them to suit his fancies, but not at creating them. He will imitate you, therefore, and tell himself that he is making something entirely new."

"So, whatever he tries is going to have a focus," Darkwind mused. "The personal link will have to be taken from Firesong, of course—but if he has to have a focus, he has to have something physical. Focus; his ideal choice would be something shaped the way the proto-Gate Looks in the halfworld. And we can attack that."

"What are you thinking of?" Skif asked, sounding just a little belligerent and definitely protective.

Darkwind looked up at the tall Herald, and shook his head. "You are not going to care for my notions," he said. "No, you are not going to like them at all."

"Probably not," Skif agreed. "On the other hand, I don't like the idea of Falconsbane with all that power."

"Nor do I." Darkwind turned back to Nyara. "Before I broach any ideas, there's something I really need to know, both from you, and from your friend in the sheath." He nodded at Need. "Do you think you can hold out against your father's control now? I mean in a face-to-face confrontation; can you hold against his will?"

:Good question, boy. My vote is yes—but she won't unless she believes she can.:

Nyara looked deeply and carefully into his eyes. "I think so," she replied after a long moment of thought. "I know that I can for some time if we are not near one another. I think that I can, if we are not in physical contact. If he had me in his hands—" She shrugged, trying to hide her fear, but Darkwind saw it and sympathized with it anyway. "I would have no chance with him, if I were in his hands. But the old means by which he controlled me no longer work. He tried upon me what he perfected upon your father. Because none of this was perfected, there were places where Need and I could break what he had done to me. He would have to work magic—perhaps even cast actual spells—to get new controls on me. And just at the moment he might not realize that."

"Part of the way he reacts in a typical fashion when he feels himself under pressure?" Darkwind asked.

She nodded. "Especially if he were distracted or busy," she told him. "The more distractions he has, the more likely he is to revert to what has worked in the past."

:Absolutely,: Need agreed. *:Half the reason I was able to help her so much was because I was watching Kethra Heal your father. His problems are a superior copy of hers. We've thrown Falconsbane off-balance by destroying the Heartstone, and he's reacting predictably, by trying to steal the power it harbored. There are a dozen other things he could do with it, or*

about it, but instead, he's doing exactly what I would have predicted for him.:

"I could prolong the moment that he thinks he still has me controlled by feigning it," Nyara offered, trembling a little inside from fear. "Need might be able to help with that."

Nyara watched Darkwind turn all that over in his mind—and she wondered. One plan, with a fair likelihood of success, had already occurred to her. She wondered if he was thinking the same thing that she was. She had been thinking about something like this for some time—fearing the idea, yet knowing it had logic to it. And knowing that if she were asked, she would follow through with it.

Skif was most definitely not going to like it.

Chapter
Twenty-two

Falconsbane stepped back and surveyed his work, nodding with satisfaction. He had done very well, given the short notice he'd had. And it had been at minimal cost to himself. There were, after all, two ways to create power-poles. The first way was to produce the power from yourself; much in the same way that a Gate was created. That was not the ideal way to proceed, so far as he was concerned.

The other way was to induce it from the body of another—as skilled and powerful a mage as one could subdue. The drawing out of the power would kill the mage in question, of course; there was no way to avoid that. A pity, but there it was.

Then, given the plan he had created, one needed to fix the pole in place—that required another mage. Fixing the pole absolutely required the life of that mage, this time by sacrifice, although Falconsbane had managed to crush the man's heart with no outward signs and no blood spilt. It would have been a pity to stain the new carpets.

And lastly, in accordance with the plan, he had needed the full power of a human life *and* the full power of a mage to establish a web of energy linking the power-pole he had created with every possible point in his territory. Naturally that had required a third mage.

It was possible to do all of that from his own resources, but that would have required exhausting himself completely. That wasn't acceptable at this point. Doing it through others was far less efficient; it took three mages to create what he could have accomplished alone.

The problem with the second method was, of course, that the mages in question would not survive the operation. Which was why the bodies of three of Falconsbane's former servants were littering the floor of his study. If he had more time, he probably would have done it the hard way, through himself. It was difficult finding even ordinary servants; mages were doubly hard to acquire.

He had thought long and hard on the best way to go about claiming the power-locus. He had not been aided by all the distractions taking place in and around his lands. The black riders were everywhere, and although they seldom *did* anything, they rattled his guards and made even his fortress servants nervous. Strange birds had been seen in the forest around his stronghold; and now the woods were reputedly haunted as well, by amorphous, ghostlike shapes and faint, dancing lights.

He had decided at last to set up a power-pole as exactly like the waiting Stone as possible, and anchor *that* within an enormous crystal-cluster he had brought from one of his storage rooms and set up in his study. When he drew the power-locus in near enough, it would snap into the power-pole as it had been intended to do at the Bird-Fools' new Heartstone. Devising the plan had taken much delving into his oldest memories, and he had been a little disturbed at how much he had forgotten. Too many times for comfort, he'd been forced to return to his library and search through his oldest books. In the end, he'd taken scraps of memory, scraps of old knowledge, and a great deal of guessing.

The difference between what he intended to do and what the Tayledras would have done was that when it snapped into the waiting vessel *here*, he would be standing between and would be linked to the crystal. When the power-locus and the power-pole merged into one, *he* would be part of them as well.

It was as inventive in its way as anything that Tayledras Adept had tried; he was quite certain of that. He was thoroughly pleased with his own cleverness. Oh, it was dangerous, surely; the mages who had been sacrificed to give the plan life had advised against it even before they knew they were going to be sucked dry of life and power to fuel it.

"You'll be incinerated by that much power," Atus had protested.

"If you aren't incinerated, you'll go mad. No one can be *part* of a Heartstone!" Renthan had told him.

Preadeth had only shaken his head wordlessly, and cast significant looks at the others.

They thought he was insane even to try it—and at that moment, when he caught them exchanging glances and possibly thoughts, he had known who his sacrificial calves were going to be.

They had doubtless been considering revolt—or at least, escape. Escape would mean they might even consider going to the Tayledras with what they knew.

It was just as well he had another use for them. It would have been a pity to kill them outright and waste all that potential.

Using his subordinates to supply the power instead of himself was the last element he had needed to make the plan reasonable as well as possible. It meant that at the end of the Working, he was still standing and still capable of acting, instead of unconscious and needing days of rest. Even at that, he was exhausted when he was done.

He sank down on his couch and considered calling in a fourth man and draining him as well, but discarded the idea. It would cause enough trouble that he had killed three of his underlings. There were those who might read it as a desperation measure. It was, on the whole, a bad idea to kill anyone other than a slave or one of the lower servants. It made everyone else unhappy—and inclined to think about defection. Unhappy servants were inefficient servants. They should know the taste of the whip—but also know that it was only there in extreme circumstances, and that they could bring that whip onto their own backs by their own actions.

He lay back on the soft black velvet of the couch, and considered his next few moves. First—find a reason for the deaths of his underlings that would disturb the others the least. The mages in particular were a touchy lot; they tended to think of themselves as allies rather than underlings. They were given to occasional minor revolt. It would not do to give them a reason for one of those revolts—not now, when he could ill-afford the energy to subdue them.

Should he claim they had died aiding him in some great work? That was a little too close to the truth, and the next time he called for help in magic-working, he might trigger one of those mass defections. He did not, as a rule, lose even one of his assistants, much less three of them.

The mages weren't stupid; they might well guess that "aiding" in a great work meant becoming a sacrifice to it.

The deep red light flooding in from the window was very soothing to his eyes, and eased the pain at his temples, pain caused by nothing more than overstressing himself. Both temples throbbed, there was a place at the base of his skull that felt as if someone was pressing a dull dagger into it, and sharp stabbing pains over each eye whenever he moved his head too quickly. Hard to think, when one was in pain. . . .

But he must think of a way to explain those bodies. He wished he could simply burn them to ash and pretend that he did not know where they had gone. But *that* might only make the others think their colleagues had run off, and if those three had done so, there might be a good reason for the others to follow their example.

Complications, complications. Everything he did was so complicated. Not like the old days, when he didn't have to justify himself to anyone. When he only had to issue orders and know he would be obeyed.

The cowards. If they hadn't been quite so quick to think of conspiring against him he might not have—

Ah. That was the answer. He would have the bodies dragged from his study and hung from the exterior walls in cages, as traitors were. That would be enough. The rest of his underlings should assume that the three had attempted to overcome him and had fallen in the attempt. A good explanation for why *he* was so weary.

He would not even have to *say* anything himself; just look angry. No one would dare ask him. The rumors would fly, but there was no reason for anyone to guess the truth.

He rang for a servant, and feigning greater strength than he had, contorted his face into a mask of suppressed rage and ordered the bodies taken away and displayed in the cages. Then he called for stimulants, food and drink, as he always did after a battle. Sometimes habits were useful things. When he demanded rare meat, red wine, and *kephira*, with a body-slave to be waiting in his bed, the servants all assumed that a fight had aroused his blood and his lust.

The servant left and came back with several more; Falconsbane ignored them as they carried the bodies away, lying back on his couch and staring at the shadow-shrouded ceiling. He often did that after a battle of magic, too. When the servant returned at last with the food and drink he had been sent for, he told the man in a flat, expressionless voice to set it down and take himself out. He did his best to look angry, and not tired. The illusion was what mattered right now.

If I were not so pressed, I would manipulate their minds to reinforce the tale that is spreading, he thought, slowly mustering the strength to reach for a cup of drugged wine. *Perhaps I should do so anyway.*

But at that moment, there came a hesitant tap at the door. He started, and cursed his own jangled nerves, then growled, "Yes? What is it?"

If it's nonsense, I'll kill him. If it's a defection, I'll set the wyrsa *on the fool who ran and see if he can outrun and outlast a pack of forty!*

"Sire," came the timid voice of the servant, muffled by the door, "I beg your pardon for disturbing you, but I'm following your orders. You said to let you know immediately if one of those riders—"

He sat up abruptly, exhaustion and pain completely forgotten. "The riders? Open the damned door, you fool! What about the riders?"

The servant edged the door open, nervously. He peered inside, then slid into the room with one eye on his escape route. There was a small box in his hand.

A small box carved of shining black wood.

Falconsbane's eyes went to it as if drawn there; he stood up and strode over to the man, and stood towering over him, his hands twitching at his sides.

"Sire, one of the riders came right up to the gate just as they were— taking out—" The man gulped, his face pasty white, and Falconsbane repressed the urge to strangle him. He simply tried to ease some of the anger out of his face so that the servant would be able to continue.

"Go on," he said, more gently than he wanted to. He cursed his own weakness; if he had been stronger, he could have seized the man's mind and pulled what he wanted right out of it.

"The rider came up and tossed *this* to the Guard Captain, Sire," the servant continued, after visibly trying to calm himself. "Then—he was just gone. The Guard Captain brought this straight to me, like you ordered."

"By 'just gone,' do you mean that he rode away?" Falconsbane asked carefully. *Why didn't they call me? Or was there no time? Can those riders move that fast? Why isn't someone chasing them?*

"No, sire, I mean he was *gone.* Like smoke. There, and then not there." The servant seemed convinced, and there was no real reason for him to lie. "The Guard Captain said so. Said he was gone like he'd been conjured and dispersed."

Falconsbane pondered the box in his hand; this was the first real evidence that the riders were the manifestations of magic. Was his unknown enemy—or friend—showing his hand a little more? They could not have gone through a Gate; he would have sensed that. Therefore they could only have been temporary conjurations, given life and form only so long as the mage needed them, or creatures from another plane. Minor demons, perhaps? Those he might not be able to sense unless he was actually looking for them.

Of the "gifts" that had been sent to him, only one was magical—and it was useless. He cast an eye at the lenticular scrying crystal as the servant waited nervously for his response, and snorted a little.

Scrying crystal, indeed. It was an excellent crystal. The clarity was exceptional, the lenticular form ideal for scrying, the size quite perfect for a detailed image to form. The problem was, no matter how he bent his will upon it, it would show only one thing. The view of some remote mountain peak, and halfway up the side of the mountain, a strange and twisted castle that he did not recognize. A snowstorm swirled about the castle when the crystal was moved.

He dismissed the servant, and reached for the wine, drinking it down in one gulp, before he returned to his couch and contemplated the box. Like the other, it was beautifully carved, and about the same size. There was no sign of magic anywhere about it.

Like the other, this one held something.

Nestled in a nest of black velvet padding was a ring. Not just any ring, either—it held no stone, and was not metal, although it was an intricately carved or molded band. Like a wedding ring, exactly like a wedding ring, it was carved with the symbols of harvest, wheat-ears and grapes—except that this ring was made of a shining, cool black substance. He tried, experimentally, to break it, but it was probably of the same stuff as the horse.

In this part of the world, widows sometimes laid aside their wedding bands to wear a black band like this, made of jet, signifying mourning. Was he being warned? But he had no spouse to mourn, and the very last thing he would weep over was the death of his traitorous daughter.

His predilection for black was apparently well known to these riders— or whoever sent them. There had been the rose, the velvet, the horse, and now the ring. And this would certainly gain his attention far quicker than a simple peasants' gold or silver wedding band.

So, was this an invitation to a "wedding"—an alliance?
Or a funeral?

"I don't like this," Darkwind told Firesong unhappily. "I only told you *my* plan because I hoped you'd have another way of handling this, something that wouldn't put anyone into danger like this. Even if it is my plan, I don't like it."

He had intercepted Firesong as soon as the Adept had anchored the proto-Gate for the night. They had walked back to Firesong's *ekele* together, while Darkwind laid bare his thoughts on Falconsbane and what might be done about him.

To his dismay, Firesong had agreed, completely.

"Nor do I care for your plan," Firesong replied, wearily sagging back against the cushions of his couch. "I dislike sending Nyara into peril of this sort. She is a frail prop for all our hopes—and yet there is a certain symmetry in it, in sending her to avenge her own hurts upon her father."

Darkwind snorted. "Symmetry was not what I had in mind," he said. He would have gone farther than that, but at that same moment, Nyara and Skif arrived, summoned by one of Firesong's ever-present *hertasi*. Skif was unarmed as far as Darkwind could see, but Nyara, as always, had Need; the sword at her side was so much a part of her that he couldn't imagine her without it.

He took a moment to examine her with the dispassionate eyes of a stranger and was a little surprised. He'd thought of Nyara as small and slender, maybe even spidery; well, perhaps she was, compared to himself and to Skif. But she certainly carried her sword with authority—and from what he'd seen, she knew how to use it well. And what skill *she* did not possess, the sword could grant to her, if Elspeth was to be believed.

"Sit," Firesong said, before the other two could say anything. "Please. We have somewhat we need to ask you." He waved to one of the hovering *hertasi*, who converged upon the two Outlanders with food and drink.

They took seats; Nyara a little apprehensively, Skif reluctantly. Darkwind didn't blame them. He'd had the feeling that Nyara knew what he'd had in mind all along, from the nebulous ideas that had formed when he asked her to locate Falconsbane's stronghold, to the crystallized plan that had sent him looking for Firesong. Skif probably didn't know what was in Darkwind's mind, but if it required involving Nyara, he was going to be immediately suspicious.

"I'll come straight to the point," Darkwind said. "Before we take this to a larger forum, we need to know something from you." He waited until they had settled a little, then turned to the Changechild. "Nyara, this afternoon I asked you to help me find your father's stronghold on the map. You thought you located approximately where it is, correct?"

She nodded, slowly, accepting a cup of tea from one of the *hertasi*. It was very hard to read her face; long ago she had probably learned how to control her expressions minutely, and that was a habit that was hard to break.

He hated to ask this of her. He hated to put her back where she might *need* that kind of control. "Well, this is a different question, but related. Could *you* trace your way back to it—and if you found it, get into it?"

Skif yelped and started to rise; she shook her head at him, and placed one hand on his knee to calm him. It didn't calm him a bit, but he subsided, looking sharply at both Firesong and Darkwind.

Hmm. Interesting. I thought he was unarmed, but the way his right hand is tensing—he has a knife hidden somewhere near it. If he had a choice, he probably wouldn't be looking *daggers at us, he'd be throwing them.*

"Yes to both questions," she replied steadily. "My problem with finding Father's hold upon your map was that I could not see the things I know as landmarks. I have a perfect memory for trails, it seems. I never had occasion to use it before I escaped my father, but it is very difficult for me to become lost. I can easily find the stronghold." She licked her lips, showing the tips of her canine teeth, then took a drink before continuing. "I can find it—and having found it, I know many of the odd ways into it. He does not guard all of them, for many are hidden. Some I was taught, but some I found on my own."

"Yes, but will *he* not know of them as well?" Firesong asked gently. "I would not send you into a trap, dear child. Candidly, that would not serve either of us."

Her lips curved in a faint smile. "I do not think there will be a trap. Since I am only interested in fleeing from him—he thinks—I suspect that the last thing he would look for me to do is return. The ways that I would take inside will be those that only I know, or those that I think he will not bother to trap."

:I can hide her some, if that's your next question,: Need said. *:I can hold a "reflective" illusion on her, the kind that makes her look like part of the*

landscape to Mage-Sight. More importantly, while *I'm doing that, I can hide myself as well. Watch.:*

At that instant, Need ceased to exist, from the point of view of Darkwind's Mage-Sight. She was nothing more sinister to ordinary sight than an ordinary broadsword, and to Mage-Sight, she and Nyara did not exist, and Skif sat alone on the couch.

Then Nyara was "back," all in an instant, and the sword with her.

"Good. Very good," Firesong said, leaning forward a bit, his voice warm with approval. "Well, then, you must know that we have a plan, but the one in greatest danger will be you, Nyara. That is a great burden to be placed upon you, and no one will fault you if you say no."

She shook her head, but not, Darkwind sensed, in denial. "I have been partially to blame for much harm that has come to you," she said. "I feel that I owe some recompense."

:It's not like she's going to do this alone,: Need added dryly. *:I've handled what Falconsbane can throw before. Hmph. Maybe if he throws the right stuff at us this time, I can transmute it and take off a little more of what he did to her.:*

"I will not count upon that," Nyara told her blade, and Darkwind thought he detected a tone of friendly chiding in her voice. "I will not even think of it. It serves little purpose, after all. If you can, I shall be grateful, but do not put yourself into jeopardy by an attempt."

Need couldn't shrug, but Darkwind got the impression she had. *:At any rate, as Nyara and Skif can tell you, I took on this form because there are times when one person can do what an army couldn't. I'm no expert on Falconsbane, but I don't think the odds are any worse now than they were back when I froze myself into this blade.:*

Darkwind looked at Skif, who growled, but shrugged. "She's her own woman," he replied unhappily. "If I tried to make her change her mind, I wouldn't be doing either of us any good. She wants to go through with this—I'll do what I can to help."

Darkwind raised an eyebrow skeptically. Skif grimaced.

"I don't *like* it," he admitted. "I'm scared to death for her, and if I could take her place I would. I won't pretend otherwise. But let's just say I learned how stupid it is to try and stop someone from doing something they have to do. It's even more stupid if you care about them."

Darkwind read the *look* Skif gave both of them, however. If Nyara came to any harm at all, Skif would personally collect the damages due.

"More than good!" Firesong applauded. "Well, then, if Nyara is agreed, I think it is time that we took the idea to the rest. We will discover if anyone can knock holes in this plan—or make it safer in any way."

The gathering in the Council Oak clearing held only part of the usual gathering. Both gryphons, Nyara, Skif, Firesong, Wintermoon, the Companions, Elspeth—and Darkwind himself. No other mages; this would not be a plan that required more mages than they had right here. Starblade and Kethra were back to recovering; Iceshadow and Nightjewel were conserving their strength. And they added no more fighters than Skif and Wintermoon, either. As Need had said, there were times when one—or a handful—could do what an army could not.

Firesong had lost a great deal of his jauntiness in the past few days, and he had put aside his elaborate costumes in favor of simple, flowing clothing like any other mage wore. He could hardly hide the flamboyant bondbird that perched on his shoulder, but other than that, and his incredible beauty, there was nothing that set him apart from the other mages in k'Sheyna.

"Here is the situation as it stands," Firesong began. Using a handful of stones and a bit of string, he began laying out something that looked rather like a very simple spiderweb. "If I had been looking for this earlier, I might have seen it being built—but it has the feeling of something assembled with haste, and we may be able to take advantage of that."

"What is it?" Darkwind was baffled. "I assume Falconsbane has something to do with this, whatever it is."

Firesong flushed, the first time Darkwind had ever seen him truly embarrassed. "Pardon. I forgot that none of you have been working with me upon this. The enemy wants to capture the proto-Gate; to that end he has constructed this web of power-points and interconnecting lines about his stronghold. If you look in the direction of his stronghold with FarSight and Mage-Sight, you will see it."

Treyvan examined the model, and growled. "Thisss isss a new thing, isss it not?"

Firesong shook his head. "Only new to Falconsbane. I have seen this sort of construction before, and it isn't half as effective as those who use it think. It has a vulnerability, a severe one. If the connections were weakened all about the edge so that they might snap beneath a good shock, he likely would not note the weakening. And *if* they snapped, the power would backlash against him in some profound ways."

"What kind of ways?" Wintermoon wanted to know. "Something grievous, I hope."

Firesong smiled faintly. "If he was not prepared with a way to ground it or to escape, he would likely be cast into the void between the Gates— as if he entered a Gate and both the Gate and the terminus were then destroyed. That is because of the way he has set up the tensions among his power-poles and his center. Great concentrations of power warp the world-space as Gates do."

Darkwind shuddered; he had once had a glimpse of that void. He would prefer not to see it again. "That's not a fate I would wish on anyone," he said.

"Not even Falconsbane?" Elspeth asked. "I can think of one or two others I would like to see contemplating their deeds for all eternity!"

Firesong continued, as if they had not interrupted him. "Any shock to him would snap these threads of power once they were weakened— that would be the best way, in fact. A shock at the center will have more effect than one at an edge. But the weakening—that would have to be done quickly, so that he did not have a chance to notice what was being done." He looked up into the gryphons' faces, expectantly.

Treyvan blinked slowly, his eyes distant. "You rrrequirrre ssswiftly trraveling magesss," he said. "And at the sssame time, you rrrequirrre sssomeone to infiltrrrate the beassst'sss home."

Firesong nodded, and waited.

"The ssswift onesss mussst be usss, I think," Treyvan continued. "And the otherrr—Nyarrra."

"If you are willing, yes," Darkwind said awkwardly. "I hate to ask you, but if Falconsbane gains control of the proto-Gate, he'll have an enormous amount of power. It would be the kind of power that normally goes to establish and maintain an entire Vale; protections, Heartstones, Vale-sculpting, and all."

"He could dessstrrroy usss all with a thought," Hydona replied flatly. "He mussst not have that powerrr."

"Bring the little ones here," Darkwind urged. "With the Heartstone gone, there's no longer a danger to them in staying here."

Hydona nodded, but Darkwind sensed that she had something else on her mind. She looked to her mate.

After a moment of wordless exchange, Treyvan sighed. "We wisssh sssomething in return," he said.

"What?" Firesong asked. "If it is in our power—"

"It isss. We requirrre a pricssse. We want k'Sheyna to not dissolve the Vale when you leave. To give it to ussss. Veil, shieldsss, and all." Treyvan tucked his wings closer in to his body. "We had planned to take it oncssse you left, but—"

"But if you leave it asss it isss, it will be betterrr forrr ourrr new *kla'hessshey'messserin,*" Hydona interrupted. "We might asss well brrring it into clearrr sky, *asshkeyana.*"

Darkwind blinked, trying to identify the two words they had just used. They sounded like Tayledras, but weren't. They weren't Shin'a'in, either.

"Kaled'a'in?" exclaimed Firesong, as he brought his head up, eyes wide with startlement.

Treyvan sighed, as Hydona nodded firmly.

Now that Darkwind knew the tongue, he could translate the words. The second was simply an endearment; "beloved." But the first—it was complicated. The strictest translation would have been "family," or "clan," except that it implied a family made of those who not only were not related by blood—but who might not even be of the same species.

Once again, Firesong beat him to identification. "Pledged-clan?" he exclaimed again. "You're—you can't be Clan k'Leshya!"

Wintermoon quite fell off his seat. "The Lost Ones? The Lost Clan?" he exclaimed, his eyes going so wide with surprise Darkwind was afraid he was going to sprain something. "The Spirit Clan? I thought—but— they were nothing but legend!"

Treyvan's beak gaped in a gryphonic smile. "But we arrre legend, arrre we not? Orrr we werrre, to you."

Elspeth, Skif, and Nyara were looking completely bewildered, as well they might. As Firesong stared and Wintermoon picked himself back up, Darkwind essayed a hasty explanation.

"At the time of the Mage Wars, a group of Kaled'a'in from several clans, a group of outClansmen, and some of the nonhumans all formed a kind of—of—brotherhood, I suppose. They called themselves—"

"Kena Lessshya'nay," in the Tongue," Hydona supplied. "It meansss 'clan bound by ssspirit.' Sssomething like yourrr Heraldsss, but without Companionsssss. *Lessshya'nay* could not join, they could only be chossssen, then agrrreed upon by thrrree morre. Ourrr leaderrrsss werrre

two. The great Black Gryphon Ssskandrrranon, and the *kessstra'cherrrn,* Amberrdrrrake.''

Treyvan chuckled. ''Though neitherrr everrr *admitted* to being leaderrr of anything!''

''The Spirit Clan supposedly held many of Urtho's mages, all of the gryphons and *hertasi, kyree, tervardi* and *dyheli,* and a fair number of the Kaled'a'in shamans and Healers,'' Firesong said to the three Outlanders, leaning forward so that they could hear him. Then he turned to the gryphons, watching them intently. ''But during the evacuation of the stronghold, you disappeared.''

Treyvan shook his massive head. ''No. Herrre isss what happened. We did not ussse the Gatesss the lessser magesss crrreated to evacuate. We had been sssent away—sssupposssedly to find a rrrefuge forrr the rrrest of you and a mysssterriousss weapon. Ssso we werrre not *in* Urrtho'sss landsss when the evacuation came. Inssstead of sssouth or easst, we had gone wesssst, we had with usss a Gate made by Urrtho—hisss verry own Grrreat Gate, anchorrred on a wagon. We usssed it while you evacuated to brrring the rrrest of *ourr* folk to ourrr rrretrreat in the wilderrrnesssss. But therrre wasss not time to take everrryone thrrrough it—only *Lessshya'nay.* The ressst of you had to take what Gatesss werrre nearrressst you.''

''And the dessstrrruction of the Ssstrrronghold thrrrew you farrrtherrr than intended. We thought you had perrrisshed,'' Hydona continued. Then she, too, gaped her beak in a grin. ''Imagine ourrr surrrprrrissse to find the legendarrry *Kena Trrrevasho, Kena Sheynarsa,* and the rrresst still in exissstence. To you, we arrre the Losst Onesss. But to usss, you arrre!''

Firesong shook his head, bemusedly. ''Quite amazing. And you still speak the Mother Tongue!''

''Not quite purrrrely, I expect,'' Treyvan admitted. ''But we have not had the prrresssuresss of the Ssstar-Borrrn to sshape our language differrrently. Sssshe doess not meddle ssso much with usss asss with you.''

''Thisss all can wait, I think,'' Hydona interrupted firmly. ''What we need to tell you isss thisss. Sssimply—you knew, Darrrkwind, that we werrre forrre-rrrunnerrrsss. Of ourrr kind, you thought. Well, morrre of ourrr people arrre coming, and not jusssst 'ourrr' kind.''

Darkwind shook his head, not quite able to figure out what she meant.

''Not just gryphons, you mean?'' Firesong said.

"Gryphonssss, humanssss, sssome *hertasssi*. And sssoon." Treyvan turned to look at Darkwind. "When k'Sheyna began itsss trrroubleesss, we called them. You rrrecall the booksssshelvesss you helped hang? They werrre not meant forrr us. We knew that thisss place would ssshelterrr usss well, and knew you needed help and would not asssk for it—asss Ssskandranon oft sssaid, 'it isss eassier to beg parrrdon than get perrr-misssion.' Sssince they did not wisssh to ssstir thingsss up by sssetting too many Gatesss, they have been coming acrosss countrrry."

Darkwind had the vague feeling that he should have been outraged by this. He wasn't, but he knew plenty in the Clan who would be. Treyvan, on the other hand, did not look in the least contrite.

"But now, we need magesss, sssswift-trrraveling magesss. Immediately." He turned his attention to Firesong, who nodded, then back to Darkwind. "With yourrr perrrmisssion, I shall usss the lessser Gate in the rrruinsss and the powerrr of the node to meet *their* Gate, and brrring them herrre in time to help. But for that help, we wisssh the Vale. Intact."

"I can't promise—" Darkwind began helplessly. Firesong interrupted him.

"Is there any reason why k'Sheyna *can't* give them the Vale?" he asked. "Any reason at all?"

The only reason Darkwind could think of was, "because we've never done it before," and that did not seem particularly adequate. Nor did he feel that this would be a true breach of Tayledras territoriality. After all, these people—beings—*were* Tayledras. Sort of.

"Not that I can think of," he admitted. He licked his lips thoughtfully. "All we know of the Spirit Clan is out of legend—and by knowing you two," he told the gryphons. "Leaving a Vale intact—that halves what little power we still possess. And it leaves you with a stronghold. What will we be leaving it to?"

"A Clan like any otherrr," Hydona replied carefully. "A Clan with perrrhapsss only one thing you do not have, and that isss the trrrained *kessstra'cherrrn* crraft. But you have bondbirrrdsss that we do not. We have ourrr lazy folk, ourrr ssstupid folk, ourrr occasssional trrroublemakerrr. I think that no one lazy, at leassst, is likely to make the jourrrney—the ssstupid would likely not surrrvive it—and the trroublemakerrr—" she bobbed her head in a gryphonic shrug. "Therrre will alwaysss be thossse. The humanssss, at leassst, *are* Clansssfolk. We will take any oathsss you rrrequirrre, and willingly, to have the Vale."

"I say that this is aid we dare not reject," Wintermoon said firmly, surprising his brother. "Whatever the cost, ridding us of Falconsbane is worth it."

"Darkwind, I think that anything you, your brother, and I together supported, the Elders would agree to," Firesong told him. "But let's take the advice of the Black Gryphon—that it is easier to beg pardon than gain permission—and go with Treyvan to bring his people through tonight."

Darkwind wavered for a moment, doubtfully. He would be helping to bring an army into the ragged remains of his own people. Would he destroy them? Or would he save them?

He looked into Treyvan's soft-edged raptor eyes, and saw there the friend, the surrogate parent, the ever-present, gentle guide.

The one who had put up with having his feathers pulled by a rambunctious small boy—and his crest snatched by a wayward bondbird.

He smiled, and nodded firmly. "Let's do it."

Silverfox & The Returned Tribe

Chapter
Twenty-three

The Vale was full of sunlight and gryphons. Elspeth had never seen anything like it, and the sight took her breath away. Everywhere she looked, there was a gryphon—bathing in a pool, lying along a massive branch or the roof of an *ekele*, sunbathing on the cliffs around the Vale. Gryphons with colors and markings like peregrines or forestgyres, cooperihawks or goshawks. Gryphons in solid colors of gray, gold, rusty-red. Gryphons with accipitor builds, and gryphons as slim as the lightest of falcons. The only markings they all had in common were patently artificial; the final arm's length or so of their first six primaries on each wing were white for four hand-spans, then red for another four hand-spans to the tips. Every time a gryphon moved a wing, the flash of red and white caught the eye like a flash of bright light.

And they had arrived hungry. Fortunately, Treyvan and Hydona had explained to all their fellow flyers just what the bondbirds were and that they were *not* to be eaten. Otherwise there might have been true havoc by now, and a number of damaged Hawkbrothers *and* gryphons. The poor little *hertasi* had worked themselves to exhaustion, finding enough to feed all of them, and probably enjoyed every moment of their work. Hydona had promised that after this, they would hunt their own food.

She thought she had never seen *anything* to match this, not even when the full complement of Heralds and Companions turned out for her mother's wedding. She would much rather look at the gryphons disporting themselves than at the chaos of arguing Clansmen. She would much rather be doing something about Falconsbane or the Heartstone than either. . . .

She shifted impatiently, and tried to concentrate on the meeting below her. The Council Oak clearing was full and overflowing with every Tayledras who could walk, and all of the newcomers—plus Skif and Nyara, up at the front, but she could scarcely see them past the press of bodies. The people who came with the gryphons had been less of a shock than the gryphons themselves; so much like both the Tayledras and the Shin'a'in that she couldn't tell any differences, except in speech and a certain uniformity of dress. They had arrived through the Gate bringing with them curious land-boats; like shallow-draft barges, but with pointed prows and places for rudders. These barges were roofed over and equipped with shutters, fitted up inside for sleeping and storage. Luggage, boxes, and bales of goods were piled upon the roofs and lashed down, and they floated above the ground at about knee-height.

Elspeth had thought her eyes were going to pop out of her head when *those* came through the Veil. She was secretly relieved to find that the Tayledras were equally astonished by the "floating barges;" it made her feel less like a country cousin. Forsaking his place with the Elders, Iceshadow had latched onto one of the mage-pilots of the peculiar constructions, and both of them were whispering to each other even now, ignoring the arguments. She had the feeling that they were planning to spend those waking moments not devoted to moving the proto-Gate to explanations of how the barges were enchanted and worked, and how Heartstones were created and functioned.

The full Clan immediately went into session on demand of a minority of Tayledras who were outraged over this violation of their territory. Wintermoon turned out, surprisingly enough, to be the steadiest voice of reason, reminding the contenders, over and over, that these "Outlanders" *were* Tayledras—or rather, the Hawkbrothers were Kaled'a'in, and that the coming of those of their own blood could hardly be counted as invasion. Elspeth wished that she could have left him to this thankless task, but she was a member of the Clan, and she had to be there, like every other member of the Clan.

There are several other things my time could be spent more profitably on.

Wintermoon could probably wear them down into consent within a day or two, with sheer persistence, with or without her help. *I wish they'd simply give up and let the rest of us deal with them later, after things have been settled. Dear gods, this is like having an argument over precedence on the eve of a battle!*

She had been here since sunrise, perched on a shoulder-high tree branch at the back of the mob, and she hadn't heard any variation in the arguments. She stifled a yawn and looked down, catching the amused eyes of Firesong and his new friend, and the shrug of the former.

Firesong was particularly taken by a young man who was supposed to be a *kestra'chern,* whatever that was, and who had offered to teach him some of the craft when there was time. "I think you would have a talent for it," Silverfox had said, with a hint of some kind of innuendo that *she* couldn't read. "You are a Healing Adept, after all—it would be a useful skill to have."

Well, that meant that Firesong was not going to be thinking about Darkwind. Not with the lithe and graceful Silverfox, he of the knowing blue eyes and ankle-length ebony hair, giving silent invitations Firesong seemed to find irresistible. And that was just fine with her.

That left one less thing for both Darkwind and herself to worry about, and they certainly had enough on their hands right now. Even without the contention within the Clan.

A stir of activity near the Elders' seats caught her eye; she was too far away to see what was going on, but there was certainly *something* happening besides the dreary old arguments.

She sent a silent inquiry to Gwena, who was somewhere on the edge of the clearing, but her Companion sent back a wordless negative. Gwena couldn't see anything either.

She narrowed her eyes and peered carefully through the screening of branches and bodies. There was someone coming into the Council Oak clearing from outside—

No, *lots* of someones!

She craned her neck to see, bracing her hands against the branch, and jumped when someone grabbed her wrist. She looked down to find Darkwind tugging her, indicating she should jump down into his arms. "They are calling for us," he said. "The Shin'a'in have arrived."

The Shin'a'in? What did *they* have to do with this mess?

But she obeyed; she jumped and he caught her waist, easing her to the ground with that carefully controlled strength that she never noticed until he did something like this. Together they wound their way through the crowd to the front, where the Elders sat.

As they broke through the final group of Tayledras screening her from the Elders' circle, she stifled a start of surprise. There was old Kra'heera—but with him were six other Shin'a'in—Shin'a'in of a kind she had seen only twice before. Shin'a'in of the kind called "Swordsworn."

They crowded in behind Kra'heera, black-clad, some veiled, some not, leading night-black horses. And the veiled ones seemed to shimmer with power, as if they were not quite of this world.

:So we are not,: said a voice in her head, and she stifled another start. One set of ice-blue eyes over a black veil caught her attention; one of those eyes winked, slowly, and deliberately. *:Be at peace, little sister-in-power, student of my student.:*

"Of course we have known of the coming of the Kaled'a'in," Kra'heera was saying impatiently. The faces of the Elders remained inscrutable, but there was no doubting the surprise and consternation in the expressions of those who had been arguing against permitting the Kaled'a'in to remain. "*She* told us they were coming, and bid us find a place for them on the Plains, if they could not find one here, or chose not to dwell here. We did not expect them to come so soon, or we would have told you long before they arrived." He turned to fix one of the Kaled'a'in spokesmen with an acidic glare. "You were not *supposed* to arrive until midsummer!"

The Kaled'a'in shrugged. "So it goes."

"*She* told you?" one of the most ardent opponents said to Kra'heera, feebly.

"We are here to stand as proof of Her word," one of the veiled ones said, in a strange voice that sounded as if it was coming from the bottom of a well. "Although we are not wont to appear to any save our own. She sent us to prove to you doubters that She approves. Unless you choose to doubt us as well."

The Tayledras in question paled, and shook his head. Kra'heera snorted, and turned back to the Council. "We have been doing what we can, within the limits of Her decree and our own resources, to give you help with your troubles," he told them, sharply. "So, I think it little enough to grant *our brothers* their request, given that they will help us all *deal* with this Great Beast, our enemy! And so, too, does *She* think!"

Skif, who was standing near Starblade with Nyara at his hand, blinked, as if he had suddenly realized something. "Now I know where I saw you!" he said to one of the black-clad Shin'a'in. "Not just at the ruins— you were out in the forest, when we were hunting for Nyara!"

The Shin'a'in shrugged. "Some of us," she said. "Two or three. Keeping an eye on our younger sister, as *She* asked us to, so that we could vouch for her to you as well. The rest—" she chuckled. "The rest of us have been sending the Falconsbane little trinkets, and harassing his borders, to keep his mind puzzling over things with no meaning, and to distract him from *your* doings as much as we could."

:It is no coincidence that we are black riders upon black horses, little sister,: said the voice in her head again. *:The Falconsbane knows of your enemy to the north and east—knows that you and yours are white riders. We simply counterfeited something he would expect if that enemy of yours were courting or challenging him; gave him something to think upon, a dangling carrot, as it were, with as many misdirections as we could manage.:*

Elspeth stuffed her hand in her mouth to keep from giggling with a kind of giddy relief. The *Shin'a'in* had been teasing and tormenting Falconsbane. No wonder they'd been able to do as much as they had been! No wonder it seemed as if Falconsbane's attention was divided! She wondered why they'd been doing this, but whys didn't really matter at the moment, only that they had.

She turned her attention back to the Council meeting, but after that, there was very little debate—and a great deal of constructive planning.

The plan was set; they were about to put it into motion. While most of the gryphons frolicked in the Vale, and barbarically beautiful Kaled'a'in occupied the attentions of most of k'Sheyna, the Council of Elders had already listened to and given consent to what the little "war council" had put together. Surely Selenay would have had a fit if she'd known what her daughter's part in this was to be. Thank all the gods that Gwena had decided to keep discreetly silent on the subject, telling Rolan only that Elspeth's studies "continued."

Well—they did. Sort of.

The gryphons—those dozen or so of the wing of thirty that were full mages, at any rate—were going to solve one problem for them. With seven pairs making the rounds of Falconsbane's web of power, the work of weakening his power-threads should be done between sunset and sunrise, easily. Under the cover of darkness, they were less likely to be spotted from below.

Nyara was going to be the arrow striking for Falconsbane's heart. That was a task Elspeth did not envy her, and she could not imagine how the Changechild managed to be so calm about it. Perhaps it was Need's steadying effect. Perhaps it was because she knew that if *she* betrayed any nervousness, Skif would probably fall to pieces.

Meanwhile, as Nyara crept closer and closer to her father's stronghold, she and Darkwind got to play target to distract him, if they could. The Shin'a'in could no longer play that role; he had started to look for them, and had laid traps for them that would catch them. They had no magic to disarm those traps, not as Darkwind and Elspeth had. The *leshya'e Kal'enedral* would be occupied in another way; helping Kra'heera and Kethra, confusing Falconsbane's FarSight and FarVision spells with their shamanic magic, so that he would not See the newcomers to the Vale, and the special energies of all the new mages there. That was vital to their purposes; if Falconsbane had any idea who and what had arrived to augment the powers of k'Sheyna, he would not hesitate, he would throw everything at them that he had, knowing their massed power could take him. Even with the help of the Kaled'a'in, there was no one in all of the new Council who thought the Vale and the three peoples there would survive that unscathed.

So Darkwind and Elspeth were on their own in supplying a needed distraction. Without distractions, Falconsbane might well notice the gryphons, Nyara, or both. If he noticed them—

She shuddered. Better not to think about it.

With Need's help, she had fashioned a blade that would counterfeit Need at a distance. It had no real power whatsoever—like the sword meant to select the rulers of Rethwellan, *all* it did was burn mage-energy in a spectacular fashion, radiating power to anyone with Mage-Sight. Gwena would supply the energy for that blade. Elspeth would go imperfectly shielded, at least on the surface, looking as ill-trained as possible. Darkwind would simply be himself. That alone should bring Falconsbane down on them.

They would ride north and west, skirting the edge of what was probably Falconsbane's territory, as if they were heading in search of something. Any time they met with one of the enemy's traps, they would destroy it. Any time they found one of his power-sinks, they would drain it. Meanwhile Firesong and the Kaled'a'in mages would be moving the proto-Gate, but with none of the speed they were capable of.

Darkwind hoped that Falconsbane would assume the obvious—that they were trying to distract him from diverting the proto-Gate—and therefore he would not look for something *else* they were distracting him from.

"I really ought to be used to playing target by now," she said, as she tightened Gwena's girth and prepared to ride out into the snow and cold with Darkwind. They looked like a pair of fancy-dress Heralds, the two of them; he wore winter scout gear, which was just as white as any Herald's uniform, and she had *finally* pried her Whites out of the grip of the disapproving *hertasi.* Gwena was champing at her nonexistent bit, ready to go—and Darkwind was going to be riding Firesong's very dear friend, the *dyheli*-mage, Brytha.

What was even more amazing than a *dyheli* mage, was the fact that Brytha had instantly volunteered for this, before Darkwind could ask any of the other stags to carry him.

:I am not much of mage,: Brytha had said, in the stilted thought-forms of his kind. *:I channel power, like Companion. I channel to you; you are less tired, then.:*

No one could deny the truth of that; any power that could be *given* to Darkwind without effort on his part increased his stamina tremendously. But now Elspeth knew why Brytha was white—and why Firesong could accomplish some of the incredible things he'd already done. With that extra reserve of power available, one Healing Adept could act like two, or even three.

That was the edge they had needed to turn this from suicidal to merely horribly dangerous, in Elspeth's opinion. Or at least, to less suicidal.

"I suppose you should be used to being a target, in those 'here I am, please, shoot me,' uniforms you wear," he replied with a grin, carefully tightening Brytha's girth.

"Not you, too," she complained. "Kero calls them the 'oh, shoot me now' uniforms. There are perfectly good reasons why we wear white!"

"I like you better in colors," he said simply and reached out to touch her hand, briefly but gently. "They suit your quiet beauty. White only makes you look remote. An ice-princess. Your spirit is brighter even than my best scarlet."

She flushed and hung her head to cover it. "Thank you," she replied carefully. Slowly, she was learning to accept his compliments without any of the doubt she'd have had if they had come from anyone else. And for a moment, she was back in his *ekele* in memory, surrounded by color and soft silk, warmth and admiration.

Then she shook off the memory. For now, all that was important was the task ahead of them. And for that task, she could not have asked for a better partner than the one she had now. Should they come out of this well enough, they would celebrate in the *ekele* again, in a similar way.

She mounted up; he followed a moment later, and looked into her eyes. She nodded, and he took the lead, riding out through the Veil and into the quiet cold and the snow.

The gauntlet was cast. There was no going back now.

Treyvan launched himself into the wind, his wings spreading wide to catch the updraft, spiraling higher above the Vale with every wingbeat. Behind and below him, Hydona echoed his launch, and once she reached height, the others followed. It was good to see other gryphons taking to the air again; better still to know that they were here to stay. Counting himself and Hydona, there were thirty-two gryphons in the Vale now, a full wing. The little ones would have many teachers, and doubtless there would be playmates for them before too long. The gryphons who had volunteered for this settlement were all paired, and the balmy temperatures of the Vale had sent several of the pairs into pre-courting. It should be very interesting to see the effect on the Tayledras if they had not moved by the time the true courting began. . . .

But that was for later; now there was a job to be done.

They all knew what they were to do. Seven were to go to the south, seven to the north. The web of power gleamed to their inner sight, seen from far above the world; a construction of entirely artificial lines of energy and their anchors, overlaying the natural ley-lines and often conflicting with them. Not exactly a web in shape, only the power-poles were connecting-points. That was what held the whole construction stable—it was *all* that held the whole construction stable.

That would be to their benefit and Falconsbane's detriment. Anything that ran counter to the earth's own ways was subject to extreme stress. Maintaining this web would be much like flying against a headwind. The moment the pressure was released, the entire construction would implode.

The swiftest of the gryphons, two of nearly pure gryfalcon lineage, would take the farthest points on the web—those two were *not* Treyvan and Hydona, but a much younger pair, Reaycha and Talsheena. Treyvan and Hydona, as senior mages, would take the nearest points, but they would take more of them, making up in work what they were not putting into flight time. All had agreed that this was the fairest way of apportioning the work; since the time of Skandranon, nothing was decreed within a gryphon wing without a majority consenting to it.

The two older gryphons held the middle heights, providing a marker point for the others to use to orient themselves. It was a moonless night, and on such nights, despite mage-enhanced night-sight, distances were often deceptive.

The first pair gained height above Treyvan and his mate, and shot off, barely visible against the swiftly-darkening sky, heading southwest and northwest. Then the second pair gained altitude and took to the sky-trail—then the third—

Finally, only he and Hydona were left, gliding in lazy circles on the Vale-generated thermal. The sky was entirely dark now, with wisps of cloud occluding the stars, and a crisp breeze coming up from below. A good night for a flight.

:Well, my fine-crested lover,: she said, her mind-voice a warm purring in the back of his mind, *:are you prepared to enchant me with some fancy flying?:*

:Ever so, my love,: he replied, and drove his wings in powerful beats that sent him surging upward and outward, as she did the same. He glanced at her, and felt the familiar warmth of love and lust heating him as she showed her strength and beauty, angling against the wind. *:We shall meet at dawn!:*

Nyara also left at sunset, riding *dyheli*-back. She had not expected that boon, but the *dyheli* themselves had insisted on it. Her partner for this first part of the journey, until the moment that she *must* go on afoot, was a young female, Lareen. Fresh and strong, she promised laughingly that *she* could keep her rider well out of any trouble by strength and speed alone. That suited Nyara perfectly; she had no wish for any kind of a confrontation—it would be far better to reach the borders of Falconsbane's territory without anyone ever getting so much as a glimpse of her.

She had thought that this would be the worst moment of the journey, for Skif had been stiff and silent all during the Council meeting, and she feared he would remain so during the ride. She had not been looking forward to spending what might be their last hours together aching with the weight of his disapproval.

But instead, once the meeting was over, he had taken her aside where no one could overhear them. Except for Need, of course, for the sword had not left her side except for sleep; but the sword had remained silent, and he had ignored the blade entirely.

"Nyara," he had begun, then faltered for a moment, as he looked into her eyes and gripped her shoulders with hands that shook with tension. His usually expressive face had been so full of anxiety that it had become a kind of mask.

She had remained silent, unsure of what to say, only watching him steadfastly. Should she break the silence? Or would that only make things worse?

He had stared at her as if he thought she would vanish or flee with the first word. "Nyara, you know I don't like what they're asking you to do," he said, finally. His voice was hoarse as if he were forcing the words out over some kind of internal barrier.

She had stared deeply into his eyes, dark with emotions she could not read, and fear (which she could), and nodded slowly, still holding her peace.

"But I also *won't* deny the fact that—that you have a right to do anything you want, and you're *capable* of doing it. And I won't deny you the chance to do what you think is right, what you have to do. You're your own person, and if I tried to stop you, tried to manipulate you by telling you I love you, which I do, absolutely, completely—" He shook his head with a helpless desperation, his eyes never once leaving hers, a frantic plea for understanding in his gaze. "I won't do that to you, I won't manipulate you. Please, understand, I *don't* like this, but I won't stop you, because I know it's something you have to do."

She had reached up to touch his cheek gently, a lump born of mingled emotions briefly stopping her voice. Then she had smiled and said lightly, "But I think you have also learned the futility of trying to stop someone who is set on a course from dealing with Els-peth. Yes?"

Her attempt at lightening the mood had worked. He had growled a little, but a tiny smile crept onto his lips, and a little of the worry eased from his face. "Yes. Minx. You *would* remind me of that, wouldn't you?"

She had sighed as he relaxed his grip on her shoulders and had moved forward so that he could hold her—which is what *she* had wanted him to do, with equal desperation, ever since this morning.

For a long time they simply stood together, holding each other, taking comfort from each other's warmth and nearness. "I think what I hate the most is not what you're doing, but that I can't be with you," he had said, finally, his arms tightening around her. "I feel so damned helpless. I hate feeling helpless."

"We all hate feeling helpless," she had reminded him.

Well, so they did, and she was not feeling less helpless than he, though for different reasons.

Her eyes adjusted to the growing darkness as they rode out into the snow, following, for a while, the tracks of Darkwind and Elspeth. The clean, cold air felt very good on her face; in fact, if their situation had not been so tense, she would have enjoyed this. She had discovered out in her tower that she enjoyed the winter, even with all the hardships she had endured once the weather had turned cold. Now she was adequately clothed for winter in Tayledras scout gear; now she was riding upon the back of a creature built for striding through snow, rather than forcing her own way through the drifts. This was winter taken with pure pleasure.

But tension had her stomach in such sour knots that she had not been able to eat much; her back and shoulders were knotted with anxiety, and she was terribly aware of the burden of the sword at her side and what it meant. Need was cloaking her, presumably, as well as itself, but she absolutely required that cloaking, and she would require every bit of her mentor's skill and learning to come through this alive.

The alarms and traps should not react to me, she told herself, once again. *Father has been otherwise occupied. In no way would he ever expect me to return to him of my own will after attacking him and betraying him. Surely he will not have tampered with the defenses since I left him last. He has been beset by the Shin'a'in, launching his own attacks—when has he had time to reset them? Once I leave Skif and Wintermoon at the border, there should be no difficulty in getting within the territory or the stronghold—*

—so why am I as frightened as a rabbit walking into the den of a Change-lion?

She shivered, though not with cold, and touched the hilt of the sword unconsciously.

:I'm here, little one,: the sword said calmly. *:I'm screening us both for all I'm worth. You can do this; I trained you, and I know.:*

Some of the sword's calm confidence seeped into her own soul and eased the cramps in muscles and stomach. There was no point in getting so knotted up that she would accomplish nothing, after all. No point in worrying until it was time to worry.

The trail widened at that point, and Skif rode up beside her; she turned to smile at him, but it was so dark that although she could see his face, she doubted that he could see hers.

:We should talk like this, Wintermoon says,: came his mind-voice deep inside her head. Although she had never heard it, she knew it for his and it gave her unexpected comfort, like feeling his hand holding and steadying her. *:I'm not—very good at it, I should warn you. Have to be this close to you.:*

:I will—try,: she replied the same way, stumbling a little despite her practice with Need. Her father had never spoken mind-to-mind with her; he had only used his mind to coerce her, and to hurt her.

:You'd like Valdemar, I think,: he said unexpectedly. *:Especially the hills in the south. They're very beautiful in the winter. You'd probably like the Forest of Sorrows, too; that's way in the north. There are mountains up there so tall that some of them have never been climbed.:*

She Saw the image of the mountains, and the forest at their feet, in his mind; saw it drowsing in the heat of summer, alive with birds in the spring, cloaked in flame in the fall, and sleeping beneath a blanket of snow in winter. *:Why so sad a name?:* she asked.

:Oh—that's because of Vanyel,: he replied, and told her the tale, embellished with images out of his own experiences and imagination. That tale led to another—and another—and soon it was midnight and time to stop for a bit of a rest and a chance to check their bearings against the stars.

Wintermoon oriented himself; she and Skif dismounted and walked a short distance. *:This—being a Herald, I do not understand,:* she told him, as he held her within the warmth of his arms and coat, and they waited for Wintermoon's two bondbirds to report with their findings.

:Sometimes I don't understand it either,: he admitted. *:I suppose the closest I can come is to say that it's something I have to do—just as what we're doing now is something you have to do. But what I do is not because of hate, or anger, or the feeling that I owe it to anyone.:*

She moved her cheek against his chest and closed her eyes. *:Then why?:* she asked simply, longing, suddenly, to understand.

:Would it sound entirely stupid to say that it was out of love?: he asked. *:That's not the whole of it; that's not even the largest part, but it's the start.:*

She waited, patiently, for the rest of the answer, and it came, in bits and pieces. They were pieces that did not yet fall together to make a whole, but like the pieces of a mirror they reflected bits of *him* that made her see him a little more clearly. When one assembled a broken mirror, one could still discern an image. . . .

Some of his reason was gratitude—the Heralds had literally saved his life and given him something like a real family. That revelation made her feel kinship and a bitter envy; she had known only brief affection and never any sense of real family. She had, now and again, spied upon the lesser creatures of her father's stronghold with wonder and jealousy. She had seen fathers who caressed their children with nothing ever coming of those caresses but care; she had seen children greeting their fathers with joy and not fear. And she had seen that strange and wondrous creature, a mother . . . a creature that could and would die to save the offspring she had given life to. A creature that gave life and love without asking for anything other than love in return—no matter what the child became, no matter what darkness it turned to.

Skif had not known a mother like that either; in that much, they were kin.

Yet he received that kind of unquestioning love from—his Companion.

She suppressed another surge of envy. To have that kind of love— what did he need from her?

Somehow he sensed that doubt, and answered it. Not with words, though; with feeling, feelings that she could not possibly doubt. In her mind, he held her close and warmed her.

Their peaceful reverie was broken by his Companion, who stole up beside them and nudged his shoulder. He turned to her after a moment of silent dialogue.

:*Cymry says that Elspeth and Darkwind have managed to attract some attention by springing a trap. She doesn't think Falconsbane is personally involved yet, but now would be a good time to move on while his guards are occupied with trying to catch them.*:

She nodded and sensed Need's agreement as well.

The moment passed, but something of it remained. She examined herself carefully, trying to figure out exactly what it was, and finally gave it up.

The terrain became uneasily familiar, and she felt that cold fear rising up her spine and chilling her throat. Soon now—soon. The first of the border-protections was not that far from here; soon she would have to dismount, shed cloak and coat, and key herself up to the point where she could ignore pain and exhaustion, and run like one of the *dyheli* herself.

By dawn, if all went well, she would be inside the fortress itself. Alone. . . .

:Alone, like bloody hell,: the sword snorted scornfully. *:What am I, an old tin pot?:*

The image that Need sent to her, of Nyara wielding a tin pot against fearful guards, made her smother a giggle, and completely dispelled the fear. Of course she wasn't alone! She had Need beside her, Skif behind her—she would never really be alone again!

:That's the spirit. Just keep thinking that way.:

And somehow, she did, as she and Skif followed Wintermoon deeper into the forest, past the valley where the *dyheli* herd had been caught by one of her father's traps so long ago, closer to the border and the first of the barriers that she must cross.

Treyvan & Hydona

Chapter
Twenty-four

Elspeth had been feeling eyes on the back of her neck for the past league and more, ever since they had sprung the trap meant for a bondbird. A particularly nasty thing, Brytha had spotted it and had alerted them to the fact that there were both physical and magical defenses in the trees as well as on the ground. If Vree had encountered such a thing unprepared, it would certainly have caught and hurt him and might well have killed him. But then, Falconsbane was well aware that harming the bondbird meant harming its bondmate.

The night-shrouded forest had held plenty of traps, not all of them Falconsbane's. Rocks and roots lurked beneath the snow, to trip even the wariest. Shadows could hide anything—or nothing. Elspeth's night-sight was not of the best, and she was forced to rely on Gwena's physical senses entirely—although, truthfully, that meant she could devote most of her attention to her mage-senses, spying out trouble.

Trouble there was, right enough, and it increased the closer they got to Falconsbane's lands. Alarms, and more traps, some meant to hold, and some meant to kill. Places where Falconsbane's underlings had simply left things to trip up the unwary, to make them delay. Nothing living, though; Elspeth was not sure if that was a good or bad sign.

Now, with the gray light of dawn creeping over the forest and Vree scouting overhead, she was so tense with anxiety that she felt like a spring too tightly wound—and would have been starting at every little sound, if she had not held herself under careful control. This was the first time she, personally, had played decoy—the Heir to the Throne of Valdemar was far too important to risk as a decoy or bait—and now she knew how Kero and the Skybolts had felt when they were playing this little game.

I can't show I know we're in danger, or we stop being such attractive targets. . . .

If everything was going according to plan, the gryphons would be completing their task if they had not already done so. Nyara would be deep inside her father's stronghold. And very soon *they* would be free to sprint back for the shelter of the Vale and the protections of a Vale full of mages and Adepts.

Nyara was already inside her father's lands, if not his stronghold; Skif had relayed that via Cymry just past midnight. He and Wintermoon had seen her safely past the first line of defenses, and had gone to the rally-point, the place she would reach if she could when this was all over. But there was no way of knowing how far she was at this point.

Please, whatever gods there be—Star-Eyed, Kernos, Astera, whatever you call yourselves—let us all come through this with bodies and minds and hearts intact—

Elspeth was exhausted and getting wearier with every passing moment; this business of springing traps was not as easy as it had sounded. Yes, they could use the power of the ley-lines to augment their own— *when* they could reach them. Some of Falconsbane's own lines overlaid the natural ones, rendering them inaccessible. And some of the lines were protected against meddling by Falconsbane's own power. No, nothing was as simple as it had sounded when they first made this plan, and it had not truly seemed all that simple then!

She caught Darkwind's eye; he smiled at her, but it seemed more than a little strained.

:He's in about the same shape you are,: Gwena said gently. *:And your imagination is not acting up. You* are *being watched. Imperfectly—the Shin'a'in are doing what they can—but Falconsbane knows you're here and he knows* who *you are.:*

Well, that was the object of this little excursion, wasn't it? To take the attention off of Nyara and the gryphons? Nevertheless, she felt a chill run up her back as the feeling of *being watched* increased, and the malevolence behind the watching "eyes" made itself felt.

:Vree says the gryphons are done!: Darkwind exulted, suddenly. *:The last line is loose!:*

Distance-Mindspeech was a hazard around Falconsbane—the kind he was watching for, at any rate. But they had something he didn't; the gryphons Mindspoke to Vree, and he in turn to Darkwind—and all at a level it was doubtful Falconsbane was even aware of, much less could eavesdrop upon.

She and Gwena turned, following Darkwind's lead as if they had decided they had come far enough on an ordinary patrol, and were turning back.

Ice crawled up her spine, her stomach was one huge knot of fear and nausea, and she kept looking out of the corners of her eyes for the first signs that Falconsbane was going to attack. *We can't run. If we run, he'll chase us. We can't hold him off if he goes all-out against us. So we have to look as if we're just changing directions, and hope that he doesn't lose interest. . . .*

Huh. Better hope that he doesn't decide he's not going to let us slip away when he realizes we're headed away from him!

At least we know the gryphons succeeded.

If only they had some such bond with Nyara. She licked lips gone dry with a tongue just as dry with fear, and felt her stomach tighten a little more.

Nyara crept along the dusty passages between the walls of her father's stronghold, moving as quietly as only she could. In this, she was her father's superior; he had never mastered the art of moving without noise, without even the sound of a breath. Then again, he had never had need to. He had never had anyone to fear or avoid.

In all his life, he never had to hide from anyone.

Not like a certain small girl, who had huddled for hours in these passageways to avoid him—to avoid what he had in store for her.

She felt fear starting to cramp her stomach, and sternly told it to relax. *Deep breaths. Slowly. Tension brings mistakes; fear is his weapon.*

She was glad of the dust, for all that it might have choked her, had she not come prepared for it. She breathed through a silken cloth wrapped closely around nose and mouth; slowly, evenly, taking each step only after testing the surface before her. The dust meant that no one had walked this passage since she had last been here—and that had been years. The last time—certainly it had been two years and more. The last time she had been here was long before she had even dreamed of escape from her father's power. And then it had taken a year of planning before she dared to try.

How bitter it had been to learn that the attempt had been watched and planned by Falconsbane all along. . . .

That thought plays into his hands again. No, Nyara; once you were free of him, you did things he had never anticipated you would. You won free of him. You turned his own plan against him. Surely it is he who tastes bitterness now.

She put that old disappointment behind her, throttled her fear again, and concentrated completely on setting each foot down carefully, noiselessly. At the moment, this was the only thing in the universe that was important. What was past could not be changed; the future lay beyond this passageway. *This* was all that she controlled, this moment of *now*, and she must control it completely. . . .

So far, Need had detected no alarms or traps in this passageway itself. Perhaps her father did not feel he needed any. Perhaps he trusted in the narrowness of the passage to keep anything of real danger out of it. Certainly it was much too small to permit the movement of an armed man.

But not too small for one small, slender female, armed with only the sword that she kept out and pointed into the darkness before her.

Thirty steps from here was her goal; her father's study. One of his workrooms; it lay in a suite in the heart of his stronghold, the heart of his power. There was an entrance into this passage from that room; behind a tapestry at the farther end, through the back of a wooden wardrobe that Falconsbane kept some of his special garments in. He knew all about it, of course, for he had built it—but because he knew about it, she did not think he ever thought about it anymore. The passage and the entrance had been there since before she was born, and no one that he knew of had ever used it but him in all that time. If she was very lucky, he might assume that since no one ever had, no one ever would.

Twenty steps more.

:*He's ahead up there*,: Need cautioned. :*In the suite. No one but him, and he's busy.*:

Ten steps.

She had never prayed before—

:Don't worry about that, kitten. I'm praying enough for both of us. And I'm an expert at it.:

Five. . . .

Elspeth sensed something change, like the sharpness in the air before lightning strikes. Alarm shrilled along her nerves, and every hair on her body stood on end. A bitter, metallic taste filled her throat. Gwena snorted and froze where she stood, sensing it as well—Darkwind and Brytha beside them did the same at the same moment. They were no longer being watched. . . .

They were being targeted!

No use to run now—they couldn't escape what was coming.

:Shields!: Darkwind cried. He stuck out his hand, blindly, as they had planned if it came to this; she linked to Gwena and caught his hand, and with it, his link. *He* was better at shielding; she flung her power to him, taking whatever Gwena could pour into her.

She sensed the blow coming and cringed over Gwena's neck; he met the blow with one of his own—a defense of offense, something she hadn't even thought of.

The two bolts of power met over their heads in a silent explosion of power and a shower of very physical sparks that landed in the snow all around him, sizzling and melting the drifts wherever they landed. He took the moment to weave a hasty shield about them both, but it had none of the layering or complexity he needed.

The next bolt came, splashing and burning against the shield, scorching it half away and blinding her. Physically, as well as in Mage-Sight. A thunderclap of sound deafened her in the next instant. They hadn't had enough time—they hadn't known Falconsbane could strike like this.

Where did he get all that power? Falconsbane should have been wounded, should have been at less power than he'd had before, not *more*.

Unless he was already tapping into the proto-Gate?

Or unless he had ruthlessly sacrificed *many* of his underlings, building a network of death-energies stronger than anything they had. Or unless he'd found an ally somewhere. . . ?

Darkwind couldn't shield all of them; the group was just too big. He reinforced where the shield had burned away, and this time she aided him, weaving light and snow-glare into a dazzle, trying to recreate the kind of shielding they had learned to make in the safety of the Vale.

But Falconsbane was keeping them both off-balance, destroying the rhythm of their dance of power with sheer, brute force. *He* controlled the situation now; it was *his* land they walked on, and the land held energy away from them. She whimpered in sudden pain as a lick of flame burned through and across her hand, the hand that held Darkwind's— but she would not let go, not even if she died in the next moment. Instead, she kneed Gwena closer to Brytha, until their legs were half-crushed between the two mounts to make the physical gap between them smaller. She closed her eyes and sheltered against Darkwind's back, sweat of fear and exertion running down her back under her coat, feeling him tremble with strain.

Falconsbane did not let up, not even for a heartbeat. Blow after blow rained down on them, driving all sense from her, until the last of the shields eroded, and they clung together, waiting for the strike that would take them both.

Together, at least—she thought faintly.

The blow never came; they opened their eyes, fearing something worse.

Then a scream from above made them jump, and look up.

Like two golden streaks of light, the two gryphons plummeted down from above. They crashed through the thin lace of branches, ending their dive barely above the ground, and pulling up with wingbeats that sent the snow spraying in all directions. Both screamed again, an unmistakable note of taunting in their voices, as they plunged upward through the tree canopy.

"Run!" Darkwind found his voice. *"Run! They've made targets out of themselves. If we give him too many to choose from, we may all get away!"*

Brytha broke from his paralysis and hurled himself down their back-trail. Gwena followed a moment later, but not directly behind, making herself and Elspeth into yet another target to track on. Above the interlace of bare branches, Hydona and Treyvan had separated as well, skydancing as if they were courting—but far enough apart that Falconsbane would have to make a choice of victims.

Four targets. . . .

When the two young fools rode along the edge of his territory, at first Falconsbane could not believe the testimony of his own senses. *It must be an illusion*, he thought at first. *It is meant to distract me.* But the closer the pair came, the clearer they were, despite the best attempts of—

whatever it was—that was trying to cloud his scrying. Between midnight and dawn, he knew that the pair were something more than they seemed. By false dawn he knew that one of them was the young Outland woman he had wanted so badly to take for his own. By true dawn, he knew that the other was the fool called Darkwind, and that the girl still carried her artifact.

By then, he could not withstand the temptation to attack any longer.

He had not lived this long by neglecting an opportunity when it was given to him. And he would not botch this chance by holding back, or making testing feints.

He gathered all of his power together, prepared his weaponry, and attacked.

Darkwind would die; then the girl and the sword would be his.

There was no point in being prudent or cautious now! Not with *this* prize in his grasp! He rained blow after blow upon them, heedless of the expenditure of power, heedless of anything about him. Elation held him like a powerful drug, making him laugh aloud with every shred of shielding burned away, giving him an elation he had not felt in decades. He held his arms high and power crackled between his hands, power from his network made of the death-energies of his mages. He was draining that network, but it did not matter, for in moments he would have *her*, and the Bird-Fool's power as well, and there would be nothing standing in the way of his revenge and his glory.

And then, just before he was to strike the blow that would take them both—

Gryphons!

The sight of them in his scrying bowl struck like a physical blow, driving the breath from him.

They dove down out of *nowhere*, interposing themselves between him and his quarry; taunting him, flaunting themselves at him, flying as if they thought agility alone would protect them.

Gryphons!

He snarled with overwhelming rage. How *dared* they step between him and his prey?

Anger and hatred filled him, granted him a strength far beyond anything he normally possessed. They thought to confuse him, did they? They thought he could only strike one of them at a time.

They would learn differently—in the few heartbeats it took for *all* of them to die!

He gathered his powers—readied the blast to destroy that entire section of his borderlands—

Nyara took three deep breaths; focused herself.

There is no future. There is no past. There is only now, and the target. There is no fear. There is only balance. There is only myself and the task.

She slipped through the false wall in the back of the wardrobe and slid soundlessly into the room. Her eyes focused quickly as she swept them from left to right, once, to orient herself.

There. The target. *Yes!*

She took two steps, raising Need high over her head to give additional momentum to her swing—

And brought the mage-blade down squarely on the huge crystal-cluster that Mornelithe Falconsbane had invested and anchored with all of his power—a crystal that cried out to her of death and pain, and even now was glowing with internal fires of red and angry yellow as he drew upon it—

Drew upon it to destroy her friends.

NO!

Sword crashed down upon crystal—and crystal exploded.

Falconsbane brought his hands up, rage a hot taste of blood in his throat.

Then—*What*—

A fractional instant of *something wrong;* no more than that.

—an instant of disorientation—

—searing *pain*—pain, engulfing every nerve, every fiber—

—out of the pain, the void, rushing upon him like the open mouth of a giant to devour him—

—and then, oblivion.

Elspeth picked herself up out of the huge drift of snow she had landed in, slowly. One moment they had been running for their lives, and the next—

Gwena!

She scrambled to her feet, flailing in the deep snow, trying to get herself turned around.

:*It's—all right. I'm fine. Mostly.*: Elspeth stopped trying to flail her way out of the snow and relaxed.

Thank the gods. Oh, thank the gods. Although Gwena's mind-voice sounded—odd. As if—

:*I feel as if I have a hangover,*: the Companion replied. :*I—think I may be sick.*: The overtones of nausea that came with the thoughts almost pushed Elspeth into sickness herself.

She got herself back to her feet and turned around, her head pounding, her stomach heaving along with Gwena's. The Companion was on her knees in another snowdrift, sides heaving as her breath hissed between clenched teeth.

:*I will—never again—mock you—when you are—wine-sick,*: Gwena managed, closing her eyes as if the sun hurt her.

Elspeth staggered to her side. "Eat some snow," she urged, holding a handful up to Gwena's muzzle. "Do it; I think this might be reaction-sickness, and eating snow will help."

:*If you—think so—*: Gwena opened her jaws gingerly and accepted a bite of snow, swallowing it quickly. The nausea subsided, and she took another bite. :*That helps. Thank you.*:

"It's not going to help the headache though," Elspeth warned, squinting against the pain in her own head. *We're all alive, I think—*

A shadow loomed beside her; Darkwind, leaning on Brytha. He smiled wanly, and the joy that flooded her almost made her forget her pounding head. She would have jumped up, if she could; as it was, he simply let go of Brytha's shoulder and fell into her arms.

"What happened?" she asked, holding him, being held, and ignoring the chill of the snow penetrating her clothing.

"I think he must have had something ready to hit us with when Nyara destroyed his focus," Darkwind replied unsteadily. "Most of it aborted, but there was enough left to knock us all head-over-hind. I hope Treyvan and Hydona—"

:*Were out of range, thank you.*: The hearty mind-voice made her wince, and snow blew up in all directions as the gryphon backwinged to a landing. "Arrre you unwell, childrrren?" he continued, folding his wings and cocking his head to one side. Vree landed beside him, imitating his pose in a way that would have been funny if Elspeth's head had not hurt so much.

And not only her head. It felt rather as if someone had been beating her with blunt clubs all over her body.

"I sssee," the gryphon said, although none of them had replied. "Wait a moment."

He walked over to a little sheltered area amid a cluster of bushes. Within a few moments, he had the earth scraped bare and overlaid with pine boughs. "Herrre. I have made you a nessst," he said, turning back to them. "Go and wait therrre, all of you. I ssshall brrring back sssome help. Meanwhile, eat sssssnow."

With that, he launched himself into the air again, vanishing into the bright sky in a few wingbeats.

"Well?" Elspeth said to Darkwind. He shrugged.

"I can't go any further," he replied. "And Brytha's not feeling much better than Gwena. Let's let someone else take charge for a change."

"Good idea," she replied, and the four of them collapsed together into the "nest" that Treyvan had made, to share the heat of their bodies and await *their* rescuers.

Nyara prowled the complex of three rooms, study, library, and workroom, and found only the destruction of a whirlwind in the workroom; Need went quiet for a moment.

:He was here. Kitten, this was mad; he meant to anchor the proto-Gate partially in himself. He's gone now—pulled right into the void, along with half of the stuff in this room.:

"Can he return?" she whispered.

:Don't know. But if he does, he won't be the same.:

She shivered and started back to the hidden passageway. The sound of people murmuring on the other side of the door made her hurry her steps. They might welcome her as savior—but more likely, they'd welcome her with the points of blades. Mornelithe's servants were steeped in suspicion and fear. Time to go.

:You did great, kitten. I was impressed.:

The Vale had never looked better, and Elspeth felt as if she would like to drink tea and stay in bed for a week. The tea she got, but she wasn't allowed to seek her bed yet. There were a number of people waiting for all of them, chiefest of whom was Firesong.

Firesong actually looked chagrined. Elspeth had never seen that particular expression on his face before and had not ever thought that she would.

"I have some strange news," he said, as she sipped the tea that was slowly dulling her headache to a bearable level. She looked at Darkwind, who only shrugged and accepted another mug from the Healing Adept.

"I'm beginning to think that's the only kind of news we ever have around here," she said dryly, pulling her blanket a little closer.

Firesong sat back on his heels, and shrugged. "This is—news that will probably not please most of k'Sheyna," he opined. "It is concerning the proto-Gate. It did not settle where I intended. It was pulled away—*very* strongly."

"Not Falconsba—" Elspeth exclaimed, alarmed, when he interrupted her with a shake of his head.

"Nay. But it also did not go to the new k'Sheyna Heartstone." He sighed, and shook his head. "I am at a loss to explain this. It has gone east and north. *Far* east and north." He looked up at her from under long white eyelashes. "To *your* land, to be precise."

She blinked, feeling suddenly very stupid. Was there something here she was missing? "Valdemar?" she replied. "But—why? How?"

"Better to ask, *who*," Firesong replied, standing up again. "There was a force came out of the north, at the moment of backlash. It used the force of backlash to snatch the power-point out of *our* hands, and when all was done, it had settled nicely as a Heartstone in the center of your crown city. Or so I surmise, since I cannot imagine any other place with so many of your Companions in one small area." One corner of his mouth crooked in a slight smile as he nodded at Gwena. "I do suspect that all of them are suffering as much as your—friend—is. The settling of that much power is not an easy thing."

"North?" Elspeth managed, trying not to look too stupid. "North?"

"North?" Darkwind shook his head. "What in the name of the gods is *north* of Valdemar's lands that could do *that?*"

"Nothing—" Elspeth began, then stopped.

"What?" both of them snapped at once.

"The Forest of Sorrows," she said hesitantly. "The Forest—has always had a reputation for strangeness. Since Vanyel died there, anyway."

At the name of "Vanyel," Firesong's eyes narrowed, and he nodded thoughtfully. "You are ready now," he said directly to her. "The rest of your training is largely a matter of practice and learning what will work for you. *I* think you both should go to this Forest."

"Go?" Darkwind said faintly. Elspeth took a glance at him out of the corner of her eye; he was pale, and looked as if someone had just struck him.

"Yes," Firesong repeated forcefully. "Go. And *you* should go with her. It is obvious to a blind man that you wish to—and with all the Kaled'a'in here, there will be nothing that the Clan needs that you alone could provide." He shrugged. "They may even choose to move back here, which *I* think would be an excellent thing. But you should—*must*—go with Elspeth."

"But—I *cannot!*" Darkwind cried out, and winced at the sound of his own cracking voice. "I cannot," he repeated, at a lower volume. "Tayledras never leave their Vales."

"*Sheka,*" Firesong said rudely. "My own foster forefathers did so, to help Herald Vanyel *in Valdemar* when he needed their aid. They have not in centuries, it is true, but this is a time of changes. Or," he finished, his tone heavy with sarcasm, "had that fact escaped you?"

"But the move—" Darkwind said feebly.

"Can be accomplished with the help of the Kaled'a'in. Either bringing them here, or your mages there. Now that the Stone is gone, you could use the node in the ruins to create a new one, or build a Gate to the new Vale." Firesong shrugged, carelessly tossing his hair back over his shoulders. "It matters little to me. My task is done here, and I am returning home."

"Father—" Darkwind began, then shook his head. "Father has Kethra and the Kaled'a'in and Shin'a'in healers. And Wintermoon. I am being foolish. But—" he licked his lips nervously. "This is not easy."

"Fledging rarely is," Firesong said dryly. "I shall leave you to make your decision."

Firesong stood and smiled, and now they saw that he had been toying with a black rose. At Elspeth's curious look, he smiled a little wider and said only, "A gift. Brought to me by a scarlet-crested firebird."

Darkwind's brow creased in concentration. "But—that breed is from the far north."

Firesong closed his eyes and sighed, content as any maiden paid a compliment. "Yes, Darkwind—north of Valdemar."

Elspeth sat quietly as Firesong left them alone in the little clearing below her *ekele*. She wanted to look away from him, but she was afraid that if she did, he would take it as a rejection.

And that was the last thing she wanted.

He stared into his cup for a long, long time, while the tea cooled and both of them were locked inside their own thoughts. Finally, he looked up.

"This will not be easy," he said awkwardly. "I am—I have never been outside our own lands. I know nothing of the Outlands."

"There are good people, bad people, and middling people," she replied as casually as she could. "Just more of them than you're used to, perhaps. But I would like you to come. I need you; not just the mage—but yourself; Darkwind."

That last slipped out before she could stop it, but once escaped, she did not want to take it back.

He let out a breath he had been holding in. "I had hoped you would say that," he said, and took her hand. "I had hoped, but I had not expected it."

She felt her heart racing, as she put her own hand over his. "So," she said, dizzy with elation, "Shall we go see where all these changes are taking us?"

"Together," he replied. "Yes. I think we should."

Once again, Elspeth made up her full packs, with everything she owned, and more—all the possessions she had accumulated in the Vale. It was still the deep of winter, but the expedition that prepared to set out from Kena Lesheyana Vale was not one that was likely to be daunted by a little cold and snow. Not only were there three Adepts in the party, Firesong electing to guide them as far as k'Treva, but there were four gryphons. Granted that two of them were barely fledged, and would make their ground-bound way alongside the riders in between their short flights, but even a *young* gryphon was likely to give predators pause.

That was something Elspeth had *not* expected, but she welcomed them completely. Treyvan would not say what his ultimate intentions were, but since he had begun asking for lessons in her tongue, Elspeth suspected that he and Hydona had been elected as the Kaled'a'in ambassadors to Valdemar. It made a certain amount of sense—and the gryphlets would be their wordless assurance to the people of Valdemar that they intended no ill.

I can't wait to see them in Court. How is the Seneschal going to call their credentials, I wonder?

Besides, with gryphons to gawk at, Nyara was going to seem almost commonplace.

Changes indeed.

It would take several weeks to make all the preparations; weeks during which she and Darkwind could help the Kaled'a'in to build the Gate to send the mages and scouts of k'Sheyna on to their new Vale. Once that was complete, there would be nothing more holding Darkwind here—except dark memories of a kind he would do well to leave behind.

Then—

The unknown—for both of us—

She started to shiver, then a hawk-cry made her look up. She wasn't certain *why*, since hawks cried out all the time in a Vale, but something about that cry compelled her to raise her eyes to the sky.

Above her were two vorcel-hawks, skydancing, courting, circling higher and higher into the sun.

Author's Note:

Falcons and horses; bondbirds and Companions. The latter are a *what-if* portrait of the former—but a bondbird is as unlike a real-world hawk or falcon as a zebra is unlike a Companion.

Yet there is always that longing to have something *like* a bondbird or a Companion. Dragons are not possible in this world—but this world does hold hawks and horses.

The demand on time, money, and special resources is similar for both the dedicated horseman and the falconer.

First, outfitting the human. Both require specialty items not found in stores. A falconer needs a hawking glove, specially constructed for extra protection where the hawk's talons will be yet flexible enough to handle leash and jesses; he must either make this—expensive in terms of time—or buy it—expensive in terms of money. The horseman requires riding boots if he is going to ride seriously—also expensive.

Next, outfitting the bird or horse. The bird needs a hood—an object very difficult to construct properly, and again expensive either in terms of time or money. She also needs bracelets, jesses, leash, portable perch, transportation box, training lure—all of which *must* be made to her size by her falconer. The horse requires tack; hackamore, halter, bit, bridle, saddle, saddle-blanket, and grooming materials—all of which must be bought.

Housing bird or horse; here is where the horseman has an advantage over the falconer. The bird *must*, by federal regulation, have a house of a certain size and construction, a weathering-yard of certain size and construction, and a permanent perch in the weathering yard. All these must be constructed on the falconer's property, for by federal regulations, he must have the bird available for inspection at any reasonable time of the day. There are no boarding-stables for birds.

Feeding and veterinary care; expensive propositions for both bird or horse. The bird must have fresh, high-quality food every day—of the kind he would normally eat in the wild. Not hamburger, steak, or chicken one can buy in a grocery. Horses eat like—a horse! It is a great deal more difficult to find a vet who will care for a raptor than one who will care for a horse, however, and there is an additional worry. Because hawks and falcons are *protected species*, if a bird becomes ill and dies, the federal government automatically becomes involved to ensure that the death was due to accident and not mistreatment.

Time and training; again, this is something where the falconer has no choice in the matter. He *must* work with his bird on a daily basis, whereas if a horseman has boarded out his horse, he can arrange for other riders to take leases to ride on those days when he may not be able to. In training the birds, there *are* no "bird-breakers." The falconer must do all of his training himself. Unless, of course, he happens to be so wealthy that like the nobility of old, *he* can employ a falconer to man "his" birds—though in that case, they will never be "his", for they will truly answer only to the hand that trained them. By contrast, papers and magazines are full of advertisements for horses in all stages of training. The falconer must have access to land in which to train, exercise, and hunt with his bird. That means that training and hunting with the bird will put many miles on his vehicle. The trained bird requires working every day of the year.

Acquisition; there are captive-bred birds available to the General and Master falconers, but for the Apprentice, obtaining a bird means hours—days—weeks spent attempting to trap a passage redtail or kestrel. The horseman must visit many breeders or dealers and try many horses before he finds one to his liking.

Care; once again, since there are no boarding-stables for raptors, the entire burden of care falls to the falconer. And a big bird like a redtail produces an astonishing quantity of . . . leavings. Houses must be scraped and scalded periodically, as must perches; the sand in the house and weathering yard must be raked daily. The bird must be offered his daily bath under conditions that will not leave him open to catching disease. Yards must be inspected and repaired, since many predators— including the large owls—regard a bird on a perch as a meal waiting to be taken.

Outside dangers. Horsemen have to contend with people who honk their car horns at horses being ridden along the side of the road, with dogs who attack horse and rider, and with people who, out of pure maliciousness, will attempt to injure horse, rider, or both. Falconers have to contend with those who are under the mistaken impression that all birds of prey are lawful targets, that birds of prey are taking the game that "belongs to them," and with those who regard birds of prey as "vermin." And with those who, out of pure maliciousness, will attempt to injure or kill the bird.

Both sports require substantial investments of time and money. Neither should be undertaken lightly, or without serious thought. For someone considering becoming a horse owner, there are usually excellent stables offering training in care and riding. For someone considering falconry, the best place to consult is the State Fish and Game department; they will have further information on falconers and regulations in your area.